JUDGMENT OF HONOR

GODDESS'S HONOR
BOOK FIVE

JOYCE REYNOLDS-WARD

Ebook ISBN: 979-8-950306-24-2

Paperback ISBN: 978-0-9898473-4-6

Hardcover ISBN: 979-8-950306-25-9

❀ Formatted with Vellum

LOOKING FOR ANSWERS

"By the Goddess's gold necklace, how did Chatain's forces capture my daughter?" Katerin ea Miteal, Leader of Medvara, dug her fingernails into the pine chair's arms. She glared at the shamefaced Council. It had taken her five days to get back to Medvara from Waykemin so she could learn just exactly what it was that had happened to Witmara.

Five days.

The need to know her daughter's fate kept building once she had arrived in Medvare-the-city—and not one word had been said about her daughter.

Five days.

Why won't they tell me what happened?

Granted, Witmara was almost eighteen and married to Toran, but…it was hard to be just the Leader and not mother as well.

She would have yelled, except that her cousin Rekaré, Medvara's former leader, straightened up from slouching against one of the Great Hall's support posts and shook her head at Katerin.

Maybe you should return as Leader!

Katerin scowled at her cousin.

Not that Rekaré would do that. She made her choice seven years ago. And after recent events in Waykemin, it was even less likely that she would return to the Leadership.

Katerin sighed and softened her grip on the chair. "Witmara should not have been so easily taken prisoner," she said in a quieter tone.

Rekaré nodded approval of her softer voice.

Katerin resisted the temptation to rub her aching forehead. It wasn't going to relieve the dull throbbing caused by three days travel on water—*waterstruck*, an ailment limited to sorcerers—and a fast, hard military campaign requiring her to wield far too much magic for—oh Gods, she couldn't remember the exact number of days since she'd ridden out with a small force to confront the Witches Council of Waykemin.

Too many days had passed, filled with worry and sleepless nights. Not just about Witmara, but about Waykemin, and war with Chatain, Emperor of Daran, on the other side of the ocean—*just how are we to fight an enemy overseas?*

But battling Waykemin had to be done, for the future of the lands of Varen. It was a first step toward confronting Chatain. He wasn't going to stop meddling in Varenese politics. He manipulated Waykemin into that battle. He had sent an apparent exile, Chiral, a distant Ralsem cousin, to destroy Rekaré's leadership of Medvara seven years ago. It was possible he was organizing a larger invasion fleet than the one that had kidnapped Witmara.

More than Chatain, there was her worry about Rekaré.

Katerin let go of the chair and tapped her right fingers on the arms as no one responded. Rekaré resumed her slouch.

Am I really that frightening?

She wouldn't think so. Then again, if her face was as lined and grim as Rekaré's, even without the red cap and cowl her cousin wore—that might be good reason for her Council to hesitate before answering.

She eyed Korien, commander of Medvara's defense forces. He glanced sideways at the other Council leaders as he flinched under her scrutiny, clearly waiting for them to speak. Tilyet and Tilvi, the twins who had stepped up to manage Medvara after Witmara's abduction, nodded at each other, then both looked at Korien. Tilvi gestured toward Korien to indicate that it was his position to speak.

Korien frowned at them, then heaved a heavy sigh. "We miscounted the surviving number of iron ships that pursued Witmara and the sailships upriver, Leader Katerin. There were seven, but we only accounted for five during the battle. Afterwards, Toran waited only to have his wounds treated before he set sail, hoping Setkin's sorcery could drive the *Heart's Desire* to a faster speed than Chatain's magitech-powered iron ships can sustain."

Setkin *was* the most adept of the Sorcerer-Captains. Katerin let herself hope. Perhaps Toran had succeeded in rescuing Witmara and they were on their way back.

"How did the abduction happen?"

Tilvi cleared her throat. "We found signs where two of the ships pulled ashore on the other side of Rocky Point, stole some horses—or possibly had horses waiting for them—and rode cross-country to the battlefield at Melanut Plains. They captured Witmara from behind. An unexpected attack."

"Was anyone injured?"

"Two of Witmara's guards were killed. Witmara's daranval Daro and Toran were wounded."

"So they knew enough to separate her from Daro and Toran."

Tilvi nodded. "They rode back to their ships once they had Witmara. No messages. No ransom demands." She looked directly at Katerin. "I had warned of the likelihood of just that sort of attack. Suggested that Witmara needed a heavy guard."

"After Witmara left to lure the ships into the Chellana, the Tapestry warned us of approach by land," Tilyet added.

"And Finniarn did not listen to you?"

That didn't sound right. Chancellor Finniarn was cautious. He should have listened to the twins' warnings, especially since the alert had come from the magical Tapestry that tied the land's magic to its leader—or her surrogate. Why hadn't he?

And why had the Tapestry chosen to speak to Tilvi and Tilyet, and not Finniarn? He was the one who had been given the authority.

"He argued that we needed more forces to deal with the ships," Korien said. "And I was in the field, preparing for battle, implementing Witmara's plan to lure Chatain's forces to Melanut when Tilyet tried to tell Finniarn about the Tapestry. Had I known sooner, Witmara would have had a heavier guard."

The Tapestry hanging on the wall to her right billowed slightly, as if to confirm Korien's words.

Gods, didn't Finniarn have more sense than that? Then again, he had gotten himself killed in the battle at Melanut.

Fabric rustled to her right as the veiled Hidden One, Leader of the sagebrush desert Saubral and a recent ally, shifted her weight.

"Finniarn brushed Tilvi and Tilyet off as nothing more than mere record keepers," she said, scorn echoing through her harsh and scratchy voice. "And would not listen to any of us who clearly saw that they spoke with the authority of the land. But because Witmara had left him in charge while she lured in the ships, we couldn't do anything else. Not without violating our honor."

Katerin inclined her head respectfully toward the Hidden One. "I thank you for respecting your honor and the land. You could have chosen otherwise." She softened her voice so it would not be seen as a rebuke. The history between Saubral and Medvara was fraught and the recent alliance so very new.

The Hidden One waved a red-gloved hand dismissively. "Let it not be said that we Saubral are a dishonorable people. Though in this case, perhaps I should have pushed. I am sorry I did not, Leader Katerin."

"Not much to be done about it, but I thank you." Katerin scratched her chin thoughtfully. "This does not sound very much like the Finniarn I have known and worked with for seven years."

"It *wasn't* like him," Tilvi said.

"And of course we can't figure out why he did it since he's dead," Katerin growled. "I suppose no one examined him or his belongings to see if he was possessed?"

"Alas, no," the Hidden One said. "There was a wrongness about him, but not something I could identify. He was also quite worried about the approach of the Darani fleet, and that sort of concern can sometimes project as wrongness."

Before anyone else could speak, Rekaré straightened up again. "What was done with the items on him at his death?"

Korien turned to face her. "I had them secured in the treasury vault in hopes that either Katerin or you could examine them later, Lea...Rekaré. The priests of Staul guard them. They examined his possessions but other than a sense of wrongness—they could not identify more."

"Then I will look at his effects after we are done here to see what I can discern," Rekaré said. "By your leave, cousin."

"Gladly. We will do this together."

Their eyes met, and Rekaré nodded in agreement. Since she was no longer Leader Rekaré couldn't use Elithtra's Veil and Gloves to examine Finniarn's possession, but Katerin could under her guidance—she had never tried to manipulate them herself, fearing to bring on the circumstances that had forced Rekaré out as Leader.

"And Korien," Katerin continued. "By the Goddess's golden tits, why was my daughter *on a ship going out to sea* instead of staying safely on shore?"

"She had worked out a defense using a projection of herself to attract the Darani forces upriver. She and Toran worried that the Darani warships might attack Cooscol, for one. Or Florinol," Aldan, the heir to Larij as well as the older brother of Witmara's husband, Toran, said.

Katerin exhaled slowly, hissing softly through her teeth. Witmara and Toran were adepts at mixing technology and magic. *That* part of the plan was sound, even though she still didn't like it. And a Darani attack on Cooscol—or Florinol, two of Medvara's limited ocean ports—would have wreaked much more havoc on her land.

But as a mother—

And then there was the land. Why hadn't it defended Witmara? She was sworn to be its Regent, after all. Or had the temporary transfer to Finniarn broken that link?

Her token of Leadership, the citrine pendant known as the Light of Medvara, pulsed twice on her chest. Her sense of the land stirred, a presence nuzzling her legs like a friendly house-cat. Then Medvara manifested itself more fully, taking the form of a frowning dust-brown boy with black hair and troubled malachite-green eyes, lingering near the Tapestry.

I could not see them until it was too late,

Medvara complained, a petulant note in their young voice.

Their magic hurt me. It stung.

The Hidden One next to Katerin roused, staring toward the Tapestry and Medvara's manifestation with a surprised expression on her face.

Can she see it?

Normally only the Leader could see such solid manifestations of the land. Katerin sent thanks to Medvara and turned her gaze back to those standing before her.

"The land tells me that they could not see those attackers. That the magic hurt them."

"That would make sense," Tilyet said.

He and Tilvi exchanged glances, and a faint buzzing sensation briefly added to the throbbing in Katerin's forehead. Katerin pursed her lips thoughtfully. *Mindspeaking?* It *felt* like it. Still—mindspeaking was not common between humans. She and Rekaré occasionally mindspoke—but not casually, and it drained their magical strength.

Still. Twins. Twins with magic are different.

"The land was very distressed when the Tapestry spoke to us," Tilvi added. "Not only was it in pain, but it couldn't sense Witmara. With you gone...." She shrugged as her voice trailed off.

"We were here, guarding the Hall and the Tapestry," Tilyet said.

"And so the land picked you two." Katerin bit back another sigh.

Another problem. While Leadership was often hereditary, it wasn't always so in the lands of Varen. Leaders needed to be able to control and manipulate the land's magic.

How do two Agricultural Record Keepers end up being selected by Medvara to run it when I am not here?

Oh gods, this land was complicated. With Witmara gone and Finniarn dead, she needed the twins. The land had chosen them. Why? Not that Tilvi and Tilyet were incompetent—they knew the agricultural production of Medvara and Medvara's trading status by heart—but could they lead? Was their magic strong enough to deal with the land?

Then again, if they can mindspeak to each other....

Twins *were* supposed to possess special skills. This pair might well have mindspeaking capabilities.

"There is another issue," Tilvi said. She exchanged another one of *those* looks with her brother, accompanied by that same buzzing sensation. "We have reason to believe that we have Darani spies at high levels in our councils."

"Not just war councils. Trade," Tilyet said.

"How can that be?" Katerin asked. "Every one of my appointees has been vetted. Korien, is this possible?"

"Unfortunately yes," Korien snapped, turning sideways to glare at the Council members behind him. "It's not the appointees and the leaders themselves, but their high level staff. Some of us were not cautious." He glowered at Mekenth and Fisan, respectively Chief of Manufacturers and Chief of Lumbering.

A flush darkened Mekenth's olive skin. "Inwhal came recommended by Larij! How was I to know?"

"If you had asked, one of us could have told you that he left my father's service in disgrace," Alden said. "*I* would not have issued him a recommendation."

"Poliniece *did* have approvals from Keratil," Fisan said. He twisted some strands of his dark curly beard around a finger only a couple of shades paler than his hair. "I confirmed them myself. We have just discovered that an impostor replaced Poliniece before he came here."

"How bad is our infiltration?" Now Katerin let herself sigh, slumping.

Gods. Such a mess.

She rested her right elbow on the chair's arm and leaned her head on her hand.

I should not have gone to Waykemin. I should have realized this was happening.

But she was the only one who could have overthrown the Witches. How far back did these problems go? Rekaré and

Cenarth as Leaders…perhaps even further back? She glanced at Rekaré but her cousin's face remained tight and expressionless.

I will ask what she thinks later.

Rekaré's last years as Leader had not gone smoothly. Perhaps this explained why.

"Possibly a quarter of the high-level staff has disappeared since the battle at Melanut," Tilvi said. "Not all were on the battlefield."

Katerin raised her head again. "Were they in different sections or concentrated in one or two areas?"

"Concentrated," Tilyet said. "Lumbering. Manufacture. Treasury."

"Standard manufacture or magitech?"

"Magitech."

Gods.

Of course Chatain would want to know how advanced their magitech was. How much had he learned about Witmara and Toran's skills? And Treasury…. Yet there was one area as yet unmentioned.

"What about Agriculture?"

How much had Chatain learned about the magical properties of the Coos berry bushes? Medvara's production of magical fleeces? Gods, if he had spies in Treasury, he *had* to know just how valuable agriculture was to Medvara.

Tilvi pursed her lips, lowering her eyebrows in annoyance. "*That* area is one that Tilyet and I can vouch for. No spies in Agriculture. Those were the first records we checked."

Well, that was a relief. "So. A quarter of our Treasury, Manufactures, and Lumbering staff have disappeared. Is there any idea of where they went?"

And why Lumbering if not Agriculture?

An attempt to figure out what was happening with Agriculture?

"As Tilvi said, the invaders may have had help. We think that some of those helpers were on the two ships that escaped," Korien said. "And as for the others—my suspicion is that they have slipped into the desert and mountains around Medvara, hoping not to be found."

"I've had Shadowwalkers and Houndriders tracking several leads," the Hidden One said. She cackled mirthlessly. "Those in flight will soon learn they cannot outrun my riders. If they haven't been taught that already."

"All right." She turned her attention back to Tilvi and Tilyet. "Do we know yet how compromised our systems are? What's been sabotaged, if anything, and who we can or can't trust?"

"We are almost finished examining records," Tilyet said. "We should be able to report by morning."

"I will plan to hear from you then." Katerin sighed again. "I'm assuming we have had no ransom messages from Chatain?"

Other than his gloating projections when the abduction happened, that is.

"None, Leader Katerin," Korien said.

"Then we will meet again in the morning. Rekaré. Let us take care of this business with Finniarn's effects."

Her cousin nodded. They waited until the others had left the Great Hall. Katerin finally stood. Instead of going directly to Rekaré, she went to the Tapestry and stroked it.

Sadness and regret mixed with shame came to her.

You tried to warn us. It is not your fault that your warnings were not regarded.

The Tapestry nuzzled her hand. Katerin kept her hand on the fabric, letting it draw reassurance from her. She had woven it early in her Leadership, infusing the fabric with magical links to her, part of the proof of her ability to be the Leader of Medvara. The contact soothed both her and the Tapestry. As it settled, so did her throbbing head.

Rekaré clucked impatiently. Katerin patted the Tapestry,

promising more contact later, and turned to Rekaré. Her cousin studied her, brows arched quizzically, lips tight.

"Is your Tapestry always like that?" she asked.

"Oh yes," Katerin said. She stroked it again.

"My Tapestry was never that friendly," Rekaré said wistfully.

She turned away from the Tapestry. Katerin gave it a final pat and walked toward the door.

"You still have custody of those items?" Rekaré asked as they left the Great Hall, clearly not wanting to refer openly to the Veil and Gloves.

"In my office, locked in a drawer."

"Just like I used to do."

Katerin wasn't certain if she heard approval or concern in Rekaré's voice. Not that it mattered.

Her Leadership is not mine.

But she still didn't have a solution for retrieving Witmara. Rekaré would go to Daran to help Toran if necessary, as part of her vow to kill Chatain. What Katerin didn't know was how to successfully retrieve Witmara from Daran—especially given what resources Medvara possessed.

I hope Toran finds Witmara soon, and brings her back home before any of us leave Varen.

More than leaving Medvara, the thought of any of them traveling across the ocean to Daran bothered Katerin. She wasn't sure if that worry came from the land, or her own fretting.

FIRST IMPRESSIONS

Betsona ea Ralsem struggled to force her wicker and iron wheelchair down the stone pathway from the main house to the outdoor kitchen required in the heat of these damnable islands, sweat already forming under her sleeveless silk tunic. Her cousin Larien used to push her wheelchair along the stone walk. But now he—

She flinched away from that thought.

Why had she sent staff away for the next few days? She clearly hadn't thought things through in her rush to get her people safely gone before Chatain's men took a notion to harass them. She wasn't going to risk her people after Chatain had screamed at her about Larien's death, raging that Larien had lost the foreign princess he had been sent to capture. She wanted to get them away and dispersed, not stopping to think about what that might mean for her daily routines.

Spells couldn't completely protect memories, and she didn't want any of them seeing the hoped-for arrival of that fugitive foreign princess late this afternoon or early evening. Bad enough that Seijina and Petronin were with—Witmara, was it?

Her memory was fuzzy after countering Chatain's psychic battering this morning.

I hope she's worth the price we've paid to bring her here. Oh Larien....

But at least Seijina and Petronin had sufficient magic of their own to keep Chatain from ripping their minds apart should he decide to question them. Not so the rest of her staff. They might be *her* property, but Chatain showed no regard for anyone else's possessions, living or inanimate.

And never has.

Even with gloves, the iron wheels were already almost too hot to handle as she tightened her hands to stop the wheelchair just before reaching the kitchen. Betsona drew a deep breath. She snapped her fingers to open the magical shield around the thatched, open cooking area that kept bugs, snakes, birds, rodents, and larger scavengers out of their food. It was the least she could do for her staff in this bug and critter-cursed exile imposed on them.

She wiped the sweat off of her brow, wrestled the wheelchair over the threshold of the cooking area, and snapped the shield shut behind her. Maybe if she thought more about her cousin's laughter, his pranks, his earnest support of her goals, she could shove the fact of his death away. And yet she couldn't. Betsona buried her head in her hands.

Oh cousin... I thought you were stronger. That you could keep evading Chatain.

Her stomach rumbled. Betsona wearily raised her head, the slightest throb of a hunger-induced headache pressing behind her left eye. She had been in such a hurry to dismiss her people for their own safety that she hadn't thought about feeding herself, the most complicated part of being alone in this abominably hot place. It would be a problem if Seijina and Petronin were delayed beyond this evening—entirely possible given

Chatain's anger. It would take them longer to evade both his magic and his men.

Get on with it, she goaded herself. *You put yourself in this position. Now find yourself some food.*

She parked the chair by the post where a set of crutches hung for just this sort of circumstance. For once she got the crutches down without dropping them. Pulling off her gloves, and struggling to her feet, she hobbled over to the tin-lined cabinet for prepared food. Maybe Mayte had left rice balls stuffed with yam paste to tide her over. The thought of *yam paste rice balls* made her stomach rumble louder. She hoped something edible was there. Stasis spells didn't keep food palatable for long in this heat, and she hadn't lived in the Islands long enough to figure out survival food that would last.

Betsona leaned her right crutch against her left arm and fumbled with the hook and eye clasp on the cabinet.

I thought heat was supposed to be good for stiff joints!

The fingers on her withered right arm didn't want to flex enough to lift the hook out of the eye. She fumbled with her free crutch and thumped it against the bottom of the stubborn hook. One. Two. Three. The hook flew free and Betsona lost her balance, falling hard on the cobblestone floor.

"Gods *damn* it."

She scrabbled for the offending crutch. Using both crutches, she pushed herself to her knees, struggling to keep the bulky fabric of her culottes from interfering with legs and crutches. Then she got her good left leg in position and, leaning against the cabinet, started to work her way to her feet.

She banged her head on the cabinet door as it swung toward her, and collapsed back to the stones. Drew several deep breaths. This time she scooted over to the central worktable. Bracing herself against one of the posts, keeping her head away from the lip, she managed to scramble onto her feet and hobble back. Gasping for breath in the heat, she leaned her head against the cabinet.

Larien had been so proud to find it in one of the secondhand stores on the main island. Had replaced the tin, outlining her initials *BR* in delicate perforations to let air into the cabinet, enhanced by depictions of the raucous, brightly colored local birds that thankfully were silent today. Her pounding head couldn't stand their screeches. Maybe Chatain had driven them off. She wasn't going to thank him for that favor, though, because if it hadn't been for him, she wouldn't be in this situation.

Larien is dead.

That thought pushed her into action, any action to keep from thinking about Larien. Opening the door wide, she spotted the rice balls and picked one up, checking it for mold first. Nothing. She gobbled the rest down right there. Mayte deserved a reward once she returned. Freedom for her young daughter with Larien, perhaps, with her own release to come in later years?

Larien is dead.

The thought was no more palatable than it had been. Betsona leaned against the cabinet. She sank to her knees and buried her face against one of the bottom drawers.

Larien is dead, and it would not have happened except for my ambitions.

She pounded her good left hand against the wood.

Gods, when would something go right?

As if in answer to her not-quite prayer, one of her wards tingled. Betsona sat up. Had Chatain returned?

She extended her awareness to investigate the link. A familiar, warm presence sent reassurance.

Seijina.

Betsona crawled to her chair and wrenched herself back into it. She spun it around, barely remembering to open the protective shield, then close it behind her before wheeling back to the main house.

Gods. Gods. Gods.

Hopefully Seijina and Petronin would figure out quickly that she was alone. If they didn't already know. There were several of her people, Mayte amongst them, who might have drifted down to the secret dock in the tiny cove to warn them. But if they saw—Witmara, was it? Then her actions in trying to keep them safe would have gone for nothing, and she'd have been deprived of staff for no reason.

Their own choice at this point.

She had to get ready for Witmara's arrival. She didn't want the woman's first sight of her to be in this wheelchair. Not with what she wanted Witmara to do.

Heat against her hands reminded her of the forgotten gloves. Betsona bit her lip and continued to wrestle the chair up the ramp into the long, low building that was her Island exile home. It was bigger than her house in Adalane, but more open, with shutters on the doors and windows that would be closed during storms. Rickety wooden shades hung at the openings to provide privacy—otherwise, the house was open, save for the interior bedrooms.

Easier to be spied upon.

One reason, for sure, for Chatain to exile her here.

She wheeled her way into the large great room that served as a reception area, heading for the windows, unfastening the ties which controlled the shades, rolling them down for a limited privacy. That done, she spun her chair, looking around the room for things to straighten up from Chatain's tantrum this morning. She couldn't do anything about the broken vase, not unless she wanted to tire herself out using magic. Nor the scattered flowers or the water stain over the table. Or the books scattered on the floor—at least they were by the couch. She could reach some of them from her chair, but not all. He had knocked over a basket-type chair before leaving. At least it was wicker. She could right it from her wheelchair.

Sharp pain lanced through her back as she bent over to right the chair. Betsona hissed as her eyes watered. But she got the chair upright and managed to shove it back close to where it was supposed to be. Then she rolled her wheelchair over and reached down to pick up the books and papers scattered by the couch as best as she could.

"Betsona?" Seijina's voice echoed from the front entry.

"In the parlor," she called back. She pushed the wheelchair against the wall, and grabbed two of the waiting canes, hobbling over to her preferred wicker chair on a platform.

She heard steps, but only two sets. Had Seijina failed? Then they entered, Seijina first, followed by Petronin carrying a tall, dark-haired woman who leaned her bandaged head against his chest. Her skin was lighter than Seijina's, a soft rich true brown the shade of mainland dust, lighter even than Petronin, but definitely still brown.

Brown skin. That could be a problem.

Betsona's golden skin had caused issues with the Succession, perhaps even more than her withered arm, leg, and twisted spine.

But she is one of the Miteal, Betsona reminded herself.

Granddaughter of Alame en Miteal. One of Elithtra's descendants. That should count for something. Even if her skin was something other than Aireii fishbelly white.

Witmara raised her head, blinking her eyes.

"Where are we?" she asked in old, formal High Aireii.

Not completely uneducated, then.

Her correspondence with Witmara had raised Betsona's hopes—good to see that they were justified.

"Welcome to my humble abode, such as it is," Betsona said, also in the High Aireii. "I am Betsona, and you must be Witmara?"

"Yes." The girl—because now she did momentarily look very young—sighed. "I do not know much Darani. Yet."

Petronin jerked his head toward the couch and scowled at the pile of books on it. "That's the best place to put her."

"Taking care of it." Seijina hurried over and started picking up and organizing things. "Betsona, what happened?"

"Chatain. He burst in here this morning to accuse me of harboring her." Betsona nodded toward Witmara, whose eyes were now closed again. "What's wrong?"

"Heat, a head injury, and the land is pulling hard at her," Seijina said abruptly. "We dare not let her feet touch the ground. Not unless we want to let Chatain know where she is. Until she's stronger, she can't control her magic."

Seijina stepped back as Petronin eased Witmara down on the now-cleared couch.

"I am sorry," Witmara said faintly, again in the old High Aireii. "Once my head settles, then I should be able to control the land's response to me."

Betsona bit her lip.

The land reacts to her?

Chatain must have sensed it. Oh, that would drive her half-brother *wild*. Clearly *had* driven him to worry. The land of Daran was indifferent to him and was only slightly more inter-ested in Betsona when she poked at its magic. For it to get excited about a new person....

Despite everything, hope started to rise in her.

Maybe she is what we hoped for, after all.

"Petronin," Seijina said. "Bring me water and healing supplies from the infirmary, please."

"What happened to her?" Betsona rolled close as Seijina unwrapped Witmara's head.

"Rearnex was more enthusiastic about knocking her out than he needed to be when he captured her," Seijina said curtly. "It took me two days to convince Larien to let me tend to her.

The compulsion that Chatain put on him this time was very strong."

Betsona gulped. "Chatain told me that Larien was dead."

Seijina sighed. "I was afraid of that. He expected to die. I hope he didn't suffer too badly." Petronin returned with supplies in a bowl and a pitcher of water. Seijina poured the water into the bowl and washed the deep cut on Witmara's head. "Thanks to this one, not only was the compulsion removed long enough for us to discover who his controller was, but his memory of seeing us was destroyed."

"Securely?"

"If you call the work of the Messenger of Staul and the Speaker for Dovré secure, yes."

"*She* did that?" Betsona looked again at the young woman lying on her couch. She didn't appear to possess that much power. Did she?

"My late father is Staul's Messenger," Witmara whispered. "And my mother was the healer for Dovré's Speaker."

Chills needled through Betsona in spite of the muggy, cloying heat.

Gods, the possibilities.

Betsona eyed Witmara with a more discerning eye as Seijina worked on her wound. High cheekbones—definitely of the Aireii, despite her tan skin. Aireii eyebrows and chin. More than that, Witmara *reeked* of magic. Even with her eyes closed and lying still on the couch, the young woman projected an aura of graceful strength. Her hands were slender and refined but not soft, a small tattoo between the thumb and first finger of her right hand. No excess fat or loose skin on her arms, right arm slightly more muscular than her left—an archer? Power swirled around Witmara, a silvery-blue aura that reminded Betsona of the Star of Elithtra, the token that her late father Dunaran had given her to provide protection against Chatain. Black edged the silver-blue of her aura, the black of the God Staul in his aspect of the Balancer.

She must be dedicated to the Two-faced God.

Staul the Balancer, Staul the Destroyer. Witmara seemed to be more of the Balancer than the Destroyer.

Another shiver overtook Betsona and it was all she could do to choke back her glee.

Oh brother of mine, be afraid, because I have finally found the tool to counter your tyranny. Vengeance will be mine.

INVESTIGATING BETRAYAL

REKARÉ HAD THOUGHT IT WOULD BE HARDER TO RETURN TO Medvare-the-city. Even though she knew that Katerin had rebuilt the Leader's House and Great Hall after a massive fire, she still dreaded the prospect of return.

At the very least, when Rekaré had stepped off of the stern-wheeler dock that afternoon, her daranval Basnen beside her, she expected to encounter the same violent reaction of burning, pushing, the land all but shouting *get out of here!* that she had experienced the past few years whenever she set foot on Medvaran soil.

She put one foot down tentatively, waiting for the land to react, holding Basnen back in case they needed to retreat to the ship. Katerin waited for them impatiently, tapping one foot, scowling, fretful about the lack of information about what had happened to Witmara.

The land pulsed against her foot, a faint warmth but not the shocking heat from before. Then it withdrew. Rekaré dared another step. No further reaction. She let Basnen step off the dock. Her mare also delicately placed first one foot, then the other, before completely stepping off of the dock. Then they had rushed to the Leader's House to meet with the Council, looking for answers.

Not that Rekaré liked what they heard in the meeting. She hadn't brought her Mer Galad Seconds Sesenth and Detaluna into the discussion, directing them instead toward settling their tens and preparing to leave Medvara for Daran. But Gods, after the way Katerin was acting once they were done, she wanted Sesenth with her. Not that Senth could be a part of this scrutiny of Finniarn's effects, but she would have been a steadying influence next to the tension that Katerin projected.

Katerin's in a fell mood today.

To be expected—but Rekaré dreaded what that could mean based on recent experience. Immediately after Katerin had learned of Witmara's capture, she had almost burned her birth town of Chiyan in her initial anger. This mood was close to that reddest of red days, and kept Rekaré close to her cousin, just in case she reacted in a similar mode. The contact with her ruling Tapestry seemed to settle Katerin—but there was still that warning edge that kept Rekaré alert.

At least Katerin's House was a different place from the old Leader's House, haunted as that place had been. It didn't trigger memories. Still, the contrast between the Leader's Houses struck Rekaré hard as she followed Katerin to her office. This building was smaller, no longer the grandiose would-be palace that her great-grandfather Alexran had built and her father Zauril had turned garish with gold foil and gaudy wallpaper.

She liked this version better. No more gloomy dark wood paneling with shadowy corners that no light could quite reach. Light-colored pine paneling, pine floors covered with boldly colored rugs, ample lighting, and light green draperies. Very much a Katerin sort of place, almost reminiscent of the Leaders' House in Dera. Open, airy, and full of light.

New paintings on the walls, depictions of Medvara's various products the most prominent. No family portraits—hadn't

Katerin said they disappeared in the fire? No loss. The damned paintings had haunted Rekaré during the eleven years she ruled as Leader. But she had been hesitant to dispose of them, the land's subtle disapproval stopping her whenever she contemplated doing so.

Different for Katerin.

She was Alexran's granddaughter, so not a direct descendant of most of those pictured. Katerin's father Alame had been painted out of most portraits when he had been exiled.

Rekaré's musings halted when Katerin stopped at a door guarded by two women in the blue and green of Medvara's Home Guard.

"It is good to see you back, Leader Katerin," the woman wearing the higher-ranking silver-edged patch on the left shoulder of her jacket said.

"It's good to be back, Delria," Katerin answered. She held out her right hand and Delria placed a key in her palm. After unlocking the door, Katerin handed it back to Delria. She opened the door.

"Lady Rekaré," Delria said politely as she passed. Rekaré nodded in response, startled by the title, rarely used for anyone short of a God in Medvara.

Lady? Me? At least she didn't call me Rekaré Kinslayer. But I am no Goddess.

She stopped just inside the doorway as Katerin snapped on a glow light.

Katerin's office was big, in one of the building's corners, with shuttered windows on both outside walls and a little stove against the west-facing wall next to a window. Bookshelves filled the spaces under the windows, except close to the stove. Rocks, bags, and what looked to be a small shrine to Katerin's long-dead beloved Metkyi, Witmara's father, dominated those shelves. A table held papers and assorted leather bags. The third wall had two great bookshelves and a worktable with bottles of herbs and oils on racks above it. Katerin's Blue Starry Robe clan mask hung on the wall above the racks.

Katerin still makes her own potions.

Not surprising. Her cousin clung to pieces of her former identity as a Healer.

Katerin left the office windows shuttered. She snapped on another glow light before reaching for a small cedar bentwood box sitting on her desk. Rekaré swallowed hard, recognizing it.

Inharise's gift to me.

Unless Inharise had given Katerin one very much like it once she had become Leader. Katerin pressed the top in an unlocking sequence that Rekaré didn't recognize, so perhaps it *wasn't* the same—but then, why would she be able to see it? One property of those Clendan cedar boxes was their invisibility to all but those for whom they were intended.

Katerin extracted a twisted iron key from the box. She inserted it into the lock on a lower drawer of the desk. After it opened, she pulled out a transparent veil that shimmered with a purple-edged green light.

Elithtra's Veil.

Katerin delicately placed it on the desk, handling the veil as little as possible. Rekaré swallowed hard, fighting back a lump in her throat at its sight, remembering the last few times she had used these tools. The lump grew as Katerin brought out a pair of green-edged purple gloves.

Elithtra's Gloves.

Magical heirlooms brought to Medvara by their ancestor Alexran, stolen from the Emperor Etikar before Alexran's exile from Daran.

Rekaré stared at the Veil and Gloves as Katerin closed and relocked the drawer, carefully replacing the key in the box. Her fingers itched to pick them up, to say the words that would activate these powerful tools.

You are no longer Leader of Medvara. You do not have the right to use them anymore.

Katerin cleared her throat and Rekaré jerked her focus away from the Veil and Gloves, acutely aware that she had been staring at them.

"I've not dared to do anything with the Veil and Gloves," Katerin said softly. "I don't know what to do to activate them."

"I—I can tell you what to say and do," Rekaré said, forcing words past the huge lump that choked her throat.

Katerin gave her a sideways glance. "Sure you don't want to do more than that?"

Rekaré shook her head. "I no longer have the right to use them. They are the property of the Leader of Medvara."

Katerin nodded curtly in acknowledgment. She tucked the Veil and Gloves into a deerskin bag that she pulled out of another desk drawer.

"Let's go to Treasury and get this over with." Her lips tightened. "Gods, if Finniarn has been co-opted...." She shook her head. "And I thought things were going so well."

"The land would not be as happy with you if they weren't."

Katerin's lips tightened. "Then why did this happen?" She headed for the door.

"It's not always what you do or don't do that causes these things to happen," Rekaré said softly as they left Katerin's office.

Katerin didn't answer as they walked down the hallway.

The Treasury was located in a stone building on the same grounds as the Leader's House. They donned oilcloth slickers before going into the gray drizzle that was one of Rekaré's least fond memories of life in Medvara.

Nine months of this.

She was glad she didn't need to endure it anymore.

Two other members of Katerin's Home Guard fell in behind them as Katerin and Rekaré walked through the grounds. Katerin took a shortcut through one of the gardens. It had been primarily floral when Rekaré had been Leader. This particular garden had been replanted to thorny berry plants trained upon trellises and some sort of vines twined on lattices—hard to tell what those were but from the bark on the vines' rootstock she suspected grapes. Further on, green shoots just barely poked out of straw-mulched beds.

At Treasury's door they hung their slickers in the entrance before going in.

"Leader Katerin. Le—Rekaré." One of the four men at the door stepped forward to greet them as the others saluted. "Commander Korien sent word that you want to examine the late minister's effects?"

"Yes."

He gestured toward a younger man. "Neskin will escort you to the vault."

Rekaré fell in behind Katerin as they followed Neskin down a flight of stairs into the basement, a passageway lit by glow lights that flashed on as they approached, switching off after they went by.

That's new.

She shivered as they went underground, suddenly aware that Medvara still watched her warily, her skin prickling as if small, multi-legged insects were crawling over her now that she was below the surface.

Not completely forgiven. Rekaré Kinslayer is welcome here with minimal tolerance.

she mindspoke quietly to the land.

The prickling sensation ended, but she still felt as if her every move was being closely observed.

They passed by several closed doors, all lesser vaults that held Medvara's treasury.

Memories of auditing yearly accounts in this basement flitted through Rekaré's thoughts. Gods. While there were things about being Medvara's Leader she missed, those yearly audits in this clammy, damp basement weren't one of them. Even with annual renewal of the spells to keep moisture at bay, they weren't infallible…and there was always some damp down here.

Actual torches burned at the end of the hall. A man and a woman attired in elegant Court blacks stood at each side of this doorway, both wearing tooth and bone necklaces. Neskin hesitated at the sight of the priests of Staul.

"You may go back," Katerin said to him.

He bowed to her, then scurried quickly away. The man and woman bowed low as she approached them.

"Leader Katerin. Rekaré Kinslayer," the woman said as she straightened up.

Kinslayer was not a curse in the mouth of one of Staul's acolytes.

"Has anyone else seen these items?" Katerin asked.

"Not since they were placed here," the man said.

"Thank you for your service."

The man opened the door. "May Lord Staul guide your search."

"I thank you in the Lady Dovré's name," Katerin responded. Two more of Staul's devotees awaited them inside the vault.

"The items you want to see are here," one of them said, gesturing at a table.

"I see. Thank you. Now I must ask you to leave us alone."

"As you wish, Leader Katerin." They bowed to her, noticeably ignoring Rekaré.

Once the door closed behind them, Katerin sighed.

"I hope these tools work underground," she said.

"No reason why they shouldn't."

Rekaré took another deep breath, glancing around the room. Several sconces burned steadily, the flickering flames reflecting the flow of air through narrow vents near the ceiling. Simple items lay on the table before them. A pouch full of something—probably coins. A couple of daggers. A smaller folding knife. A handkerchief. A locket. A leather-wrapped metal flask. Nothing out of place, nothing Rekaré would find suspicious in any non-magician's pocket. Except—next to the flask was a small, empty, glass vial with a carved wood stopper.

Is that—?

If it was what she suspected, then that cast a different light on Finniarn's motives.

Katerin placed the deerskin bag on the table, then carefully extracted first the Gloves, then the Veil from it.

"What do I do?" Her voice trembled slightly.

"Veil first," Rekaré said. "As you put it on, say 'In the service of Medvara, I call upon the Seven Crowned Gods to heed my voice.'"

Katerin nodded sharply, then carefully draped the Veil over her head. "In the service of Medvara, I call upon the Seven Crowned Gods to heed my voice."

The Veil flashed green, then went quiet.

Did it do that with me?

Rekaré wouldn't know. She never looked in a mirror when donning it.

"Now what?" Katerin reached for the Gloves.

"Stop!" The command came out sharper than Rekaré intended.

Katerin jerked her hand back. "What?" Her voice was just as edged.

"Before you put on the Gloves, you need to decide which

Gods you are going to call upon, which one to protect you, which one to answer your question. The Gloves work with the Veil but while the Veil is general, the Gloves are specific."

"Does the hand and the order matter?"

"Yes. The right hand belongs to your guardian. The left hand to the God you are querying. You can only ask one question."

Katerin nodded, chewing on her lower lip. She stared at Finniarn's effects for what seemed to be a long time but was most likely only a thirty-count. Then she looked up.

"I am ready."

"All right. Pick up the right Glove. Say, 'In the service of Medvara I ask—whichever God you're invoking for protection —to guide and protect me.' Then put it on. Got that?"

Katerin nodded again.

"Before you pick up the left Glove, you say 'Protect me in what I do next, oh God or Goddess—whomever you chose for protection. Then say, 'In the service of Medvara, I demand that—again, whichever god you are choosing to answer your question—explain and answer my question', and put the glove on."

Another nod.

"Immediately after that, say 'In the service of Medvara I use the Veil, the Right Hand, and the Left Hand to uncover these secrets. In the service of Medvara, I seek the open path, the way which serves and protects. In the service of Medvara, I ask for protection, command, and guidance. So do I request of the Seven Crowned Gods, with preference to—whichever gods you are invoking."

"And then?"

"Depending on who you call upon—you may need to ask them to manifest themselves, if they are reluctant. Otherwise, you ask your question."

Katerin tightened her lips. She took a deep breath and picked up the right Glove.

"In the service of Medvara, I ask Dovré to guide and protect me."

No surprises there. Dovré was Katerin's patron Goddess.

Katerin eased the right Glove on, flexing her fingers within it.

"Protect me in what I do next, oh Dovré." She picked up the left Glove. "In the service of Medvara, I demand that..." her voice faltered slightly here. "Artel explain and answer my question."

Rekaré raised her brows, surprised. She would have thought that Katerin would have invoked Staul. After all, Witmara's late father had been a priest of Staul. But Artel? The Judge rarely responded to such queries.

I should have warned her of that.

Too late. It was done now.

Katerin pulled on the left Glove, flexing like she had done before. "In the service of Medvara I use the Veil, the Right Hand, and the Left Hand to uncover these secrets. In the service of Medvara, I seek the open path, the way which serves and protects. In the service of Medvara, I ask for protection, command, and guidance. So do I request of the Seven Crowned Gods, with preference to Dovré and Artel."

For a moment Rekaré thought it wasn't going to work, that her failure to warn Katerin about Artel's probable refusal would doom their request. Then she felt the air grow heavy about her, cool and dense as befit an appearance by both Dovré and Artel. A silvery glow shimmered next to Katerin as rich wheat-gold light flared across the table from them.

Katerin.

The Goddess Dovré manifested in the silver glow, and Rekaré's throat tightened. The Goddess had chosen features which resembled her dead mother, Alicira.

Another death that Chatain must pay for.

"I thank you, Goddess." Katerin's voice was low and husky. She had been Alicira's personal Healer for eleven years before her death. Surely she also saw the resemblance.

The Goddess bowed to Rekaré.

It is good to see you in Medvara again, Rekaré.

Rekaré swallowed hard and bowed back, unable to respond. Even the Goddess's voice reminded her of her mother, made her miss Alicira's presence.

Pressure grew heavier. The golden light on the other side of the table took form, then the God Artel stood there. He had taken the shape of a stocky, mature man from the Two Nations, long dark hair plaited into two braids with a tall forelock, red-brown skin the shade of fire-struck pine. He looked so much like Alicira and Inharise's husband Heinmyets, now bereft of both his wives, that it hurt Rekaré to look at him.

Leader Katerin.

Artel's voice rumbled deep.

Rekaré, sometimes called Kinslayer. You have a question for us.

"Yes." Katerin gestured toward the items on the table. "These items belong to my late prime minister, Finniarn. Reports were that his behavior was changed in the last days of his life, to the degree that he did not take adequate precautions to protect my daughter, Witmara, when she was serving as Regent."

We are aware of the situation, Leader Katerin.

Katerin swallowed hard, then met Artel's gaze fearlessly. "I want to know. Do these effects show any indication that Finniarn was under the influence of Chatain, Emperor of Daran, during his last days?"

An interesting question.

Both the God and Goddess studied the items. Dovré picked up the bag and shook it.

Let us start here.

As Rekaré suspected, the muffled clink-clank of heavy coins rattled inside the bag. The Goddess loosed the ties and poured the contents onto the table. Silver, gold, and copper coins clattered out, more than what had appeared to be inside the pouch.

Artel bent over and picked up a silver coin. It glowed faintly red in his fingers. He put it to one side, fingering through the rest, sorting out two more silvers and four golds to go with the first silver. All of them shone red as he separated them from the others now glowing purple, green, blue, or yellow. He inspected the seven coins again, frowning, then handed them to Dovré. The Goddess winced as the coins touched her hands, quickly returning them to Artel.

You agree?

he asked her.

Yes.

The God turned to Katerin.

These particular coins are Darani in origin. Not unusual, of course.

"We have enough smuggling trade that the occasional Darani silver or gold shows up in our coinage," Katerin said.

And these others show signs of being part of ordinary trade.

Artel pointed to a purple-edged gold, and three purple-shaded silvers.

But these.

He pointed to the seven.

They have been part of a magic-based transaction. Not a definite answer, but one which suggests that yes, Finniarn was engaged with some sort of magical business. Chatain, or one of his agents, has handled these coins.

Rekaré bit her lower lip as Dovré picked up the daggers. She examined them, then handed them to Artel. His inspection was shorter. He put the daggers by the ordinary coins. The God and Goddess went through the same process with the folding knife, the handkerchief, and the flask.

The golden locket glowed bright red as Dovré touched it. She bounced it back and forth between her palms, as if it were red-hot, then dropped it into Artel's waiting hands. He scowled as he studied the locket, then popped it open. Magenta, purple, and red lines flashed out of it, snaking around each other like bees from a disturbed nest.

Freeze,

Artel commanded.

The frantic twists of light stilled, forming a shape. A red-haired man glowered at them. She had never seen Chatain in real life, but he had appeared to her often enough in projections that Rekaré recognized him.

"So it is true," Katerin said slowly. "Finniarn was compromised."

Artel nodded.

A device such as this is rarely given to one who cooperates willingly. I do not sense that Finniarn cooperated with Chatain of his own free will. You have not touched it?

"No," Katerin said.

Good. It would still have an effect upon you if you had.

"Do I need to fear for those of my people who emptied his pockets?"

Dovré shook her head.

Not unless they are sorcerers.

"I'll have them checked. Some do have magic."

That would be a good idea.

"There still had to be a means for Finniarn to get it, and activate it," Rekaré said slowly, looking more closely at the locket. She didn't recognize the style.

Items such as these are often passed from hand to hand without appearing to be magical until they reach an acceptable target,

Dovré said.

Once that person opens the locket—then they are captured by the sorcerer who sent it out into the world.

Her fingers brushed against the outer case.

There is a picture in there. Do you know who it is?

Katerin leaned in carefully to study the picture without touching.

"Finniarn's wife and eldest daughter," she said finally. "Lost at sea two years ago when traveling by sea from Cooscol to Medvare-the-city." She paled. "The bodies were never recovered. Is it possible that Chatain holds them hostage?"

They no longer live,

Artel said softly.

Our sister Terat gathered them in that storm. They have her mark in this picture. But Finniarn would not know that. This device carries a secondary enchantment that makes them appear to be alive, even make them seem to speak to him. Someone with more magic would see that they are not alive, but if your minister did not have that skill, he would not know.

"He was not a magician. He could work small magics created by others, but nothing more than that," Katerin said. "But he was a skilled negotiator."

The God shook his head, sorrow lining his face.

This is foul. And it provides your answer. Finniarn was influenced and affected by Chatain.

Dovré picked up the small glass vial. She pulled the stopper and sniffed inside. Her brows rose, and she handed it to Katerin.

Be careful with this one.

Katerin took a cautious whiff and flinched away, raising her free arm protectively to her nose. "Poison! Essence of Darsnai!" She handed the vial back to the Goddess.

Rekaré's skin crawled. Essence of Darsnai was a fast killer, highly toxic, and had been implicated in the death of their ancestress, the Empress Elithtra.

I suspect that Finniarn either learned the truth about his beloveds or else decided that the price of betrayal was too high to endure,

the Goddess said.

It has been used. Do you know how he passed?

"Only that he died during the battle."

That would be a good cover to consume it.

Dovré sighed.

"Chatain will pay for this as well," Rekaré growled. "He owes me many lives. *He will pay.*"

Thus speaks the Kinslayer,

Artel said.

Are you reconsidering your previous vow not to ascend to Empire, Lady Rekaré?

Rekaré shuddered, repelled by the idea.

"No. I spoke truly when I said I would never accept Empire." Her fists tightened. "Chatain has chosen to attack those I love. For all those deaths—my mother, my daughter, my husband—he will pay for what he has done. That is most important to me. What happens to Daran when he is gone is not my concern."

Are you certain of that?

the God asked.

"Yes. I utterly renounce any claim I may have to the throne of Daran," Rekaré said firmly. "It is not mine, nor will it ever be mine."

But it could be.

Rekaré shook her head, unable to speak for the sorrow and rage that washed over her at the thought of the Darani Empire.

The God turned to Katerin.

And you, Leader Katerin?

"Medvara is more than enough for me," Katerin said, her voice steady.

Then we are done here.

Artel turned to Rekaré.

And as for you, Lady Rekaré....

"I will walk whatever path comes my way," Rekaré husked. "Where ever it takes me—except to the Throne of Daran."

A faint smile twisted the God's lips.

> Lady of Sorrow, you could have made a great
> Empress.

"And I would have brought much sorrow to Varen and Daran, along with the greatness," she retorted. "You know the visions I have seen as *benghaalph*."

He bowed to her.

> A wise choice, Lady Rekaré. We shall meet
> again, Lady of Sorrow.

Then he turned to Katerin.

> Leader Katerin, do you know the words to
> dismiss us?

"I have not yet been told those words," Katerin said.

"You dismiss Artel in the name of the Left Hand of Medvara, and Dovré for the Right Hand," Rekaré said.

The God kept his eyes fixed appraisingly on Rekaré as Katerin dismissed him. Rekaré wrapped her arms tightly around herself once he was gone, shivering from the weight of the God's scrutiny.

Only the Gods were addressed as Lord and Lady in Varen.

What does it mean that the Lord Artel called me Lady?

Artel the Judge did not do such things lightly. Did that mean she would become Empress instead of Witmara? Or did it hint at something else?

There might be worse fates ahead of her than becoming Empress of Daran.

Rekaré shivered again, wishing for the comfort of Sesenth's arms.

CLAIMING DARAN

WITMARA STIRRED, HER THOUGHTS NO LONGER MUDDLED AND cloudy. Quiet watchfulness surrounded her. The throbbing ache in her head had faded. Cloying, damp warmth reminiscent of a Medvaran summer pressed against her skin, but she no longer felt like she was burning up inside. Muffled excitement from the land instead of a frantic, desperate plea for attention pressed against her as she became more awake, opening her eyes to darkness except for a nearby faint light.

I've survived. Still free, I think. Thank you, Lord Staul.

She needed to figure out where she was. What was happening. What she could expect. What offerings and thanks she wanted to give Staul could wait until she was in private. And perhaps the shade of her father might appear to her again. She hadn't seen him since she left her cell on the iron ship.

Witmara eased herself up, surprised at her weakness, using the pillows to support her. The light radiated from a small oil lamp burning on the table next to her. She lay on a firm but comfortable narrow bed with a thin silken tent covering it. What she could see of the walls looked earthen, left natural and not whitewashed. Seijina sat in a chair by the light, knitting something dark-colored that was yet to take form beyond a small square. A distant scent of offal mixed with a faint musty smell that went along with the damp tickled her nostrils.

She sneezed.

"Do you need the bedpan?" Seijina set her knitting aside. "Or are you going to be sick again?"

Witmara's cheeks burned. Seijina's words brought back memories of several times with the bedpan in this darkness. But Seijina had been discreet and skilled, seeming to know exactly what to do. At least the nausea was gone.

"I—my head doesn't hurt any more," she said. "And I think I can use the privy without help."

"Good." Seijina nodded toward a brown curtain across from the bed. "It's back there. Glows on the table."

Witmara fumbled with the silken tent until she found an opening, pushed herself to her feet, picked up a small glow, and made her way back to the covered porcelain chamberpot. When she was finished, she washed up in the matching porcelain bowl, pouring fresh water into one hand from the pitcher to splash on her face, then wiped it with the towel that—surprisingly—was a floral design that matched the ones on the chamberpot, the pitcher, and the bowl.

Everything matches.

That struck her as odd. And the porcelain was of fine quality.

Seijina had resumed her knitting. She set it aside as Witmara made her way back to her bed, helping her find the opening in the netting over her bed. As Witmara straightened the covers and adjusted the pillows to support sitting up, she noticed that the pattern on the bedspread and netting matched the towel, the chamberpot, the pitcher, and the bowl. She choked back laughter. This was clearly a hiding place. Who had the resources to have everything matching here? Or was Betsona simply that wealthy?

She is Chatain's sister. I wonder what her status is with regard to the throne?

She had the impression—based on what Seijina had said—that infirmity kept Betsona from challenging him for the throne. But was that the only thing?

You need to be cautious.

Especially since she now knew that the supposed slave she had known as Nereast during her imprisonment on the iron ship was actually Seijina, Betsona's long-term companion and Sorcerer-Captain Setkin's cousin.

Anything you say around Seijina is going to be told to Betsona eventually.

Witmara leaned back against her pillows with a sigh. She wanted to leave Seijina with the impression that she was weaker than she really felt. At least until she had some idea of what Betsona might want from her.

"Perhaps you could drink some broth?" Seijina asked.

"Perhaps."

More memories flooded back. She had tried to drink broth earlier, and vomited it right back up. But now, at least, her stomach seemed to be steady.

"Good.

Seijina put aside her knitting and went to a rickety cabinet by the door, taking out a brown ceramic cup. She filled it from a pitcher—which matched everything else. A flash of green magic, then Seijina picked up the cup. She carried it over to the table that held the lamp, parted the silken curtains, and slipped inside, sitting on the side of Witmara's bed and reclosing the curtains before offering the cup. Witmara's hands shook as she wrapped her hands around it. Seijina's hands supported the cup's weight as Witmara guided it to her lips.

Witmara's stomach grumbled loudly. The savory scent of chicken broth made her want to gulp the liquid down, but she knew better than to do that, taking a careful, slow sip. Then she waited for a few moments, and tried again. Her stomach rumbled louder as she drank another mouthful. She waited, but it didn't roil any further.

"I think I'm hungry," she said.

The worry lines softened in Seijina's face. "Good. It has been two days since we came here."

"I've been sleeping the whole time?" Her head injury must have been worse than she thought.

"Yes."

"Where are we?"

"In the slave quarters of Betsona's property. We dared not leave you in the main house. Chatain's men have been here several times searching for you. We're underground right now."

Slave quarters?

That was right. The Darani were slavers. Witmara swallowed hard. Not a good time to react, though the thought made her nauseous again.

"Underground?" That explained the musty smell, and the damp, and the dark earthen walls.

"A dugout under the main slave residences," Seijina clarified. "You are not the first person that Betsona has concealed in this hidey-hole. It's a risk to keep underground spaces like this in the Islands due to flooding—usually such cells are reserved for prisoners—but the prison holes are good hiding places for people on the run. Betsona had this one made to hold her spies. It's easier for Betsona to work the spells to keep people hidden if they're underground."

"I—see."

Witmara reached again for the cup, pleased to see that her hands no longer trembled. So this was all matching by Betsona's design.

She focuses on details. Need to remember that.

She drained the rest of the broth. "What happens now?"

She remembered Seijina's words as they sailed to Betsona's from the main island where they had landed.

Betsona cannot rule as Empress—it would consume her far too quickly, before she could fix our broken land. It would fall back into foul hands. We have been preparing to make things right for years, hoping that one of our exiled kin would return. And now you have.

Betsona would want to put her on the throne, but at what cost?

But she had already spoken her own ambition in the hold of the ship of her kidnappers to the Gods Artel, Staul, and Dovré.

I will be Empress.

And Artel the Judge had acknowledged and supported her goal.

So how do we get there?

"It depends on your strength. On whether you want to challenge Chatain for the Empire," Seijina said. "We have received word from my cousin Setkin. He brings support for you from Medvara. They should be here tonight."

"Do you know who he's bringing?"

Her heart leapt. She had not dared to worry about her husband Toran and her daranval Daro for fear that she couldn't keep going if she heard they were dead. No one would tell her their fate. She hoped that meant they had survived the attack—and the restraints she had worn during her voyage confined her magic so she couldn't reach out to them herself. Afterward, she had been sick, in pain, and not ready to manage the effort.

Seijina shook her head. "All I was told is that they are riders from Medvara."

Well, that was something.

The land poked at Witmara, tentatively at first, then more insistent, demanding that she acknowledge its claim on her.

I have to do something about this and soon.

Before now, she hadn't had the strength to accept its welcome of her and keep its reaction under control, for risk of attracting Chatain's attention. Dare she try it at this point, or should she wait?

No more waiting. She wanted to find out if she could reach Toran and Daro. But first she had to connect with the land and keep it from betraying her.

Witmara took a deep breath and extended her awareness cautiously, sending out delicate golden tendrils. They struck the white fabric around her and bounced back, threads of magic springing around her.

"Stop!" Witmara commanded. The magic filaments froze in place. "What is this thing?" She gestured at the tent around them.

"Additional protection to keep Chatain from detecting you. What are you doing?"

Witmara summoned the tendrils of magic back to her. "It's time. I have to do something to settle the land." She closed her eyes, raising her awareness higher, and took a fold of the silken fabric between the thumb and forefinger of her right hand.

"What are you *doing?*" Seijina repeated, fear making her voice quaver.

Witmara ignored her, tracing through the spell on the fabric. A shield, yes, but also a constraint—tied to the floral pattern.

Aha. A means of monitoring and control.

Did she have the strength to deal with this magic and then the land?

"So this is meant to *confine* as well as *protect*," she said, letting a sharp note creep into her voice as she kept her eyes closed to better focus on the spell elements. "Convenient, that."

"We—we didn't want you reacting unconsciously." Seijina's voice wavered even more. "Perhaps we shouldn't have done it, but Chatain *could* have provoked you somehow while you were sleeping. We don't know how your magic works, and we didn't dare take the risk of you bringing him down on us!"

Ah. There it was. She could trace through the elements in this spell easily enough. Witmara placed her left hand on her necklace—thankfully no one had dared to remove it. She pressed her wedding ring against the main stone in the necklace.

Restore and protect. Remove that which shields and restrains me from outside magic. Re-shield me.

Warm tingles ran through her left hand. Witmara kept her eyes closed as she traced a glyph on the silk. Heat followed her fingers, and Seijina yelped as if she had been poked. Weight lifted off of Witmara, followed by a cool flow of power surging through her body as her full magic returned and the land's awareness begged for her attention.

Witmara opened her eyes. The silken tent had disappeared. Seijina now sat in her chair, staring at Witmara's hands. They glowed dark purple, edged with black. Witmara smiled at that sight.

My magic has returned in full. Thank you, Lord Staul.

"You risk exposing us to Chatain," Seijina whispered.

"Then I suppose I should take steps to prevent that happening."

Witmara slid to the edge of the bed. It would be safer to work this magic here, with earth around her. She pointed to the ceiling.

"Is that earth or wood?"

"Wood," Seijina husked.

Then she needed to be on the earth for this to happen. Witmara pushed a rug aside and placed her feet on the floor. Cool earth, firm and smoothed by many feet. She eased herself off the bed and lay face down, arms spread wide.

"What are you doing?" Seijina demanded from above her.

Witmara raised her head. "Getting control of the land. Let me concentrate!"

She pressed her forehead to the ground again.

I am here,

she said to the land.

I am Witmara ea Miteal, daughter of Metkyi the Messenger of Staul and Katerin ea Miteal, Leader of Medvara. I have come to make you whole.

You are here!

The land snatched desperately at Witmara, like a fretful half-grown pup would chew at a bone it had snatched away from larger dogs.

Sh. Sh. Shh.

She rested her palms flat on the ground. Then she extended her magic deep into the earth to find the nearby current of its power. She located the line and grasped it hard, marveling at the intensity and power within that particular channel.

She is here!

Daran exulted.

A Miteal returns to me at last!

It surged against Witmara, trying to take her over, to turn her strength to its will.

Quiet! Now is not the time! Be still!

Why?

it demanded, still trying to consume her.

Because I say so. It is not yet time! Do you wish to lose me to Chatain?

She seized the flow of power hard, tightening her hands as she concentrated on stilling it, quieting its wild frenzy.

I would protect you!

Not like this.

She whispered a spell of control. Gods, this magic had run wild for *years*. Just as she thought she had tamed the feral force in her grasp, it spat flame at her, struggling against restraint, stinging her in its desire to *control* while resisting *being controlled*.

There was so much power. So much intensity. Nothing like the land's magic she knew from Heinmyets and his deft manipulation of the land's power in the Two Nations, or her mother's skilled handling of Medvara. This was untamed, ungoverned power. It threatened to overwhelm her, swamping her in its desire for control and possession as they battled for dominance.

You—will—listen—to—me!

Suddenly an image from the early training of her daranval Daro came to her.

Daro pulling hard and bucking against halter and lead after she put a saddle on his back. He reared high, throwing his head from side to side in an attempt to break free of her hold on his rope, then dropped down to all fours, kicking high, blindly fighting against her, crashing against the fence of the round corral.

"Steady, steady," she said to him, her heart breaking to see him fight against the restraint.

"Loosen your grasp and send him forward," her mother said calmly as she leaned on the fence watching them, her own daranval Rainin, Daro's dam, standing next to her with ears forward. "He runs to escape restraint. That's normal. Don't box him up. Let him run a couple of laps, then reel him in gently, gradually."

It had worked. After spooking him into a run around the pen for several laps, the lead loose, she had slowly tightened it to slow him, until his strides slowed and he turned to face Witmara, then walked toward her.

Witmara loosened her grip on the land's power slightly, keeping a light hold on it as it ran and bucked under her. She met its attempts to overpower her with a firm resistance, but did not try to restrain it. Not yet.

After what seemed to be ages, the struggle eased, until the flow of magic lay quiescent within her grasp. Now she exerted her power, delicately threading it over the core of the land's strength with the same light touch she would use to halter Daro when he was in a playful mood. As she closed her binding over its core, it shuddered, then submitted, pushing gently against her hands.

I am yours, to do with as you will,

Daran said to her.

She tamped back the sudden exultation flowing through her.

Chatain must not know yet.

Why?

the land challenged, sulky in tone.

You are my new mistress. I do not want to deal with him anymore.

I am not ready to confront him. We must prepare. Until then, you must deceive him about my control.

I don't want to.

Whiny.

Would you lose me?

No.

Slow, reluctant to admit it.

Then hide me, as best as you can.

What if he demands that I tell him? He will have sensed our struggle.

Then you will need to misinform him.

He will hurt me.

Hurt the land? How could Chatain hurt the land? That didn't make sense.

> Then turn to me and I will help you. But we must wait until the time is right.

> As you wish. But how am I to contact you? What token can you bear for me?

Medvara had given her mother a deepest piece of its heart, forcing a stone through the soil. Dare she ask Daran for that kind of token?

No, Witmara decided.

That required too much power and would definitely draw Chatain's attention. What jewelry did she wear regularly that she could use for a token until she could proclaim herself? Her necklace was dedicated to Staul. Her ring was a sign of her bonding to Toran. But her bracelet was a matching stone to the necklace and ring…and was untied to any other power.

She slipped the bracelet off her wrist and pressed the stone against the earth.

> Mark this bracelet as your token for me.

The bracelet warmed against her palm as she felt the land's power probe the stone. Then a flow.

> It is done.

> Good. I will summon you as needed through it, and you can do the same for me.

> I will, Lady Witmara, Empress-to-be. Oh, I look forward to our time together!

So do I. Now hush! Do not betray me any further.

I hear and obey.

The sensation of power faded away. Witmara slowly rose to hands and knees, rocked back on her heels, then slipped the bracelet back onto her wrist, resting her hands on her thighs. Fatigue pulled at her, but it was a different tiredness from her injury, a familiar feeling that followed the working of magic. She looked up to meet Seijina's wide-eyed gaze, staring at her in shock.

"It is done," she said, surprised at how raspy her voice was. "Daran is mine."

Seijina slid off of the chair and prostrated herself in front of Witmara. "Empress Witmara. I am honored to have witnessed your winning of the land."

"No," Witmara said, leaning forward to try to pull Seijina up and falling onto the good earth beneath them. "I am not yet your Empress. We have a lot to do before then."

Seijina helped Witmara up, shaking her head.

"You are my Empress. Proclaimed or not, you are my Empress."

"That will not be certain until Chatain falls." Witmara heaved a heavy sigh. She closed her eyes again.

Shield me,

she said to the land. Then she sent out a tentative searching thread through her ring, seeking any sign of Daro and Toran's presence.

Gods, she hoped Daro was with Toran. The bond between her and her daranval was easier to manage than mindspeech, even with the magic enclosed by the tattoo that the Hidden One had gifted her when she and Toran had spoken their vows.

The small tattoo on her hand throbbed as Daro perceived her. Wordless joy surged through the link. She projected thoughts of scratching his forelock. He sent back images of cookies, mounds of the mint and oat treats she made for him.

> Toran lives?

she thought at Daro.
Affirmation.

> Link us.

> Witmara!

Joy in Toran's mindvoice, as strong as if he were nearby and not across the ocean.

> I feared the worst!

> Toran! You live!

She was remotely aware that tears formed in her eyes.

> Oh Gods, Toran. Where are you? You sound so close!

> We are on the Heart's Desire. Setkin says we will be there tonight.

> Oh Gods, Toran. Oh Gods.

She drew a ragged breath.

Tonight, then. We dare not use more magic. Chatain is searching for me.

Stay safe, beloved.

I will.

Daro protested as she closed the link.

"Are you all right?" Seijina asked as Witmara wrapped her arms tightly around herself, letting the tears flood her eyes as she curled tightly on the ground.

"They live, praise be to Staul," she whispered, blinking her eyes to clear them, fighting back the fatigue that threatened to make her sleep again. "My husband and daranval *live*."

A REQUEST FROM KERATIL

DREAD OF THE DAY AHEAD TIGHTENED KATERIN'S GUT AS SHE gazed around the familiar bedroom of her suite in the Leaders' House. Just enough light spilled through the window shutters that she could recognize shapes in the room.

Home. And she had many things to do besides make sure that her daughter was safe, including dealing with the consequences from Finniarn's co-optation.

Gods only knew what sort of mess *that* would be. Oh well. She had awakened early enough that perhaps she could sort through parts of the problem before others would be up and demanding her attention.

At least she was back home, in her own land, in her own bed, in the capable hands of her majordomo Cantiste. She didn't have to *go* anywhere or do anything other than her usual responsibilities as Leader, at least for today. After the past month, it felt good to be staying in one place.

And how long will that be?

If she didn't go to Daran-over-Sea to confront Chatain, then she had to deal with the situation she learned about in

Waykemin—not Waykemin itself, but the potential disaster that lay to its southeast.

She didn't want to think about leaving home again just yet. But her desire to stay in one place was certainly a change from the years she spent traveling on a healing circuit, where after a few days she was eager to move on to the next village.

Sooner you get moving, the sooner you can get things done.

Katerin rose and went into her combined sitting and dressing room. She almost burst into relieved tears when she found a *clean* daily tunic and trousers in her usual plain brown laid out, a heavy gray sweater thrown over the back of a chair. Leather slippers waited by the chair. On the small round table next to her chair, her usual breakfast of two sweet biscuits, cheese slices, and a handful of dried apples and peaches sat on a plate next to a pot filled with berry tea. Katerin poured herself a cup of tea, then nibbled on the food and sipped tea as she dressed, pulled on her slippers, and hung her nightclothes. So different from traveling, so different from conditions in battle camp.

Home.

After visiting her birthplace Medvara seemed to be a veritable paradise. She could handle the problems her land handed her.

Waykemin, on the other hand—once again she fought back the sorrowful sick feeling that *I should have known, I should have done something sooner.*

Instead, Katerin quickly ate one of the sweet biscuits, and refilled her cup with the rest of the berry tea, her mood already improved. Cantiste would have left another pot of tea in her office.

Make time to see Cantiste this morning.

Not just to thank him, but to hear about Witmara's vowing. He most likely had played a major part in organizing it. She put on her belt with a sheathed knife, her key ring, and the pouches that carried her everyday potions and goods. Then she pulled on the gray sweater, and carried the plate with the remnants of her breakfast and her cup down the hallway to her private office. One of the guards—Uvnen—opened the door for her.

"Admit visitors or turn them away?" he asked.

"While I'd like to say turn everyone away for the morning—there are those I will need to speak to. Introduce and admit Rekaré, Korien, Tilvi, and Tilyet," she said. "Anyone else—if they insist that it is urgent, check with me. I will tell you if I want to see them."

"I will do so, Leader Katerin." He closed the door after her.

After setting plate and cup on her desk, next to the waiting teapot, she heaved a sigh and looked around her.

Cantiste had already kindled a fire in the little stove. She checked on it—no need to add wood right away. She sighed again at the piles of paper on the main meeting table that hadn't been there before everything happened with Waykemin—clearly reports from Finniarn, Witmara, Tilyet, and Tilvi, amongst others.

It was tempting to throw them into the fire, tired as she was, but no, they needed to be checked.

A folder sat on her desk that hadn't been there last night, when she had returned the Veil and Gloves to their drawer before going to bed.

Delaying dealing with the papers, she opened the shutters and leaned her head against a windowsill, sipping on her tea. The glass fogged from her breath as Katerin stared into the West Garden, where she had built a small folly for entertaining guests. She straightened up, watching the small wisps of early morning fog fade as a drizzle began. Apparently that was where Witmara and Toran had said their vows.

She turned back to study her office, stifling another sigh, cupping her teacup in both hands. Where was she going to start?

Desk, and that damned report.

She set her tea down on the desktop, then sat and pulled the folder over to her. Tilvi's stamp marked the front cover. Katerin scanned it.

That didn't take long for them to prepare.

She wondered if the twins had been ready for just this sort of situation. If so, why hadn't they approached her about their suspicions before? A good question to ask Tilvi and Tilyet.

She read the report in more detail after eating the last of her breakfast, pausing after several paragraphs to sip tea and think. When she was finished, she slumped back in her chair and stared out the south-facing window. The drizzle had intensified to a gray mist.

Things were not quite as bad as she had feared. Most of the problems came from recent promotions within those ministries, and those involved had not been there long.

So this was a recent attempt to infiltrate her government, not a long-term plan. And those involved had connections back to Rekaré's father Zauril. A case where they were taking advantage of new leadership to ooze back into power.

But. They had to be dealt with.

Someone knocked at her door.

"Yes?"

Uvnen opened the door. "Rekaré is here." He stepped aside to let her enter, then closed the door.

"Good morning." Katerin leaned back in her chair and waved Rekaré to a seat. She noticed that her cousin also carried a cup of tea.

Must tell Treasury to increase Cantiste's pay.

Not just for taking care of Witmara and Toran's vowing, but for his overall mindfulness. After Waykemin....

Gods, she hoped she never, ever had to deal with slavery ever again. Especially slavery that stole the souls of the enslaved.

Dark circles underlined Rekaré's eyes, and she moved stiffly, hunched over, as if her back hurt.

"Did you sleep all right?"

"Good morning," Rekaré said. "My sleep?" She winced, staring down into her mug. "Fitful. But that had nothing to do with your hospitality and everything to do with—well, being back here. *Benghaalph* stirs within me but is reluctant to come forth. We face a turning point but I don't see the right pathway. Yet."

Benghaalph.

Rekaré had somehow assumed the mantle of being the Saubral prophet after she had left the Leadership of Medvara. Sometimes it rode her lightly, and other times it drove her hard.

Benghaalph and Kinslayer.

Both roles struck Katerin as more difficult than being Leader of Medvara.

"I might have a mixture that would help with sleep."

"You don't need to do that." Rekaré's protest sounded half-hearted.

"Would you prefer a tea or a tincture?" Katerin went to her mixing bench. This was something she could work on while they talked.

"Probably a tincture."

Rekaré got up and leaned against the edge of the bench top, watching Katerin sort through her mixtures. Katerin found what she wanted and began to measure it into the polished stone bowl she used to prepare her healing potions.

"How bad is the infiltration into your government?" Rekaré continued.

"Surprisingly not as bad as I thought, at least after looking at Tilvi and Tilyet's report."

Katerin poured her base mix into a wooden mixing bowl. What else would she add to it, especially for Rekaré? Perhaps a pinch of cirelen, to balance out her magic. She had to grind it separately from the other herbs.

She continued. "For the most part, the spies they've identified appear to be former lackeys of Zauril trying to sneak their way back into favor. Why those particular ministries I don't know. Treasury and the magitech part of Manufacture are obvious, but Lumbering?"

"That doesn't make much sense to me, either. I would be more inclined to think Agriculture instead of Lumbering."

"Unless they feared Tilvi and Tilyet, and thought they might be able to get information about Agriculture through back channels."

Katerin crushed the dried herbs in the bowl, grinding harder than usual with her pestle. A good way to rid herself of tension.

"But even so, I'd think Fisheries would have been a better choice—no, wait, Tilyet would notice irregularities there."

Rekaré raised her brows. "They have that much influence at their age?"

"They're Senior Record Keepers in the Agriculture ministry, and would notice any irregularities quickly. That's why they're so high-ranked even though they're young." Katerin studied the powder. Was it sufficiently fine? No. She needed to grind some more. "They're also Miteal family. Distant cousins of ours—descended from a cousin of Alexran."

"I remember a little bit about them. Mainly being surprised when they first entered service in my third year of Leadership because they were twins with magic, born and raised under Zauril's regime." Rekaré scowled. "Not many twins lived under Zauril's rule. Especially any with magical ability who were tied to our family."

Katerin nodded. "I've heard a few stories about them since I became Leader. Their mother died in my first year and they had to go to Cooscol for the ceremonies. I attended, to honor her, and heard stories. Tilyet went to sea with the fishing fleet when he was barely old enough to pull nets, and Tilvi to the herders. Their father was a Cooscol fisherman—drowned in a storm. The community protected them, probably because their mother was one of Artel's shamans."

And perhaps because they were distant kin to the Miteal family— even then someone was thinking about replacing Zauril, I'd wager.

"I remember that. But gods, they're young. Younger than me —can't remember by how much. Not many years."

Katerin paused, staring at her bottles of herbs, oils, and premixed potions as she thought.

"Let's see. They entered service the first year they were eligible, during the third year of your leadership. So they're three years younger than you are."

"So thirty-two, thirty-three. Fifteen years of service, in Agriculture." Rekaré sipped her tea. "And influential. That speaks to their competence, that they've risen this high in a ministry as big as that one."

Katerin sifted the powder through her fingers to make sure it was finely ground. She poured it into the base liquid, then reached for the bottle filled with dried blue cirelen flowers. As she pulled the wooden stopper out of the bottle, the haunting sweet scent of cirelen wafted around them.

Katerin picked out three flowers that glowed silver at her touch and dropped them into the stone bowl. A brief melancholy touched her as she capped the bottle, then faded—normal for exposure to that much cirelen, even that briefly. She ground the cirelen with a softer touch than she had the other herbs. A less-intense version of cirelen's sweet scent filled her nose as she worked.

"No. Not a bad rise at all for Agriculture."

"You said there were some spies who weren't connected to Zauril's rule."

"Yes. A few. Not anyone who has been vocal about problems

with my Leadership. But those unconnected spies worry me the most."

The cirelen powdered almost too easily—*beginning to reach the end of this batch's usefulness.* Katerin carefully poured it into the mixture, making sure she got the last crumbs of powder into the liquid. Cirelen was too precious to waste.

"For good reason. They're most likely the ones who betrayed Witmara, rather than any legacy from Zauril."

The hair on the back of Katerin's neck tingled with worry at the harshness of Rekaré's tone.

The Kinslayer speaking—or was that benghaalph?

Whichever it was, Rekaré's voice carried the authority of prophecy.

"You think so?" she asked, adding a touch more chamomile to the mix.

Ah. That was it. A little more mint and it would be a perfect combination for Rekaré.

"Is that *benghaalph* or the Kinslayer speaking?" She kept her voice steady.

Rekaré snorted. "Neither. Say, rather, the former Leader of Medvara who saw opposition rising during the last years of her Leadership. You're a popular Leader, Katerin. It makes no sense for you to attract opponents who support Chatain's goals."

"There is always opposition to any government."

"Not to the degree that they'd willingly spy for a known enemy, especially against a Leader loved by the land and her people. Zauril's lackeys?" Rekaré shrugged. "They would aid Chatain no matter what, because they support Daran resuming colonial rule over Medvara. It's the new ones who aren't tied to Zauril that are problematic—and would be in better positions to spy, plus receive direction to betray Witmara." She chewed on her lower lip thoughtfully as Katerin added more liquid to the mixture. "No. As I think further, it doesn't make sense. You would have heard murmuring. I would have heard about unrest. My Mer Galad riders hear a lot of things in our travels. If you had been a target—I would have known."

"That's true. Could they have been unwilling, forced? Like we saw in Waykemin?"

"The land would have been aware of that and warned you."

"I guess we won't know until they talk."

"*If* they talk. How many have been captured?"

"None."

"That suggests outside infiltrators rather than collaborators from within."

Katerin sighed. "And further problems that won't be solved overnight." She chewed on her lip. "I don't know what to do about Witmara. By now she has to be in Daran. Leave it to Toran to rescue her, or do we go?"

"Dare you leave the land again? Tilvi and Tilyet appear to be excellent guardians…" Rekaré's voice trailed off.

Katerin thought she heard the tone of the Kinslayer present, perhaps also a bit of *benghaalph* speaking.

"They are, in normal circumstances. But. We have two things happening. First, that handful of betrayers." Katerin said. "Second, and potentially worse, what we left behind in Waykemin. Or, rather, the threat that looms there, and on the edge of Keratil."

"The Divine Confederation and the Outcast God? I don't know what to think about that situation—and *benghaalph* is silent on the subject." Rekaré fingered her chin thoughtfully. "But the Keratil still safely hold the Nerean Gate. As long as the Divine Confederation doesn't breach it, we should be all right."

"And that's the problem. I don't know what to think about that menace to our east, either. Except that I feel I don't dare go haring off over Sea in pursuit of Witmara, much as my heart tells me I should." Katerin sniffed the mixture, and decided it would work. She poured it into a vial, then stoppered and handed it to Rekaré. "Two doses. If you need to carry more than that, let me know. It should be mixed freshly for best effect."

"Thank you." Rekaré tucked the vial into one of her belt pouches. "I may ask for more, but this will do for the next night or so."

"Good. So I don't know what to do about Witmara. I suppose I could consult with the Gods—but Staul has been uncommunicative both about her and about the Divine Confederation. If he won't speak on those subjects, then the Goddess won't either. My heart says *go*. Find out if she is safe. Defend her against Chatain if needed. But my head tells me I need to stay in Varen. That Medvara—and perhaps all the lands of Varen—need me more than Witmara does. I'm torn."

Rekaré's lips tightened. "Sesenth and Detaluna have been down to the docks. Vered is back, after returning the Mershaunten to Leithra."

Vered was the second-in-command of the Sorcerer-Captains who piloted the sorcerous sailships. While the Sorcerer-Captains were nominally unallied with any nation, over the past few years their allegiance had leaned toward the nations of Varen instead of Daran.

"I'm assuming the Mershaunten has taken his fleet back to Larij?"

She had been grateful that the leader of the neighboring country of Larij had been so generous with his support of Witmara during Chatain's attack—then again, his youngest son had married Witmara.

"Well, that's the thing." Rekaré looked down at her mug, then back up at Katerin. "He is willing to split his fleet. Half to provide you aid and support in the defense of Varen."

"Not necessary, but I do appreciate that sentiment. So he's ordering the half not committed to me back to Leithra?" Katerin automatically began cleaning up her supplies.

Tell Cantiste I need more dried cirelen.

She reached for chalk to write a reminder on the inventory slate.

Rekaré shook her head. "If I so desire—if *we* so desire—he has pledged that portion of his fleet to support me in an attack on Daran."

Katerin stopped writing. "He *what?*" She turned to face Rekaré.

"He has given me command over half his fleet if I want to take them to retrieve Witmara—or help her overthrow Chatain, if it comes to that."

"I—Gods, Rekaré. That's a generous offer."

The Larijian navy was much, much stronger than anything Medvara had. The Mershauntens of Larij had always been focused on sea defenses.

"I told him I needed to speak with you first. He agreed—but that's why half the fleet stays here, should I decide to go to Daran. Alden will command those who remain, to defend Varen. Both the Mershaunten and Alden are concerned about where the rest of Chatain's fleet went. They can't all have returned to Daran."

Katerin finished her note. She swept up the crumbs of dried herbs on the counter and wiped her mixing bowl clean. The Mershaunten's support made sense. Witmara was his lawdaughter now, and his son had gone to rescue her. Medvara and Larij were united as they had not been before.

"We need to think about this," she said, returning to her chair. "We'll need not just the fleet but riders if we're going to mount a credible invasion challenge to Daran. And how are you going to track down Witmara?"

"Vered believes that Setkin will return swiftly, either with Toran and Witmara, or not. That's a start." Rekaré dropped back into her chair. She placed her tea on Katerin's desk, and leaned back, interweaving her fingers and studying her hands thoughtfully. "Setkin should be able to tell us what the situation is with

Witmara and Toran—if they aren't already on the *Heart's Desire* with him."

"So you are waiting for his return?"

"No. A couple of days at most before I leave. I plan to sail with Vered in the *Morning Star*. The Sorcerer-Captains can communicate with each other across the waters, thanks to the aid of the Goddess Terat. Intercept Setkin, find out what he knows of the whereabouts of Witmara and Toran, and go from there."

"And if Witmara and Toran are with Setkin?"

Her cousin grinned mirthlessly. "I have sworn to take Chatain's life. If the Gods so will it, this will be the time it happens. One way or another, I will continue to Daran, and will not return to Varen while he lives."

Amber flecks shone bright in her gray eyes—*the Kinslayer rides her now*, Katerin realized.

"I—see." She wanted to cry out against this plan, especially since she couldn't aid her cousin like she had for so many years, but could not find the words to do so.

Uvnen knocked again.

"Yes?"

He opened the door. "A man named Doryits is here. He brings news from Leader Kintarit of Keratil."

Katerin and Rekaré exchanged worried looks.

"Keratil now?" Rekaré said.

"That means issues with the Nerean Gate and the Divine Confederation. Send him in," Katerin said.

At least it's Kintarit and not Yitlisk of Waykemin sending a messenger.

Waykemin was quiet, and that was what mattered at this point. But Keratil...Gods, she had hoped that the Divine Confederation would not be a problem for just a few years more. At least until they knew Witmara was safe and—whatever was to happen with Daran and Chatain was settled.

Battle on two fronts. This is not a coincidence. Chatain has a hand in this, I'll wager.

That had to stop. Katerin clenched her fists tight. She was right to stay here.

Goddess Dovré, I swear I will not rest until I have rooted out every little piece of poison that man has planted in this land!

Just as Rekaré wanted to kill Chatain, she wanted to wipe his influence from Varen.

Uvnen opened the door. "Commissioner Doryits from Keratil." He bowed and stepped back as a burly man slipped into the room, lighter-skinned than most but still darker than Katerin, more brown than red in his coloring. "Leader Katerin?"

Katerin rose. "I am she, and this is my cousin Rekaré." She didn't add *Kinslayer.* "Commissioner Doryits?"

"Yes." He shifted on his feet uneasily. "I give you the regards of my Leader Kintarit and the best wishes of the people of Keratil...." His voice trailed off as Katerin fixed him with a steady glare.

"You can skip the formalities," she said.

He sighed with relief. "By Artel, I am not good at this."

"That's all right. Speak directly."

He cleared his throat. "Well. Then. I lead the Guardians of the Wall. Leader Kintarit felt I was the best one to bring you this message. He sends word that Keratil has been threatened, and begs support from Leader Katerin and any others of Varen who can answer his call." Doryits's voice was deep and steady, but his face sagged in lines of fatigue above his gray-streaked, curly dark beard. "The Divine Confederation has sent a delegation through the Nerean Gate. They demand a tribute of souls, or else they follow with an invading army of—the dead that walk, first to conquer Keratil, and then the rest of Varen. And other sorcerous creatures." He swallowed hard. "They carry this sigil. You have fourteen days. If no tribute is provided, they invade."

He held a copper disk out to them. Rekaré took it first, her face hardening after she looked at it, then handed the disk to Katerin.

Chatain's face was stamped on the disk, a visage almost identical to that on the coins in Finniarn's bag.

"So Chatain has allied with the Divine Confederation," Katerin said. "What does Keratil need from Medvara?"

"The Divine Confederation's demand for tribute includes Medvara, the Two Nations, Larij, Saubral, and Waykemin. We knew the Hidden One was here, and, well…" Doryits paused. "The messenger spoke of you by name, Katerin Leader. You are to lead the tribute."

"Lead the tribute?" Katerin snorted. "Only if the Confederation considers a war party to be a tribute. That's the only tribute they'll ever get from me!"

A faint smile twitched Doryits' lips. "Then you will help us turn them back?"

She bared her teeth at him. "Of course. They should have been paying attention to what happened at Waykemin."

"I think they were, along with Chatain, and that's why they did this," Rekaré said. "All right. That settles matters." She bowed to Katerin. "I wish you well in your battle against the Divine Confederation, but if Chatain is allied with them, then he needs more distraction. I am more than happy to be the source of that diversion. Let me know how many riders you can spare. I'm leaving for Daran tomorrow, with Vered and my half of the Mershaunten's fleet."

Katerin pressed her lips tightly together. She didn't like this, not at all. But if Chatain could fight on two fronts, so could she.

MEETINGS

THE DARKNESS IN THE HIDEY-HOLE WAS ALMOST AS OPPRESSIVE AS that of the hold of the iron ship that had hauled her here. The only difference was that Witmara had her magic—and her new link with the land of Daran.

She curled up on her bed, alone now that she was feeling better. Seijina had joined Betsona once they were told that Chatain had left the island, promising to bring Witmara out as soon as it was dark. Just because Chatain was gone did not mean that the watchers were.

Now that she was alone, she could speak with her patron God. Seijina had left more broth and soft rolls. Witmara set a roll on a plate, wishing she had huckleberry jam or something like that to offer the God. Not that it mattered—she trusted that the God would understand that there were limits to what she would procure right now.

My Lord Staul. *Your servant Witmara gives you thanks and praise for keeping me safe and bringing me out of captivity. Please accept my humble offering in this place of hiding.*

She bowed low before the plate, touching her forehead to the bedclothes, palms turned upright. The warmth around her turned heavy, pressing down hard on her body. Then it lightened.

> I am pleased to see you have made it this far.
> Rise, Witmara.

The God sat cross-legged on the bed across from her, attired in formal black Court dress. His necklace of teeth, finger bones, and miniature skulls glowed bright white in the dim light. He grinned at her as he ate the roll.

> I could not have done it without the guidance
> and protection of you and my father.

> True. But it also required your own boldness
> and courage. Your mastery of the land of Daran
> is commendable. Few have been able to
> restrain its power.

> Why is that?

The God rolled his eyes.

> Past history that I am constrained from
> revealing in detail, unfortunately. I would tell you
> if I were allowed. But it is tied to the dangers
> that your mother faces. I can only say this—
> there is a tie between the Divine Confederation
> and the land of Daran. A curse that will take
> both of you to lift.

Gods. A curse? She'd have to deal with that too? And what was the Divine Confederation? Witmara exhaled deeply.

> What sort of curse, Lord Staul? I do not know
> what the Divine Confederation is.

> The Divine Confederation comes from the lands beyond the Nerean Gate, and is tied to the Witches of Waykemin.

The God reached out and pressed one hand against her forehead and the other on her bracelet.

> My blessing on your new link with Daran. This land will challenge you—your struggles with it are not finished. It has not been under a magician's complete control since Elendor, Elithtra's father, and it was dominant even over him. I have no doubts that you will tame this magic, but it will be a continuous process.

He lifted his hands.

> Take your next steps. Reunite with your husband and daranval, and trust what they will tell you. Be cautious in your dealings with the Darani. Tricksters walk everywhere, encouraged by the wild magic of Daran, the greatest trickster of all.

> Betsona has her own goals.

> She intends well. But…she dreams of power, and Daran gives her a trickster's hope. Remember Daran carries a curse, and that one encounter will not keep its magic under restraint. Guard that you do not fall into the temptations of Daran's curse. Do not be seduced by the dreams and not the responsibilities of the power it can give you. I watch over you, my beloved.

The God smiled, then faded away.

Witmara moved to the chair. She started to explore parts of her link with Daran's magic, careful not to do anything that might attract Chatain's attention. She sensed Betsona's presence, a fiery but wounded and vulnerable power source roiling in the mix around her.

If Betsona had not been so badly injured...she might be the ruler that Witmara was dealing with. A good thing? Witmara wasn't sure. There was a twist in the magic around her that she could now perceive. Part of the curse that the God had mentioned? It did match certain things—*wrongnesses*—that Witmara had sensed from Chatain's projections. But Chatain and Betsona were siblings, so that kinship could explain the flaws she felt. Or it could be an artifact of the magical damage done to Betsona years ago. Or a foundational flaw in her deepest self tied to that curse—Witmara lacked the tools to determine this further. Yet.

Something to be wary of.

It would be wise to keep some of her abilities hidden from Betsona. Better to be underestimated. She had felt some of Betsona's ambivalence toward her at their first meeting—the reaction to her brown skin, and her age.

Not a new experience for her. While her mother's councilors in Medvara did not have the Darani bias against dark-skinned peoples, some of them did not seem to grasp that she was no longer a child. Especially Finniarn. Something had not been right about him those last few days in Medvara. It was almost as if he viewed her as a potential threat and not a prospective Leader.

Not that I will be Leader of Medvara now.

Rekaré seemed to understand the power churning within her.

Rekaré and those twins from Agriculture. She had noticed Tilvi eying her speculatively, as if she were measuring Witmara's magical potential in the same manner that she would do with a prize ram from the Stardance line. It hadn't bothered her like it would when she saw it from others, because Tilvi *understood.*

Tap-tap-tap from the door above interrupted her thoughts. Witmara alerted. Another search? No, the land would have warned her—wouldn't it?

Wait for the rest of the code.

Chatain might not be the only one searching for her. It was also likely that his lackeys here might have decided to follow up on his concern.

This is not Varen.

And the God had warned her of multiple tricksters.

A pause. Then *tap-tap, tap-tap, tap-tap-tap* followed the first sequence. The code Seijina had whispered to her before leaving.

"Yes?" she called.

"It's me," Petronin said, as he lifted the top off of the hole and climbed down the stairs. He carried a big bag. "Her ladyship sent these to you." Petronin dropped the bag on the table beside her and pulled it open to reveal several scrolls and a couple of small books. "Maps of Daran. And a couple of Darani-High Aireii primers—plus a dictionary."

"Tell her I thank her for this support." Witmara picked up the biggest scroll.

Maps. She could get some idea of what this land was like.

"I will." He turned to leave, glancing around the room. "All's well here? Do you need anything—food? Water?"

Something about Petronin's concern felt more trustworthy than Seijina's, especially since they were back with Betsona. Seijina was concerned about her standing with the future Empress. Petronin saw her as a person and not a potential ruler.

"Nothing right now," she said nonetheless. "I thank you for your concern. Both on the ship and here."

He shrugged. "It is the right thing to do. Word is that the *Heart's Desire* will reach Lanivar this evening. I have been told to bring you up then."

"What time of day is it now?" she asked.

"Three bells past midday."

"And evening comes when, here?"

"Between seven and eight bells."

"So between seven and eight bells."

"Perhaps closer to nine," he said. "But no later than ten."

Still later than she wanted for getting out of this hole, but this was not the time to press for concessions.

Not until I have Daro and Toran here to support me.

"Thank you, Petronin," Witmara repeated. "And thank her ladyship for the wise choice of things to occupy my mind until then."

But then, Betsona *had* always sent her useful books and scrolls to read. Witmara had looked forward to the possibility of sharing insights with her.

Hold on to that thought when dealing with Betsona.

Petronin nodded. "I will do that."

He climbed up the ladder.

Once Witmara heard the door slide into place, she unrolled the scroll. It was a large map of the land of Daran. Aha. At last she could get more than a vague idea of how large Daran was, and what lay around it. Betsona had not sent any maps of Daran, nor had Witmara sent Betsona any maps of Varen. Old books were one thing to share; but access to maps was even more restricted. The maps of Daran available in Medvara were incomplete, especially since Etikar, Dunaran, and now Chatain had expanded Daran's reach through conquest.

She found the Ourigny Islands on the map. Lanivar was the furthest to the southeast, the farthest away from the mainland and the closest island for any ship sailing from Varen. The mainland of Daran was further north jud west of the islands. The land directly across from the Islands was marked as Ternar—a conquered colony of Daran, and it spread north for quite a distance. She remembered learning a little bit about Ternar in her readings from Betsona—its natives were golden-skinned.

If she remembered correctly, Betsona had once said her mother came from Ternar.

That might explain her golden skin—

The one feature that Witmara vaguely remembered from meeting Betsona. So she wasn't pure Aireii, either—those were pale-skinned like Rekaré.

She became aware of a lighter version of Staul's ponderous presence.

Fascinating,

said her father Metkyi, Messenger of Staul. His spectral finger traced the coastline north from the border of Ternar. He poked at the border port of Fenras, where Setkin and Vered had originally been based before Chatain's rule.

That's probably where you should go from here.

I agree. The longer I spend on the ocean, the more exposed I'll feel.

She stifled a shiver. The restraints on her magic during her captivity had kept her from the worst effects of being a strong magician traveling on water. She wondered how the Sorcerer-Captains kept from being waterstruck. Perhaps because they were blessed by the Goddess Terat?

Fenras is a safer port than further north. After you land, I would go here.

He pointed to the city of Adalane.

She recognized the name. Betsona had been exiled there first, before Chatain moved her to Lanivar Island. It was the home of the Great Amphitheater, where the Spring Festival celebrated the work of Daran's playwrights and poets.

It's over a divide from Daraelen.

She pointed to the capital city of Daran, Daraelen, further north and west, on the other side of the mountains.

I need to go there if I intend to become Empress.

You need to build support first. Fenras and Adalane will be more open, due to their proximity to Ternar.

He hesitated.

Chatain will take this route to Daraelen eventually, after he opens the Festival.

He tapped a marked path over the mountains.

The Daraelen River runs west to an inland sea and not east to the ocean. Adalane and then the mountain pass will be his best path to the capital.

I see.

She studied the map further.

How had Daraelen had become the capital of Daran?

Unlike Medvare-the-city, located at the junction of the great Chellana River and the smaller Saktrin, there was no direct water access to Daraelen from the ocean. Besides the mountain pass from the Fenras River at Adalane, there were connections over land from a smaller port on the other side of those mountains, and from the north.

None of those ties made sense. A capitol *needed* easy travel access, usually by water. Even Dera, in Keldara, was on the Keldara River. Had Daran once been landlocked, with another realm between it and the ocean? Had that inland sea once been strategically important?

Nothing in either Medvara's records or the books Betsona had sent her explained why it would be so. This barebones map laid the dilemma of Daraelen's location out clearly, though.

Another thing to learn.

With a sigh, she rerolled that scroll and opened the next one. This was a detail of the city of Adalane. Several locations were marked in red on this map, not landmarks as far as she could tell, but places in the lower city. One place was identified as the Barking Dog. Another was the Actor's Playhouse. Taverns?

I wish I knew what these markings meant,

she said to Metkyi.

He shrugged.

I would memorize them. They clearly have some significance.

She nodded, and whispered the names over and over until she had them solidly fixed into her mind. Barking Dog. Actor's Playhouse. Sten's Brew and Bull. Corniea's Hats. Weaver's Supply. The Grand Stage. The Little Library.

The other scrolls were maps of Fenras and Daraelen, all with similar notations. Witmara memorized those notes as well. Her father sprawled on the bed, peering at the maps, but not commenting.

Then she turned to the primers, sorting through them before finding a small one she liked.

I need to learn common Darani,

she said to Metkyi.

Agreed. I will practice with you.

They worked on the simple phrases available in the primer. Witmara consulted the dictionary as she worked to form basic sentences. Her father quizzed her, until she could ask and answer simple questions about food, lodging, supplies, and count money.

She startled as someone tapped on the door. Her father faded away. How long had she been focused on this? Was it already dark?

"Yes?"

Seijina lifted the door, holding a lamp high.

"Safe to come out now. Betsona thought you might want to meet the incoming ship."

"Of course!" Witmara gathered up the scrolls and books. Only now did she notice that Petronin had taken the bag he had used to bring them down the ladder with him. "What should I do with these? I don't want to leave them here."

Seijina dropped down a bag tied to a rope. "Load this and I'll pull them up. You might want to be careful," she cautioned as Witmara finished loading the bag. "You've not had a lot of time to recover from your injuries."

Witmara bit back the snippy response she wanted to make.

I'm not ignorant. My mother was a Healer before she became Leader, after all.

"I'll be careful," she said instead.

She gathered up the clumsy long split skirt that someone had put on her—probably Seijina—and wondered where her usual trousers and tunic had gone. Probably for cleaning. Then she grabbed the sides of the ladder and climbed out. The skirt was awkward, wanting to cling to her legs and interfere with free movement.

I'll change as soon as possible.

Unless she needed to wear the cursed things to blend in?

That could be likely, though when they had landed at the main island she had seen that slaves, male and female both, wore trousers and tunics. Perhaps that was it. If she wore trousers, with her dark skin she would appear to be a slave.

She blinked in the darkness broken only by Seijina's light as Seijina lowered the door and kicked loose hay over the top of it. They were in a shed of some sort with animals—a barn? A donkey glared at her from its stall as it munched on hay, flattening its ears for a moment. Chickens muttered short chirps from their roosts, one red hen squawking louder than the others, shoving at a black and white neighbor. The neighbor moved over two steps, clucking in annoyance.

"Ka, ka, ka, sh, sh," Seijina crooned, imitating a hen's happy song. The squawker and her neighbor settled.

Seijina handed her a scarf that matched the one draped around her head and shoulders. "Wrap this like I have mine. We'll bring a fold up over our mouth and nose when we leave the barn." She demonstrated. Witmara copied her. "Good." She handed Witmara a cane. "Betsona thought you might need this for support."

She didn't, but Witmara detected a sensing spell to measure her strength once she touched it.

Aha. So I am right to be suspicious.

On the other hand, Betsona would not have survived this long without using such tactics to explore the vulnerabilities of those who might be a threat to her.

Remember, she has endured under Chatain.
You could learn something from her,

her father whispered without manifesting himself.

You need to be cautious.

Instead of completely blocking the spell, Witmara fed a

projection of her remaining fatigue back into it, along with a healthy dose of her worry. She leaned on the cane more than she needed to, hobbling alongside Seijina as they walked to the main house, Seijina carrying the bag.

Thin shades covered the openings in the house now that it was evening. Witmara noted how easy it was to see outlines behind them.

Not much privacy.

But not that different from summer camps in the Two Nations, when she and her mother had ridden with Heinmyets and his wives alongside the sheepherders to watch the summer flocks—and resume official contacts with the roaming clans of Clendan herders as well as the villages nearby.

Seijina led her through an exquisite courtyard with a walkway of flat-slabbed stone framed by carefully trimmed bushes. Glow lights accented the presence of certain stones— shrines to Dovré and to Artel. They passed under a tree with bright white flowers that shone in the light from the house. A faint sweet scent wafted from the flowers, but faded two steps later.

A short ramp led from the courtyard to a vertical-slatted blind next to a shuttered opening. Seijina held the slats aside so that Witmara could precede her. Once inside, she took off her scarf and hung it on a hook on the wall. Witmara copied her, looking around. This was a different room from the one she remembered when she arrived. Boxes and a clothing rack lined the three walls of this room, chairs by the open side.

Storage? On the outside walls?

Perhaps a means of increasing privacy further inside.

A solid door set into a solid wall was on the far side of the room. Seijina knocked on it.

"I am here," Betsona said.

Was that irritation or pain in her voice? Witmara wasn't certain. Seijina opened the door. Once again, she gestured to

Witmara to enter first. The faint tingles of a strong protective spell prickled her arms and then the rest of her.

Harmless,

Witmara thought, projecting

no threat, no challenge.

The spell flickered away.

This room had walls on all four sides, though it lacked a ceiling, the only cover being the thatched roof overhead. Another door paralleled the one that Witmara had entered. Betsona reclined on a red-cushioned daybed placed on the top tier of a series of risers, pillows behind her and under her right arm. She wore a loose-fitting, long-sleeved, red gown of a shimmering material that seemed to have golden undertones—*silk?* Witmara wondered. If so, it was a finer make than what smugglers brought to Medvara. The other chairs in the room were on the main floor, so that their occupants had to look up at Betsona.

"Be seated," Betsona said, gesturing toward one of the chairs. "I am sure you still need the rest after all that time sleeping."

"I thank you for your consideration. The *Heart's Desire* is nearby?"

Witmara scanned the indicated chair. More probes. She kept up her façade of greater weakness than she actually felt, letting the spell proceed so far but no further.

Betsona nodded, surveying Witmara. "Yes. You have connected with the land and can now control your linkage with it?"

"Yes." Witmara met her gaze, not allowing herself the temptation to give Betsona a knowing smirk. "At that point I became aware that my husband and daranval were not only alive, but traveling on the *Heart's Desire* to meet me."

"*Daranval*," Betsona mused, her voice caressing the word longingly. "That would be one of the magic-gifted horses of your people?"

"Yes," Witmara said cautiously. "They bond to one rider and will not allow any other, unless their rider has died."

"Alas." A world of disappointment hung in her response. "I had hopes that one of your daranvals—"

"*Daranvelii* is the plural," Witmara said.

"*Daranvelii*, then," Betsona repeated, voice slightly irritated. "That one of them might help me compensate for—well—such as I am."

"Perhaps if we were to bring a young, unbonded daranval, or an older one that has lost its rider, then you could have the opportunity to bond with one," Witmara said carefully.

"Well, it's not going to happen right now." Betsona waved impatiently. "And that's not the issue, anyway. I cannot order up a cart to carry both of us to the dock. Will you be able to walk there?"

"With a cane, I think I can manage," Witmara said.

I can ride Daro back.

Though she had to wonder—if Betsona could not come with her, then why had she summoned Witmara?

"How soon before you anticipate their arrival?"

"Very soon." Betsona drew a deep breath. "Before you meet your family—what are your plans? Return to Varen or—the land has claimed you. What do you intend to do about that?"

"I have much to learn before I dare assert myself against Chatain," Witmara said. "I had hopes that you might be able to provide me with guidance in how I can best do so."

A thin smile twitched Betsona's lips, one that didn't quite reach her eyes. "Of course, cousin. When would you like to begin?"

"Once I have returned with my husband and daranval, and know what actions my people may be taking," Witmara said.

"We will speak in the morning, then." Betsona gestured to the inside door. "There are several enclosed rooms such as this for sleeping. I would recommend that you sleep under a net since this place—" she grimaced, "does not have ceilings for ventilation's sake and there are bugs and other vermin. We do have walls for some privacy. Plus spells for silence. I would be happy to provide you with the key spells for your reunion with your husband."

"Thank you," Witmara said.

Betsona reached for two canes that sat in a stand next to the daybed. She sat up. For the first time, Witmara realized the extent to which Betsona was crippled. She hunched to her right side, head angling over her right shoulder rather than straight up and down. Her right arm was smaller than her left, apparently withered. When she stood, she leaned precariously to the right. Her gown was of a stiff material that masked the crooked angle of her body, but couldn't disguise the tilt of her shoulders.

Seijina hovered protectively as Betsona carefully made her way down step by laborious step to the floor. Witmara looked down so that she wasn't staring at Betsona's infirmities. No wonder Betsona couldn't challenge Chatain herself. Coping with her body took enough effort.

How had this happened—that's right. A magical accident when she was young—and involving Chatain.

"So you see how crippled I am, thanks to my brother," Betsona said bitterly. "Are you repelled by my imperfect self? Do you consider me cursed?"

Now Witmara dared look at her, feeling like she had been given permission.

"No. I am a Healer's daughter, after all. I know that the body's condition does not always reflect the spirit within it."

"More enlightened than most of Daran, then," Betsona growled.

Witmara shrugged. "Alicira ea Miteal battled injury and

illness for years, but was still one of the Three Leaders of the Two Nations. My mother was her Healer—oh, since before I was born. I grew up around Alicira."

Betsona tightened her lips. "A much more reasonable attitude than you will find common amongst the nobility here. Fortunate. It is—one of the things I admire about Medvara. Your mother. Rekaré. Alicira. A place where ability matters and not—other things."

"We have our own challenges."

"Doesn't everyone?" Betsona sighed, and her face softened. "Let me show you the room prepared for you, and give you the key spells," she said.

"I thank you again," Witmara said.

And I'll wager you hope to hear something useful from our bed conversation.

She would have to warn Toran on their ride back to the house—the daranvelii would screen any conversation if asked.

Gods, this land's politics were convoluted.

She followed Betsona through the inside doorway. It opened onto a narrow hallway with several doors opening off of it. Betsona led Witmara to the furthest door.

"This is where you two can stay," she said as she opened the door.

Witmara noticed that the bedcover, bowl, bed net, and pitcher had the same floral pattern on them as the items in the hidey-hole. Little pink and blue five-petaled flowers on vines with heart-shaped leaves. Had she seen a flower like that here? She hadn't been outside with a clear head in daylight. It looked vaguely familiar, though.

Everything matches. Definitely spell-laden.

She idly wondered if Betsona had the same patterns in her private room, or if the patterns were just shortcut spells so that she could monitor those around her. Betsona hobbled past Witmara to sit on one of the two chairs beside the bed, her long gown rustling as she settled. Witmara turned around to assess the room. A brown dresser and mirror with bowl and water pitcher on top, several towels neatly folded next to the bowl. A wardrobe. Two chairs. Most likely a chamberpot under the bed. Everything they needed for a night's stay, or longer.

She opened the wardrobe to find more divided skirts like the one she wore, along with shorter tops, some with longer sleeves.

"Is this common wear in Daran?" she asked, trying out her common Darani.

Betsona raised her brows. "I thought you didn't speak Darani?" she said, using Darani instead of the High Aireii.

"Seijina gave me a primer. I am learning."

"I see." Betsona switched back to the High Aireii. "You are a fast learner. That's good. As for the clothing—yes. You will wear heavier underthings on the main continent because it is colder there than here."

"Good."

Gods, she hoped that Toran had brought her clothes to wear. She couldn't see herself wearing such lightweight clothing on an extended ride.

"Also…" Betsona's voice trailed off. "I thought you might appreciate the opportunity to freshen up for your husband's arrival. A change of clothing, perhaps. If my staff were still here and not dismissed for their own protection, I could offer both of you a bath this evening." She gestured toward the pitcher and bowl. "Unfortunately this is all I have available this evening, since only Seijina and Petronin are here."

"Thank you." Witmara turned back to the wardrobe. "I had not expected such consideration."

Betsona snorted. "Even though my body is such that no man will want *me*, I am aware of such niceties. After all, once Dunaran discovered that I possessed the potential for strong magic, he rewarded my mother by making her the Royal

Concubine. I grew up amongst his concubines, and was privileged even after the accident that did—this." She gestured at her body.

"It sounds like a difficult life," Witmara said. "I am sorry it was so for you."

"Ah, well, it was good until my father died," Betsona said softly.

Witmara wasn't sure how to respond to that, so she turned to the wardrobe and selected a pale green skirt and matching short tunic.

"An excellent choice. I'll leave you be to get ready. Here are the spell keys."

Betsona held out her hand. A green ball swirled above it. Witmara snapped her fingers, and the ball floated toward her. She opened her right palm. The ball hovered over it. Witmara extended gold tendrils of her own magic to absorb and enfold the green ball. She concentrated, and the spells woke.

"I have them," she said finally.

"Good. They will expire when you leave for the mainland." Betsona struggled to her feet. "I will wait for you in my private reception room. Do you remember where that was?"

"Far end of the hall, on the right."

"Good. Smallclothes are in the drawers." She hobbled out.

Witmara slipped out of her clothing. She splashed water on her face, then used a small washcloth and soap to wash herself. At least at some point someone—probably Seijina—had cleaned her up from the voyage. But still she yearned for a real bath, where she could wash her hair and get completely clean.

She checked herself in the mirror, wincing at the dark circles under her eyes and the paleness under her normal redbark brown. At least the bruises had faded and she didn't need to wear a bandage on her head any more. Even though she'd slept for a while, she still looked tired and strained. Her dark hair was partially out of its braid, and there didn't appear to be a comb or brush around for her to take care of it.

Surprising that it's been overlooked.

Or perhaps not, since Betsona was clearly used to having attendants. Witmara unbraided her hair and used her fingers plus a little bit of water to undo the snarls in it as best as she could, then braided it again. She frowned at her reflection. Her hair still looked ratty, but better than it had been. She retrieved smallclothes from one of the dresser drawers, and dressed quickly. Another check in the mirror—these clothes didn't look half bad. But she still wanted her trousers and tunic.

A last rinse of her hands, and then she went down the hallway. Betsona sat in one of the chairs rather than on her daybed. Her face lit up as she studied Witmara.

"That color looks good on you."

"Thank you. I appreciate all you have done," Witmara said.

Betsona flicked her right hand dismissively. "It's a small thing in the face of all that is needed to put things right. I am grateful that you are willing to help us fix Daran." She took a deep breath. "I am tired and will most likely be in bed when you return. I will speak with you and your husband in the morning. Seijina!"

Seijina came in from the outside room, carrying their scarves. "Everything is ready. Setkin should be here shortly." She turned to Witmara, holding out one of the scarves. "We have a donkey ready to carry you."

"You were able to persuade Sweetikins to accept a saddle?" Betsona raised her brows.

"A packsaddle."

"That's all?" Disappointment shaded Betsona's voice.

Petronin shrugged. "She was more tolerant of the packsaddle than harness tonight."

"That silly beast. Sweetikins will either pull a cart or pack a saddle," Betsona said to Witmara. "But we never know which she prefers—it's different every time. And often it takes more staff than I have here right now to get her tacked up for the cart, even when she is in a good mood."

"I thought you might want to ride rather than walk, Lady Witmara," Petronin said. "I hope that's all right."

"Thank you. This is not the first time I've straddled a pack-saddle, and I'm grateful for the ride. And thank you for your hospitality," she said to Betsona. "We will speak in the morning."

"Yes. We will."

Witmara draped her scarf around her head and shoulders, then followed Seijina back through the garden. Outside the main fence Petronin waited, holding the lead to a small donkey wearing a packsaddle—the same donkey that had been in the shed.

Sweetikins. What a name.

The donkey glared at Witmara as she let them help her onto the equine. She reached for the lead but Seijina shook her head.

They'll be surprised by Daro.

Petronin led the way, carrying a torch. Witmara settled in, listening to the chirps and hoots coming from the thick vegetation around her. None sounded familiar. Rich floral scents occasionally wafted by her, some pleasant, but once she gagged at the stench.

"Deathflower," Seijina said casually. "It doesn't bloom often, but when it does, it stinks like something dying." She paused. "It is usually an ill omen for whomever rules the Islands at that time."

"Oh?"

"It is said that the land only makes deathflower bloom when it judges its leader to be unfit. We have had an uncommon run of deathflower blooming over the past two years, ever since Chatain exiled Betsona here."

"I see. Does he know?"

"Oh Gods, yes. It's worse whenever he visits." Seijina

coughed as another wave of the strong odor drifted past them. "He can't miss that."

Witmara covered her nose until the stench faded.

The faint whisper of waves on shore grew louder. At last they broke free from the vegetation and onto a white sandy beach. Witmara caught her breath as she spotted the familiar form of the *Heart's Desire* approaching the small dock that ran out from a rocky outcrop in the sand. She slid off the donkey, hurrying to the dock, no longer bothering with the cane.

She felt Daro first as he reached out impatiently to contact her. Eagerness, worry, and a desire to *be off this water* came to her, along with the faint sound of hooves on wood.

Patience,

she told him.

She sent him images of being petted and reassured. He sent back images of kicking his way free from the ship.

Don't do that.

Reassurance came back that he was not that foolish, though he had been on this ship, on this water, absolutely *forever.*

The ship eased up next to the dock, her masts glowing blue as Setkin sang guidance to it. Sailors leapt off the ship and tied it to the dock. Witmara fretted as they put the ramp in place. Toran waited on the deck, his daranval Gernar on his left, and an increasingly impatient and pawing Daro on his right. As soon as the sailors stepped back from the ramp, Daro reared high against Toran's restraint, shaking his head as his silver-flecked black mane glowed bright. His red coat shone in the reflection of the witchlight from the masts. Then Toran set him free. Daro charged down the ramp and over to Witmara, whickers rumbling deep in his chest as he slid to a stop in front of her, placing his head gently against her torso.

Oh Daro, Daro.

She leaned her forehead against his poll, wordlessly sharing her joy at their reunion. Power surged into her from him, easing the fatigue that had made her legs wobble. She extended her awareness to check him. Where had he been injured? She knew it had happened—she felt his pain during her capture.

She found it, a deep wound on his left hindquarter. Healing well.

He backed a step, issuing low, deep chuckles as he rested his head on her shoulder. She slid in closer and hugged his neck, burying her nose deep in his mane.

Footsteps. She raised her head to see Toran and Gernar waiting. She gave Daro one last hug and went to her beloved. She couldn't see *his* injuries either, but Gods, she felt his pain too. But there he stood, solidly on both feet.

He took her tightly in his arms. She felt the bandages on his back and traced them.

"How bad?" she whispered.

"It feels worse than it is," he said. "Especially now that I am with you. Oh Gods, Witmara...." He bent his head to kiss her.

"Gods, I've missed you," she finally said as they pulled apart. "I thought you were dead."

"As did I at first, about you." He pulled her close again, lips resting on her forehead. "Collaborators helped them—Finniarn was one of them."

"You're serious?" She straightened up, reading his solemn expression. "You *are* serious. Collusion with Chatain that goes as high as Finniarn."

He nodded.

"Then Gods, who's in charge in Medvara since you're here?" She held her breath.

She failed her mother in this duty—she hadn't kept Medvara safe! Hopefully either the Mershaunten or the Hidden One had kept those turncoats from taking control of Medvara.

"The land speaking through the Tapestry chose Tilvi and Tilyet as temporary Regents. My father and the Hidden One verified that choice."

She exhaled in relief. "They will do a good job."

"They had already started rooting out infiltrators," Toran said. "I—I was torn between following you and staying with the land. I knew you would want me to protect the land—but all I could think about was them carrying you off in the chaos during the attack." He scowled. "Your kidnappers scattered glimmer dust and worked a confusion spell. By the time Daro and I came to our senses, they were long gone. Daro charged after you anyway. Gernar and I followed him. But the two iron ships they used to launch their attack were gone, already out of sight." He shivered. "Daro's cries were...awful to hear. He tried to swim after you, actually got chest deep in the river. It was all Gernar and I could do to stop him."

Daro shoved his muzzle between them. Witmara laughed and scratched it.

"Silly daranval," she scolded. "You would have drowned!"

Smugness radiated from him, as well as the firm conviction that he would have caught up with those ships, even though they were on that cursed water.

"Silly daranval!" Witmara repeated. Toran laughed, too.

"Setkin said he could bring me to Betsona, and from there we could track you down. It was a relief to feel your mind and learn that you were with her."

Setkin coughed. Witmara turned to him. "Thank you, Setkin, for bringing Toran here."

"I knew we needed to work with Betsona and Seijina." He

studied them. "So what's next? Do I take you back to Varen? The impression my Goddess left with me is that such is not the case."

"No. We are not going back. I'm not quite sure how I'm doing this yet, but I am planning to confront Chatain. It's time."

Setkin nodded, unsurprised. "Do you think you'll have need of the *Heart's Desire*?"

"Can you still travel safely to Fenras?"

"Not directly to that port, no." Setkin scratched his chin thoughtfully. "But there is a cove used by smugglers. The daran-velii will need to swim."

"Fenras?" Toran asked.

"I can show you on the maps Betsona gave me. We'll talk to her in the morning."

"I did bring a ten of riders," Toran said. "Enough for support but not so many that we would attract attention if I had to ride through Daran to find you."

"Good. We're still going to be riding in a small group. Chatain has returned to the mainland. I want to challenge him before he reaches Daraelen."

"Good luck," Setkin said. He handed her a smooth, round crystal. "Use this to call me in. I'm taking the *Heart's Desire* back out to sea once we finish unloading our cargo. It's less likely we'll be found there."

Witmara tucked it in her shirt.

I need a new belt, and knife, and pouches.

"Cargo is right," Seijina grumbled. "Poor Sweetikins is going to be overloaded with all this." She gestured at the pile of boxes and bags behind Setkin that kept growing as Toran's ten riders unloaded supplies.

"It'll be no problem once my ten have gotten everything off the ship. We'll be able to carry most of the supplies—we did bring a couple of daranval mules," Toran said.

"And how is Witmara getting back to Betsona's?" Seijina frowned at her. "Do you plan to walk the entire way?"

"I'm riding my daranval," Witmara said.

"Is it safe in your condition?" Seijina eyed Daro with a skeptical expression. "He seems very—excitable."

"He's the safest mount I'll ever throw a leg over."

Witmara reluctantly eased away from Toran, intending to check what he had brought.

Daro snaked his head and neck in front of Witmara, stopping her. Toran gently laid a hand on her shoulder.

"Let's get you up on him, and I'll tie your bags to his saddle. I brought clothing, your comb and brush, and your bow and sword, among other things."

She glanced at him.

> Magitech?

He nodded.

> Crystals blessed by the Hidden One. I'll tell you later.

> We will need to be discreet at Betsona's. Listening spells everywhere—and I would not be surprised to discover that they monitor mindspeech.

His hand closed on hers.

> Understood.

He added, out loud. "Let me give you a leg up."

Once she was up, she discovered another issue with the split skirts. Slick. She slid easily in the saddle. Gods, she'd be glad to get back into tunic and trousers!

At last things were organized on Sweetikins (albeit with her loud brays of complaint) and the daranval mules. She and Toran followed Seijina and Petronin back to Betsona's, his ten riders following behind. The land poked at Daro and Gernar, making both daranvelii dance fretfully. Witmara and Toran tried to soothe them.

Why are you bothering our daranvelii?

she demanded of the land.

What are these things? They have magic but aren't human! Danger!

They mean no harm. Accept these creatures and their magic.

Not-humans with magic are dangerous!

Not these daranvelii. I am bonded to one, and my bondmate and the other riders are tied to the others. They mean no harm, so do not bother them!

Alien magic,

the land grumbled. But it left the daranvelii alone after that.

"That was—interesting," Toran said.

"You felt that?"

He nodded.

"The land of Daran is—not Medvara or Larij. I have some control over its magic. But from what the God tells me, it is not used to being controlled." She sighed. "I've learned a lot over the past few days. I am so glad that you and Daro are here."

"I'm glad to be here."

They took hands again. The rest of the ride to Betsona's was quiet. By the time they reached the barn to put away the daran-velii and found places for Toran's riders to spend the night, she was more than ready to sleep.

At least tonight she would be resting in Toran's arms.

DOLPHINS

THE COOL OCEAN BREEZE SOOTHED THE PAINFUL TINGLES ON Rekaré's face as she leaned on the railing of the *Morning Star*'s bow. *Railing* was probably the wrong word for whatever the dark-polished wood was that capped the *Star*'s sides, but then again, she was a creature of land, not water. At one time Dovré had been her patron Goddess, not Terat of the Waters. Now she wondered just which God was in charge of her these days. Possibly Two-Faced Staul, especially given her connections with the Saubral.

It felt good to be moving again, even on water. In spite of the sharp pinpricks on her skin and the queasiness in her gut that came along with being a magician on water—*gods, I hate being waterstruck*—the relief of being *on her way at last* outweighed the drawbacks. It seemed as if Vered's guidance of the *Morning Star* was smoother than Setkin's with the *Heart's Desire*. Both *Desire* and Setkin were rough-hewn in build and in action, and their movement on water reflected that. Somewhere she had read that the sorcerous sailships matched the personalities of their Captains. Although the only sailships she had ridden on were

Heart's Desire and *Morning Star*, that statement matched her experience.

All the same, it was their second day on water, and the nausea, prickly skin, and the displaced *not-my-place* sensation that went along with being on the ship pulled hard on Rekaré's magic, making her feel slightly ill. Katerin had made her several more doses of the sleeping tonic, but she didn't want to use it until they were closer to landfall. She wanted to be at her best once they arrived in Daran. No telling if she would be able to get more once she used it all up—and the tonic worked well not just for sleep, but also for managing waterstruck.

Sitting as close as she could to the furthermost point of the bow seemed to help with waterstruck, especially as the sun oozed down over the flat line where ocean and sky met, illuminating the distant clouds in shades of orange, gold, yellow, and magenta.

Rekaré frowned at the distant clouds ahead of them.

Gods, I hope that doesn't mean a storm. I don't want to deal with rough seas.

These were supposed to be smooth seas, and they were bad enough. They had passed over the Chellana's bar opening late in the afternoon of their first day. Seven and a half days from the Chellana's mouth to Lanivar Island, where Betsona was currently living. Or so it would be if they didn't have the fleet following them. That added two more days to the travel time, because the Larijian ships couldn't travel as fast as the sailship.

She was glad to have the Larijian fleet with them. What was left of Chatain's invading force? There were at least two more ships out of those nine that were unaccounted for—and others that had not been magic-powered iron ships. Had they just followed Witmara's captors? The half of the Larijian fleet that remained behind patrolled the coasts of Medvara and Larij. Hopefully they would intercept any potential attackers.

Basnen's mind nudged wistfully against hers. The daranval

mare was unhappy about being on water, especially since she was deep in the hold with the other daranvelii of the Mer Galad. But there just weren't any other options. Not on an ocean-going sailship that was fully loaded. The deck wasn't big enough to hold twenty-five horses and mules, and it was difficult to bring only one or two up to get fresh air. Rekaré tried to spend time with Basnen, but being down in the hold just seemed to make her waterstruck worse. Sesenth and Detaluna spent more time with the daranvelii, as well as organizing their tens for training in close combat. Waterstruck didn't seem to bother them.

Gods only knew what they would face in Daran. Detaluna knew Daran well from her years spent there first as slave and then spy, but even she was hesitant to predict what things would be like now, seven years further into Chatain's rule. Would they need letters of safe conduct to travel on the mainland? Sponsorships? How guarded would the roads be? Those were all questions Rekaré hoped Betsona would be willing to answer once they arrived at Lanivar.

Katerin had given Rekaré what she could find of the letters Betsona had written to Witmara. On the surface they seemed nothing more than an informal correspondence, Betsona telling Witmara the history of Daran, gossiping about current events, sharing the latest set of plays debuting on the Great Stage of Adalane, and sending old records. Some of Betsona's literary allusions read like a private code—did Witmara and Betsona have an arrangement? It was too much like what Rekaré had experienced with Chiral for her comfort.

She would almost believe the innocence of Betsona's words if she hadn't spent eleven years in that haunted old wreck of a Leader's House where such seemingly innocuous words were common.

Gods, she'd been happy when Katerin told her that the damned thing had burned down. The malevolent presence of her father had haunted Rekaré ever since she first walked into the place. Bits and pieces that she found of his things had created a different picture of Daran than she had been told. A land where slavery was common. Where wild magic ran rampant, unrestrained by first Etikar and then Dunaran. And once Chatain had become Emperor, he sent their cousin Chiral to Medvara so that she could destroy Rekaré.

Would I still be Leader of Medvara if Chiral hadn't come?

Some things would have been different. Her mother probably would have died by now—she was already fading. But her daughter Melarae would still be alive. So would Cenarth.

Trusting Chiral was my mistake. Is Betsona going to be Witmara's mistake?

Point against that assumption. Betsona's words were more straightforward about the situation in Daran than Chiral's had been. So whatever she was telling Witmara was closer to the reality of life in Daran than anything Chiral had said.

Point for the assumption that Betsona was problematic—she was Chatain's half-sister, part of the royal family. Granted, she had been exiled by Chatain. But what had been her status before their father's death? Could Betsona be using Witmara as a tool to become Empress? They only had Betsona's own words that she lacked the physical strength to lead. Chiral had portrayed herself as being a discredited member of the Ralsem family, a distant relative of Chatain's, and had not disclosed that her father was Rekaré's uncle. Was Betsona also downplaying her position in Daran?

Point against the assumption that Betsona was a problem— Rekaré's discreet probe of any magic involved in the letters only revealed the sense of a magic that was both canny and devious while being good-intentioned. As near as she could tell, Betsona *meant* what she wrote to Witmara.

Point for it—there were masking spells which could make Betsona's intent look innocent. And if she had the power and strength to wield such spells, then she was most likely capable of ruling. But there would be no possibility of knowing the reality of that possibility until she clapped eyes on Betsona herself.

Rekaré sighed. Gods. If only Cenarth had survived. When they had been the Leaders of Medvara, she had relied on his steady good sense to help her discern the motives of people like Betsona. The ache she had been trying to ignore tightened her gut. It had only been a few days since his funeral pyre. She should not have encouraged their reconciliation, should have sent him to battle alongside their son Linyet instead of letting him follow her and Katerin into the Witches' Great Chamber.

Selfish of me, but I wanted something that wasn't Rekaré Kinslayer or benghaalph in my life again.

His father Heinmyets had forgiven her. He shouldn't have done it. Even though it had been the Chief Priestess Tranarin who had actually killed Cenarth, Rekaré hadn't made him turn back before that last magical battle. If she had done that, forced Cenarth to protect Linyet, then he'd still be alive.

But she had been greedy and wanted the comfort of both her loves.

Rekaré groaned and buried her head in her hands. She bore a number of deaths on her shoulders, even before she killed Chiral and earned the epithet *Kinslayer*. But Chiral had been the one to bring the curse upon her. Chiral her cousin, uncle's daughter, a closer relative than Katerin. She hadn't known that when she'd allowed Chiral to come to Medvara, seeking refuge from alleged persecution. Had trusted that Chiral was telling the truth. Had only realized too late that Chiral was a spy for Chatain, meant to weaken her control of Medvara.

And that was another of my mistakes. Gods, when will I stop making mistakes that kill those I love? Mother. Daughter Melarae. Inharise. Cenarth. Who else will end up dying because of me? Staul. Dovré. Artel. Can't someone keep me from harming my beloveds? Answer me, please!

Perhaps the smartest thing she could do would be to strike out alone once they reached Daran. Take herself someplace where she knew no one, was related to no one. Then she wouldn't bring the curse of the Kinslayer down on anyone else she loved.

None of the Gods answered her—or at least the three she appealed to. She didn't think Terat would respond, and as for the other three—she would not welcome any answers from Nitel, Karnoi, or Cirdel.

Light footsteps behind her broke into her thoughts. Sesenth gracefully slid one arm around Rekaré's waist, pressing close to her side. The soft warm scaliness of the edges of Sesenth's skin where flesh still remained felt oddly soothing. Rekaré raised her head from her hands to smile weakly at her beloved. Sesenth squeezed her gently, giving her a soft smile. Like her arms, Sesenth's face was partially covered by gray-green scales against brown skin, mostly on her cheek and jaw bones.

"I felt the weight of your thoughts five strides away," Sesenth said. "Dear one, you know well that Cenarth would begrudge you sorrowing so. He chose to walk with you and me for those last battles. I regret that he followed you into the Great Chamber to fight the Witches, but *he* made that choice. Not you. Not Katerin. Not me."

Rekaré exhaled a shuddering breath.

How did she know?

The bond between them was sometimes bewildering, deeper than anything else she had experienced.

"Maybe it's just being waterstruck. Gods, I've never been on water this long and we've still got days ahead of us. It's like someone's poking me with red-hot needles. By the Goddess's gold-glazed tits, how did my ancestors stand it? Now I know why the past Emperors sent minions to Medvara and didn't come themselves. They couldn't face the ocean with their magic."

"One tolerates what one is capable of tolerating."

"I suppose." It *did* feel better to have Sesenth's arm around her. "But you don't feel the curse of the water? Even with your magic?"

"No. If anything I wish I could swim. Just look at those colors. All this water around us. The smell of the water. Nothing like home. Nothing like the desert—even sailing the Inland Sea you can still see land. I'm just—I could never imagine what this was like before now. It's amazing. And *dolphins*." Awe filled Sesenth's voice. "So beautiful. So graceful! Vered said their visit meant we had a blessing from her Goddess."

"I wish I'd been able to see them."

Rekaré had been doubled over the railing on the other side of the *Star* when the dolphins had appeared, puking her guts out. They hadn't deigned to appear since then.

"There'll be another time for you to see dolphins."

"I hope so."

"I wish I could lift you out of this melancholy."

"I wish I knew what lay ahead of us," Rekaré said. "*Benghaalph* is silent." She swallowed hard. Senth would understand her doubts and not judge her. "There are times when I wonder if it wouldn't be best for me to just disappear into Daran, never to be found again, once Witmara is located. After all, Detaluna knows Daran. I could be the lurking threat to Chatain, a ghost that haunts all he does."

"Is that what you really want?"

Rekaré tightened her lips, staring as the sun slowly sank behind the waves.

"No," she said finally. "He owes me many deaths. I have sworn to kill him and I want to do it outright, face-to-face. But I wish I could do it without bringing any more sorrow down upon my family and friends. I see nothing ahead but darkness, and I tremble."

"Look!" Sesenth pointed toward the sun as it dropped from

sight. Just as a flash of green illuminated where the sun had been, a graceful great fish with a pointed nose leapt in a great curving arc. "Dolphin!"

"Many dolphins."

Rekaré marveled as one after another, dolphins leapt in the air, silhouetted against the reds and yellows of sunset. She counted—there were at least ten. So beautiful. So graceful. And there was something about them that suddenly lifted her spirits.

She leaned on Sesenth and watched the dolphins play in the sunset-reddened water, the darkness that had weighed her down somehow eased by the playful creatures. Even the hot pinpricks on her face seemed to be duller.

She finally felt the graceful presence of the Goddess Dovré, starting with a gentle forehead caress that settled her melancholy.

Fretting about what lies ahead does you no good,

the Goddess chided.

Oh Gods. The Goddess almost sounded like her late mother Alicira. Rekaré swallowed hard and closed her eyes as her tension rose again, clinging to the voice without daring to look at what form the Goddess might take. She didn't *want* to look, for fear of disappointment that it was *not* Alicira.

I would not bring harm to Witmara, and I fear I am a danger to all I touch.

Katerin is all right, and you are close to her,

the Goddess countered.

Which makes me worry about Witmara.

Child. Her fate is not bound up with yours. You have a goal. Focus upon it. Chatain must be stopped.

"And I am the one fated to do it," Rekaré said out loud, exasperated. Couldn't the Goddess just say soothing things, not provoke her mood again? Gods!

Goddess,

Sesenth suddenly mindspoke.

Can't you ease the weight on my beloved? Don't you see how she struggles with her fate? Losing Cenarth was hard on her. Can't you acknowledge that?

Rekaré rested her head on Sesenth's shoulder momentarily, grateful that her beloved had spoken up.

As long as she doesn't bring Dovré's wrath down upon her.

The Goddess was usually tolerant, but—she was a Goddess, after all, and even though Dovré was frequently predictable, she *did* have her enigmatic moods.

Sesenth the Faithful,

the Goddess said.

I honor your concern. I am pleased that you are so devoted to Rekaré. Your courage and your dedication will keep her safe.

Sesenth persisted.

But at what cost to others who are important to her and still live? Witmara. Katerin. Linyet. She's already lost so many she loves!

The Goddess shook her head.

I wish I could reassure both of you. Unfortunately, her fate was laid down at her birth and naming.

Sesenth scowled.

So we have no ability to change our fate? That is not what the Lord Staul has taught us in Saubral. Otherwise we would not have changed our ways to follow Rekaré as benghaalph.

The Goddess sighed.

That was—different. And unexpected. But no matter what path Rekaré choses, there will be pain and loss and sorrow along the way. Rekaré, even if you try to walk away from your fate, it will find you.

Then what choice do I have?

Rekaré said bitterly, the joy from seeing the dolphins fading, the pinpricks under her skin burning.

If I am meant to be sorrow and a curse to many, what difference does it make what I do?

The difference lies in your motives,

the Goddess said gently, in tones that once again reminded Rekaré of her mother.

You have seen what would have happened had you gone back to Medvara. If you chose to become Empress.

But I have not seen the losses that will happen as a result of my current course. That remains hidden from me.

Not hidden from you alone.

The Goddess's voice suddenly carried a sorrowful weight, the tone no longer reminding Rekaré of her mother.

Things are in motion that the Seven, divided as we are, cannot foresee. I cannot give you any consolation, my dear, because I cannot see anything beyond the need to stop Chatain. Neither can Staul, or Artel, or Terat. We do not know what Nitel, Karnoi, or Cirdel are doing. We do not know what alliances they may have made with forces beyond us.

Her voice grew colder and more remote.

As the Outcast God makes his moves in the east of Varen, things change even more, and his choices muddy our vision. One of you has to deal with him—and it cannot be you, Rekaré, because you are needed to help against Chatain. I wish I could give you more reassurance. But I am almost as blind as you are, dear one. Just know that our blessings ride with you, and with Witmara.

That's not much consolation,

Sesenth insisted.

No. It is not.

The Goddess took Rekaré by the chin. The contact soothed the prickles once again, and she opened her eyes. Even if it was the Goddess in the form of her mother, she needed to acknowledge her presence.

To her relief, the Goddess's form was not that of her mother but the same as it had always been.

I fear I have brought you more sorrow and worry when my goal was consolation. I failed to do what you needed.

My moods are dark these days, Lady Dovré. Any joy I feel is fleeting.

I understand. All I can promise is that it will not always be this way.

The Goddess kissed her forehead and faded away. Rekaré tensed, expecting the hot prickles under her skin to start up again. They didn't.

"You matter to me," Sesenth said fiercely, tightening her grip on Rekaré's waist. "As did Cenarth."

Rekaré shook her head, unable to speak as grief washed over her at the thought of Cenarth.

"You have made it possible for me to become what I am," Sesenth continued. "I ache to see you hurt. I feel your agony at the absence of those who are now missing from your life."

"I tire of being Sorrow, and bringing sorrow," Rekaré whispered, shaking with the effort to keep from crying.

"But you would not be Sorrow if you did not feel regret," Sesenth said. She squeezed Rekaré even tighter, then eased her grip. "Come, now. Deta has prepared a light dinner for us and pulled out some maps. We need to think about strategies once we reach Lanivar—and then the mainland."

Rekaré straightened up, wiping her eyes. "I will be there. Give me a moment."

"As long as you join us soon. Don't make me hunt you down!" Sesenth scowled at Rekaré.

"I promise! Just a few moments." Rekaré choked back a sniffle.

Sesenth softened. "We will be waiting for you. But not too long! I'm looking forward to tonight's dinner—fresh fish."

"I will be there."

"Good." Sesenth gave her one final hug, then walked away.

Rekaré refocused on the sunset red waters. Another dolphin leapt high, followed by a second one. She watched them leap. Then one fixed its eyes on her, and emitted what sounded like a chuckle, seeming to dance away on its tail as it cackled at her. Another long, high leap, and then it was gone.

She pushed away from the railing. It took two steps before she realized that the melancholy pulling at her had faded. Her steps quickened as she headed for the Captain's cabin and dinner.

Perhaps going to Daran wouldn't be as bad as she feared.

As long as she didn't have to deal with a battle at sea. Oh Gods, if they would just spare her that.

THE NEW THREAT

DRIZZLE WRAPPED MEDVARE-THE-CITY IN A GRAY MORNING FOG, just cold enough to sink into a creature's bones. Rainin sent images of —*sore, hurt, need to move* at Katerin from her stall, grumpiness underlying her mindspeech. Katerin sighed, looking up from the papers on her desk.

> Patience, dear one,

she thought back to Rainin.

> We will be traveling soon enough. I'll be out to work you later in the day. I promise. Rain or shine.

Rainin's only response was a derisive snort. Then she turned back to her hay, and the contact faded.

Katerin continued to gaze at the grayness outside, leaning her chin on her hands. Just another spring day in Medvara. The damp was the price they paid for the later lush greenery that supported several of Medvara's major magical exports—Stardance wool and Coos berry products the most prominent. Over the past seven years she had worked to establish Medvara as a source for low-level magical supplies—and had hopes that Witmara and Toran would create more magitech devices to add to Medvara's offerings.

Well. For better or worse, Witmara—and hopefully Toran—were in Daran. Would they come back? She didn't think so. Not unless things went terribly wrong.

And even though the drizzle and damp brought good things to her land, that didn't rule out finding the drizzle tiresome during days like this. Especially after returning from the drier inland.

Nere and Keratil will be back to drier weather and hopefully more sunshine.

That was the only upside to this forthcoming trip to deal with the Divine Confederation's tribute demands.

A force with an army of undead. At best it would be like fighting *shalkendar* in Waykemin. But the prospect of invasion from the Divine Confederation had driven the Witches Council in Waykemin to drastic measures—including the creation of *shalkendar.* So whatever the Confederation possessed must be worse, if the Witches had feared them so.

The Confederation had to be dealt with, and quickly.

She glanced at her paperwork again and decided it was time for a short break. Katerin stretched, rose, and checked the small fire. After adding a couple of sticks to the stove, she stood over it, holding her hands just above the metal surface to help warm them further. But that didn't stop her thoughts.

There was so much to do before she led that battle force to Keratil to face the Divine Confederation—an entirely different sort of confrontation from her recent trip to Waykemin. She hadn't grown up in Keratil, didn't have personal connections with any of the Divine Confederation.

Though it was quite concerning to remember that Nenanim the Golden, the great scholar of Waykemin that she and Rekaré had freed from the bonds of the kendar, thought that the former rulers of Waykemin had fled from the Divine Confederation several generations ago.

It was only a theory, one she didn't want to think about. No, she absolutely did not want to consider that possibility unless forced. Some things needed to remain in the past.

This march was bigger than the one she and Rekaré had led to Waykemin. The Mershaunten's brother Haran and his beloved Orlanden would lead an army from Larij—their ships had already departed for Cooscol. A larger Medvaran force was gathering in Cooscol. The Hidden One had sent orders to Gulter for a Saubral force to meet them in Cooscol as well. It would be the second time in the same month that she led a multi-national force to deal with a threat to the land of Varen. What did that mean for her future? Was she meant to unite Varen in an empire of its own to counter the Darani Empire and the Divine Confederation?

Katerin shuddered.

No. Don't think of that as a possibility. Just happens to be coincidental.

Oh really?

Deep inside, she knew better than to dismiss these circumstances as coincidence. She wanted to believe that the Divine Confederation and the Outcast God would go back to ignoring Varen if Chatain was no longer around to stir things up. But experience suggested that such a hope was nothing more than wishful thinking. They needed to exhibit a strong force to repel the Confederation from the Nerean Gate, and afterwards would probably need to reinforce the guard in Keratil.

In any case, thinking about those possibilities didn't help with the current demands on her time. Better that she focus on those.

Katerin ticked off the things she needed to do this morning on her fingers.

First, she needed to leave Medvara operating in smooth order for Tilvi and Tilyet. That meant signing off on assorted pieces of paperwork, performing the ceremony which conferred that authority on them, as well as ensuring that they were aligned with the land. That would not be a problem. She just had to dedicate time to ensuring everything was completed.

Unless Finniarn has left us an unexpected mess somewhere.

She groaned at that thought. She hadn't needed to think about the Regency process for at least five years. Finniarn knew what to do on his end, had covered many of the tasks needed so that Katerin could slip out of Medvara to meet with Rekaré on a regular basis without a lot of preparation and ceremony.

Perhaps his corruption reflected why the land had been so clingy when she had left for Waykemin.

Then again, Tilvi and Tilyet probably already knew about compromised areas within the government. She hoped. The twins were quite thorough. She would have to trust to their competency.

Second, check on the provisioning status of her forces and make sure arrangements were on course for their departure tomorrow. She wasn't worried about that process. Last night's reports suggested that, if anything, preparations were running ahead of schedule.

Third, ensure that she had sufficient supplies not just of healing herbs and potions but the tools she might need for working magic—glimmer dust. Neutralizing paste. Charms— perhaps she should ask Doryits about the potential effectiveness of those devices against the Divine Confederation and its forces.

Uvnen's *tap-tap, tap-tap-tap, tap-tap* that meant *visitor not already cleared but one you might want to receive* echoed on the door. She stifled a sigh and turned her back to the stove.

"Come in."

Uvnen opened the door and stepped inside. "Doryits is here," he said, keeping his voice low so that he could not be overheard easily. "Shall I send him in?"

"Yes," Katerin said.

At least she wouldn't need to summon him. She checked on the supply of hot water in the iron kettle that sat on top of the wood stove. Good. Enough for tea. In her experience discussions like the one ahead of her went better with tea. She found it to be more productive—and sometimes she learned things she hadn't expected to discover over a shared cup of tea.

Doryits entered, hesitating. "Leader Katerin?"

"Yes." She turned to face him. "Would you like some tea?"

She noted his slight relaxation. "Why yes. Yes I would."

"Rosehips, mint, or a mixture containing the two?"

"Whatever you would prefer to have," he said.

"Well, you make it easy." Katerin moved to her mixing bench. She carried the iron water kettle with her and set it on a trivet on the counter. She ran her fingers along the glass jars on the shelf until she found her favorite morning blend, which included some dried Coos berries. "Do you have magic?" she said as Doryits stood by the door.

"A little. Not much."

"Will Coos berries be a problem?"

Not every minor magic practitioner reacted well to the dried form of Coos berries. It was only polite to check.

"No."

Katerin put enough for two cups into a strainer, then dropped it in the teapot and poured the hot water into the pot. She looked up to see Doryits still standing uncomfortably by the door.

"Sit down," she said.

Katerin carried the iron kettle back to the stove, then placed the teakettle by Doryits while she fetched two cups. Then she sat in the chair facing his, their knees separated by two arm lengths.

Perfect.

She rested her right arm on the table, noting that Doryits relaxed as she took the more casual posture.

"So. Do you have further news from Kintarit? Does the Divine Confederation still wait for our answer—or are they planning to move?"

"So far I have not heard from Kintarit. I am hoping that no news is good news." He frowned. "I do find myself wishing—please forgive me for saying this, Leader Katerin, but I do wish that Medvara had a faster means of communication than your messenger birds. Once our rider reaches Cooscol, we're dependent on the birds."

"Call me Katerin," she said. "I agree about the speed of messaging within Medvara. But we've not had the ability to set up messenger relay stations like you have in Keratil. The birds work well for Medvara and, well—until Rekaré made peace with the Hidden One, such relay stations were targets for Saubral attack except in the heart of the Saktrin Valley. It is easier to protect and shield messenger birds."

"True."

She poured them each a cup. Then she sat back in her chair and rested her hands in her lap, hands wrapped around the cup's soothing warmth.

"So. Besides a complaint about communication speed, what brings you here, Doryits? I trust that you approve of what you see of our preparations?"

"I'm quite impressed," he said, mirroring her posture, gazing down into his tea. "I had not thought of Medvara as capable of forming a large army for anything other than defense. The small force you took to Waykemin—yes. But from what I see gathering on your Western Parade Ground—pardon my forwardness, but I've not seen this level of strength from Medvara."

Katerin took her time to answer, taking a sip of her tea before speaking.

"Rekaré and Cenarth before me created a Home Guard, based on what the Two Nations have done over the years, and I've continued the tradition. For the most part they've provided security along the border with Saubral—at least until they stopped their raids thanks to the liaison with Rekaré. I've kept them in active duty on the coast in anticipation of a possible raid by Chatain. But the rest have kept in training and ready to be called up. We'll see more in Cooscol."

"I would not have known that these forces were a Home Guard," Doryits said carefully. "Their skills are greater than I would expect." He sipped his tea. "We are on track to leave tomorrow?"

"As far as I know, yes. The ships load first thing tomorrow morning."

He heaved a relieved sigh. "I have been worrying," he admitted. "Kintarit is young, and I have been afraid that the Divine Confederation's representatives may try to push him further than if he were older and more experienced. I've not received a response from the message I sent to him about Medvara's bringing an army to help."

"He has good advisors, right?"

She drank more tea, thinking about what she knew of the young Keratil Leader. He'd come to power a year ago, earlier than expected when the previous Leader, Mauryat, had been thrown from a horse. There had been several possible Leaders put forth, including a cousin and a son of Mauryat, but the land and the Gods had chosen Kintarit, the son of the Prime Minister, instead.

"I'd like to think so," Doryits said. He half-smiled. "Especially since I am one of them."

"Oh? I'm surprised you did not stay and send someone else."

What exactly is your role in Kintarit's government?

He had been announced as Commissioner—of what? Was he was affiliated with spying operations? Maybe he would tell her more, disclose what he was without her needing to ask. But she definitely wanted to know this before their meeting ended.

He shrugged.

"Wentosk, Kintarit's father, still holds office as Prime Minister. If anyone can keep Kintarit steady—not that much of that is required, he is a strong young man!—it will be Wentosk rather than me. The Council decided that I was the one most likely to persuade Medvara into action." His lips tightened and a haunted look crossed his face as he stared down into his teacup. "There is more, Leader Katerin. I am not a safe person when it comes to dealing with the Confederation. I have a weakness. I—my family lived on the border as part of my role as Commissioner." He rolled his lips even tighter until she couldn't see them any more. "There are regular probes and incursions by those who walk with the Confederation in the mountains near the Gate. Primarily from the dead that walk again. They—took my wife. My son and daughter. I gave my beloved the final death myself, as well as my son. But my daughter got away from me, and is now one of their generals."

"I am sorry to hear that," Katerin said softly.

So that's why he came.

Not only an example of the challenges Keratil faced and one who could speak to those particular circumstances, but—*yes. Spymaster, I'll wager.*

He glanced up at her, then back down to his cup. "She is also the general of the army we face." He drew a deep, hard breath. "So you see, that is why I'm the best option to send for help. I am compromised and should not be privy to their inner councils, even if I am Commissioner of the Border."

"Can your daughter be won back?"

He shook his head. "At this point a fast death is the kindest thing I could do for her. The person that Sariost was is already dead. Her spirit—I do not know. What exists is just a body, not her spirit, possessed by—I don't know what. Perhaps the

Outcast God himself walks in her. But we've learned that kin to the undead are a special risk. Even though we know full well that the only thing they have in common with our loved ones is the shell of their body. We've—tried to save them, in the past, to no avail. I would not want to put even the shell of her body through that kind of torture. But the temptation and lure of her presence is too great. I will want to save her if I get too close."

"Similar to *shalkendar* in Waykemin." Katerin shivered.

During their reign the Witches of Waykemin had three classes of those that they possessed and stripped of their will—the *ushar belost*, the empty ones that were easily directed and retained no initiative or thoughts of their own; the *kendar minost*, the expedient ones who still retained bits and pieces of their old selves and could be trusted to act on their own—and the *shalkendar*, the walking dead who could never be brought back, unlike the *ushar* and *kendar*. But the *shalkendar* did not have an attraction for their living relatives. Magic? She wondered why these beings would be that way.

A difference between the Outcast God and the Seven?

Gods, more information she needed to figure out.

He nodded. "Very much so," he said in a monotone. "She is like something between *kendar* and *shalkendar*. Completely theirs. And I—I have failed once already at giving her the final death. I cannot be reliable once it comes to battle. I can speak to her without danger, but in battle—" He wearily shook his head.

Katerin instinctively reached out and rested her hand on his forearm. "If you want, I will guarantee that she dies fast and cleanly." The Leader in her cringed at this promise, but the parent and the former Healer knew it was the right thing to do.

He shuddered. "You would promise me that? How can you guarantee that you can give her the final death?"

"I was raised in Waykemin until I went to the Healing House in Keldara," she said. "My mother Terani-the-God-Killer forced me to help her make *ushar, kendar,* and *shalkendar.* I know the way of their making and unmaking. And I am Staul and Dovré's designated Banisher of Shadows. I also wield the Spear of War and Unmaking."

"If you could do that—since you have the Spear—" He set his cup down and placed his free hand on hers, now meeting her eyes. "Sariost is the greatest threat they could have sent against us. Not only am I at risk, but Kintarit and others as well. The Council all knew Sariost. She and Kintarit were playmates."

"Oh Gods. I am so sorry, Doryits. I vow to you as the Leader of Medvara and as the Banisher of Shadows. I will do this for you." A title she hated, but—when the Banisher was needed, it was for circumstances just like this.

"If you can take her down, Katerin Leader, that would be the greatest gift that Medvara could ever give Keratil," Doryits said.

"Then it will be so."

Their eyes met, and she felt something stir that she had not felt for years. Something about those mournful dark eyes called to her heart. Told her that he shared her sorrow. Perhaps they could make each other happy.

You're being silly.

But even as she scolded herself, she thought she spotted the same hope in his eyes.

Doryits sighed, and released her hand, gently extracting his arm from under hers as he picked up his cup once again.

"So you see, that is why I am so worried about returning to Keratil in a timely fashion. It takes—what—three days on the ocean to reach Cooscol?"

"Unless we use sailships—and those have been committed to aiding my daughter."

Doryits nodded. "And another two days to ride to Nere, with the Gate yet another day beyond. Who knows what has happened there since I left? That is why I worry."

"I understand."

Gods, she had thought it was bad enough when Chatain's

forces had kidnapped Witmara. But to have a daughter turned into something like *shalkendar*?

What she was going through now was nothing like what Doryits had experienced.

She hesitated, then decided it was time to ask. "From what you say, it sounds as if you will be my best resource in preparing to counter the Divine Confederation."

"I am Keratil's expert on them as the Border Commissioner," he said wryly. "Even before I lost my family."

"Spymaster?"

A faint grin touched his lips. "Yes. Precisely. Though my focus has been on the Confederation—I am but one of several working for Kintarit." His face tightened again. "I have just enough magic for safety, but not so much that it would attract the Confederation's attention. Or so we thought. Sariost—" he shook his head. "I should have moved them away when we first learned that she possessed stronger magic than Jarilyn or me. Sariost was the Confederation's target. But we thought—wrongly—that our magic was strong enough to shield a young girl."

"How old was Sariost?"

"Thirteen," he said flatly. "The attack happened on her birthday."

Thirteen. The traditional age when magicians came into their first flush of real power.

"How long ago was this?"

"Five years ago."

"Has she aged? Mentally, that is?" Neither the *kendar* nor the *shalkendar* aged after their making. It was one reason why Nenanim still lived, despite his great age. If Sariost was one of the dead-that-walked, and if they were much akin to the *shalkendar*…she could not be unmade without dying.

Now who's clinging to foolish hope?

He shook his head. "We are essentially facing a thirteen-year-old dead-that-walks who has been made a general. Her powers are not that of a thirteen-year-old, neither is her strategy, but—I have heard reports of tantrums and behaviors that Sariost did not exhibit in life."

"Is it the nature of what she has become?"

"I think it is very likely, though we—more precisely, *I*—am not certain." He leaned back in his chair and set his teacup on the table. "I have been in one of their camps as a spy. Years ago, as a young man gathering information. I did the same in Waykemin. Not all of the dead-that-walk behave in such a manner as Sariost is rumored to act, but the ones who do are considered to be especially blessed by the Outcast God. From what I have seen of Sariost since her taking..." His voice trailed off and he swallowed hard. "She is one of those."

Katerin nodded. "I will want to speak further with you about what you have learned about the Divine Confederation and the dead-that-walk. But I also need to prepare so that we can leave Medvara on time tomorrow morning. We will have several days worth of travel on the water. Would you care to be on the same ship as me so that I can learn more from you while we sail?"

He drained his cup, smiled, and rose. "I would like that very much, Leader Katerin. And I thank you for understanding. Though I suppose that the daughter of Terani-the-God-Killer would sympathize." He paused. "I visited your mother's body during a public viewing day in Forsim, during one of my spying assignments."

"When she was in the dreamless sleep."

He nodded. "It made an impression on me. I was young, and at the time thought myself invincible. Waykemin taught me otherwise."

"My birth land often has that effect." She rose. They walked to the door.

He took her hand and shook it before going out. "I look forward to our future conversations, Leader Katerin."

"As do I, Spymaster Doryits, Commissioner of the Border."
As she hoped, he straightened up a bit more when she said his
title. "Any further knowledge I can gain about the Outcast God
and the Divine Confederation before we arrive in Keratil will be
of use."

He bowed. "I hope to serve."

And then he left.

Katerin pursed her lips, thinking.

Perhaps she needed to add that copy of Nenanim's *History of
Waykemin* to her baggage. She had retrieved it from the Council
library in Forsim, intending to review it at some future date.
Sooner might be more important than later.

She wondered how Witmara was doing. Was she a prisoner,
or had Toran found her? Had she made it to Betsona? What
about Rekaré?

It was tempting to reach out to the Gods for whatever they
could tell her. But what could she do from here if she found out
Witmara was imprisoned? No, she needed to take care of this
situation in Keratil. That was her job.

But Gods, she hoped all was well with her daughter.

PREPARING

Betsona wearily sank back on her couch, savoring the sudden silence of the house around her as the last *clip-clop* of horse—*no, daranval,* she corrected herself—hooves echoed down the driveway back toward the dock. One of the sorcerous sailships waited to convey Witmara, her husband Toran, their riders, Petronin, and a handful of her staff to the mainland. Had it only been a single day since Toran's arrival? It seemed longer. And now it seemed likely that some of Witmara's kin were on their way to support her, from what Toran said.

Possibly even Rekaré.

But she needed time to think and consider now that she had actually met Witmara—and then her husband, and put their challenge to Chatain in motion. Especially after she got a whiff of the tantalizing magic wafting around the—*daranvelii*—she thought carefully. She had wanted to taste that magic, see if it was something she could manipulate for herself—but both daranvelii and their riders seemed to move under a shield. What she saw of the magic made her hunger for more.

What I could achieve if I had a daranval partner!

She might even have the strength to tame Daran.

But the land had chosen Witmara instead of her—and she had agreed to its decision. She needed to honor that choice. Otherwise, she was no better than her brother. Witmara would provide a significant challenge to Chatain—and that alone was worth forgoing that oh-so-tempting magical force from the daranvelii.

I have to remember. Deposing my brother as Emperor is my primary goal, not gaining power.

Witmara also had Toran. The two of them working together outstripped anything Betsona could do with magitech, even with Petronin's help. Toran and Witmara had repaired her mechanical wheelchair, using a crystal from Medvara to replace its power source. Both of them were comfortable with integrating magic and technology, more so than Chatain was. Toran in particular had been fascinated by the various devices around the house. If Witmara succeeded in overthrowing Chatain, that might be a place for Betsona in Witmara's Empire—as an advisor who had experience with Chatain's devices.

A slight rustle outside. Betsona picked up the palm-sized box which held her shield sensors. She sighed with relief as the sensors identified Seijina. Probably back from escorting the energetic horde back to their ship.

Gods, they were *so active.* Magic? Or were all Varenese like this? Toran and his riders were not from Medvara but the neighboring land of Larij, after all.

Footsteps echoed outside her door. "Betsona?"

"In here."

Seijina entered, carrying a tall pitcher of sweetened sourfruit juice and two cups.

"They are off, and messages have been sent to Adalane. Provided they can get there safely, all will be set for Witmara to appear at Festival, perhaps to challenge Chatain there." She filled the cups.

"Good."

"Witmara thanks you for the loan of Petronin and the links to our cell groups. They will put ashore near Fenras and ride the indirect southern route to Adalane. Unless Chatain changes his plans and goes directly to Daraelen."

"There is no reason for him to change right now." She took the cup from Seijina and sipped from it, then set it on a coaster atop the mottled heartwood table next to her couch. "He has to open the Spring Festival himself, since I am not there. If they can get Witmara in place on time...oh, he will regret his indifference toward the arts." She smirked at Seijina.

Seijina chuckled. "Do you think he considered the Goddess's requirement that one of the Royal Family opens the Spring season when he exiled you here?"

"I think he feared my greater popularity at that point, not further responsibilities." Foolish of Chatain, especially given the distaste that he held for plays and poets.

The last ruler to ignore the Festivals at Adalane had come to regret it. She supposed that Chatain would try to give greater honor to Nitel than to Dovré. After all, Nitel was his patroness. But Dovré could not be overlooked at Adalane, not overshadowed by Nitel. That had been a precept their father had pounded into Betsona at an early age.

You ignore Adalane and the Goddess that favors it at your own risk. Playwrights and poets do not appear to be the stuff of revolution —and yet they are. Elithtra disregarded them to her regrets.

"Petronin has the message cylinders?"

That *was* one of Chatain's magitech devices that she trusted. She and Petronin had discovered how to secure the devices that augmented mindspeech from Chatain's meddling. They had tested it, of course, sending mildly seditious messages through the cylinders and waiting for possible reactions.

When none came, Betsona had tried to break the locks when Petronin and Seijina sent messages back and forth to no avail—and when it came to that sort of magic, she was at least a match for Chatain if not stronger. So what if the attempt had left her bedridden for several days? It was worth the effort for her peace of mind that their communications were secure.

At some point even the cylinders would be compromised. But as long as the system remained secure long enough for Witmara to act against Chatain, Betsona didn't care.

After that it wouldn't matter.

"So what do you think about our prospective Empress?" Betsona broached the subject she had wanted to bring up over the past few days.

But not while Witmara was here. That one was sharp, even though she hid it well. If Betsona hadn't needed to learn the secrets of hiding her thoughts at a young age, she wouldn't have recognized the same ability in Witmara.

"She is—interesting." Seijina chewed her lower lip. "Though oh dear. We will have to polish her up quite a bit for Court. Especially given that she is clearly Varenese as well as Miteal."

"You think the nobles will accept her as Empress?"

Seijina rocked her head from side to side and rolled her shoulders before answering. "In person she can be quite persuasive. She projects an enthralling presence. She will charm most of the Court. And if she succeeds in challenging Chatain at Adalane, given the land's acceptance of her control over it—do they have a choice?"

"Some may feel they do. She is rough. She has not learned Court manners. That will matter to some."

And her skin is darker than mine. As is her husband's skin. I had a hard time getting people to accept my golden skin, even though I was the Emperor's own acknowledged daughter. Should Witmara prevail, she may find herself facing opposition.

"From what I have been able to pick up since her people arrived, that roughness would not be unusual for someone from her background. I did learn a bit more about that in the past day."

"Oh?"

"She spent her summers traveling with sheep herds until her mother became Leader in Medvara. Apparently that is common for leaders amongst—not Medvara, but the land where the lady Alicira shared leadership. The Leaders themselves roamed with the herds."

"I knew that Katerin Leader had been Alicira's last Healer," Betsona said. "I did not realize that meant camping out with the herds."

"Apparently that is common. Not so much with her husband's people, or in Medvara itself. But in the—" Seijina frowned. "Two Nations, I think they called it?" she said finally. "That appears to be typical—watching the flocks appears to be one of the summer duties of Leadership. Witmara did not quail at the mention that they would need to camp out while traveling to Adalane. Nor did she want pavilions, or special bedding. Nothing that required wagons for traveling, only pack animals. She even knows how to pack a mule—was doing that this morning."

"*Really*. I suppose that goes along with riding with the herds, like you said."

Betsona sat up and drew her knees to her chest. She hadn't spent much time with Witmara, in case Chatain chose to communicate with her during that time. Yes, she could shield herself from his scrutiny, but that could be just as damning as what he could see without it. Better that he keep thinking she wasn't capable of blocking him out. Yet.

"But can you imagine a life like that?" Seijina made a face. "Especially amongst the noble class? And Leadership living like that? How very strange."

"It is their way, I suppose." Her bad leg ached, and she straightened it out. "How easily influenced is she?"

"She did listen to me when I gave her guidance, both on the ship and here. As long as she sees that there is a clear purpose for advice she will follow it. She is young, after all, and at times unsure."

"Well, that's something."

"At least it's better than Chatain." Seijina drained her cup and poured more. "And if Witmara becomes Empress then you can go back to Adalane. You couldn't do that if you were Empress. You'd have to live in Daraelen."

Betsona stuck her tongue out at Seijina. "I'd change the capital to Adalane if I became Empress. Then I could go back to enjoying the plays year-round."

"Scandalous!" Seijina laughed. "Dearest, you know the nobles would never agree to that. Why, they wouldn't own the best property! And it would be so tempting for their slaves to flee to Ternar. Bad enough that most of them have to travel to Adalane for the Spring Festival."

"But they'd be raiding Ternar for new slaves anyway, since it's so close." Betsona patted the couch beside her. "Come over here. You're too far away. It's been so long!"

"I thought you would never ask." Seijina joined Betsona and took her into her arms. "You know, you didn't have to hide us from Witmara. She is very open. Her cousin Rekaré is in a long-term relationship with a woman."

"Better to be safe," Betsona said. "I don't know about the men around her, for one. And as long as Lord Efrenit is in high regard, we are in danger."

"He will not be in power for long," Seijina said. "I can predict that he will offend Witmara quite quickly should she become Empress."

"And if he doesn't do so soon enough—I'm certain we can find a means to make him offend her."

"Yes."

Betsona sighed and leaned against Seijina, soothed by her

familiar scent of spice and lavender.

❧

Over halfway there.

Katerin braced against the motion as the ship tossed back and forth on the rough seas, swallowing hard as her gut roiled. She fought against the temptation to grab the table and hold on. Waterstruck was worse below deck, but this storm was strong enough that it was safer to remain in her cabin.

At least the first day on water had been pleasant, apart from the roughness of passing over the Chellana's bar. But even then the waterstruck had taken hold. Luckily she knew from past experience that the ship's cook was sympathetic and would have broth and crackers ready for her.

"Anything you need, Leader Katerin," he had said.

She gave him a salve for his aching joints—a preparation she always carried in small boxes to hand out as gifts when traveling —and a large packet of the tea she used for waterstruck attacks. He promised to make her some any time she wanted.

Waterstruck was why Katerin preferred riding in the sternwheelers that put ashore every night while traveling up and down the Chellana and dreaded her annual trips to Cooscol. Twice she'd been able to ride to Cooscol across the land, making it part of a regular procession to check on her people. The other years, though, she'd had to travel by ship because of time demands. But unlike the Chellana sternwheelers, nightly stops weren't possible with this big ocean-going ship. There weren't enough ports on the rocky Medvaran coast to put in every night to ease the effect of water on magicians.

It will get better.

Tomorrow evening they should reach Cooscol. Perhaps a

day later, if the storm worsened and they had to put in at Florinol to wait it out.

Katerin sighed and turned her attention back to *The History of Waykemin*, the sheer weight of the volume holding it steady on the table despite the ship's pitching and rolling. She swallowed back the sour taste in her mouth. Nenanim had written this history early in his career, before she was born. It lacked the smooth phrasing and wit of his later writings before he had been made *kendar*, plodding along pedantically in imitation of the classic style of other histories common in Waykemin.

And Gods, it was dry, dry, *dry* reading, filled with genealogies and family intrigues.

But it was the first time she had read a history that covered pre-Witches Waykemin in any detail. During her youth in Waykemin, pre-Council history had been artlessly waved off as utterly unimportant, not something to bother learning about. If anything, she'd learned more about early Waykemin in Chiyan than when she and her mother had moved to Forsim.

Probably not as suppressed in Chiyan, she thought wryly, remembering her recent experiences in her birth land. Then burped, a sour taste filling her mouth. Katerin swallowed hard. She had to go to the galley soon to see if Cook had any of her tea already prepared. Gods, she didn't want to move, though. The sickness was better if she didn't have to walk.

The knock on her door was a welcome distraction. "Come in."

Doryits opened the door, stepped in, then hesitated. "I see you are busy. We can speak later." His skin was pale under brown with the faint sheen from waterstruck.

He must need some distraction, too.

"Oh *Gods* no, Doryits. Come on in. I swear, if I threw this thing out of the porthole it would soak up the whole ocean including that storm out there." Sour taste filled her mouth again. She reached for her waterskin and took a gulp.

He chuckled and plopped down in a chair. "That bad?"

"Absolutely." She closed the book and pushed it to the edge of the table. "I would offer tea, but I'm afraid I lack sufficient sea experience to make some without risk to both of us. And to be honest, I'm not wanting to move because I don't get quite as sick."

"I bring relief, then." He raised a flask she hadn't seen until now. "It's cold, but I got some from Cook. You've offered me tea every time we've talked. It's only fair I return the favor." He set the flask on the table and fished two cups out of his coat pockets. "There."

"I thank you."

Doryits clutched at the flask and cups as the ship crashed hard into a trough and they started to side. "Rough one, isn't it?"

"All of it is rough to me," Katerin sighed. "Supposedly this is a mild storm. I wouldn't know otherwise."

"That's what Cook said to me, too. All the same, I'm also not fond of water travel."

Doryits poured the tea during a quiet moment, then rested his fingertips first on her cup, then his, lips moving silently. Katerin smiled as she saw the wisps of steam rising from the cups. She wrapped her hands around her cup quickly so it wouldn't spill.

"Perhaps you have more magic that you thought."

"Just enough to get waterstruck, especially in a storm, even a mild one like this." Doryits scowled. "This is about the level of my magical strength. I can heat some water, cast a few minor spells, spot some traps." His face darkened. "Some of the traps I'm best at spotting are the ones cast by the dead-that-walk. I can see those better than those from the Saubral, or Waykemin."

Katerin sipped her tea. "So Cook is brewing this tea regularly now?"

There were enough magicians on board this ship, after all. Had she brought enough?

"Cook has cold flasks of it on hand between meals. He muttered something about *damn magicians who won't eat* when I stopped by, but he was boiling up a big kettle of broth. At least he understands most of us aren't going to be eating much."

"Good to know that he's doing that. Some ships are more experienced with magicians than others." She would have to take one of her own flasks to get more tea to have on hand. If she dared stir past her cabin door for more than the basics. "Thank you for bringing it."

Her stomach settled as she drank more tea. Part of her annoyance with the *History of Waykemin* had as much to do with being waterstruck as it did the quality of the writing.

"I figured you would be miserable as well. Why not share tea? Oh. I met one of the Hidden One's attendants in the galley getting tea, and she said to tell you that the Hidden One will not move until after we've put into shore. No meetings unless they're in her cabin."

"I should probably check on her," Katerin groaned. "As a courtesy. She's probably handling this storm worse than I am. At least I'm used to going up and down the Chellana and Saktrin rivers on sternwheelers, and have some degree of exposure so I don't get as sick as I used to. She lives in the middle of the desert. I think her first water travel besides skiffs on the Inland Sea was when she came to Medvare-the-city to help Witmara."

Doryits eyed her curiously. "What could you do for her?"

"I *have* been a Healer."

"You said that before." Was that surprise in his tone?

"Before I was Leader I was a Healer. A circuit Healer in the Two Nations for years, then Alicira's personal Healer."

"Oh. I didn't realize that." He flushed slightly. "It's not the usual Leader's background."

"I suppose not," she said. "But I didn't even know I was a Miteal until Rekaré became Leader. By then I'd already been a circuit Healer." Her stomach roiled again and she sipped from her cup. Ah. Relief. "Enough about me." She didn't want to talk about that time. Not with the memories of Metkyi that it stirred. It felt disloyal. "Let's talk about something else."

Doryits sighed. "You wanted to know more about the Confederation and the dead-that-walk."

"It doesn't sound pleasant, but yes." She sipped more tea. Gods, they'd moved from her discomfort to his.

"It wasn't." His voice went flat.

Should they discuss this now? From what he'd said before, he probably had memories as difficult as those she had about Metkyi. But his painful past was a part of what she needed to know about what they were going into.

"I'm sorry if this is difficult. I wouldn't push, but...." Her voice trailed off.

He shrugged. "You need to know this."

"Just tell me if it's too much to talk about at once."

He sighed. "It's been five years. I should be over this by now."

"It's been eighteen years since I lost my beloved on the battlefield. I still ache for him." *Especially since I can no longer speak to his shade, even at Staul's shrines.* "You never really get over the loss. And not knowing what is happening with my daughter in Daran—the only thing I can be certain of is that she still lives, and has not yielded to Chatain's designs. I am sure he would send me gloating projections if she were dead or subservient to him."

"Then you know what it's like."

"All too well." She sipped more tea, then took a deep breath. "All right. You saw my mother in Waykemin, so you know what that was like. My recent excursion to Waykemin was—I'd never seen anything like that before. How similar is Waykemin to the Confederation? As bad? Worse? Probably not better."

"No, the Confederation is definitely not better." Doryits stared into his cup, clearly organizing his thoughts. At last he looked up. "Like and yet unlike. Waykemin—Waykemin had an order to daily life under the Witches. People had a purpose. Yes, there were *ushar* and *kendar* in Waykemin. The *shalkendar* were unseen but we knew they were there. All the same…" he shifted in his chair as his voice trailed up, then set his cup down, lacing his fingers together, and coughed. His voice was stronger as he continued. "Waykemin had order and not chaos. Structures were there to run everyday life. I was perfectly safe in the guise of a merchant. Once I crossed the Kitskan Fords, I knew I was as safe as I would be back home in Keratil. No one would rob me, and the worst danger I encountered was being discovered as a spy."

Katerin nodded, remembering. "And the Confederation lacks order?"

He scowled at his hands. "Along the border at least. I never went further than that. Not safe to go further. Chaos, anarchy, destruction seems to be their purpose. They don't have villages or cities—though what I did hear suggested that those might be further inland. But all I saw were camps. Not even organized camps, such as you find amongst the Clendan herders. Chaotic, dirty, disorganized camps, and everyone preys on everyone else. You dare not leave anything of value unguarded unless you are rich and can hire guards. Otherwise, you make alliances and hope that your associates are somewhat honest. Or you pay someone to watch you and your things for a night's sleep—and hope that someone doesn't outbid you so that you find a knife at your throat demanding the clothes off your back. Loyalties change from day to day, depending on how valuable you appear to be to those who are supposed to be your allies. They pride themselves on being outcasts, like their God. And when they worship him? They *fight* to die for his glory during his ceremonies."

Katerin shuddered. "So the Outcast God drives most of what happens?"

"To some extent. It's all chaos."

"How can the Confederation be such a threat if they're so disorganized?"

"Numbers, a mutual hatred of anything that isn't them coupled with passionate devotion to the Outcast God, and the sort of magic they use. But mostly it's the dead-that-walk that powers the threat. There are comparatively few living people, at least on the border, and there's more of the dead-that-walk than you think." Doryits shook his head. "Katerin, the foulness goes down through the children. If you have magic in the land of the Outcast God, you get sucked into the army right away—the younger, the better. Life as a child born to magic in that land is far from good. Only the few that are very powerful do well— like Sariost." He winced.

"I am sorry."

"If she hadn't been so powerful, she would have ended up like her brother Aryetis. He was sucked dry. A shade powered by hatred and the glory of the Outcast God, until I struck him down." He didn't look at her, staring instead at the rain pounding against the porthole. "Given what I know about them, Sariost was probably the one who did it."

"Oh, Doryits."

The Healer in Katerin desperately wanted to console him. To lose his family like this, to have to kill the shades of his wife and son to give them rest—she rested her hand on his for comfort, squeezing it gently before pulling it back.

"She probably consumed Jarilyn too." Doryits drew a deep, shuddering breath. "I'm sorry. But even after five years, it still hurts. Worse, when I am close to the border, I feel Sariost's hunger. She wants to devour me as well. That's quite a prize in the land of the Divine Confederation. Being a magician who has absorbed the rest of their family. That gives her favor and power amongst them—and a certain degree of safety."

"*Is* it safe for you to go back to the border?"

"If the Confederation breaks through and establishes a presence, no place in Keratil will be safe for me. Probably no place in Varen." He laughed harshly. "Safe or not, I'm going back. We have to stop them, Katerin."

"So what is our best offense? Defense?" Katerin pushed herself up to retrieve her writing desk so that she could take notes. Vertigo made her reel for a moment and she grabbed the back of her chair, breathing slowly until the world steadied around her. She settled the desk in her lap and prepared to write. "Tell me—at least as much as you can bear to say in one setting."

"It will take several," he said, staring down at his hands.

"We have the time."

He shuddered. "All right. Let's start with the border defenses, and how one such as Sariost can evade them."

Katerin took a deep breath and wrote *Border Defense Evasion* at the top of her paper.

She was pleased to see how steady her hand was.

Even given the storm and the subject.

MAGICAL DISCOVERY

Witmara and her troop rode along a narrow trail through the grasslands behind tall sand dunes, occasionally passing through small groves of wizened pine trees. The sandy beach where Setkin had put them ashore near dusk reminded Witmara more of the beaches around the mouth of the Cooscol Bay than the alien, hot, and teeming Ourigny Islands. To be expected, since they had sailed two days north after leaving Lanivar. She had noticed the growing chill in the wind as they sailed.

The temperature was more like she would expect on Medvara's coast, cooler than the Ourigny Islands and less humid.

But there were differences. While the shorebirds seemed to resemble those she knew from Medvara, there were subtle changes in coloring and the cries they made when startled. When they rode through the groves, the trees were shorter and more twisted, needles smaller than she expected. Unlike the Medvaran coast, she didn't see much moss on the ground and on the trees. A drier climate than Medvara.

Plus the coast was to the east, not the west. She wasn't used to sunrise over the ocean and sunset over the land. Where the ocean was to her right instead of being on her left as they rode north, parallel to it. It was just like and yet unlike enough to be discordant.

Daro reached once to grab a bite from the tall, coarse grass lining the path and flinched back, sending her an image of

sharp edges, burny, be careful.

She noticed that Petronin and his horse were careful to stay in the middle of the track.

The meadows gave way to taller trees, with more brush than in the dunes, but still nowhere near as much moss on their trunks as Witmara would expect this close to the ocean. At last Petronin halted in a grassy clearing. In the center of it was a fire ring made of stone so like the ones she'd seen while traveling in the Two Nations that a wave of homesickness passed over her. Daro sniffed at this grass and took a bite.

Sweet. Good.

"This is a good place to stop for the night," Petronin said. "We're far enough away from the shore and from Fenras that no one is going to stumble upon us here by accident. Well, unless there's some smugglers from Ternar. But they won't want to be found, either. Not until they reach the slave market. So they'll avoid us."

"Slave market?" Witmara dismounted and began to undo Daro's cinch. "So slaves are not born into that life? And they're smuggled? By Dovré's golden tits, why would they be smuggled into Daran?"

"These are special slaves," Petronin said. "Concubines. After the lady Betsona proved to be so powerful in magic, there's been an illicit traffic in men and women for the nobles. Every family wants the opportunity to create a powerful magician. But only certain families from Ternar have that ability, and even then it's not reliable."

"What happens if the concubines—" she couldn't make herself use the word *slave,* not yet, "—don't produce magicians?"

Petronin shrugged. "There's always a need for brothel staff, especially in Fenras, Adalane, and Daraelen."

"That's...." Witmara fumbled for words, unable to speak. She eased Daro's saddle off, then his bridle. "Barbaric," she said finally. She carried saddle and bridle over to where Toran was unrolling their bedroll.

"It's a better life for them than in the general slave population, my lady," Petronin said as he followed behind her.

Witmara turned to face him. "Are *you* a slave, or a servant?"

"We are all slaves who serve the lady Betsona. Including Seijina, who shares her bed. She calls us her staff, but she owns us. All of us." His voice was neutral.

Witmara stared at him, speechless. Toran came up behind her and rested one hand on her shoulder.

"But Seijina's cousin is a Sorcerer-Captain," she said finally.

"He escaped the family's debt," Petronin said. "Some of us are born to servitude, while others are forced into it. I was fortunate enough to be born to the household of Betsona's mother, the lady Vespla. Once Dunaran learned how powerful Betsona was, he granted Vespla her freedom, the title of Royal Concubine, and slave ownership rights. Seijina's family was not as fortunate. While Setkin was in training to become a Sorcerer-Captain, their family lost their fortune. Had Setkin not been at sea and gained his title during the family's fall— well, it was a good thing that he earned his Captain's ring. Luckily, Seijina and Betsona had known each other before her family fell. Betsona bought her friend and as many members of the family and their servants as she could. A softer landing than most who end up being enslaved under such circumstances."

"There are no slaves in Varen," Witmara whispered. "Not since Rekaré deposed Zauril."

"That is a strange land," Petronin said. He bowed. "I beg your leave, Lady Witmara. I need to make sure that our shield points have been set around camp."

"Yes, yes," she stammered, remembering what Betsona had told her about them. Shield points. Little transmitters that enhanced the establishment of a magical shield.

Something I want Mother and Rekaré to know about. They could use them.

She turned to Toran as Petronin left them. "Did you hear that?" she asked, speaking the Clendan dialect she had taught him for private moments.

He nodded, his expression solemn.

"Gods. We *have* to eliminate Chatain. This is—unconscionable," she said.

"Changing this system isn't going to happen overnight, Witmara."

"I know. But Gods." She shook her head. "I just can't support it."

"You have to become Empress first," he reminded her. "And we have a roundabout journey to Adalane and surviving the Challenge in order for that to happen."

"True."

So much depended on disrupting a festival. From what Betsona had said, Witmara needed to issue Chatain a challenge —Petronin was supposed to know just how to do it.

She already had the land on her side. Now she just needed to win her challenge and be consecrated, in front of the people of Daran in Adalane.

"Deep thoughts," Toran said.

"Just thinking about what lies ahead. Gods, Toran."

"I believe in you, dear heart." He kissed her, then moved off to help set up camp.

Witmara looked around camp to see what needed to be done—wood. Fire. Only one man gathered wood, picking and choosing between branches that lay on the edge of the clearing. What little he picked up wouldn't be enough for even a small fire. She went to him.

"Are you looking for a particular type of wood or just anything burnable?" she asked, in halting common Darani.

"Oh, my lady, no need for you to be doing this work."

Witmara raised her brows. "I am sharing in the comfort of the camp along with you. I need to be contributing to its welfare." She gestured to the branches he held. "Is there a reason you choose those branches, or will any wood that size work here? Along the coast in Medvara we gather just about any wood. But I noticed that my daranval did not find the beach grasses palatable. Is all the wood burnable? Please tell me. I want to learn more about Daran—and practice my Darani. You seem to be a good person to teach me."

As she had hoped, asking him to teach her softened his disapproval. "Come along, my lady, and I will show you. Certain woods are best avoided. They contain various kinds of sorcery and we don't want to release that magic in the flames. It's a pity because those are the best woods for burning. But only magicians can burn them without harm, and they only do that for ceremony."

Interesting. The land's magic might help me discern which branches are useable—but best to ask him, to build his comfort with me.

"So how do we know which wood is which? By the type?" She followed along as he went amongst the trees.

"Yes." He pointed to one branch lying at the edge of the clearing. It was a nice long straight stick, with a pine knot in it. "Ordinarily that would be a good one for the fire. But see how the bark twists in swirls around the branch? It carries magic that could betray us and breach our shielding."

She studied it. "Is it safe to touch?"

"Not for me." He studied her. "You're a magician. But some woods will entrap a magician."

"I can ask the land's magic. It will tell me."

His eyes widened. "You can speak to the land?" He crossed his arms across his chest and fell back a step. "Not even the Emperor would dare to do that. The land is wild with a mind of its own. It would overwhelm him!"

"The land listens to me. But if you would prefer me not to invoke the land's magic, I can call my daranval over. He can tell me if it is safe to touch."

"Your horse can do that?"

"My daranval is from a magic-gifted breed."

She switched to mindspeech.

> Daro, can you come here? I need you to check on something for me.

He sent her disgruntlement at leaving the grass, but raised his head and trotted toward her. Witmara pointed to the branch.

"This man—" she said out loud, jerking her head toward the nameless man, oh Gods she was as bad as the rest of the Aireii, she hadn't asked his name! "—says that this branch is magic-possessed and possibly unsafe, Daro. What do you think?"

"He understands you?"

"Every word," Witmara said, watching Daro.

He snorted, then approached the branch, sniffing it carefully from the broken end above the knot down to the other, shattered end.

> Safe. Not to burn. Life within.

He picked it up in his teeth and dragged it over to her.

See?

She took the branch in both hands even as the man's eyes widened again. A weakened spirit stirred within the wood as she held it, a sense of resignation at being separated from growing life.

What are you?

she asked it.

Despair at never fulfilling its purpose filled her, a spiral that would have pulled her down with it if she had been weaker. The land's awareness stirred, and sent her an image of a tall, straight pine. It had been felled years ago, and used to make—Witmara caught her breath.

Sailship masts!

So this was the secret of the sailships!

Do all trees of this type contain this magic?

she asked Daran.

Only certain trees, with bark of this twist.

The land showed her a picture of wood with a different twist. That wood was dangerous and fell, angry with humans and desirous of drinking human blood. Chatain carried a staff made with that wood and used other pieces of it to make his devices. That was the most he could do to manage the land's magic.

Interesting.

She studied the branch further. It could serve her as a means to control Daran's magic. After all, serving as a channel to control the land's magic was one reason for the Great Tapestries of Varen, as well as the various jewels and tokens many Leaders used for that purpose. With a wild and unruly magic such as Daran's, the use of a focus might well be the wisest thing to do.

> You can still be useful,

she told the branch.

> I can use you as a staff and magical channel to the land. And your kindred can be used to make devices for me.

Plaintive sorrow that it was not destructive and could not be used to consume her foes.

> I do not ask that of you and your kindred. I ask you to serve me freely, to make life better for all.

A tendril of hope. An image of other, scattered branches further in the woods, some of its siblings that had been discarded and then dispersed, as others looking for firewood had shunned them for fear of the magic within. She sent the images to Daro.

> Help me find them.

"Lady?" The man's frightened voice brought her attention back to him.

"This is safe wood," she said. "It has a power that I can use, but not for burning fires. Thank you—what is your name?"

"Tiernin, my lady."

"Tiernin." Her mind raced. What would it take to free him from Betsona's service? "You may have just guided me to the power I need to help me defeat Chatain. Can we get someone else to gather firewood? I need your help to find more of this particular wood. In fact, I will do whatever it takes to release you from the lady Betsona's service, if you will help me. I need a forester, a guide to the woods. Will you be willing to serve me in that role?"

He knelt and bowed his head. "If you so command me, lady Witmara."

"Tiernin. Rise. Don't be so silly. I want your consent. I will not be your mistress, but your Empress, and I'm not even that yet. I want guidance, not servitude. Someone who can tell me if I've made a mistake."

Her mind raced as she looked around the woods.

So there is magic in the trees. What else?

She had always been taught that the Coos berry plants and the Stardance breed of sheep were anomalies, that magic had appeared in them by an explicit gift of the Gods to the Miteal family. The daranvelii had emerged in Clenda with no explanation that Witmara knew of. But other than those three things, magic did not regularly stir within products of the land.

In Varen, that was. Could Daran be different? Was this why its magic was considered difficult and wild—it had appeared in its land products, but those things had not been regularly used and channeled, unlike in Varen?

Is that why Daran is like this—its rulers and residents have disregarded its magic?

Definitely something to consider—later.

Tiernin rose to his feet, frowning, worry creasing his forehead. "My lady, are you *sure* of this?"

"You appear to be knowledgeable about the woods on the mainland. Is there someone else with greater understanding riding with us?"

"Well, no, my family are foresters, but—"

"Then you are the one to help me understand the forest

better, especially since different woods carry magic. Quick. I will find someone else to help us gather firewood. You and I will find what we can of this particular tree's leavings—and any other with the same sort of power."

He still hesitated. "Others will need guidance."

"So will I. But I will not leave the other pieces of this wood to rot unhappily without the possibility of becoming something greater. Toran," she called.

He was at her side quickly. "Yes?"

"Saddle Daro and bring a rider and mule. I've discovered magic wood that we can use for our devices. Bring rope to tie the branches on Daro. We'll put firewood on the mule."

"Packsaddle?"

Daro stomped and snorted.

You are the only one I can trust with the magic wood,

she told him.

"Yes," she said to Toran. "The magic wood goes on Daro."

"All right." Toran clucked to Daro. The stallion followed him, switching his tail disapprovingly.

As Witmara waited for Daro and Toran's return, she examined the stick, running her hands over it to check for weaknesses that might render it useless for her intended purpose. The limb wasn't exactly straight, with a couple of small twists, none of which would impair its use. Some of the bark was missing, revealing a gorgeous mix of dark red and pinkish fibers that twisted around each other in a pattern similar to the bark scales. That would look beautiful if lightly sanded and oiled. Her hand curled just right around the stick below the knot at the top, and if they could find someone to put an iron tip on the bottom—oh yes, this would serve her well, and be striking if carved and finished right.

By her hands only, though. If she wanted to use it as a

channel for the land's magical energies, she had to be the one to shape it—just as the rulers who used the Great Tapestries had to weave them with their own hands, incorporating their own magic into them.

If the wood consented to be used in such a manner.

> Would you allow me to carve you into a slightly different form, so that I can use you as a focus for the land's magic?

she asked.

Curiosity. Wonder at what she meant.

Witmara visualized some of the carved wood she had seen and learned to make in sheep camp during her childhood in the Two Nations. A sudden memory of Heinmyets carving a staff like this for Alicira flooded her thoughts, and she blinked back the unexpected sadness that came with the recollection.

A cautious concern at her sorrow, mixed with pleasure at the beauty of Heinmyets's carving.

> Only remembering someone who is gone,

she reassured it.

> I will not be quite as skilled as Heinmyets, I'm afraid. But I am the one who will shape you. You will be the wooden version of the Great Tapestries woven by leaders of my people, not only a sign of my strength but a participant in my use of the land's magic.

Happier thoughts. Joy at the thought of being able to serve her in such a manner.

Toran joined her, the mule and Daro following.

"We need to find branches like this one," she said to Toran, showing him her staff-to-be. "Whorls in the bark and wood like this. They contain magic that we can use. I plan to carve this one to be my staff."

"Fascinating." Toran studied the whorls, and the colors of the wood where the bark had fallen off. "That section without bark almost looks like the wood in the masts of the sailships."

"It is the same, or so Daran tells me," she said. "Those who took its tree only took the tree and not the branches. I think we can make use of those branches."

"I would agree—look! I see one there!" He pointed. "Isn't it?"

"Tiernin?" She turned to him.

He nodded. "My lady, it's definitely another one of that type."

"Good. Tiernin, this is my husband Toran. Toran, this is Tiernin. He is going to help us find more of this wood, and I have commissioned him to advise me about the forest. Toran, there are other kinds of wood as well—malevolent wood, some that Chatain uses." She glanced over at Mennit who had come with Toran—another of Betsona's people. "Mennit. We are gathering firewood but I also want to find more wood like this." She pointed to the whorls. "Avoid these but call us to them. Tiernin, are there other woods here that contain magic? Or just those marked like this?"

"There are others, my lady." Tiernin frowned. "Perhaps we could gather together? You can pick up the safe enchanted wood, and the rest of us could gather that safe wood which does not contain magic."

"That sounds like a good idea. Lead us."

He hesitated, then began to walk. Some branches Tiernin pointed out as dangerous. Witmara sensed the angry red glow emanating from those pieces, and her staff quivered in their presence, a faint vibration coupled with worry. The two types together, especially fallen and dried, reacted to each other— sometimes bursting into flame. Her staff fretted about that likelihood.

> Do not fear,

she told it.

> We will leave those be.

For now, she added to herself. If that particular wood was that magically volatile, she needed to consider a means to deal with it once Chatain had been deposed. Perhaps losing his magic might render those woods innocuous…and then again, it might not.

Not something I can change right away.

But definitely something to be considered for the future, once she became Empress. If she became Empress.

They continued gathering wood, leaving the dangerous pieces alone. The safe ones Mennit and Tiernin picked up. Once one or the other had an armload, Toran helped him tie it on the mule. Witmara picked up the magic branches and tied them to Daro's saddle, all except for her staff.

At last they had gathered a towering stack on the mule. Mennit and Tiernin also carried armloads of wood. The pile tied to Daro's saddle was much smaller than the one on Gernar, but she couldn't find any more of the magical wood as dusk thickened around them. Time to return to camp and start a small fire.

> Do we have all of your kindred?

she asked her branch.

Satisfaction came back to her.

"I think we're done," she said.

"Good," Tiernin said. "We have enough for a fire."

Tiernin and Mennit led the way back to camp. Toran walked on the other side of Daro, resting his hand on the daranval's neck. Witmara used the staff as a walking stick, still feeling out what power lay within the wood.

"This was a find," he said. "Lots of possibilities using wood with magic. I was curious about some of Betsona's devices—wooden, no crystals, no other source of magic. Now I know. Magic in the wood. We've gathered enough for me to experiment with."

"It makes me wonder what we could have done had we been able to use something like this during that battle in Medvara."

While gathering, she had taken advantage of one period where they were away from Tiernin and Mennit to whisper to Toran what she had learned about the malevolent woods and how Chatain had used them.

"That might explain why Chatain's men were able to sneak up on us and abduct you. Devices using that malevolent wood to conceal their presence—I felt *something*, but not until it was too late. If I'd known, we could have searched the dead for them." He scowled. "I wonder how many were left in Medvara after they took you?"

"It does explain some things—and Chiral could have scattered devices of that wood in Medvara as well." She rubbed her thumb on the wood, wanting to imprint more of herself into it. Her mother should be told about this, but when? How?

Perhaps I should wait to worry about that until I can communicate with Mother. Until then—trust to the bond she has with Medvara. The possibility that Chiral scattered tokens is quite high—and would have been something Mother had to deal with long before now if that were the case.

"I'm going to start work on my staff tonight," she continued.

"It would probably be best to save the bark and shavings as you work."

"I agree. No waste."

They went over to their bedroll and unloaded the branches from Daro's back, then turned him loose to graze. Witmara knelt by her bags as Toran bundled the wood into a tighter bundle that could be tied to a packsaddle.

"Did you bring me a knife? They took the one I got from Inharise years ago."

Toran smiled and handed her a small knife. "No, they didn't. I found this close to where you had fallen, along with the Light of Medvara and the Regent's Ring. Apparently they didn't like the feel of it."

"Oh Gods, Toran, thank you!" She hefted the light knife, smiling. She had missed the blade, and feared that her captors had taken it, never to be returned. "It will be perfect for carving my staff."

He kissed her forehead. "I had intended to give it back to you sooner. But with everything, and repairing Betsona's chair before we left—it slipped my mind until now. A magical knife to work on a magical staff."

"Yes." She picked up a cloth to catch the pieces of bark and shavings when she worked, and carried the stick with her as they joined the others around the fire. Spreading the cloth, she began debarking the branch, careful to ensure that every scale and chunk landed on the cloth. She could already visualize the possible pattern she wanted to carve in the staff. She just needed to see what the wood grain pattern was along its full length.

CHALLENGES

"SHIP AHEAD!" ONE OF THE SAILORS CALLED FROM THE CROW'S nest.

Rekaré startled up from her seat in the shade of the *Morning Star's* forecastle, where she had been playing the elaborate *shaling* game with Vered. Shaling came from Daran—supposedly one of Chatain's favorite games—and used a black and white checkered board with assorted playing pieces. It was also a preferred entertainment amongst the *Star's* crew, and Rekaré was starting to develop a degree of skill using the strategy required to win.

One way to get into Chatain's mindset.

"Is it Setkin?" she asked Vered.

The other Sorcerer-Captain had contacted Vered through their sorcerous channels last night to tell them that he was on his way back from Daran. No word about whether Witmara or Toran were with him—it had been the shortest of contacts, with most of the discussion about Setkin finding them.

"Yes," Vered said.

She left Rekaré and the game to coordinate their meeting. Rekaré gathered up the game pieces and inserted them into the box that the game board was part of. She put the box in Vered's cabin.

"Senth. Deta," she called into the hold. "*Heart's Desire* draws near."

Soon enough they could see the *Desire*. Vered sang softly to the *Star* and it put about gently, as did the *Desire*. The two ships glided toward each other until they were side-by-side.

"I'll come over there," Setkin called from his deck. "I have news to share."

They waited while the rigging was set up between the ships and Setkin transferred over. He knelt and pressed his hands to the *Star's* deck, then touched his forehead to it.

"*Morning Star* accepts your presence, captain of the *Heart's Desire*," Vered said.

Setkin straightened up. "*Desire* acknowledges *Star*."

"And *Star* acknowledges *Desire*," Vered responded.

Rekaré reined in her impatience as the two captains continued with the boarding ritual. The sentient sailships had their own necessary protocol when another ship's captain came on board, and she knew better than to interfere with the process.

At last they were done with the formalities.

"Come to my cabin," Vered said. Setkin, Rekaré, Detaluna, and Sesenth followed her inside, taking seats around the sturdy table in her cabin. "So. You have news?"

"Witmara is safe, and free in Daran—or at least as free as any outsider can be in Daran," Setkin said. "I put them ashore with their daranvelii on the mainland three days ago, and have been sailing as hard and fast as I can push the *Desire* to meet you."

"The mainland?" Rekaré asked.

They're together, safe, and free. And Witmara has Daro with her. Good.

Relief flooded through her, and she wished for a means to let Katerin know that would not take days to reach her.

Goddess Dovré, if ever you've heard my pleas, please do this for me. Send Katerin a sign, for we are too far apart for me to reassure her.

She wished she knew how Chatain managed to send projections over the ocean. Perhaps she could do it once they were on land and she no longer struggled with being waterstruck?

Setkin nodded. "Betsona gave Witmara and Toran forged safe-conducts that will get them past Chatain's patrols. She also provided them with links to the secret cells she has been nurturing ever since Chatain exiled her to Adalane. Witmara is planning to confront Chatain in a duel of magic."

"How?" Rekaré frowned. Toran hadn't taken that many riders with him, just his personal guard. "Would those cells provide enough support for Witmara to take on Chatain?"

"The Emperor or a member of the Royal Family performs a ritual at the Spring Festival of Plays that is significant for the survival of the Empire. Witmara will have sufficient support from his opponents to challenge him in that setting. She won't need numbers—just the right people in the right place."

"Why hasn't Betsona used them to elevate herself, then?"

It didn't make sense. Betsona was already there, with support. If she already had an effective secret organization, why wasn't she using it to promote herself?

"Betsona does not have the advantage of being unknown like Witmara is. Since Chatain exiled her, if she appears at the Festival without his express command, then she can be accused of treason and executed along the way there. He didn't start coming to Festival until after he exiled her," Setkin said.

"I'm surprised that I haven't seen anything about a possible challenge in the letters she wrote to Witmara," Rekaré said.

"Security," Setkin said. "Betsona can shield conversations better than she can written messages. I knew she had a spy network—I carried messages for her—but was not aware that she also was organizing a resistance to Chatain."

"I asked Chiral if there had been an organized opposition to Chatain when she was gathering information for me," Detaluna said. "She denied any knowledge of it. I'm surprised at its existence because in spite of Chiral's many faults, she did have a finger on what drove things in Daran."

"I don't think she and Betsona knew each other very well, except by reputation," Vered mused. "From all I have heard, Betsona is wiser and more cautious than to ally herself with Chiral's branch of the Ralsem family. Chiral's father Zauberin wasn't much loved by the late Emperor Dunaran. That meant that Betsona would keep her distance from him and by extension Chiral. She was Dunaran's favorite. Betsona understood his whims and if he condemned someone—she would share his opinion, at least in public. Their father's preference for Betsona was one reason why Chatain turned on her once he became Emperor."

Setkin raised his brows at Vered. "Don't forget how Betsona's crippling came about."

"Unless you're part of the royal family, suggestions that there was more to it than a simple accident are just rumors." Vered frowned at him.

"What do you mean?" Rekaré asked. "I had heard that her disabilities were caused by a magical accident, and that Chatain was involved. Is that what you mean?"

"Chatain was fortunate that he was not banished for what happened to Betsona," Setkin snapped. He shook his head at Vered as she tightened her lips and scowled. "Seijina told me the truth of it years ago, Vered! Her relationship with Betsona definitely puts her—and me—adjacent to the royal family. What we don't know is if Chatain purposefully caused the injury to Betsona. Betsona believes it was deliberate, but that was never proven. They were both young and powerful magicians as children, both leading contenders to rule after Dunaran. Either explanation is possible."

"So what happened?" Rekaré asked.

Setkin sighed. "Seijina was at Court and part of Betsona's circle. Betsona is more adept at magical manipulation of technology than Chatain is—he is more proficient at the technological manipulation of magic. Their tutor had given them a cooperative project, to adapt a piece of magitech that used volatile magical and chemical elements. Chatain was the one manipulating the magic when the compound exploded. Both were injured, but because Betsona was handling the actual project when it blew up, she was the one who suffered the most harm. It took days before they were certain that she would survive, and there was worry that her magic would be impaired. It didn't impact her magic—just her body—but it left her with a weakened constitution. Major magical workings leave her exhausted for several days afterward."

"That would give her sufficient reason to be unhappy with him," Rekaré said.

Setkin nodded. "Dunaran gave her several magical tokens in the last years of his reign which helped her survive. Chatain ruthlessly purged his rival siblings in his first years as Emperor—all save Betsona."

"So she's a survivor," Rekaré said thoughtfully. "And she organized opposition to Chatain? How?"

"Yes. Do you have time to hear the details?"

"Please. Sesenth and I know little of Daran, compared to you, Vered, and Detaluna, and anything you can tell us would be useful."

"All right." Setkin stretched, then rested his hands on the table, studying them as he spoke. "Betsona started to organize a resistance to Chatain's rule when he exiled her to the city of Adalane upon his ascension to Emperor. While she has always liked Adalane, when Dunaran was alive, she preferred to split her time between Adalane and the court in Daraelen. Adalane is the oldest city in Daran and at one time was the original capital.

It's also home to Daran's greatest amphitheater. It has been traditional that the Emperor, Empress, or their designated family representative presides over the Spring Festival's opening dedications—which is the most conventional of the four seasonal festivals. The ruler who avoids or scorns the Spring Festival risks Godly wrath." Setkin shrugged. "The last ruler to ignore the Festival was Elithtra. Make of that what you will. Neither Etikar, Dunaran, or now Chatain have avoided that responsibility."

"Chatain regularly goes to the Festival?" Rekaré pursed her lips.

A possible place to attack him. How long would it take them to get there?

"No. Until two years ago, the lady Betsona presided in Chatain's stead, as she had done during the last years of their father's reign. Then Chatain decided that she was becoming too popular with the people, and exiled her to Lanivar."

"But by then she had established her information and opposition networks, right?" Rekaré said.

"Yes, and she's kept in touch with her organization since her exile. I've—carried a number of messages for her over the years. Never knew the content. In any case, Betsona sent Witmara with letters of introduction to her cell leaders. They can place her in the ceremonies so that she can confront Chatain at the dedication. Witmara has gained control over Daran's magic—as much as any sorcerer can. She will have that advantage over Chatain." Setkin paused. "If she gets there in time. She's riding a roundabout passage to get to Adalane. Over land, along the border with Ternar, rather than directly upriver from Fenras to Adalane."

"Why not go direct?" Rekaré tapped her fingers on the table nervously. "And when does this happen?"

"Festival starts in ten days. Witmara's brown skin would call attention if she were on a sailship or riding a more direct route as anything but a slave to a master or mistress," Setkin said. "For her to travel the river route successfully, she would need to have Betsona or someone else of paler hue accompany her as her mistress. And Betsona dares not leave Lanivar this close to Festival opening. Chatain has a tracker set upon her, and will know if Betsona leaves Lanivar without his permission. If she does, there's an open warrant for treason upon her. For Witmara to triumph she needs to be stealthy and not be in Betsona's presence."

"I see." Rekaré chewed her lip thoughtfully. "Witmara couldn't just hide below decks on a ship?"

"Ships heading to Adalane are searched thoroughly with Spring Festival coming on. Taking this particular land route allows Witmara to meet supporters who aren't nobility. There are many more of those—especially the middle level guild and craft workers—who would initially follow her than among the nobles. Plus she and her followers can blend in better with those coming to Adalane for the Festival if she's coming in on the road from the west, than from the eastern coast region."

"I see. Do we have a map? I'd like to look at the layout. The Islands. Fenras. Adalane. Witmara's probable route."

"Easily done," Vered said. She rose and went to a cabinet filled with rolled parchment. Selecting a big scroll, she unrolled it on the table. "Lanivar Island." She pointed to a small, eastern-most island on the edge of an island chain in the ocean. Her finger traced a curve around the other islands. "This would be the route to Fenras. Where did you set them off on the main-land?" she asked Setkin, fingertip pausing in the narrow passage between the biggest island and the mainland.

"Hagni's Rest," he said, his voice suddenly flat.

Vered's face tightened momentarily, then eased. She resumed tracing the route, stopping before it touched a city at the mouth of a big river.

"Hagni's Rest." Sorrow echoed in her voice, and she closed

her eyes for a moment as Setkin tightened his lips. Then she opened them and moved her finger to touch the city. "Fenras, and the Fenras River." She followed the river. "Corean. Penteph. Then Adalane. That would be how she would travel if she took the river route."

Setkin poked at the map between Penteph and Adalane. "Two more stops have been added since this map was drawn. Chatain installed those as shipping checks after he exiled Betsona. They are held by his followers. Those would be the places where Witmara would be most at risk if she were traveling by ship, and Betsona lacks any supporters there." He traced a route on the map. "This is the way Witmara is taking. There are small villages along the edge of the mountains. Some are heavy with slave smugglers from Ternar, but when she turns from the border with Ternar she crosses the upper end of the Fenras Valley to follow the Darldinnei range until she reaches the West Road from Daraelen. That makes it appear that she is coming from the inland, not from the coast." He pointed to another city on the other side of the mountains from Adalane.

"How very strange that Daraelen is the capital," Rekaré said. "There's no ocean access. Just river access to that inland sea."

"At the time, inland trade with the western nomads was more important," Detaluna said. "They had contact with peoples further west who had access to mines and spices. Eventually Daran's conquests overtook the nomads. But it is still a center for overland trade."

"There were also fears of invasion by sea," Setkin added. "Plus, the growing season is somewhat better around Daraelen. It's also closer to the mines in the Darldinnei—" he pointed to the mountain range between Daraelen and Adalane. "They're on the Daraelen side of the mountains. Once the Empire expanded to that side of the Darldinnei, the primary noble families bought up as much land as they could around Daraelen."

"Could we sail upriver to Fenras?" Rekaré squinted at the map, an idea starting to form. If they could time it right….

Setkin shook his head. "I can't. Not only am I known as Seijina's cousin, but I've been publicly identified as one who works with Betsona. Vered—possibly. She's never carried things for Betsona. The other factor? You are unquestionably Aireii, albeit one who spends a lot of time outside. Unlike Witmara, you won't stand out. But you will still need forged safe-conducts and passes."

"And to get those, I suppose I need to meet with Betsona."

"That's the safest way," Vered said. "I don't have the clearances or the cargo that would give us automatic passage during Festival season. Trying to do so would call attention to us. The port authorities at Fenras will be aware that you're not one of the nobles they recognize. But if I come into port with permissions and papers in order already, especially if we have a good cover story and a reason to be sailing upriver, then they won't look closely at us."

Setkin scratched his jaw. "Maybe she can be from one of the eccentric Island families who hold to themselves most of the time. Some of those people *rarely* leave their estates, much less the Islands, except for their ten-years."

Vered quirked her lips. "That sounds possible. Rekaré could pass as a scion from one of those families who needs to make a ten-years pilgrimage to Spring Festival. The timing is right. It would also explain her sun exposure and lack of knowledge of the customs. But. We'd still need Betsona's help with the paperwork." She turned her attention to Rekaré. "You'll have to learn the family rituals. That will also require Betsona's help."

"I'm willing to try." Anything to give her the opportunity to strike at Chatain. "So this will get me close to Chatain?"

"Closer than you'd like, perhaps."

Rekaré nodded, thinking. "I'll need a glamor or disguise. Chatain and I have seen each other through projections."

"Betsona should be able to help with that," Vered said.

"All right, then. I like this idea. Let's do it."

"There is another factor," Vered said. "What about the Larijian fleet?"

"I'm assuming we can't just drag them along upriver." Rekaré paused. "If I go to Adalane, we'll need to sail faster than the fleet can travel, especially if I need to stop and get papers from Betsona. One of you stay with the fleet, hold them off the shore until we know what is happening. Witmara and Toran may need that support in establishing herself as Empress, even if she succeeds in defeating Chatain."

"That makes sense," Setkin said.

"Are you willing to go upriver?" Rekaré asked Vered. "Setkin can't, as he said, and we're already on the *Star*."

"It has been a while since I sailed up the Fenras," Vered said thoughtfully. "It's not the size of the Chellana—more like the Saktrin River. But yes, I am willing, and the *Star* is comfortable traveling that river. We need to get paperwork from Betsona. Otherwise, it's not worth the risk."

"And you'd be willing to work with Chespir and the Larijian fleet?" Rekaré asked Setkin.

"Makes more sense for me to do so," Setkin said.

"He has more battle experience than I do," Vered agreed.

Rekaré took a deep breath.

"Well then. How long will it take us to reach Adalane?" she asked Vered.

"One day to Lanivar," Vered said. "Two more on a direct route to Fenras—not a problem for us once we get the paperwork. Three days upriver."

"So that's six days out of the ten left before the beginning of the Festival. Does that put us in Adalane too early?"

"It would if everything worked smoothly, with no interference from weather or bureaucrats. That's an ideal schedule," Vered cautioned. "We will spend time along the way teaching you not just the Festival rituals but making sure that you can pass as one of the Islanders. Once we get the papers and passes we need from Betsona, it might be wise to take a day or two of that extra time so that you also have the appropriate attire and manners."

"Manners," Rekaré sighed, remembering little quirks of Chiral's behaviors that had annoyed her. "Does that include simpering, whining, and fussiness about dirt?"

"Ritual and manners are important considerations for the Darani court," Detaluna said. "You can be a little bit rough as an Islander, but there are certain routines that—you need to learn. As well as how to move in the women's styles common in Daran."

"And you can teach me?"

Detaluna nodded. "I was a lady's maid before you bought my freedom and returned me to Varen," she said softly. "A minor noble, but still—enough of one that I learned court etiquette. *That* we can begin before we reach Lanivar."

"There is one problem." Rekaré tapped her fingers on the table again. "My hair." She pulled off her cap and cowl, running her hands over the brown stubble on her shaved head. "Unless this is a woman's fashion amongst the Islanders. I'll need a wig."

"That *is* a problem," Vered said, tapping her chin thoughtfully. "We'd have to have you appear as someone recovering from a severe illness."

Detaluna frowned. "But then it would be unlikely that she was traveling from the Islands."

"That's right," Vered sighed. "Sanctions for any ill person coming from the Islands. Plus that would also draw more attention to her. All the chronically ill from the Islands are on record. We'd have to explain why she wasn't."

"So that's not a possibility. What if I passed as a man without taking on a glamor, or a minor glamor? Doable? Not doable?" Rekaré studied the others. Setkin pursed his lips thoughtfully, scratching his chin. Vered squinted at her, and Detaluna frowned.

"I think it's doable. You'd have to bind your breasts, but you do that already," Sesenth said. "It would just need to be snugger. Wouldn't that also get her past attention for sun exposure?"

"It would," Vered said.

"I did it when spying for you in Daran," Detaluna said. "Just not as a noble."

"Again, though, records," Setkin said. "Even the most obscure male members of the Island families are recorded."

"Not to the same degree as the sick are," Detaluna said.

"She *could* pass as a younger Family member who has not been to Adalane before," Vered said.

"That might just work," Setkin said. He rose. "I think the faster you reach Lanivar and get this scheme started, the better. I'll tell Chespir what is happening, and send a message to Seijina advising her of your coming."

"We should be able to reach Lanivar in a day sailing at *Star's* fastest speed," Vered said.

Setkin nodded. "I will let Seijina know."

Vered left the cabin with Setkin. Rekaré took a deep breath, and studied Detaluna and Sesenth.

"So are you both with me? We'll need to create cover stories for you, especially if I'm traveling as a man from the Islands. And what do we do with the rest of the riders? Their cowls and hats?"

"I've disguised myself as a man before," Detaluna said. "I don't have any problems with that. The cap and cowl, especially red, will not draw particular attention. But Senth—her skin will draw attention. However, if she travels as your wife—there is a custom of veiling amongst the more isolated Islanders."

"I could do that," Sesenth said.

"Well. Then. I suppose it's to Lanivar and then Adalane," Rekaré said.

Just what she needed. More time on water. Still....

Not long, Chatain. Not long.

She fully intended to be there to help Witmara defeat Chatain.

FIVE DAYS NOW.

The quiet after Witmara's departure should have calmed things around Betsona's compound, especially since Seijina rounded up the staff from their various hiding places on the Big Island and put them back to work. But a continuing fretfulness plagued Betsona, roiling her gut and making her not want to eat, even though Mayte concocted her favorite tempting foods.

She glared at the half-full plate on the table next to her couch, along with a glass of her favorite sweetfruit drink and the carved wooden communicator link with Petronin. Seijina had coaxed her into one of the open-walled outside rooms with a sunset view and refreshing breeze off of the ocean, saying she needed more fresh air. The problem wasn't in the food. Nor the enclosure of the house, though Seijina liked to blame the stuffy inner rooms as causing Betsona's nervous stomach.

No. It was the lack of news. Petronin's communicator had gone silent after he confirmed their safe arrival on the mainland, though she still carried her link to it, just in case. Witmara had started gathering goodwood. Was carving one piece to be a staff. She could only assume that the silence meant that Witmara's work was interfering with the communicator—a known problem with goodwood. A good thing? A bad thing?

Whatever it is, I can't do anything about it now.

Seijina had gone down to the beach to receive a message from Setkin. He'd advised her a messenger bird was en route. Whatever he had to tell her was clearly something he didn't trust to their linked devices.

Betsona lay back on this room's couch, staring at the torches that outlined the porch below. If she wanted, she could walk out of the room, down a set of steps, and onto the porch. Right now, though, her throbbing gut made her tired and her joints ached. Even though her shields kept the bugs away from the house, she would have pulled the shutters closed to lock out the night if she had the strength and energy, not wanting to see the too-bright stars against the dark sky.

Her thoughts kept spinning.

Witmara was gathering goodwood. Had figured out that it possessed power. How had she discovered that? True, her having that knowledge would cause problems for Chatain—but *Gods*, hadn't anyone warned Witmara that at some point working with goodwood would attract his attention? If he found out too soon and focused his attention on her, could he track her down? That worried Betsona more than anything else. Confrontation at the Festival fit a predictable pattern and had rules that would aid Witmara. But if Chatain engaged her any place else….

The communicator twitched slightly, warning of an incoming projection. Betsona sat up as the twitching progressed to vibration, then smoke. This wasn't from Petronin. Not with that warning intensity. Did it mean that Chatain had captured Witmara and those with her—or had he decided it was time to let her know he could break the protocols that protected these communicators?

Betsona grabbed her canes and pushed herself to her feet, whispering a spell to bring the communicator along. No matter what this was about, she would *not* let Chatain see her in a position of weakness. Not now. She hobbled over the threshold and down the steps to stand on the patio. Air shimmered in front of her, shaping into a bright red whirlwind. The communicator exploded into burning pieces.

He's very angry, she thought at the sight of the whirlwind, and took a deep breath, calling upon her shields.

Ever since Witmara had left Lanivar Island, Betsona had taken the precaution of wearing the magic-laden blue topaz brooch known as the Star of Elithtra during the day. At night, it rested on her nightstand. It was a dying gift from their father Dunaran—and her greatest defense against her brother. She rested a hand on the brooch, calling up its power to give her strength and shielding.

Chatain's projection took shape in the whirlwind.

What have you done?

he roared.

How dare you?

"What have I done, *brother?*" She injected a touch of malice into the last word. "Nothing more than waste away here in Lanivar. What else is there to do here for one such as me? I'm certainly not going to drink myself to death like the Island Families do."

He pointed his right index finger at her.

You sheltered and aided that woman!

A purple-red flame lashed out at her. Betsona diverted it with a casual flick of her left hand.

Mechanical, not pulling from his magic. Conserving his strength. Anticipating an attack from Witmara? Most likely.

"I'm sorry, but I don't have any idea who you mean." This time she used her most sickeningly-sweet Court voice as she flicked a blue and silver ball seething with magical energies at him.

I warned you not to have anything to do with
that prisoner! I WARNED YOU!

Another small spurt of flame emitted from Chatain's index finger, puncturing the ball before spluttering out, testifying to its diminishing charge. Good. He'd either have to activate another device soon or draw on his own magic.

"Who says I have done anything to help—who was it?" She faked a bored yawn. "Mitmara? From Wedvara? No, that's not right. So many *aras*. It's *confusing.*" *Slip in just a tiny piece of expected petulance there to annoy him further.* "However am I supposed to keep your conquests straight? Isn't she the one you wanted to marry but ran away from you?"

She followed up with tossing another blue and silver ball at him. Those didn't cost her much energy and it would use up the last of the stored spells that powered that device, before they expired.

You know very well who I mean! The prisoner
Witmara from Medvara!

Chatain disposed of this ball, glowering as the flame spluttered out just before the ball exploded.

"Oh. *That* combination of aras. I was confused. Weren't you courting a Mitmara?"

She thought about flicking another ball at him, and decided against it. It would drain her strength. Besides, as long as he didn't try any more tricks this time, then perhaps he had learned his lesson and wouldn't try to flame her.

Witmara is the half-breed Varenese upstart from
that cursed House of Miteal who escaped
captivity!

"Oh. Well. I haven't seen her." She shrugged. "What does it matter? She's probably found a smuggler to take her back across the ocean by now. You surely don't imply that she's gone to the mainland instead, do you?"

He growled and clenched his fists.

Stop playing with my words and twisting them! You know what's going on! She seduced the land from me when she was still on the Islands —if I had evidence she did so on your land, I'd charge you with treason. And now I hear she's on the mainland! WHAT HAVE YOU DONE?

"Really, now, *brother*. You think I have that much influence on—what did you call her—'the half-breed Varenese upstart from that cursed House of Miteal?' *Really*. And as for seducing the land—" her voice sharpened here, "—perhaps if you paid more attention to caring for it and your people instead of conquest and plunder of other lands and their peoples, you might have more control over the land and its magic. Maybe you need to find a wife instead of buying more concubines."

You'd do the same thing if you were in my place!

"Are you certain?" She feigned another yawn. "*I* certainly wouldn't be buying concubines. Do you have a purpose beyond appearing here and yelling at me? If not, it *is* getting late and I'd like to go to bed soon."

Chatain bared her teeth at her, breathing hard, his image wavering in the projection. It steadied.

I order you to return to Adalane for trial before the Dedication. I don't have sufficient evidence to bring a charge of treason against you, but I do have enough to demand Examination. You will appear at the opening ceremonies with me, and at that time I will bestow upon you the justice you so greatly deserve. That you've been asking for over the last nine years.

She summoned a green and purple ball this time, concealing it in the palm of her right hand. "So are you naming me traitor now, *brother*? What's your evidence? How many brigades are you sending to drag your crippled sister from her quiet home in the Islands? Who do you expect to be the judges?"

He laughed.

> No brigades. No judges. I'm issuing you a formal Challenge and Examination, like I should have done when Father died. I was stupid and took pity on you because you were sick. That was a mistake. I demand that you appear and face the Challenge.

"And if I don't come?"

> Then you will be labeled as a traitor to Daran and your lands, your titles, and your slaves will be forfeit. I will call down Nitel's curses on you, to follow wherever you might choose to flee— even to Varen. I can cast that far, you know.

"So I have been told," Betsona said carefully. "But you expect the people will love you for attacking your crippled sister—the one whose injuries were caused by your arrogant mishandling of magic? Are you so strong now that you risk their love for me?"

He waved his hands dismissively.

> That doesn't matter. And besides, I add an additional provision that should appeal to the people. Should you decide to choose a Champion to battle in your place, I will not object. I can defeat the two of you. That should be sufficient for those who love you.

"Oh?" Betsona raised her brows.

He intends to lure out Witmara.

Yes. I expect you to be at the Festival nine days from now. That should give you time to round up some sort of Champion to aid you in the Examination and Challenge.

"Nine days? But the opening is in ten days."

You'll be at the banquet the night before so you can introduce your Champion to the Court. After all, even the condemned are entitled to a good meal.

With that, his projection disappeared. Betsona's lips tightened. She dismissed the green and purple ball. Much as she wanted to throw it at something, she needed to conserve her magic.

Instead, she threw one of her canes at the steps, hard enough that it cracked.

Betsona sighed. Before she could summon a spell to mend it, Seijina entered the patio.

"I did not expect to find you outside," she said. "I have news."

"So do I. But tell me yours first."

Seijina moved to Betsona's right side to help support her up the steps and back to her couch.

"The lady Rekaré arrives tomorrow evening. She seeks passes and letters of introduction to get her to Adalane."

"Really." Betsona collapsed on the bed, turning on her back to stare up at the open ceiling as Seijina clucked disapprovingly at her half-eaten plate. "Well, that is a fortunate coincidence. Chatain has ordered me to appear in Adalane to face Examination and Challenge."

"What? No! You wouldn't!" Seijina moved to her side. "Your power—it will exhaust you. We need to flee."

"He has given me the option of using a Champion," Betsona said. "And flight is not an option, as he will curse me as a traitor in Nitel's name if I do not appear. He claims the power to project as far as Varen in order to enforce his decree—and we know he can do that."

"Oh my lady." Seijina shook her head, sinking to her knees. "Are you going to be strong enough? And who will be your Champion? Witmara?"

"No. With this news, I think my Champion will be the lady Rekaré." Betsona waited as understanding sunk in. "Chatain knows that Witmara is on the mainland and has the land's favor. He will not expect the lady Rekaré instead. Nor that he will face *two* challengers."

Seijina's mouth half-opened. "But—but—Rekaré...we committed to Witmara...."

"I believe they now call her *Rekaré Kinslayer* in Varen," Betsona said slowly. "But that does not eliminate the fact that she is the daughter of Zauril en Ralsem and Alicira ea Miteal. Miteal and Ralsem both. Twice royal, you might say. *Also* descended from Elithtra the Fallen."

"And Witmara?"

Betsona shrugged. "We shall see what happens after the Challenge is completed, won't we? Will Rekaré Kinslayer hand over power to her cousin—or, after being maddened by the Challenge, will she see her as another foe? It will be an *interesting* opening for the Spring Festival, don't you think, my dear?"

"If Chatain is overthrown, and Witmara challenges Rekaré...." Seijina paused.

"Then that leaves one other direct descendant of Elithtra to step up to the throne. Unless we get more challengers from Daran."

She didn't think that would happen. Both Katerin and Linyet were bound to their lands. Which left—herself.

"Will you have the strength to carry it out?"

"As long as I have your support, dear one. And after me? Well, one thing I can do as Empress is to restore your family titles and honor."

As she expected, Seijina brightened at that prospect.

"And I can name you as my successor. You're close enough in descent to the Ralsems that you qualify."

That sealed the deal, as she knew it would.

If Rekaré overcame the madness of Challenge and yielded to Witmara? As long as someone defeated Chatain, she would be satisfied, Betsona decided.

Witmara will be grateful for my assistance. And having either one of them as Empress will still give me more power and control than I currently have.

But she would wager on the strength of the power-madness that would fuel the Challenge to fuel a battle between the two. And no matter how it turned out, the survivor would owe her favors. She would have not only more freedom than she did now, but more influence within Daran with either Witmara or Rekaré as Empress.

If neither survived?

Well, she could count on those who loved her in Adalane to call for her ascension to the throne once Chatain was gone.

And Chatain will finally get what he's deserved to have coming to him.

That was most important.

"Send messages to the staff in Adalane to prepare for our arrival," she said. "That should reassure my brother than I plan to obey his command. Be aware that he has most likely broken at least some of the codes for our secure communications."

"Shall I arrange transport for us as well?"

Betsona paused. If Rekaré was coming here to get documents to travel to Adalane, then surely she already had a mode of transport in mind?

"No," she said. "Let's wait to see what arrangements Rekaré Kinslayer may have already made. It will not be too much trouble to charter transport to Adalane if she does not have any or we dislike her choices."

"All right. I'll get things ready." Seijina rose.

"Oh. And Seijina? Let's prepare *better* for the Varenese intrusion this time, now that we have our staff back. Did Setkin say how many were coming?"

"Twenty-two riders besides Rekaré, the same number of daranvelii, and pack stock."

Betsona sighed. That much magic would require more shielding, now that Chatain would be paying attention. Then again, the magical horses *did* seem to have the ability to mask their strength if required.

But that many people arriving? That would be reported to Chatain by the spies that doubtless watched her.

Wait. There was another option, one which could provide a cover for Rekaré.

"Put the word out in the markets that not only am I going to Adalane as commanded by my brother, but that I will be traveling with an entourage from one of the Families. After all, it's probably time for *someone's* ten-year Progress. And it will provide the cover for Rekaré's documents, as well as those with her, as well as explain any delay in our arrangements."

"I'll tell Mayte. She'll be able to spread the word while shopping tomorrow morning."

"Good." She was tired already just thinking about what needed to be done. Betsona pushed herself back up, reaching for her surviving cane. Seijina handed her another one. "I'll be in the library. I need to find an appropriate Family to use as cover."

Gods, it was a good thing that she had endured what passed for literary and social life in this damnable place. She now knew enough about the Families that she could find several who would happily collaborate with her scheme. None of them were fond of Chatain. But that meant she needed to spend a lot of time in the library tonight preparing a cover story.

The goal is well worth the work.

And that included the loss of one night's sleep. There would be time to rest before Rekaré's arrival.

MARINSET

Witmara tensed as they rode through the main street of the small village after dusk, fingers closing tight on Daro's reins. He snorted and pulled a little against her hands, chomping the bit nervously, projecting worry.

> I know. Be alert. I feel it too.

He settled after her reassurance, but that still didn't stop the prickling sensation of uneasy magic on her arms. She and Toran followed Petronin, riders on all sides to put them in a protected space. That had been the routine while they rode after that first night, except for the narrowest trails. Witmara supposed it was something that would become even more common if she managed to become Empress.

Another difference from Varen.

A tall wooden barricade surrounded this village—Marinset, it was called. All the housing for humans and stock was inside the wall, with access controlled by a gate and guards.

Keeping danger out or people inside?

She had to wonder, given the aura rolling off of the place.

The shifty-eyed guards at the gate didn't wear Chatain's insignia or colors, just plain black. They glanced at the papers Petronin presented and given Daro an especially sharp look.

Part of her wanted to bypass Marinset and camp out again. But they needed to replenish their supplies, and she had to admit that sleeping in an actual bed sounded very good tonight after several days in a bedroll. Maybe a real bath instead of quick cold stream dips. Besides, if she was going to rule here, she needed to know those who would be her people—even the unsavory villages.

Behind walls. That felt so strange. Was the simple presence of walls around Marinset the cause of her worry?

No. *Something's not right.*

She allowed herself a brief contact with the land. It stirred anxiously, conflicted and unhappy with the flow of magic here. Whatever was wrong was a scar on the flow of magic. But the contact clarified what she felt. Sorrow clung close, an agony of parting and aloneness and fear.

Something bad happens here.

But Petronin and Betsona wouldn't view this place as safe if something they thought was wrong was happening in Marinset —would they? Or was it something they didn't quite see as wrong? That was a strong possibility, given what she had seen of Daran so far.

Perhaps this sensation is connected to slavery and smuggling.

"The land's uneasy," she said quietly to Toran. "Some sort of anguish. Sorrow. Pain."

He nodded and urged Gernar forward to talk to Petronin. She couldn't hear what they said, but Toran nodded again and eased Gernar back.

"Petronin says thank you for the warning. Marinset is a known smuggler's hideout, and he didn't know the guards—but that turning away would attract suspicion. He suggests we stay alert. Not an issue of Chatain, he thinks—but smugglers."

"Understood," she said softly.

Smugglers of what?

She could only think of one thing which would cause sorrow —slaves? She didn't think the land would care about jewels or drugs.

She rode silently, studying Marinset, such as it was. Most shops were closed, except for a tavern they passed without stopping. The main street seemed to go on forever, though, and she thought she spotted curtains being pulled back from second story residences above the shops to stare at their party. Witmara pulled the hood of her cloak further to cover her face. There were villages like this in Medvara, after all, places where she could still sense Zauril's influence. But none of them felt this bad.

Four days on the road. Petronin guided them to camps a distance off of the road when they stopped on previous nights. The other villages they had passed through were half the size of Marinset, mere handfuls of houses clustered around blacksmithies and taverns. Certainly no walled villages. Petronin hadn't stopped for the night in any of the hamlets they'd gone through so far.

This is one of the more dangerous parts of the trip, he had said just this morning. *Mostly smugglers through this part of the Empire. They won't tell on us—but they won't help if we have any problems, either. And they may see us as prey.*

At last, they stopped outside of an inn. *The Winking Owl,* she made out from the Darani characters. At least she *thought* that one word was *"Winking."* It matched the crude painting of an owl with one eye closed, so it was probably close if not quite precise. Petronin dismounted and came back to them.

"Everything should be all right," he said as he stood between Daro and Gernar, keeping his voice low. "But just in case, stay mounted. Mennit will follow me in, separately. If something goes wrong, he'll come back out to let you know. If you hear a commotion or we don't come out—"

"Understood," Witmara said. "The God go with you." Out of his sight, she signed Staul's horns.

Petronin nodded sharply, noticeably not asking *which* God she invoked. He patted Daro and Gernar, then headed for the doorway, his boots clumping on the boardwalk. He cleaned the road mud off his feet on the scraper before opening the door. Shortly after, Mennit dismounted and went inside as well.

Witmara strained to hear what, if anything, was going on inside. So far, what little sound drifted out was no different from what she would expect from any inn that served food and drink as well as provided rooms.

It is no rougher than the Nixyin waterfront.

And yet...perhaps it was only the difference between here and Varen, but something felt off. Sorrow. Fear. Aloneness.

Two men came out. They eyed the riders, then went on.

Mennit returned to Witmara and Toran. She tensed. He didn't seem worried or in a rush, but was that truly the case, or was he just appearing casual in case they were being observed?

"All is somewhat well," he said in a low voice. "We are not staying in this place. Smugglers are here. Petronin and a guide will take us to a safe place to stay." He glanced at Witmara. "Pull your hood up even more. These smugglers deal in slaves, and you're just the sort of woman they'd like to get their hands on."

"I'd like to see them try," Witmara growled, before Toran could speak. *That is what I feel. Slaves.* "So the inn is full of their slaves?"

Mennit shook his head. "No. The slaves occupy the barn, and are heavily guarded."

Witmara bit her lip. *Gods.* She glanced at Toran.

He shook his head. *Not here,* his lips formed. *See where they go tomorrow.* She nodded in agreement. That made more sense. Mennit frowned at them.

"You're not—"

"Let's talk about it later," Witmara said.

Petronin and another man came out of the inn. Mennit scurried to his horse. Petronin did not mount but led his horse as he walked alongside the man. They turned right on the next street. The shops petered out quickly. Modest cottages lined the streets. Unlike the houses in some of the hamlets, from what Witmara could see, these houses were kept up. Lights on some of the porches illuminated cultivated yards mulched with straw.

Probably a bit early in the season to plant here as well as in Varen.

This street appeared to head directly for the wall. Then she realized there was a barn built next to the wall, the darkness blending building and wall together. Petronin handed his reins to Mennit before he and the other man shoved the big doors open and gestured them inside.

"You'll want to leave a guard with your horses tonight," the other man said after they were all in and he and Petronin had closed the doors. "They're very fine, and with Klendaus in town, well, he's not above adding a few horses to his wares."

"Klendaus?" Witmara asked as she dismounted next to Petronin and this unknown man. She slipped Daro's bridle off, hanging it on the saddle horn. "Is he the slaver?"" Her voice sharpened as she turned to face him.

The unknown man raised his brows at her, a surprised expression crossing his face.

"Yes," he said, surveying Witmara from head to foot. "And you are?"

Witmara took a deep breath and flipped back her hood. Was this the time to reveal herself? She couldn't judge from Petronin's expression. But this was Betsona's contact in Marinset, and she had to start sometime.

"My name is Witmara ea Miteal," she said, studying his reaction. "And I am riding to Festival to meet Chatain en Ralsem in the Challenge."

The man startled. "Witmara ea Miteal? A Miteal lives? But how? Chatain has murdered all his relatives from that bloodline save Betsona...."

"I come from Varen. My mother Katerin is the daughter of Alame en Miteal, son of Alexran en Miteal."

"*Alexran's descendant,*" the man whispered. Shock, then hope crossed his face. "Oh Gods, I never thought I'd see the day that a Miteal of that lineage walked in Daran again. But lady—" he gestured at her. "Your skin—"

"I am also Varenese. My mother came from Waykemin and my father from the Two Nations." She eyed him. His skin was a shade lighter than hers. "Are you one of those fools in this land who cares about the color of one's skin?"

"Me?" He gulped. "No. But Lady Witmara, this will be—surprising for many."

"So I have seen," she said dryly. "Especially in this land where slavery is practiced. By Staul's blessing, if I do indeed become Empress, I will end that foul practice."

"Lady Witmara!" The man dropped to his knees, prostrating himself before her.

"That is not necessary." She reached down to raise him back up, but he protested, shaking his head.

"Oh Gods," he said. "My lady, if you can end the stranglehold that those such as Klendaus have on Marinset, I swear that we will follow you without question."

"Get up and tell me about it while I unsaddle my horse—where shall I put him—and what is your name?"

"Vinkel," the man said. "My name is Vinkel. Follow me."

Witmara gestured to Toran to follow as they walked down the alleyway to a spacious stall. Petronin moved amongst the riders, directing them to their stalls.

"Here is a stall worthy of your good beast," Vinkel said.

"Truly, my lady, if that is an example of the fine horses you have in Varen...."

"They are," she said, not wanting to focus further talk on the daranvelii. She led Daro inside and began to undo his saddlebags. "So tell me more about this Klendaus and the hold he has over Marinset."

"He comes through at least once a month with a minimum of five slaves to be sold in Adalane," Vinkel said. "If he comes up short, well...he is not above filling his quota here, or in the next village."

"Taking people from the villages?" She pulled the brushes she wanted out of the saddlebags and dropped them outside of the stall, noting there was a saddle stand nailed next to the door. She returned to undo Daro's cinches and pull his saddle off. He shook and snorted, then scratched his nose on his left foreleg.

Is this person speaking the truth?

she asked Daro.

Daro snorted, studying Vinkel.

All true,

came back to her. Not that it meant too much—just that Vinkel believed what he was saying. It did not mean his source was reliable.

"Yes. Young women and girls, mostly." Vinkel swallowed hard. "If we have warning, we hide them. We don't always have warning."

Toran stood in the doorway. "So what does Chatain do about this?" He took Daro's saddle and bridle from Witmara and hung it outside of the stall, then tossed a flake of hay into the stall. She began to brush Daro. He grabbed a bite of hay and nudged his head under the brush. She held it in place as he scratched his forehead while chewing on his hay. He stopped scratching to grab more hay, and she moved on to brush his neck.

"Nothing," Vinkel said bitterly. "In fact, he is one of the biggest buyers of young women every spring."

"He *what?*" Witmara stopped brushing Daro's neck and turned to face Vinkel.

"Chatain keeps a large stable of concubines," Vinkel said. "And while he claims to be seeking heirs and a spouse...to this date, none have born him a child. It is said that the same curse that injured the lady Betsona also rendered him unable to father a child."

"How many—no, no, the numbers don't matter. We have to do something about this." Daro raised his head, shifting his weight uneasily, looking for the source of Witmara's unease.

Not here, dear one,

she told him.

Just a wrongness that needs to be fixed.

"Witmara—" Toran began.

"No. It is not right. I feel their agony. Their fear. It is not right!" It brought back memories of being trapped in the ship's hold—*after all, wasn't that why he kidnapped me, to be his concubine? I know how they feel!*

"It's a distraction from your goal."

"Is it? Consider that Chatain tried to kidnap *me* for those purposes," she retorted.

Toran flinched. "I—Gods, Witmara. I'm trying *not* to consider that. Otherwise I want to strangle him."

"I can't just pass them by. Not when I can sense their emotions."

He sighed, and glanced at Vinkel, shaking his head. "Let's talk later."

Witmara turned to Daro again, brushing his back, wanting to bury her head in his neck in sheer frustration. Toran was being protective and while she understood the motivation—it wasn't useful.

"Vinkel. Do many of the people of Daran support this atrocity?"

"Primarily the nobles. The buyers. The rest of us? We do our best to avoid drawing their attention," Vinkel said bitterly. "It was not bad under Etikar and Dunaran. But since Chatain has become Emperor? The traffic in pretty young women has tripled, and they aren't all foreign."

She leaned on Daro's haunches, looking at Vinkel over them. "How much support would I gain from the people of Marinset, if we were to thwart Klendaus's schemes?"

"All but those who benefit from it," Vinkel said. "That would be five people who are part of Klendaus's organization—out of a thousand or so who live here."

"Then why do the people endure this treatment?"

Vinkel snorted. "Not many of us have magic. And Klendaus's thugs are endorsed by Chatain. To strike against them risks us being marked as traitors. We do not have a magician's protection."

"You do now," Witmara said. She held up her hand to stop Toran's objections. "Isn't this part of what we came here to do— stop Chatain's abuses? What better way to raise a following by showing that we won't tolerate it?"

"And if you fail?" Toran asked in a low voice. "If a thousand people don't dare rise against him, what chance do you have?"

"If I fear failure, I should have returned to Varen with Setkin, to prepare for Chatain's next invasion of Medvara instead of seeking to overthrow him. We have no good place to hide. He will pursue us. Toran, he would make me one of his concubines!"

"He would dare," Toran growled, and ran his fingers through his hair. "You're right. But is now the time to act?"

Witmara straightened up and set her chin firmly. "What better time than now to start? Dear one, if we pass this by, we'll just have to deal with it later. Why not start fixing Daran now?" She turned to Vinkel. "Let's talk."

He brightened, giving her a faint smile before bowing to her. "I would be honored, Lady Witmara. This is my own barn, and my house is safe."

"We'll need help," she said. "Are there others in Marinset who would be willing to ride with us?"

"Under your leadership? Yes. I will send word."

"Thank you."

Vinkel left the stall. Witmara turned back to Daro. He snorted, sending approving thoughts, and turned from his hay to nuzzle her, resting his forehead against her torso for a moment. She leaned into him, scratching his poll. He sent her images of stomping Chatain into the ground. She laughed.

"Thank you, Daro."

Toran raised his brows at her.

"He's being protective. He sent me images of him trampling Chatain."

Toran chuckled and scratched Daro's rump. "You and me, Daro, you and me both." His expression turned solemn. "I just worry about the timing. We should be discreet until we get to Adalane and you confront Chatain."

"And perhaps we should be bold instead," she said. "What will put the most fear in Chatain's heart? He must already know I am here. I can't imagine he thinks that I would just return to Varen. So should I slink along in secrecy? As I said, we'll have to fix this later. Stomping down someone like Klendaus now will earn us support from those like Vinkel."

He shook his head, smiling ruefully. "As long as I've known you, you've not been one for slinking in the shadows."

"No. And I would much rather ride into Adalane knowing that the people I want to lead are confident that I am on their side—because I have shown it to them."

He took her gloved hand and raised it to his lips. "I just hope that we survive to see it."

"We will." She forced confidence into her voice. "And if we do not—there are others who can step into my place. Rekaré. My mother. Linyet. Betsona. Even if we fall, we will be a beacon for those who oppose Chatain. And someday, someone will succeed."

Was it her imagination, or did she briefly see the shade of her father nodding approval?

"We will not fail," she continued. "The Gods will not allow it. Not from what I saw while being held prisoner."

Toran pulled her close and held her tight. "I fear for you, beloved."

"Trust me," she said. "After what I endured on the way here—just trust me. I must be bold. The Gods will it to be so."

Katerin. Katerin.

Rekaré's voice was low and crackling, rising and fading, almost a dream voice.

Katerin startled up from where she'd fallen asleep in front of the table in her suite in Kintarit's Leader's House, papers scattered around her, still fatigued from the drain on her magic after three days on water. One day hadn't been sufficient to rest —gods, she was aging. She could remember a time when one night's sleep would be enough to recover from this trip.

She rubbed her eyes, blinking hard. It must be the middle of the night—the oil lamp burned low, casting a flickering light, but had not yet consumed all its fuel.

Am I hearing things? Or has Rekaré found a way to send—but that didn't bode well, did it? Not with the strength such a sending would require.

Katerin,

Rekaré's whisper came again. Katerin blinked, looking around, until she finally spotted the glimmer of Rekaré's presence, hovering over the malachite stone given her by Medvara.

"Rekaré?" It *was* a sending from her.

Oh Gods, what has gone wrong? Is Witmara dead? Is this Rekaré's shade speaking to me? Gods, what's wrong?

Gods, you hear me at last!

Rekaré glanced around furtively.

I have made landfall in Lanivar, and am on my way to meet Betsona.

"Witmara and Toran?" she asked, fighting to keep her voice from trembling.

They are reunited and on the mainland. Witmara has a plan to challenge Chatain during a festival of some sort. I am here to get paperwork to sail upriver to Adalane so that I can support her. I can barely reach you now, and only because I am on land.

"Have you met Betsona? Is she trustworthy?"
Rekaré shrugged.

> Not yet. I feel Chatain's power strongly, even though he doesn't control the land. Witmara and Toran are implementing a plan. Daran has accepted her and she wields the land's magic.

She turned her head, and snapped something at someone Katerin couldn't see.

> I must go. Much more and we risk attracting Chatain's attention. But you needed to know Witmara is well. So far. Be safe.

"You too," Katerin said. The wisp faded out. She pushed herself up, now wide awake.

Witmara made it to Daran and is no longer a prisoner. Thank you, Goddess Dovré.

For a moment she fancied she smelled Metkyi's musky scent. Then it was gone. She paced the room, back and forth, not wanting to delve back into the papers, fretting about what Rekaré had said. What sort of time frame were they facing? How soon would their showdown with Chatain be?

A soft, distant bell sounded, tolling twelve times. Midnight. Gods, how long had she been asleep over the paperwork? Katerin sighed. Even though she was awake, her thoughts were fuzzy enough that she knew better than to go back to work, especially over approving provision details. Better to wait until morning, with a fresh mind, and not risk missing something important. She chewed her lip, looking into her sleeping area and contemplating a potion to help her sleep.

No.

Best not to do that at this time of night. She would just wake up fuzzy—she'd taken a draught after Kintarit's majordomo had shown her to her rooms last night. Natural sleep was probably the best thing she could do for herself right now. Perhaps she could find a snack in the kitchens. Investigating that possibility would certainly help her work off some energy.

Katerin checked the oil supply in the lamp, and picked it up. Keratil did not use as much magic as Medvara, and she was reluctant to start using her magic-powered glow lamps just yet. She wanted to hoard every little bit of sorcery she could for facing their foes. Ever since they had arrived in Nere yesterday, a vague foreboding had filled her, a malign pressure radiating from the East.

The Confederation waits. The Outcast God knows I am here.

Gods, she wished she could talk to Metkyi again! Perhaps it was worth a visit to Staul's shrine in Nere, to speak to her beloved's God, at least.

And the Goddess as well.

But not tonight. Not while she was still under waterstruck's influence.

I need a good night's sleep.

But she also felt the need to move after being on the ship for several days. Furthermore, the uneasiness kept building, now that she was awake again. Something wasn't right. But was it the presence she felt looming to the east, or something else?

Feeling silly, Katerin strapped her belt back on, checking the hilt of the sword that could transform to the Spear of War and Unmaking on command—or the Spear's whims. She was in a safe place. No reason to be armed…and yet something niggled at her. She checked the pouches on her belt. Glimmer dust in the right. Medicine bag on her left, with basic healing supplies. A mirthless smile tightened her lips. How many years had it been since she had learned her lesson about carrying a medicine bag on her belt at all times?

As she left her suite, it felt better to be carrying the Spear in its sword form and an adequate supply of glimmer dust. It wasn't her usual habit to walk around another Leader's house armed, and yet she felt that she needed it. Why?

Just as she reached the stairs she heard Doryits's voice echoing up from below. Katerin couldn't make out what he was saying, but his tone was clearly angry. She paused at the top of the stairs. Should she go down, or not? She didn't want to interrupt anything, and if this were a private meeting….

A woman's sibilant voice sent shudders through Katerin. The pitch was wrong for a human voice, higher and sharper than it should be, like….

Shalkendar!

The fully-consumed empty ones from Waykemin rarely spoke, but when they did, they sounded like this voice.

Shalkendar here—no—Doryits said he wasn't safe—Sariost!

She scurried down the stairs.

"Doryits!" she bellowed. "Hold firm! I'm coming!"

No response. The *shalkendar* voice had shifted to a hypnotic drone, trying to mesmerize its victim. Katerin whipped around at the foot of the stairs, trying to figure out where the sound was coming from—ah. There. A parlor off of the main hall, sliding door half-open. She ran for the door and shoved it wide, dreading what she would find, fumbling in the pouch on her right side for a pinch of glimmer dust.

Doryits was backed into a corner while a green-shaded figure swirled in front of him, mostly skeletal with an elongated bare skull. It bared long sharp teeth at him, ichor dripping from its jaws as it tried to seize him with claw-like fingernails. The faint pale shimmer of a protective shield was all that kept it off of him.

"Begone!" Katerin bellowed.

The figure turned from Doryits.

And who are you to challenge my rights to this meat?

"I am Katerin Leader of Medvara, Katerin the Banisher of Shadows!" She hurled a pinch of glimmer dust at the figure—a projection, she realized. Not the real thing, thank the Gods, but strong enough that if she had not been restless it could have harmed Doryits—

The projection's shape faded, but still loomed between her and Doryits, green and silver threads swirling around each other as it tried to reform.

Not enough to banish, needs a further spell.

The sword transformed into the Spear as Katerin drew it. Without hesitating she plunged the Spear into the projection. It disappeared, leaving a puddle of ichor in front of Doryits and on the head of the Spear. Katerin shuddered. She scattered a pinch of glimmer dust over the ichor on the floor and on the Spear.

"Goddess Dovré, I call your cool flame down to banish these remnants," she said. A blue light spread over the ichor, puffed into a brief flame, and then the goo was gone, thankfully not leaving any ash for her to clean up.

Spear transformed back into sword. Katerin checked the blade to ensure all the ichor was gone before sheathing it, then turned to Doryits. He sat in one of the comfortable-looking chairs, burying his head in his hands.

"Are you all right?" She unlaced her medicine bag. It was a good thing that she had made up a strong mixture of *protection-against-possession* before leaving Medvare-the-city. She was going to dose him after this exposure—and herself.

He raised his head. "That was Sariost—or rather, one of her manifestations," he whispered, his voice shaking. "She is strong. Very strong, more than I thought she was. I think I am all right—but I cannot guarantee that I am safe. Thank you. Thank you for—Gods, I don't know what she would have done."

Katerin set a dosing spoon on the table in front of him. "I have something which will help." She uncorked the bottle of *protection-against-possession* and poured it into the dosing spoon, thrusting it nearly in his face. "Take this."

He took the spoon, eying the dark purple liquid. "What is this?"

"*Protection-against-possession*. We used to use it against Shadowwalker attack, as well as for those attacked by Karnoi and Cirdel's Hunt."

"You've known the Hunt?" Haunted eyes met hers.

She wondered if those cursed Gods were on the side of the Outcast God. They had been allied with Nitel in the past.

"Far too well," she said grimly, gesturing at the spoon. "Take it. I need a dose as soon as you are done."

He nodded, and drank it down. She poured herself a measure and took it quickly, watching Doryits. If he had been possessed—the last thing she wanted to do was to chase down a curse within an untrained person tonight. But she would do it if necessary. At least Metkyi had been a priest of Staul, and had known how to work with her. If Sariost had left a piece of herself in Doryits…no, no, the parallels would be too close.

He shuddered again, beads of sweat breaking out on his forehead. Then, to her relief, the tight lines on his face eased.

No chasing down possession tonight. Good.

"I feel—better," he said. "That was close. Too close for my liking."

"We need to place protective charms on you," she said. "That was Sariost?"

"Not Sariost herself. But one of the entities that she can summon. Bad enough." He shook his head. "This is the first time she's been able to affect me this far away from the border."

"Kintarit needs to have priests of Staul and speakers of Dovré exorcise this place if Sariost can reach this far," Katerin said grimly. "I know what to do. As does the Hidden One."

And who better to speak for Staul and Dovré than herself and the Hidden One?

More things to do tomorrow. She sighed.

Doryits rubbed his face. "Katerin, what will it take to keep me safe? I don't know that I can be trusted to do what we planned on the border."

"I have ways to protect us, starting with *protection-against-possession*." She eyed him. "But it does mean you'll need to be close to me. I dare not expend that much magic to guard you at a distance."

He grimaced. "So what does that require of me?"

"We need to be in the same room at all times, and ride together. Regular doses of *protection-against-protection*." The Hidden One could also keep him safe, but for some reason she didn't want to tell Doryits that just yet. She stretched and reached out a hand to help him up. "I was going to the kitchens for a snack. Come with me, then we'll go back to my rooms."

"You're not worried about rumors about us?"

He pulled himself up, releasing her hand once he was on his feet. The feel of his calloused hand on hers lingered and she almost wished he hadn't been so quick to release it.

"Should I be?"

She raised her brows at him. He didn't strike her as a womanizer. That didn't fit the profile someone who still mourned the loss of his family five years later—well, some men would react like that. Doryits didn't seem like one of those.

He sighed. "No." He gestured at her sword hilt. "What weapon is that? No need to show me—just tell me. It transforms, so I know it's magical—but which one is it?"

She smiled grimly at him. "The tool of the Banisher of Shadows. The Spear of War and Unmaking."

His eyes widened. "I did not know you wielded *that* weapon. Gods, that can help us...."

"Yes. It can." She pulled at his hand. "Come on. Snack. You need it after that encounter. And then tomorrow morning we need to do an exorcism, on top of everything else."

"An exorcism?"

"Raising protective wards. Consider it an attempt to keep our base free from contamination."

He nodded. "I understand."

She started toward the kitchens. Doryits hung back.

She stopped. "Is there a problem?"

"You're sure that I need to stay close?"

"Not in my bed, if that worries you. There's plenty of space in my suite for you to bed down," she said. "Couches. Bedroll. Floor. Or I can have bedding brought in. Right now I want to nibble on something, and Cantiste sent along a hunk of my favorite sheep cheese from Keldara. Tonight of all nights you dare not be alone."

"All right." Reluctance in his tone.

"And besides, I'm hardly a young thing whose reputation might be at risk. I'm a widow and a Leader. My daughter is an adult."

He shuddered, then smiled weakly. "Just being silly. And tired."

She took his hand and pulled him along. "And waterstruck. You've just enough magic to feel the sickness's aftereffects, and you're physically close to a malevolent entity that sees you as a target—yes, between the two you need to be near someone who can protect you. We'll take further measures tomorrow. Besides. This sheep cheese is marvelous."

And it's another product from the Keldaran Stardance lines.

Not enough magic in the milk to do more than give a magician a little bit of a glow, not seething with magic like the Stardance fleeces were—but it would give both of them a boost, make them feel better after tonight's encounter.

She'd take any small measure to bolster her magic right now.

TWO POWERFUL WOMEN

THE LAND ROILED UNDER BETSONA FOR A MOMENT, THEN settled. She startled up from lounging on the couch where she waited for Rekaré. Seijina had gone to meet this latest batch of Varenese arrivals, with instructions to bring Rekaré alone to her formal parlor.

What was that?

The timing would be right for Rekaré to have stepped off of the ship. Was she that much of a power that the land stirred at her touch, more so than it had for Witmara?

Maybe I've backed the wrong horse in this fight.

Though the land had been clamoring for Witmara, had been uneasy and upset until she gained control of it. Witmara was the leader it craved. So if this was the effect that Rekaré had on the land—did this foreshadow a struggle for power between those two?

Betsona made herself draw smooth, even, deep breaths until calm descended upon her. She could afford to be less guarded with young Witmara, still inexperienced. Besides, they had gotten to know each other through their correspondence.

But Rekaré Kinslayer had not been privy to their letters. She had killed. Had ruled Medvara as Leader for eleven years. She was unlikely to be easily influenced, might need to be persuaded to follow along with Betsona's plans. At the least she was no untried youth.

Rekaré has claimed she has no interest in ruling Daran.

That—would have to be seen to be believed. Betsona had yet to encounter anyone who could walk away from the temptation of ruling. Though Rekaré had done so in Medvara, to all reports. But was that a true abdication, or did she control Medvara through Katerin? Witmara hadn't born the marks of any such meddling. That didn't mean it didn't exist.

Betsona rested her fingertips on the Star of Elithtra. Warmth seeped into her fingers from the stone, its magic rousing and fully awake. She traced the faint glyph of a protective spell in the air, drawing upon that brief *feel* of roiling magic to create the ward. It fell into place around her, shifting slightly from the enchantments she'd used to protect herself from Chatain.

Interesting, she thought, as her sense of this new magic grew. While Witmara hummed with potential that still needed to be honed, especially against a skilled sorcerer such as Chatain, this small feel of Rekaré's power was not only mature, but suggested a possible greater strength than his. But it was cloaked, carefully hidden under wards that she couldn't investigate further.

Real strength or a glamor? That magic was familiar. She had used a glamor in the past to make herself appear stronger to Chatain than she was. No reason to assume that it would be different for Rekaré.

Betsona settled in to wait, meditating, opening herself to what sensations the land deigned to pass on to her. She felt the brief stir of the alien daranval magic before it wrapped itself smoothly into a guise—a practiced hiding of magical skill that hadn't manifested from the daranvelii with Toran. She couldn't gain a clear picture of how many riders there were with Rekaré. More alien magic there, something she couldn't define yet lurked as a potential threat. Then it cloaked itself, as if it were aware of her observations.

Very, *very* different from the last group of Varenese. This group appeared to be an experienced fighting unit, not the guards for a pair of young royals who had barely come into their full power.

Well, that would match what she knew of Rekaré and her choice to lead a band of negotiators and fighters to bring the nations of Varen together.

But not as an Empire—that was curious. A union of equal nations, each keeping their own rule. That notion had drawn her attention to Medvara in the first place. Amusement at Chatain's discomfort with first Rekaré's then Katerin's rule and how it played out in the colonies.

Former colonies. The Varenese did not strike her as people who would appreciate the reminder that Etikar had tried to conquer them—until Alexran's rebellion.

It wasn't a governing process she understood. Perhaps she'd have time to learn more about it from Rekaré—that is, if Rekaré agreed to travel together to Adalane. She might not. But she was certain that Rekaré would want to go to Adalane, once she knew that both Chatain and Witmara would be there.

The faint sounds of horses and riders drifted in from outside. Betsona opened herself even further to gather what information she could. A wary response as someone detected her magical presence, and then nothing.

Powerful shielding.

Was that only Rekaré, though? Or was it that the alien, non-daranval, magic?

Betsona waited, anticipation rising, fueled by curiosity as much as worry.

Something new. Something different. Gods, I have to get off these damned islands!

Until now she hadn't realized just how *boring* Lanivar could be.

"My lady Betsona is in here," Seijina said to someone behind her, opening the door. "My lady, Rekaré ea Miteal and her staff, Sesenth and Detaluna."

Minor annoyance at the presence of the others faded away as Rekaré strode into the room, her staff following. All three wore red cowls.

"*Rekaré Kinslayer,*" she corrected Seijina, irritation in her tone. "And these are my Seconds and Captains, Sesenth and Detaluna." Rekaré marched up to the dais and met Betsona's eyes steadily. "I am not Rekaré ea Miteal. That person no longer exists."

Unlike Witmara, Rekaré's common Darani was smooth and fluent. She'd learned it somewhere and been able to practice it.

Betsona inclined her head respectfully. No, the hidden strength she sensed was not a glamor. Power hummed under Rekaré's shields, flaring every time she said *Rekaré Kinslayer.* Real force lurked leashed under her command, greater than that of any magician Betsona had ever encountered, and somehow shared with those others, especially the one....

"And I am Betsona ea Ralsem, ni Vespla, Rekaré Kinslayer." She kept her voice steady and quiet. No need to provoke that flame lurking within Rekaré.

"Betsona ea Ralsem, ni Vespla," Rekaré repeated. "Ni Vespla? I am not familiar with that usage."

"I carry that addition under my brother's order, to indicate that my mother was but *one* of our father's concubines," Betsona said dryly, biting back the anger that statement provoked.

"There's supposed to be a difference?" Rekaré quirked a brow. "Oh. I forget. Daran concerns itself with such trivial matters as marital status. You don't need to add it around me."

She *liked* this woman. "I thank you."

Betsona studied Rekaré under lowered lashes. Unlike

Witmara, Rekaré's skin was pale under a tan, but unquestionably a base of pinkish-white, unlike Chatain's fish-belly white. The red cap and cowl hid her hair. Tall and lanky, flat-chested enough to pass as a man in her tunic and trousers. Command sat lightly on this woman, a self-confidence that would annoy Chatain in its lack of submission to male authority. Power roiled around Rekaré as Betsona raised her head. Her gray eyes met Betsona's, unflinching.

Gods, she would make a powerful Empress.

And yet that power didn't seem to be a match for Empire. Chatain's sorcery didn't feel this way, neither had their father's magic nor what little she could remember of their grandfather Etikar.

The women flanking Rekaré also projected that ease with power, a calm acceptance so unlike Chatain's angry floundering. One—the darker-skinned one—looked faintly familiar. The other—Betsona frowned as she realized that gray-scaled ridges lined her cheek and jaw, fading into a gray-brown.

What is this?

No, Rekaré was not at all what she had expected after seeing Witmara. On the other hand, that *potential* she had sensed in Witmara had clearly reached its fulfillment in Rekaré.

"Sit." Betsona gestured toward the single seat facing her couch. "Seijina, would you bring in more chairs?"

"I will."

Rekaré stood silently until the chairs were provided. She waited as Betsona used her crutches to hobble down from the dais, and settle herself in the most padded seat. The three sat down simultaneously after Seijina brought in the last chair, Rekaré choosing the middle seat, directly across from Betsona.

"So we meet at last." Betsona finally broke the silence.

"This is not what I expected from Daran," Rekaré said. "Nor are you what I expected." She gestured to the crutches.

"An injury from long ago." Did she really have to explain

herself to this woman? *Yes. If I want her assistance—yes.* "My brother—that is, Chatain—and I were working on a magitech experiment under the supervision of a tutor. It blew up. My father executed the tutor for treason."

She watched Rekaré closely to see what reaction that might bring.

"So I have been told," Rekaré said, no change in her expression. The one with the scales on her face did not react, but the other one winced slightly. "It is one thing to be told about someone's physical weakness, and another to actually see it. It is reflected in your magic."

Was her vulnerability really this obvious? Betsona bit back uneasiness. "Not everyone is capable of seeing how my disability impairs my magic."

"Rekaré is *benghaalph* as well as Kinslayer," the captain with scaly skin said—Sesenth, was it? Her Darani was halting and careful. "That allows her to see things others do not."

Rekaré's lips tightened. "Senth, you don't need to explain me!"

Ah. She was close enough to this person to use a diminutive in company—and sufficiently comfortable with it.

"I do appreciate knowing this," Betsona said placatingly. "If I may indulge a further explanation—I do not know what *ben—ghaal-ph* is." She stumbled over the unfamiliar word's harsh gutturals.

"Prophet to the Shadowwalkers of Saubral," Rekaré said sharply. "The One Spoken Of. *Benghaalph* comes over me unpredictably, sometimes only as a whisper of revelation, other times of complete vision. Sesenth—" she gestured toward the scale-skinned one, "—is becoming Shadowwalker. Even though I am not a Shadowwalker, *benghaalph* makes me capable of guiding a developing Shadowwalker. We are *quixnahi* and *quixnafal*." They exchanged a quick glance before Rekaré returned her attention to Betsona.

I'll wager you two are more than that to each other, given that look.

Betsona studied Sesenth carefully. *This* was the non-daranval alien power she had sensed earlier—at least part of it. She shivered as she realized what God's power this woman carried. *Staul.* But it was Staul of the Balance, not the Destroyer —though both Rekaré and Sesenth projected more than a little bit of the Destroyer about them. Betsona shivered.

Staul.

Witmara was also dedicated to Staul. These were the first of his devotees that she had met.

"Shadowwalkers are dedicated to Staul, then? But how can you…?" Betsona's voice trailed away. "At least it's not Nitel. Chatain and his lackeys fawn over her."

"I *have* carried Nitel in the past." Rekaré's voice was hard. "I've also banished her from Medvara, and seen her driven from the Two Nations. She, Karnoi, and Cirdel are no longer welcome in Medvara."

"Karnoi and Cirdel have never walked here. Until now, neither has Staul."

"That you know of."

Gods, Rekaré was prickly! On the other hand, what could she expect from a battle-hardened sorcerer?

Chatain is going to be so intimidated by this woman.

Betsona pressed her lips tightly together to stifle her amusement at that thought. How many times had she heard her brother proclaim that female magicians were weak and that no women were cut out to be warriors? Witmara was a younger, softer version of this woman. But still….

Betsona took a deep breath.

I must defuse this situation. This woman needs to be favorable to me.

"I'm sorry," she said. "I suppose you're seeking information about Witmara."

"That would be helpful. We have heard she is traveling a roundabout way to reach the city of Adalane, so that she and Toran can challenge Chatain during a festival. I intend to help her. Chatain owes me many deaths—and I want to collect."

Betsona nodded. "Because she is dark-skinned and Chatain knows she is here, it's safer for her to travel by land. I sent her with my master of spies, so that she can make contact with his networks and raise support amongst the common people. The nobles will eventually follow her—except for the rabble who drool after Chatain."

A faint smile twisted Rekaré's lips at that one. "The nobility is not favorable to your brother?"

"The older families have retreated to their holdings rather than dance attendance upon him in Daraelen," Betsona said. "I was supposed to keep them persuaded that he was worthy of their support. Alas, I failed in that endeavor."

"And that failure would coincide with your exile here?"

Betsona let a matching smile twitch her lips. "Exactly."

"I'm surprised you're still alive. How far along are you in trying to seize power for yourself?" Rekaré's eyes drilled hard into Betsona's.

She sees much.

"My support is aging but real. Chatain's managed to eliminate any other potential heir to the throne, so until now, I've been the safest successor to keep around because of my health. As for my ambitions—you see what I am. I lack the strength to rule a nation as challenging as Daran. That doesn't mean I don't want to see a change in leadership. Chatain's rule has been a disaster for Daran."

"I see. No heirs of his body?"

Betsona shook her head. "Several conceptions, all miscarriages or stillbirths. If he has a heir of his body, I don't know about it—and since my mother is remembered well in the royal quarters, I have friends there who keep me informed of such matters."

Rekaré exhaled, relaxing slightly. Sesenth and Detaluna remained alert and wary. "That is one possible effect on rulers who devote themselves to Nitel."

"I did not know that."

"I learned that while reading through my father's journals," Rekaré said bitterly. "There are—reasons for rulers under Nitel's thumb to behave in certain ways."

"Our father was dedicated to Artel, so I would not know. It explains a lot." Betsona paused. "I hope I've explained myself to your satisfaction. I want to see Chatain gone, but I lack the strength to step into his place myself to do what is needed. Either you or Witmara are qualified—you perhaps more due to your experience."

"Not me. Never me. I renounced all thoughts of becoming Empress years ago."

"Then what can I do to help you assist Witmara?" A twinge of disappointment pulsed through Betsona. And yet—she had no doubt this woman could kill Chatain.

"I need paperwork and a false identity to travel upriver without challenge to attend this—festival, is it?—where Witmara intends to challenge Chatain. I am told you can provide me with what I need."

"Yes to both. Papers are almost ready, and I have a suggestion for a cover story. Chatain has ordered me to appear at the Festival to face Challenge. There is a requirement of the Families of the Ourigny Islands for each significant member to make a pilgrimage to Spring Festival every ten years." She studied Rekaré. "I had planned for you to travel as the Lady Finkarna. Alas, you're less of a match for Finkarna than I had realized. While she hasn't been at Court, she's smaller than you."

"I had plans to travel as a man," Rekaré said. She pulled off her red cap and cowl to reveal a brown-stubbled head. "I shave my head as part of my role as Kinslayer. Easier for me to pass as male than as a woman."

Especially here hung between them.

"I agree." Relief washed over Betsona. Finkarna was the only unattached woman who was remotely eligible to travel to Adalane this year from the Islands. Witmara would have been a better match for Finkarna than Rekaré—but on the other hand, she knew of several men who would be delighted to not have to swear allegiance to Chatain this year. "And setting that up will actually be easier, as Finkarna was the only unmarried woman going to Adalane from the Islands, besides myself." She tapped her fingertips on her chin. "But your captains—Detaluna will pass, but Sesenth, with those scales?"

"Vered and Setkin both say that she can travel veiled, as a wife," Rekaré said.

Oh, that was even better, that Rekaré came provided with a companion close enough to pose as a wife. "Giolanth of the Stanils would love to have an excuse not to go to Adalane this year, as would his lady wife. She has recently miscarried and neither were particularly happy at the thought of traveling."

And Giolanth would owe her even more favors if she made it possible for them to avoid Chatain and celebrate Festival at home.

"That sounds like a possibility, then."

"And it's easily arranged. I can advise you on expected behavior as we travel to Fenras, and then upriver."

Rekaré squinted at her. "Did I hear you say that Chatain has demanded your presence at this festival? I thought he didn't want you there at all."

"Chatain sensed Witmara's grasp of the land's power. He cannot prove that I am connected to it. But he knows that it happened on Lanivar Island and rightly suspects that I gave her shelter. I have been called to face Challenge and Examination. None of our siblings have survived that call."

"I see," Rekaré said slowly. "Why now? Chatain's been in power for nine years. You said no heir of his body has survived —has that changed?"

"Either that or he thinks he's found immortality."

Rekaré snorted. "Good luck with that. So Nitel's delusions are strong within him. That's good to know."

"How?"

"It's a weakness. I've seen it elsewhere. But still. Why challenge you now?"

"Rage over losing Witmara. I think—I do not know for certain, but from what Seijina says, he intended to force her into concubinage in hopes of creating a stronger sorcerer. Still hopes to do that."

"Like my father did with my mother," Rekaré growled. "And Seijina's information is reliable?"

"She helped Witmara escape. While there, she overheard much."

"I see."

"Until Witmara fell into my lap, I've tried not to give him a reason to pay attention to me as a potential threat. Oh, I have power. But thanks to what happened at his hands years ago, it's not consistent. As long as I remain quiet, I have protection. The older families would not look well on him if he harmed his crippled sister without reason. I just had to ensure that I didn't give him evidence to provide that justification."

"What changed?"

"Besides Witmara's arrival? My support is aging, and he's elevated a score of new wealthy families who follow him to replace the old families. His grasp on power has not always been pretty, and he's actively purging magicians. Additionally, he's become much more reckless about alienating the people and the land than in previous years."

Rekaré nodded. "And harming you would not sit well with

the land. If the land was solidly with him, Witmara would not have been able to harness its power."

"Exactly." At least she didn't have to explain *that*.

"I understand the feeling when the land withdraws from you," Rekaré added.

Betsona drew a deep breath. "Yes. And that is why he has issued the demand that I now face Examination and Challenge. Due to my injuries and the inconsistent nature of my magic, I can recruit a champion's assistance."

Rekaré's brows raised and she tightened her lips. "So who is to be your champion?"

"Why, Giolanth of the Stanils. Why else would I ask him and Estarel to travel with me? He is respectable, with a small amount of sorcery, so that I could legitimately give him magical strength without doubling our combined power. Even more importantly, he has not yet left the Islands for Adalane."

"So you would have me serve as your champion?" A slow, predatory grin that didn't touch her eyes spread across Rekaré's face.

"Chatain expects that I would use Witmara. But he would know by now that she is on the mainland and not here. Giolanth will surprise him."

"Especially if I'm Giolanth. I like this idea." Rekaré leaned back in her chair. "Chatain owes me for several deaths. I look forward to the opportunity to obtain my vengeance on him." Her face twisted. "My mother. My daughter. My husband. My lawmother. Those are just the primary deaths he owes me." A pitiless chill crossed her face. "And what do you get out of this besides your brother deposed and my cousin Witmara on the throne?"

"You do not wish it for yourself?"

Rekaré flicked her right hand dismissively. "I have been a Leader. Empire does not fit me. Vengeance does. Witmara is the future, and I am but the tool to bring her to power." Her face hardened. "What do you expect to gain from us deposing Chatain?"

"Freedom," Betsona said, and meant it. She could say nothing less to this hard-eyed woman. "Freedom, and the chance to be my own woman, like I was under my father."

No need to mention that she would gain influence at a court ruled by Witmara.

❦

"IF ONLY THE HIDDEN ONE COULD SEE ME NOW!" SESENTH chuckled as she examined her veiled and cloaked self in the mirror the evening after their arrival on Lanivar. "By Staul, I think she'd decide I need to apprentice to her instead of you."

That day had been a bustle of fittings and meetings, as the actual Giolanth and Estarel had arrived early in the morning. Rekaré had closeted herself with Giolanth to learn what she could of Stanil business and Giolanth's concerns in order to present herself properly as him, while Sesenth and Estarel spoke. Estarel's veils did resemble those the Hidden One wore.

Rekaré studied Sesenth. "It is a good look on you, dear heart."

Sesenth snorted and pulled the veil off. "We can all dream. The Hidden One most of all. I'm not about to give up the Mer Galad to take over her role."

"Even if I fall here?"

"If you fall, I fall," Sesenth said. "You know that."

"I know. But if—no, *when*—something happens to me, do not turn your back on other options, dear one."

"We shall see if that time ever comes." Sesenth pulled off the veil. "So confining, especially in this climate. And how were your meetings with Giolanth?"

"Nothing unexpected. And it's a good thing I knew some dandies while Leader. Giolanth claims to be one of moderate taste, but ay. The details! I can just imagine how complex the female aspect of being at Court must be."

Sesenth nodded. "Estarel has a habit of being quiet and retiring. She told me that she finds the dress details of Court abhorrent, which is one reason she veils once she leaves the Islands. Convenient for us because that practice makes it easier for me."

Rekaré groaned and rubbed her head. "No such luck for me. Giolanth tries to be stylish. I will have to let my hair grow out a little more and make a big deal of how I shave my head regularly after it reaches a certain length. Giolanth says that I can explain my practice as the desire to establish a new style, something he has a reputation for." She rolled her eyes. "And I'm thankful that Orlanden taught me how to tie a stylish cravat when I was young. This won't be the first time I've passed myself off as a man."

Sesenth grinned. "I love it when you tell me stories. I've not heard this one."

"From my years running from my father. Later." Rekaré tapped her fingertips on the arm of her chair, delicately tracing a spell on the wood that distorted their voices. A mild one, not anything that would attract Betsona's attention. "What do you think about our hostess's protestations that she has no interest in the throne?"

"You'd believe her?" Sesenth hung the veil and dress in the wardrobe, slipping her tunic back on.

"No. Oh, the issue of her strength is a true one. She lacks consistent magic. Her body is weak. But if those were not a concern, then oh yes, she'd be a contender. She will be a worry to anyone sitting on Daran's throne, because she *is* well-liked, and is opinionated enough that if she takes a dislike to any policy...well, any opposition to the Empire's ruler will be in her circle. I listened to Giolanth raving about how wonderful Betsona is, how generous to those in need here on the Island. He'd put her on the throne in a heartbeat."

"Estarel was the same. Betsona possesses a hidden power."

"It's a good thing that Witmara raised the land's magic," Rekaré said thoughtfully. "It leaves no question about Chatain's potential successor—as long as she survives."

"And that is the question, isn't it?"

"I will do everything to ensure Witmara's survival. Otherwise…." Rekaré's voice trailed off.

She didn't have to say more. The only way she would assume the title of Empress would be if Witmara couldn't.

And I will do whatever it takes to ensure that doesn't happen.

KLENDAUS

I HOPE WE CAN TRUST VINKEL.

Witmara's hand tightened on the grip of her bow, arrow nocked and ready to be drawn. Daylight brightened the road she watched from behind a jumble of tall boulders. Vinkel and the leaders of Marinset had vowed allegiance to her in secret visits throughout the night, so as not to warn Klendaus that Marinset was no longer loyal to Chatain.

She should be able to trust him. She hoped.

Daro had witnessed each vowing. But did people here in Daran honor vows made to daranvelii like they did in Varen? She wouldn't know for certain until after this battle.

Witmara had dipped all of her points in glimmer dust and whispered a disabling spell on them so that even a minor wound would bring down a rider. Her half-carved staff hung from a scabbard fastened to Daro's saddle, within easy grasp. She wasn't going to use it as a primary weapon. Not until it was time to work magic. Right now it was time for bows and swords.

Next to her, Toran held his unsheathed sword low, by his side. Their riders, along with Vinkel and a carefully recruited band of fighters from Marinset's leading families, hid in scattered spots along the narrow road through the canyon. The plan was to allow Klendaus and his men to enter the canyon unchallenged. Petronin and the others would fall in behind them, until they reached Witmara and Toran in the middle. Toran had tossed a scattering of wards at the last bridge before this canyon. Just before they took their places, the wards signaled the passing of riders and several people on foot. It wouldn't be long before they entered this narrow, rocky canyon.

Faint scuffle of hooves on rock near the entrance. Witmara and Toran glanced at each other. She nodded at him. They eased Daro and Gernar into the middle of the road.

Clip-clop. Clip-clop.

More hooves.

Please let Vinkel be true.

The faint buzz of daranval-to-daranval communication pressed on her forehead. Then it faded, and Daro sent her an image of

riders entering the canyon

from the vantage of another daranval. Twenty riders, headed by several burly men. Eight young women bound by chains on wrists and ankles and tied together by ropes staggered behind the lead riders. One of the binding ropes was tied to the saddle horn of the shortest of the burly lead riders.

Then the image flickered out. Witmara's fingers tightened on her bow grip.

Clip-clop. Clip-clop. Almost there.

Witmara raised her bow, drawing.

"Halt!" she bellowed as the first riders appeared.

"No wisp of a girl's gonna stop me!" the lead rider snarled, and urged his horse forward.

Witmara let fly, falling into trained reflexes as his eyes

widened and he grabbed at the arrow in his chest before falling, her next arrow swiftly following the first ones.

"I'm no *wisp of a girl*," she muttered. Daro turned to give her a better angle on the next riders. Witmara shot two, three more times, trying to hit the man holding the rope connected to the women. That had to be Klendaus. She couldn't imagine someone like him turning over the control of his captives to anyone else.

Toran reached Klendaus before she could hit him. Gernar collided into his lesser horse, sending horse and rider staggering. Toran severed the rope with his sword. Klendaus turned to throw a charm at him—*no!*

Toran laughed, and deflected the charm. Witmara sent Daro charging into the man and his horse from his other side, knocking them down. She hung her bow from her saddle horn and drew her staff as horse and rider flailed, trying to get to their feet. Toran dismounted and grabbed Klendaus's mare, yanking her up and away from him. Daro pawed impatiently as Witmara kept him from stomping on Klendaus.

She pointed the staff at Klendaus as he pushed himself to his feet.

"Don't try anything," she growled. "Raise your hands."

"Who are you?" He grabbed at the staff's knot, then froze as it glowed blue. "Goodwood! Gods! Chatain's curse will be upon you for interfering with my trade! I bear his favor and you stop me at your peril!" Nonetheless he lifted his hands, though he kept his palms turned away from her.

"I don't care one whit for Chatain's curses."

He laughed as rocks rumbled above them. "Only a fool would try an ambush here! It's charmed and I have the key to the charm!" He turned the palm of one hand to reveal a tattoo. "You will be crushed while my men and I survive. *Fool.*"

"Perhaps." She reached for the land.

Quiet. Do not give him that power he claims.

The land agreed. Her staff glowed a brighter blue-white.

"Rocks fall!" Klendaus yelled, gesturing with his right hand.

Rumbles, but nothing. He stared up at the rims, a confused expression crossing his face.

"Rocks fall!" he repeated, waving his right hand even stronger.

Still nothing.

"Maybe it's this one," he muttered. "Rocks FALL!" he bellowed, pointing with his tattooed left palm at the even bigger rocks at that side.

Not even so much as a rumble.

"*ROCKS FALL!*" Klendaus screamed. "*ROCKS FALL, ROCKS FALL, ROCKS FALL!*" The last words were sobbed more than screamed, his eyes growing wider as nothing happened.

"It's not going to work, you know," Witmara said calmly. "The land is mine now, not Chatain's."

He spun back to face her. "Who *are* you?"

"I am Witmara ea Miteal, soon-to-be Empress of Daran, and I am here to purge the land of parasites like you," she said.

He blanched and staggered back, grabbing at a wooden pendant at his chest. The malign energy surging from it was identical to that wood Tiernin had identified as Chatain's preferred working. Toran knocked his hands away from the pendant.

"*Break and burn,*" Witmara growled, and pointed her staff at Klendaus's pendant. It glowed bright red and shattered into splinters. Blue overwhelmed each splinter, the cold fire turning each fragment into a brief bright twinkle before they became ash.

Klendaus's eyes widened so far that they almost bugged out of his head. He stopped struggling with Toran, his jaw working but no sound coming out as he stared at Witmara. She dismounted and strode toward Klendaus, gripping her staff tightly, Daro so close on her heels that she felt his breath. Part of her wanted to clobber Klendaus with the staff. But a second, wiser part held back. He wasn't worth it. While venting her anger on him would be personally satisfying, she wasn't the one he had harmed.

"Search him for more tokens and bind him securely," she told Toran. "I will check the women."

Toran grinned grimly at her and whistled to one of their men. "Quantri. Come help."

"You can't get them free without my key!" Klendaus gabbled as she stomped past him without so much as a glance.

Witmara stopped, but did not turn to face him. "Oh?"

He cackled a high-pitched, keening laugh. "Oh yes. Did you seriously think that Chatain would trust me and mine with the likes of these lovely young things without precautions? They bear special wards that hurt the slaves as well as anyone who tries to touch them. After all, some of these little darlings might try to seduce their way out of captivity."

Don't turn to give him more attention, don't turn to give him more attention.

The skin on her back crawled as she just *knew* he was staring at her.

"I'd think you'd have better control over your men than that," she said, keeping her voice even.

What kind of charm harms the ones it protects?

"Those little lovelies would do anything to be free of their bonds," he sniggered. "But except for the sluts from Marinset, they're all witch-bred, from the royal motherlines of Ternar, just like Betsona is. One of them will eventually conceive the sorcerer of his own blood that Chatain wants, and when she does, I'll get a bonus."

Her blood ran cold. Sorcery had kept her safe from rape during her recent abduction. After what had happened to

Alicira ea Miteal, all the Miteal women learned the wards and spells that protected them from the same fate that Alicira had suffered at the hands of Rekaré's father. Rekaré had taught those magics to Witmara. And Chatain had imagined the same fate for her....

Her fingers tightened on her staff.

"Silence him," she ordered Toran, and continued forward.

She'd find a way to safely free the women without his key.

One of their riders writhed on the ground by the shackled women. Denki, a distant female cousin of Toran's. Three of the restrained women comforted another who gasped for breath on the ground next to Denki, trembling.

So it does not matter if it is male or female who touches these women.

Witmara studied the eight captives. Six had golden skin like Betsona's, including the one in pain from contact with Denki. Two were paler-skinned, both with dark hair. One of these women held the other, who rocked back and forth, hands clapped to her ears, staring at the ground. Vinkel joined her.

"My sister," he groaned. "They took Meris!"

"Which one is she?" Witmara asked in a low voice.

"The one holding Eunir." Eunir must be the woman rocking back and forth.

"Can you free her?"

He shook his head. "Those shackles are cursed." He gestured toward Denki and the prisoner still quivering in the arms of the others. "You see what will happen. We have to get the key from Klendaus—and it's a charm, not an actual key."

If it's a charm, I can break it.

On the other hand, if they could get the key from Klendaus, then that was less magic exerted, with no possibility of drawing Chatain's attention.

"Get the charm," she said to Vinkel. "I'll talk to the women."

Hysterical laughter from behind her. "I'll never give you the key! Never!"

Witmara approached the women. "Is there anything I can do to help?"

One of the golden-skinned women, the one with the palest blonde hair, laughed bitterly. "He has no power to free us," she said, in Darani as rough as Witmara's. "The key requires an additional link from Chatain. Klendaus will entertain himself watching us suffer while the breach summons one of Chatain's projections. Better for you to wield your own magic."

"Oh? And how do you know this?" Witmara tightened her grip on the staff. Something about this woman made her uneasy. Magic stirred in her, and it didn't feel friendly.

The blonde snorted. "Ever since Vespla became elevated to the role of Royal Concubine, our motherlines have sought to breed another mother of sorcerers, selecting amongst us to sell to Daraelen. That's the price Ternar pays to Chatain for the right to govern ourselves. The six of us are sacrifices. We are doomed to be broodmares for Chatain. If we are lucky, and one of us pleases him."

"What happens if you don't please him?"

"Then it's to the brothels at the mines for us."

"What if I were to tell you that I am here to challenge Chatain?" Witmara watched this woman carefully.

Lord Staul, if ever I needed your help, now's the time.

These women were captives, but would they support her or Chatain?

There are plenty of women who would do almost anything if it made them mother of an Emperor. Or Empress.

The woman's mention of *mothers* reminded her of the Witches of Waykemin. Toran had not known how her mother's battle with the Witches had gone. She thought she would have known if Katerin had fallen in that battle—but she didn't know for certain.

"That wouldn't be possible. The only surviving ruling heir in Daran is Betsona, and she lacks the strength to rule." All the same, was that hope she saw in the blonde's gold-flecked blue eyes? "What gives you the right to challenge Chatain?"

"Heirs to the Empire have survived in the land of Medvara, in Varen," Witmara said. "I am Witmara ea Miteal. Granddaughter of Alame the Cursed, great-granddaughter of Alexran the Exile." She lifted the staff high. "The land acknowledges my right to direct its magic."

"I—see," the woman said. The sensation of *wrongness* started to fade. "But your skin is darker than the typical Aireii—how can that be?"

"I am part-Varenese," Witmara said. "My mother is the Leader of Medvara and my late father is the Messenger of Staul."

The blonde nodded. "That explains the feel of the Lord Staul about you, then." She glanced down at her shackles. "The power of the land will help you break our bonds without interference. But it may still trigger Chatain's projection."

"I will take that risk."

"All right." The woman drew a deep breath. "You need to know our names to break the spell. My name is Charis." She pointed to another woman, with reddish-gold hair. "Chaye." The honey-gold haired woman. "Chanti." Brownish-hair, the one who held the woman Denki had touched. "Chenari." Brown hair. "Chinani." Blood-red hair. "Chasi. I don't know the two from the village. Yet."

"Meris and Eunir," Witmara said absently. She wondered at the common *ch* beginning each Ternar woman's name. Real names or new names assumed once they were sent to Daran?

Are they related to Chiral somehow?

Chiral hadn't had golden skin, like Betsona...but was she also descended from the Ternar motherlines? Or did the *ch* prefix reflect a hope that the six would all become Chatain's property?

You might just be overthinking things.

And yet, magic could often work this way.

The dark-haired, pale-skinned woman who held the other one tight looked up and swallowed hard. "Yes. I am Meris and she is Eunir. Klendaus's men—oh gods, they used her horribly."

"They would," Charis said harshly. "Before the shackles. They brought her—Eunir—in before Meris. You're lucky, girl."

"Charis, you are familiar with these shackles. How do you recommend I proceed with releasing them?" Witmara asked. "All at once or one at a time?"

"I would start with these two," Charis gestured toward Maris and Eunir. "Their bonds are newer and of lesser strength than ours."

"Thank you."

Witmara knelt by Eunir. She took her staff in both hands.

Daro. Lend me strength.

She waited until she felt his muzzle rest on her shoulder, power flowing into her from him.

DaroandWitmara,

she thought at him.

WitmaraandDaro,

came back.

Sniff. Look. Tell.

She visualized the shackles. Daro lifted his head and moved

closer to Eunir. Meris shrank back at his approach, her arms tightening around Eunir.

"Daro is a magic-gifted horse," Witmara said quietly. "He will not harm you—I have commanded him to show me what spells he can see. Let him look at your bonds."

Meris nodded, her jaw tight and tense.

Daro blew gently on the two women, then lowered his head to sniff at the bonds. He sent Witmara a picture of the magic swirling around the bonds, the dark reds and magentas of the Goddess Nitel's power as forged by Chatain.

> Thank you,

she told Daro. She closed her eyes to focus on the pathways of this magic. Where was the best place to break it without doing further harm to Eunir?

> Lord Staul. Help me see what must be done to right this wrong. How do I best break these shackles?

She waited. The God's presence approached, a ponderous warm weight that loaded down her arms and legs. Then it lightened.

> See this path?

The spectral voice of her father Metkyi whispered in her thoughts. His skeletal finger traced a particular braid, highlighting the red in a blue that turned purple.

> This is the portion which inflicts harm on the bound one. And this is the portion that harms the one who would free them.

His finger traced a second section, and then a third.

And this is the piece that summons Chatain.

I see.

She chewed on her lip. The threads were complex, and ideally should be severed simultaneously. She could do two at once, but the third?

What would you recommend?

For these two, glimmer dust, then a release chant. Later bonded, less strong. I do not think breaking their link will summon Chatain.

She undid the pouch that held her glimmer dust. Concentrating on Meris's bonds, she sprinkled glimmer dust in the three areas that Metkyi had pointed out.

"Unweave the bond," she chanted in Varenese. "Break the threads, open the locks, with no harm done."

The shackles loosened. Witmara yanked them off of Meris. She repeated the process for Eunir, who barely looked up from her rocking as Witmara jerked her bonds away. Vinkel and another man from Marinset gathered them up, murmuring reassurance as they guided them away from the other women.

Witmara focused on the others.

How are these bonds different from the first two?

Start with the last one—Chasi, the injured one. Have Daro look at her ties.

The redhead groaned as she held her bonds up for Daro's exploration. The picture he sent back after careful check of wrist and ankle bonds was of a more complex spell, one that was in part of Chatain, in part an unfamiliar magic.

No. Wait. There was a similarity to what she had felt in the magic at Betsona's—did this spell originate with one of her kin from Ternar?

Now this is interesting,

her father said, tracing the links as he had with Meris and Eunir's bonds.

That new link—the yellow-green—is not influenced by Chatain. It's not Darani.

Charis said something about the mothers breeding mothers of sorcerers in their land.

So she did. Charis is the key to that particular binding.

Should I free her first, instead?

Metkyi did not respond right away.

No,

he said at last.

You have neutralizing paste?

A little, yes.

He pointed to one spot in the braid, where the yellow-green glowed brightest.

Put it there first. It will mask the disappearance of Chasi from the chain. You will need to do this for each woman. The rest can be handled just like you did with Meris and Euler.

Thank you.

Witmara fumbled in her pouch for the small bag of soft paste. She carefully spread it over that part of the link. Then she repeated sprinkling the glimmer dust over the other parts of the link. As the shackles loosened, she pulled them away from Chasi.

"Thank you," Chasi murmured, rolling to her side and raising to hands and knees, shaking her head.

Once freed, Chinani stood next to Chasi. For some reason that made Witmara uneasy, but she couldn't explain why. Daro stepped between her and the other women. The freed women shifted position so that they could watch Witmara work on Chenari, clasping hands. Once she was freed, Chenari joined the others.

They are related and they want to make sure they are all safe, Witmara told herself as she worked. All the same, something about their scrutiny of her actions triggered caution in her. She paused before freeing Chaye to sketch a further protective spell for herself and Daro out of clear sight from the women.

Be very careful,

she warned Daro. He snorted agreement.

Yes. These links are not as straightforward as they seem,

Metkyi agreed.

There is something—you need to learn more about whatever agreements Ternar may have with Chatain. These women are too accomplished to have just been captured for slaving purposes. At some point, they've given consent—or been led into giving consent. Do not trust them.

Should I wait to unbind these last two?

Too late to stop now. Four of them are freed. Be watchful.

Slowly, carefully, she put the neutralizing paste on the link between Chaye and Charis. Sprinkled the glimmer dust. Spoke the spell to break the link.

Chaye and Charis exchanged smiles as that link severed, and Chaye joined the others. Witmara paused, resting one hand on Daro's back.

"I need to rest for a moment," she said out loud. Something about the luminous glow in Charis's eyes made her uneasy. "Is there anything I should know before breaking this final bond?"

"What makes you think there's a problem?" Charis asked.

"Given the sort of magic I'm seeing, I suspect that freeing you is going to trigger a different response from the others," Witmara said.

Charis's smile spread. "You are an observant one, Witmara ea Miteal." Her voice was suddenly deeper, not quite hers.

Chasi frowned. Her expression was mirrored by three of the others. Only Chaye remained focused on Charis, still smiling.

So is there a difference between those four and Chaye and Charis? That cast an entirely different light on things. A split between the six—*pay attention to that.*

"Keep in mind that if something happens to me, you still may become enslaved again," she said, directing her words to the four. "If Chatain is bringing in others like you regularly, that's more competition for one of you to become his hoped-for mother of sorcerers."

Charis laughed, a spiky, brittle cackle that sent chills down Witmara's spine. "Ah, but the fortunate one will need attendants. And we all know who they will be, right, sisters?"

Sisters by blood or sisters by association?

The different shades of hair certainly suggested association rather than blood kin. Despite the common golden hue of their skin, facial features differed—now that she looked more closely, there was a stronger resemblance between the four than between them and Charis and Chaye.

Witmara shrugged, forcing a calmness she didn't entirely feel. "So you believe you're all going to Chatain together and not being separated?"

"That fate is unlikely," Petronin said as he and Toran joined them. "I've seen groups like this before, Lady Witmara. Sometimes the Mothers of Ternar think to game their tributes to Chatain by sending sister groups to support a strong prospect." He shook his head. "They don't realize that Chatain can see those linkages clearly, and knows better than to allow sisters to remain together. Strong sister groups like these two?" He snorted. "Once you reach Adalane, each one of you goes somewhere else to be sold. Only one will proceed to Chatain's ownership."

"That is *not* the agreement with our Mother," Charis snapped.

"Chatain lies," Petronin said. "And your Mother should have known that full well by now."

"Only because those she has sent him before have failed."

"And you expect to be different?"

Charis scowled at that question. For a moment her shields dropped. Witmara quickly sent a thread of sorcery to hold that slit open. Now she had a lock on Charis.

Witmara stepped forward. "It's time."

Petronin moved toward the four sisters who had now pulled away slightly from Chaye. Toran and Gernar stood behind Chaye.

Ready to keep her from helping Charis. Good.

Witmara spread the neutralizing paste on Charis's bonds. Took her time sprinkling glimmer dust on the breaking point of her shackles, sneaking a pinch on the knot of her staff. Then, clutching her staff firmly in both hands, she raised it high and chanted the spell-breaker.

The shackles exploded off of Charis's wrists. She lunged for Witmara, laughing as Chatain's visage twisted over her body.

"You fool! How can you ever expect to supplant me if you let a tender heart overrule your wisdom!" he shrieked through Charis.

Witmara swung her staff hard, striking Charis's body in the gut and doubling her—them—over.

"Begone from her, Chatain!" she bellowed. "By the power granted me through Daran, I banish you back to your own self!"

Charis collapsed as Chatain's projection separated from her.

It is not that easy to be rid of me, half-breed witch of Varen!

He grew to almost twice her size, tracing a spell in the air.

I will find where you are and send my men to capture you. You will regret challenging me—I am not so easily defeated!

Daro screamed and reared to his full height, head and neck towering over the enlarged Chatain. Witmara fed power into their link as the glow of daranval magic shimmered bright, the silver streaks in his black mane and tail expanding and spreading over his blood red body until he was entirely silver, the black and red of his natural color providing a shaded undertone. He lunged at Chatain and bit down hard on the sorcerer's shoulder, loud *thumps* sounding as his hooves struck Chatain's body.

He shouldn't be making actual physical contact!

She couldn't do that with her sorcery. But daranval magic *was* different....

Chatain shrieked and tried to grapple with the enraged stallion as he shrank in Daro's grasp. Daro shook him hard, then sent him flying. As Chatain's projection landed, Daro pounced on him, along with shadowy others that Witmara tried to identify. Was that the dark form of Heinmyets's late stallion, Elantai, Daro's sire, who tore at Chatain's spectral shape? And another gray figure grabbing Chatain's left foot in her teeth that might have been her mother's previous daranval, Mira? And that palomino mare snapping at his hands so that he couldn't cast a spell, who resembled but yet was not Rekaré's Basnen—Alicira's Narasin, Basnen's dam?

Begone, foul beasts!

Chatain squawked,

You have no power over me! Witch! Call off your familiars or I will lay a death curse on you!

Witmara ambled to where the daranvelii ripped at Chatain's projection, taking her time. He squealed and writhed, trying to get away from them. It was tempting to let them finish him.

He's had enough,

her father said.

Why not let them kill him? It would solve a number of our problems.

That is not the way you want to become the Darani Empress. Better to defeat him in the flesh, by your own hand. Then that discourages challengers. Plus it would be best to not have the daranvelii contaminated by his death.

True,

she conceded. Defeat him publicly, in the body. In front of witnesses, at the Challenge. Then no one could doubt her ability.

Back!

she commanded the daranvelii, living and dead. Raised the staff high, then impaled the apparition with it.

I will see you in Adalane, cousin! I am also not so easily defeated!

Chatain's form disappeared. Daro stomped at the dirt where it had been.

Enough,

she commanded Daro. Then she turned to face the spectral daranvelii that stood around her and Daro.

Father, how do I best thank them?

A piece of your essence and naming them. They have chosen to aid the bond between you and Daro, and gifting part of yourself to them will be their reward. It also strengthens Daro.

Piece of my essence—did that mean magic or something else? Sometimes workings with Staul demanded blood. Witmara drew Inharise's knife out of its sheath. She pricked one finger-tip. But how would she know the daranvelii names?

Start with the ones you know for certain.

She held the fingertip out. Elantai's spectral shape nuzzled it.

Elantai.

The black stallion snorted. He touched noses with Daro, and then his form overlaid Daro's. Daro's black markings shone bright underneath the silver sheen covering his body.

The palomino mare moved forward regally. Witmara pinched her finger to bring more blood.

Narasin?

The mare's nostrils flared delicately as they brushed the blood away from Witmara's fingertip. She nuzzled Daro, and then faded into him.

That left the gray mare standing next to Metkyi as he rested his hand on her withers. Mira, about whom she'd heard so many stories while growing up. Mira, who had been amongst the strongest of the magic-gifted daranvelii, more powerful even than Elantai. Mira, her mother's companion until her death in the fight that made Rekaré the Leader of Medvara.

The gray mare stomped. Faint images of buffalo dung covered the last image of Chatain's visage writhing on the ground. Witmara couldn't help giggling. Her mother had often mentioned that Mira visualized people and things she didn't like as covered in buffalo dung. And that when both Mira and Metkyi had fallen in the battle against Zauril, she had seen the two of them together in spectral form before they faded away.

I must remember to tell Mother about this, if I can.

She squeezed her finger for an even more generous drop of blood.

Mira.

The gray mare licked Witmara's fingertip, then pressed her forehead against Witmara's hand. An image of a younger Katerin, riding the mountains of Clenda on Mira's back, came to Witmara. Mira chuckled deep in her chest like a mare would to a young foal. Then she nuzzled Witmara before fading into Daro as the other two daranvelii had.

Her father sighed.

I will miss Mira, but she will be gone from me only for a short time.

What does this mean?

Witmara gestured at Daro.

Are they part of him?

They are a part of his heritage, either by his inheritance or yours. You will have need of the strength Daro gives you, and the wisdom those three carry.

Her father bent to kiss her forehead.

Their strength will confuse Chatain. But you must ride forth quickly, before he recovers enough to track your magic.

Thank you,

she breathed as he faded away. She blinked and looked around her. Daro still shone silver, but it faded even as she watched, though tiny silver, gold, and gray hairs now flecked his blood bay coat, and the silver streaks in his mane and tail dominated the black base.

"Lady Witmara." She startled at the worshipful tone in Charis's voice as she prostrated herself on the ground, along with the other five Ternarese. "Command us and we will serve. Your magic is clearly superior."

Witmara scowled at them. She did not trust any of them. And she certainly wasn't going to take them with her, not when she had to ride hard. But what *was* to become of these women? Leave them here in Marinset?

"What would you choose to do? Return home?"

Charis shook her head, still staring at the ground. "Once we have been given as tribute we have no place in Ternar. The Motherlines have moved on."

Oh *Gods*. And she still had those damn smugglers to deal with. "Vinkel. How many of Klendaus's men survived our battle?"

"Ten, including him."

"Petronin. We can't take the women with us. They don't have mounts and I don't trust them. What do you suggest?"

Petronin shrugged. "I would kill them, myself. Including the women."

"I won't do that. At least to the women and those who served Klendaus. Klendaus himself? I need to think on his fate."

"Slave them? I'm sure that Vinkel could use the labor."

She cringed at that thought. "Bind the men temporarily to the families of Meris and Euler," she decided. "They will serve those families as payment for their treatment of their daughters, until I return to judge them as Empress. All except Klendaus."

"And the women?"

She studied Charis's prostrate form. "Get up, all of you," she said wearily.

"But my lady—"

"*Get up.*"

Charis rose unsteadily, followed by the others. "You vanquished Chatain. Therefore we now belong to you."

"I don't own people." She tightened her lips.

Gods. What would her mother do? Rekaré? The women needed a means to support themselves.

"What does Marinset need for free workers?" she asked Vinkel.

"For women?" He shrugged. "Seamstresses. Bakers. Healers. Gardeners. Between Klendaus and those like him, our best workers end up being forced into the cities to serve. We are stretched thin here."

"Can any of you work magic besides Charis?" she asked the women. "Sew? Cook? Garden? Heal?"

Silence. Then Chasi stepped forward. "I have some healing skill. Not much magic, but I apprenticed to a midwife in Ternar."

Chenari joined Chasi. "I can bake."

"I can speak to plants," Chinani said.

"I know sewing," Chanti said.

Chaye and Charis remained silent.

"And you two?" Witmara demanded, glaring at those sisters.

"I am not meant to wither away in a backwater like this!" Charis growled. "Much less work at domestic tasks. I am from the Royal Motherline, not a servant!"

Chaye rolled her eyes. "Neither my sister nor I were trained to be anything other than concubines," she said softly. "I am a musician and poet, and she is an artist."

"So you were the two the others were meant to support?" Witmara turned to Chaye.

"Charis, mostly. I was meant to be attractive to the Lady Betsona. The Motherlines think that connection is important."

"I see." Witmara sighed, thinking over her options. "All of you. Will you swear loyalty to me as the future Empress of Daran?"

"We are yours already by conquest," Charis said sourly.

"And I free you from that obligation! I have neither the

horses nor the time to bring you with me. I am trying to find you places in Marinset."

"I will swear to you," Chaye said. The other four echoed her, all save Charis.

"And you will work in Marinset as freed women?" Witmara asked. They nodded, except for Chaye.

"I do not know if I have skills that would be of use in Marinset," she said in that same soft voice. "But I would prefer to ride with you, Lady Witmara. Whether it is through you or Chatain, I was meant to work with Betsona."

Witmara considered her for a moment.

Would a link between Betsona and Ternar be a good thing?

There was so much she didn't know—and could learn from Chaye. Plus, by herself, Chaye appeared to be more biddable.

"I will consider your plea," she said to Chaye. Then she turned to Vinkel. "Marinset can use these women, right? But they are free women, not slaves. It will take them time and work to be independent, but they can contribute to Marinset's well-being even as they gain the resources and tools they need. Can they find housing?"

Vinkel pursed his lips thoughtfully. "Those four, yes, with those they would work for. We haven't had a midwife in Marinset for several years now. Those are amongst the first women that the slavers take. Jaconi needs a second hand with her tailoring and mending work. We can always use a skilled hand in planting the common fields, and Kendrei the baker is overloaded. But the concubine and the musician?" He shrugged. "Common labor."

"I. Will. Not. Serve." Charis tossed her head defiantly. "I am meant to be Chatain's Empress. I will not serve anyone else!"

"Sister," Chaye said reproachfully. "We don't have a choice."

"You mean *you* don't have a choice. You'd sell yourself to this half-breed Varenese twit! Not for me!"

Witmara saw the spell forming in Charis's fingers. She smacked Charis's hand with her staff. "None of that now!"

"You dare!" Charis snarled, blinking back tears. "You who can't wield magic without help from your horse and Staul's Messenger! You foul wisp of Staul's nightmares—" She hurled a second spell at Witmara. "I will *die* before I submit to the likes of you!" she screeched through a choked sob.

Witmara deflected Charis's spell. Charis struck at her again and again, her spellcasts becoming more and more erratic as she sobbed and screamed. Witmara did not engage, nor did she cast spells of her own. She used her staff to deflect and demolish the spells, until Charis finally collapsed to her knees again, sobbing.

"I will not yield. I will not yield." She looked up at Witmara and Vinkel. "*I will die first!*" Before either of them could move, Charis yanked Vinkel's bloody shortsword from his hands. She could barely hold the hilt in shaking hands as she turned it to herself, but still managed to hold it straight as she fell hard on the blade, impaling herself before anyone reacted.

"*Sister!*" Chaye screamed, kneeling beside her.

"Chasi!" Witmara yelled, joining Chaye at Charis's side. Charis fumbled at a pouch at her belt, uncorking a vial and pouring it in her mouth. The telltale bitter, sour scent of Essence of Darsnai wafted from her.

"Oh no," Chasi groaned. "Charis, you wouldn't!"

Charis's bloody body stiffened, then convulsed.

Chasi shook her head, groaning as Charis's body went limp and her eyes dulled.

"Is there any more of that foul mix amongst you?" Witmara demanded.

"No," Chaye gulped. "Charis carried it all."

Witmara sighed again. She pushed herself up. "I am sorry for this."

"She was determined to be the one to bear an heir for Chatain," Chaye whispered, wrapping her arms around herself.

"She planned for us to be his most beloved, that we would elimi-nate Betsona and serve Chatain." She shook her head again, choking back sobs. "Sister. Oh, sister."

Witmara remained silent as tears ran down Chaye's cheeks.

At last Chaye sniffled, and brushed the tears away. She rose and bowed low to Witmara. "Lady Witmara. My sisters can have roles here in Marinset, if they so desire. I repeat my request to be given the favor of serving you personally. Many of our sisters have hidden responsibilities in Daran, and I can help coordinate their support of your rule. Few of them love Chatain—or at least, that is what they felt when they left Ternar. Any support for him is forced."

"I am riding hard and long," Witmara said, studying this young woman. "You need to be able to ride."

"I can ride."

"But can I trust you? Obviously I could not trust Charis."

"I have no ambitions to be the mother of Emperors," Chaye said with a half-smile. "Nor do the rest of us. That was all Charis."

"What do you know of the history of Daran?"

"I was trained to know the ways of Daran as well as Ternar, to be a resource for the Motherlines," Chaye said. "I was selected for the tribute only because our sister died."

Witmara studied Chaye further. "Daro. Sniff. Look. Tell."

The stallion snorted. He approached Chaye imperiously, neck arched high, nostrils widened in a high, rolling warning snort. He shook his head so that his long mane flew for a moment, then lowered his nose to sniff Chaye's shoulders. Chaye shivered but did not flinch away as the edge of his nostrils brushed against her torso, her legs, her arms. She stared straight ahead.

Daro snuffled around Chaye's hands. Then he flicked his ears forward and pushed hard against her torso hard with his forehead, rubbing up and down. She staggered sideways, clearly unprepared for this action.

"What? Why did you do that?" she demanded, turning to face Daro with her hands spread wide.

Daro tossed his head again, a familiar, impish light glowing in them. He shoved her again, this time more gently.

"He wants you to scratch his forehead," Witmara said. "He has accepted you."

Chaye carefully reached up to scratch under Daro's forelock. "And if he hadn't accepted me?"

"When I give Daro that command, he acts based on what he perceives. If it is bad—he will do anything from knocking you down to killing you. I have no control over what he does at this point. He will do what is needed to protect me."

"Then I can ride with you?" Hope rose in her voice.

"Yes."

Chaye dropped to her knees, raising clasped hands to her. "I will follow you, Lady Witmara, and forsake any allegiance to any others in my life. I will do my best to ensure that you become Empress of Daran, and will give my life to keep you safe."

"I accept. But know that you make this choice freely, and are still your own woman. I refuse to be your owner." Witmara turned to Vinkel. "Guard these others."

"Perhaps we should submit Klendaus to your stallion's judgment," he said.

"I would not befoul Daro so," she said.

Not if my father thought killing Chatain would do him harm. Klendaus is just as bad.

"What are we to do with him and—this one?" He waved at Charis's corpse.

Witmara took a deep breath. "Toran. Should this be of Artel?"

He shook his head. "What God did she serve?"

"Nitel, like Chatain," Chaye said. "I am devoted to Terat."

Interesting.

That Goddess had promised Witmara a favor back when they were in Medvara. Would Chaye be the instrument through which that favor was dispensed?

"None of us are devoted to Nitel in Marinset," Vinkel said. "Mostly Artel."

"Denki," she said. "Isn't she devoted to Dovré?"

"She is."

"Then we will have her call down the cool fire to purify Charis. And as for Klendaus...." She paused, then turned to Toran.

"For Klendaus, I would ask you to exercise Artel's judgment. I cannot be the one to do it. I fear I would take too much joy in harming him."

"I hear and obey." Toran bowed gracefully to her.

"And as for the rest—we must ride quickly and soon," she said to the others. "Find a mount for Chaye," she ordered Petronin. "Gather up weapons."

All the same, it was midday before they rode away from that narrow canyon, with the fallen—save for Charis and Klendaus—buried. Charis's body had been consumed by Dovré's cool flame, and Klendaus's body hung from a tree as a warning to other smugglers.

"Well done," Petronin told her quietly as they settled into a fast long trot. "But I am worried about what Chaye said about the Ternarese women having roles in Daran. It sounds too much like Betsona's networks for my comfort. What are their goals?"

"Yes. It's a concern we need to keep in mind for the future," she said.

And I will not trust any Ternarese women that have been culti-vated by the motherlines until I know more about them. Even Chaye.

Still another thing she needed to learn more about.

CONVERSATIONS AT
THE NEREAN GATE

Katerin fought back shivers not entirely caused by temperature as she led the small group of riders to answer the Divine Confederation's demands. Ever since they left Nere, the road led through a thick forest with firs tall enough to block any sunlight even at midday. Moss covered the ground adjacent to the road, carpeting fallen limbs and trunks and running up the sides of the living trees. Despite the lack of brush on the forest floor, it was hard to see very far past the edges of the road. A dark gloom shadowed and blurred any shapes more than two horse lengths from the road's opening. And even though the sun shone high overhead, it only faintly lit the roadway.

"This doesn't feel right," Linyet, Rekaré's son, the heir to the Two Nations, said from her right. He glanced around uneasily. "It was sunny when we rode in here. Even a forest this thick should have some light patches."

"They do in Medvara," she agreed.

"The most haunted thickets in Medvara are less creepy-feeling than this." Linyet shuddered. "I feel anger. Malign intentions."

"The Gate Forest has always been this way," Doryits observed from Katerin's left, where he was directing the scouts riding ahead of them, carrying white truce flags. All of them wore white truce armbands. "It changes, and a wise person does not leave the road here. But we ride under truce. We are safe."

That is, if our opponents recognize and accept the notion of truce.

Katerin wasn't convinced that would be the case. But both Kintarit and Doryits hadn't seen an issue.

They have accepted flags of truce before, Kintarit had said just last night. *And despite their demands, trade has continued.*

She had spoken her piece then. Had agreed to leave the main body of their army behind despite her misgivings so as not to provoke Sariost and her riders into an early direct attack. After all, they still had two days before the threatened deadline. It was not the pattern for the Divine Confederation to attack negotiators.

But something still didn't feel right. On the one hand, it reassured Katerin that Linyet should also be unsettled by this forest. It meant she wasn't imagining what she felt. On the other —the fact that he felt the same uneasiness she did was worrisome. Her fears were real and not just caused by an unfamiliar setting.

This place is not right.

Worse, she had that creepy-crawly, chill-down-her-back sensation that went along with appearances by the Twin Gods, Karnoi and Cirdel, and their pack of followers, the Hunt. They usually appeared as wolves but could also materialize as street predators in urban settings. She hadn't seen or thought about the Hunt for years, not since just before Rekaré had abdicated from the Leadership of Medvara. Why was she thinking about the Twins and the Hunt now? This wasn't the sort of place they preferred.

Then again, she hadn't thought that Medvare-the-city would be a place where the Hunt manifested themselves, either.

Be watchful.

Two scouts galloped back toward them. They reined up next to Doryits.

"The road's changed again, sir," one said.

"Again? Were there warnings?"

"No," the other said. "Just—instead of forest all the way to the Gate, there is now a big meadow. Like it has always been there."

"I don't like this," Doryits muttered. "All right. Ride to the guardhouse. Make sure all of your protections are fully armed before you speak to any of the guards. Do not go inside. Confirm that the guards are—who they are supposed to be."

"We have the code phrases and the protection charms that Leader Katerin gave us," the first speaker said.

"Then use them."

"Yes, sir."

"You said that the forest changes," Katerin said to Doryits. "Is this normal?"

His jaw tightened. "Not to this degree. Perhaps you were right."

"An illusion or does the forest itself move?"

"I wish I knew. I'm no sorcerer, Katerin. This worries me."

"Should we return to Nere and bring the whole army?"

That was what she really wanted to do. Especially now that the possible presence of the Hunt niggled at her.

He shook his head. "It's too late now. We'll be pursued."

Katerin turned in her saddle. She waved Korien up. "Pass the word. Activate all charms. Do not draw arms—yet—but be ready to fight. The situation may have changed."

Korien nodded. "Should I send someone back for reinforcements?"

"Yes," she said. "Have them advance carefully. This may be nothing—or we may need them."

"Remind them not to leave the road," Doryits said.

"I will do that." Korien turned his horse and galloped back.

Katerin turned forward. "So what does it mean that the road has changed?"

If anything, his expression became grimmer. "It will do that from time to time. Magic. It doesn't happen very often, and when it does…the last time was when my family was taken. Be ready. I do not *think* they will attack us magically, before we speak. All the same, this change does not bode well."

"But you would still trust them not to attack before we speak."

"Without further indication of betrayal I would trust them to speak first—their border populations still have need of the food we trade. It's not late enough in the growing season for them to supply from their own resources. Their preserved food doesn't last long."

"And if they decide they need souls more than food?"

"That would be unusual. That would mean they evacuated their own populations by the border. Sariost's soldiers are not all supernatural. They still need living beings to support their efforts."

"I hope you're right."

She couldn't explain the sinking feeling in her gut. His reasoning made sense—and yet, there was that lingering doubt. The Witches of Waykemin had shown similar off-pattern behavior at the end.

But that was Chatain's influence, and the return of Nitel to Waykemin.

So why was she sensing the presence of the Twin Gods? That was a change of circumstances she did not like.

Goddess Dovré, speak to me. Please.

The Goddess remained silent, not even lending Katerin the familiar warmth of her presence. Only that tingling chill she associated with the Hunt...and the Twins.

She spotted movement off to her right even as Rainin tensed under her.

Danger. Danger,

the mare sent.

Rainin halted, turning her head to stare into the woods. Katerin followed her gaze. Was that a ghostly wolf pack that paced alongside them? The hair on the back of her neck prickled. Now it felt too much like gods-haunted Wickmasa, before she and Metkyi had confronted the Twins. Then she heard the rhythmic *swoosh, swoosh* of the wings of a big bird in steady, measured, flight.

"*Rawk.*" A raven landed on a tree branch in front of them.

No. No. Not that.

She glanced sideways, trying to get a better sight. Was that just more of this damnable forest's shadows or did shadowy humanoid figures drift above those animals trotting deftly through the woods? The appearance of the raven combined with the pack of otherworldly wolves...no.

It can't be the Hunt...but if it is, why is it here and who is its target?

"What is that wolf pack?" Linyet asked softly.

"You see it too." Dread washed over Katerin.

The Hunt.

The Hunt stole souls, but not at random, hunting specific targets determined by the God and Goddess who led them. She had not heard that Karnoi and Cirdel were favorable to the Outcast God—so why were they here? She reached underneath her tunic and brought out the Eye of Dovré that she always wore, wrapping her hand around the clear crystal with gold threads inside of it.

Goddess. Lend me strength.

Maybe invoking the Goddess through her token would help.

A faint twinge of the usual warmth of Dovré's presence heated her hand. But nothing more than that, coupled with a sensation that the Goddess wanted to reach for her but could not.

What is restraining her?

Rainin shook her head and snorted, ears flicking back, then forward.

"I remember mother and father's tales about the Hunt in Wickmasa," Linyet said. "And Grandfather's."

"What are you seeing?" Doryits asked.

Katerin pointed with her chin toward the luminous shapes that she could just barely make out.

"You don't see them?" She was reluctant to mention the Hunt.

Doryits shook his head.

"Karnoi and Cirdel," she said softly. "The Hunt."

"I have never seen them here before."

Katerin glanced behind them. "I hope that messenger tells Haran and the Hidden One to hurry. We're riding into trouble."

Doryits leaned forward and squinted hard. "Those luminous figures?"

"Yes."

She remembered when the Hunt appeared in Medvare-the-city, before Rekaré's abdication. Then they had taken up the forms of scruffy and sneaky street gangsters—fitting for urban predation.

"I have never seen those in Keratil before," he said. "But yes, I have seen them on the other side of the wall. I thought they kept me from attack."

"That's not the usual state of affairs with them. You must not have been their target."

Doryits shrugged. "They weren't hunting anyone when I saw them."

Katerin urged Rainin on, watching to the side. The luminous figures continued to pace them. Why were the Twin Gods here? The Twins thrived on chaos. Did that mean their force faced betrayal from Sariost and the Divine Confederation—or was the Hunt there for one of them?

Gods, could Sariost call upon them to stalk her father?

Doryits *had* been taking *protection-against-possession* regularly, as had she, ever since that incident in Kintarit's House. She remembered what had happened in Wickmasa—and even with *protection-against-possession* in them, she and Metkyi had still been drawn out to battle the Hunt in the middle of a blizzard.

Perhaps it was a good thing that they would soon be riding out into an open field. Katerin strained to see ahead, but could not see any change in light that indicated an opening was nearby. To all appearances the forest continued to stretch on without any breaks in the darkness that surrounded them.

"Is this an illusion or an actual change in the land?" she asked.

"I do not know," he said.

Rainin pinned her ears and stopped as the forest around them suddenly opened onto a large meadow dominated by last season's dry grasses. She raised her head and snorted, a loud rolling warning with her nostrils flaring wide.

No warning, no light change.

She should have been able to see some brightening as they rode. Shouldn't she?

At least the cold prickling sensation that testified to the presence of the Hunt was gone. If it had really been the Hunt, and not some masquerading shadow. If Dovré was restrained, wouldn't Karnoi and Cirdel be as well?

Anything is possible.

Katerin wanted to turn Rainin and ride back for the rest of their forces. Every instinct in her screamed a warning. But they were here. She had to face whatever this was, not avoid it.

Goddess, protect me!

The Eye of Dovré tepidly warmed again on her chest, much weaker than usual. She wished the Goddess would speak to her, but then again…who knew what limitations she was under, this close to the Outcast God's realm?

She urged Rainin into the meadow and halted halfway through it. Katerin blinked her eyes, trying to adjust to the sudden light after the darkness of the woods behind them, and raised her right hand to signal a pause to those riding behind. She took this opportunity to study the setting, calculating what was likely to be a battleground. The field ended at the foot of steep gray shale slopes with a narrow ravine between them. A tall black stone wall blocked the gorge, a lower extension of that wall running up the shale slopes and along the top of the tree-lined ridges as far as Katerin could see.

Rainin tossed her head, blowing that warning roller snort again.

Foulness. Foulness,

she sent.

Katerin stroked her neck, returning reassuring thoughts as she noticed that Doryits swallowed hard and tightened his lips. Was it her imagination or did the same murky shadows that obscured the forest depths also lurk around that wall, not allowing her to make out its details?

"So that's the Nerean Gate," she said, her mouth feeling dry and stuffed with cotton. "There is actually a gate in that wall, isn't there? I can't see it if there is."

"Yes. As we get closer you'll be able to see more. Sorcery keeps you from being able to see things clearly from here." Doryits signed a glyph as she spoke. Katerin recognized it as a simple protective charm. "What you can't see—yet—is the guardhouse. The gates are wooden and infused with spells. They're replaced every five years to keep the spells from fading. The guards are rotated monthly. Otherwise they become haunted."

"How long since the last gate replacement?"

"Four years."

"That's a spooky place if ever I've seen one," Linyet muttered.

"How did the one who carried the Divine Confederation's demand for tribute get through the wall?" Katerin asked. "Is there a protocol for traveling through the Gate?"

"We only open the Gate at set intervals," Doryits said. "Limited trade, mostly food from our side, and starberry and other delicacies from theirs. There are—other routes to cross the gate. We guard our side. The Confederation—they depend on their chaotic nature to deal with those who would venture into their land unasked." He paused. "The demand was issued by one of Sariost's projections."

"And how do they know we want to speak? Is there a signal?" Linyet's lips tightened as his voice cracked slightly. It was only at moments like this that Katerin remembered he was younger than Witmara, thrust into a leadership role by the death of his father.

"Yes," Doryits said. "When we can see the guardhouse and the gate, I will signal that we are ready to speak to their delegation."

They rode forward. The black mist around the stone wall

seemed to thin as they drew closer, lightening until the black turned dark red, then a paler red. At last she could make out the shape of the gates and the structure next to them. Tall, broad gates wide enough to allow twenty riders to pass through side-by-side without obstruction. She couldn't tell how they were barred or locked. The structure was a single-story long building, with shuttered windows. It almost looked like a stable next to that great gate, the moss covering the wood-shaked roof testifying to the forest's normal presence close by.

Five more steps, and she made out the shapes of their advance guard, seemingly frozen in place.

"Doryits?" She gestured toward them. "What is this?"

"Spellbound," he said harshly. "Both they and the guards are compromised."

Katerin halted Rainin. "So have we been betrayed?" Her neck prickled again and she looked around for the Hunt. Nothing—so far. But they were present, somewhere.

Whose side are they on?

"Not yet. This may just mean that Sariost and her guard do not want their interference. Spellbound does not yet mean possessed. But I will not trust any who have been touched in this manner. These guards must be rotated out—today."

"I see. So what do we do next?"

He shuddered, then dismounted. "I will send the sign." He strode ten steps in front of them and spread his hands wide. "Tell the Great One that we are ready to answer her demands!" he bellowed. He snapped his fingers, first the right, then the left. A magenta thread flashed bright from them after each snap.

Doryits held himself stiff. The red mist swirling around the Gate intensified. Then riders emerged from the mist, led by a skeletal shape that resembled the figure Katerin had seen arguing with Doryits at Kintarit's House. She rode a blood bay stallion almost the same shade as Rainin, followed by ten other riders on gray horses, the riders skeletal on their apparently normal mounts.

They halted ten strides from Doryits.

So this is your answer,

the lead rider screeched.

Are you the first offering, Father?

Katerin urged Rainin forward five steps, drawing her sword. It transformed to the Spear, and she smoothly adjusted her grip.

"There are no offerings for the likes of you," she said harshly. "Nor will we give your Outcast God any tribute of souls. Go back to where you came!"

The lead rider shrieked again, a keening wail that sent chills down Katerin's spine.

Katerin Banisher of Shadows, she who would be the savior of Varen! You would dare defy the will of the Outcast God?

The Eye of Dovré flared bright on Katerin's chest, along with the Light of Medvara.

At last the Goddess responds!

"The Outcast God holds no power over me and those I protect!" she answered.

Then know that it is Sariost, servant of the Outcast God, who brings your doom!

she howled.

And I will take my first soul NOW!

She stretched one hand toward Doryits. He shuddered but did not move, his eyes fixed on Sariost.

"By Dovré's gold necklace, NO!" Rainin shot forward as Katerin yelled. Linyet and his daranval charged with them. Linyet pulled Doryits up behind his saddle as Katerin rode between Doryits and Sariost, thrusting the Spear at Sariost.

So you have doomed Varen,

Sariost snarled.

You will be amongst the first tribute! Divine Confederation, it is time to strike!

A force larger than theirs manifested in the field around them, riders separating Katerin and the others from the main force. Sariost laughed as Katerin leveled the Spear, disappearing to leave her surrounded by a host of skeletal riders. Rainin reared high, startled by Sariost's disappearance. For one brief moment Katerin regretted that it was Rainin and not the former war mare Mira underneath her. Mira would have struck at their opponents without exposing her belly in panic.

Then Rainin dropped to all four feet. The Spear shrunk back to its sword form, and Katerin slashed at those attacking her. Rainin lunged at the other horses with her teeth bared, squealing and kicking, but much less skillfully than Mira would have done. They were able to hold their own, but just barely.

How long before our reinforcements get here?

She was disabling the skeletal riders, but there were so many....

A flash of blue-white light sent her opponents flinching back.

"This way!" Linyet yelled.

Katerin wheeled Rainin, blinking as she focused on Linyet,

still holding the brightness high. She urged Rainin toward Linyet and whatever it was that he held. As she approached, she realized the brilliance radiated from something on his brow and not in his hand. Then she recognized it—the gem known as the Gift of Clenda that had once belonged to Inharise, often worn on a browband. She had never seen it glow before.

Her opponents recovered but by the time they resumed pursuit, she was with Linyet and Doryits, now remounted on his horse.

"We need to catch Sariost," Katerin called to Doryits as she fought. "How can we find her in this melee?"

He shook his head. "She's retreated!"

The tingling that signaled the presence of the Twin Gods grew stronger. Suddenly the Hunt was among them. To Katerin's surprise they did not strike at her fighters but at the Divine Confederation.

What is this?

She spotted an opening back to the forest, which the Hunt seemed to be creating for them.

Was it another trap? Were the Twins living up to their Trickster natures? Would they remain true? No time to worry, just take the opening. Even if it was provided by the Twins. She had dealt with the Twins before. She could do it again.

"Riders, to me!"

Katerin sent Rainin through the gap that the Hunt had created, tensing. She expected the wolves to turn on them while they rode by. Instead, the shadowy figures widened the breach so that they could gallop through the field. Katerin kept the Spear in her hand, riding hard, not pausing as they reentered the shadowy forest.

A shimmering figure appeared in front of them after their forces were completely within the trees. Rainin skidded to a stop.

Katerin gasped as the shape became firmer. Her mother

Terani-the-God-Killer stood there. Her hand tightened on the Spear. The last time she had seen her mother's form, she had cursed Katerin. Had they truly escaped?

An enigmatic smile close to that preferred by the Goddess Cirdel touched her mother's lips, but not her eyes. Not that Terani's eyes had ever been anything but measuring and unfriendly, from Katerin's earliest memories.

Katerin my daughter, I give you friendly greeting,

she said finally.

The Hunt's wolves trotted past Katerin and her riders to flop around Terani's feet. Katerin recognized the biggest and sleekest pair. Karnoi, his pelt an even mix of black and silver, eyes burning bright red. His tongue lolled out of his mouth as he sat next to Terani. Terani rested a hand on his head. On her other side, Cirdel stood on all fours, eyes flashing green and gold against her silver-tipped black coat. And next to her, lying down, was a silver wolf. Makri, brother and would-be betrayer of Metkyi. She had killed his manifestation in Wickmasa—but it was not surprising that he would reappear here. After all, he was now part of the Hunt, and that would never change.

"Terani." She would not, could not call this being mother to her face. Not after seeing what real mothers were like. Not after becoming a mother herself. "I give you greeting and thanks. At least I suppose it is your patrons' choice to save us from the forces of the Outcast God."

Your manners are as rough as ever,

Terani sighed.

But she was still not the twisted virago that Katerin had encountered in Waykemin. Katerin wondered if that had truly been Terani, or if it had been a distortion created by one of the Witches.

> But yes. Much as my beloveds enjoy chaos and war, this is not the battle we seek.

She caressed first Karnoi, then Cirdel. Cirdel finally sat on her haunches, her gold-flecked green eyes focused on Katerin.

"Then I give you even more thanks. Do the Twins side with us in this upcoming battle?"

> It was through my wishes and my influence that we came to your aid. They are bound as I am not. That is why I am speaking to you.

Terani was that powerful amongst the Gods? Katerin wanted to shiver but forced herself to remain calm, steady.

"Why?"

Terani sighed again.

> A long story, daughter of mine. Had you not been in this party, had the Outcast God not cast his eyes upon you to be one of his own, then we would not have intervened. Could not have intervened, by Artel's dictate.

"Very well, then—but *why* are you doing this?" It was confusing and annoying that Terani would not answer directly. The last time she had encountered a wraith wearing her mother's form, that being had shrieked curses at her for interfering with Terani's goals. She had known that she was an unwanted child.

Priestesses in Terani's position did not bear children, and both her mother and her followers had not hesitated to remind Katerin of that fact. Even if they took lovers, the priestesses used contraceptive powders. But the usually reliable powders had failed Alame and Terani.

The Balance is wrong. The Outcast God seeks to overthrow the Seven. He seduces Nitel yet again, to ride with him and rule.

She gestured to the Gods in wolf form who sat beside her.

Karnoi and Cirdel are the children of the Outcast God and Nitel. They are forbidden to strike against their parents. But they do not support their parents' aim. That was why I dedicated myself to the Twins.

"Why would they not ally with their parents?"

Karnoi and Cirdel the children of Nitel and the Outcast God? It made sense from their chaotic nature, but it was not something she had known before now.

The Outcast God tolerates no other beside himself. Nitel does not believe he will banish her, thinking that if she works hard enough to help him prevail, he will accept her as an equal and not a subordinate. The Twins do not share her opinion.

"Is Nitel foolish or deluded?"

Nineteen years ago she would have been appalled to discuss one of the Gods like this. Much had changed in that time.

Wolf-Karnoi answered.

She hopes to raise Chatain to replace the Outcast God once the Outcast God has overthrown the other Gods. Betrayal upon betrayal, as it has ever been with our parents.

We are not our mother,

Cirdel added.

> We know our father's goals far too well. In a
> world where he would reign, there would be no
> place for us.

"But surely the Outcast God could not overthrow the Seven, even with Nitel's aid!" Katerin swallowed hard.

> His power grows strong.

Karnoi pointed a paw at Katerin.

> We can only be here now because we are his
> children. We dare not appear in any other form.
> He cannot control us in this shape.

Oh Gods, she needed to get her people out of this damned forest, needed time to devise a strategy.

"What do you want from me?" Not that she would sell herself to Karnoi and Cirdel, but if any of this were true....

Karnoi focused on her.

> You carry the Spear of War and Unmaking. And
> Linyet Lightbringer carries the Gift of Terat to
> Clenda.

Cirdel nodded, showing her fangs before she spoke.

> If you bring down Sariost, you defang his
> primary weapon. We cannot touch his
> supporters for very long. But the Banisher of
> Shadows and Linyet Lightbringer may.

> No more of these half-measures against the
> Divine Confederation,

Karnoi said.

> You must ride with your full force the next time you approach. Sariost retreats to build her strength. We will give you the tool needed—but you dare not underestimate them again.

Katerin tightened her hand on the Spear, not wanting to look at Doryits just yet. She had been right after all. "I thank you for that help, Lord and Lady, and agree with your concern." Gods, it was hard to admit that she needed the Twins' help! "Now what can you do for us? How do we defeat Sariost?"

> You will find the information you need in the libraries of Nere,

Terani said.

> My journals will tell you how.

"I don't understand. How can your journals tell me about the libraries of Nere? *Which* library? *Which* book?"

Terani sighed yet again.

> Gods. Listen to the magic in you, your gifts from me and your father. That will guide you. You have my black journal, the one in which I wrote my studies on the nature of Nitel. There are references to what you need there.

"That's a help." By the Goddess's gold necklace, there were so many notes in that black journal! "Can't you be more specific? Time is limited. We have—or perhaps now *had*—two days before Sariost's deadline."

I am aware of that. I cannot tell you more. But Sariost also needs time to prepare to strike against you. Chatain is distracted and that diverts Nitel's attention. The Outcast God cannot attack at full strength without Nitel's support, and she will not abandon Chatain since he has served her well.

Terani's smile widened.

Your daughter troubles him, while the real danger to Chatain approaches unnoticed.

"Rekaré."

Yes. You have done well with your daughter, my girl. She has given us an opening. But you must strike while Nitel's focus is elsewhere. That will help both you and them.

"So give me more of a clue. What am I to look for?" Terani laughed.

You will find it. That task will not be hard for the daughter of two dear to their Gods. But be prepared to battle in two days.

Katerin sucked in a breath. Her father Alame had been dedicated to Artel, the Judge of the Gods in life, and was now his Messenger.

"Both of you?" Then that meant that Terani was—oh, now it made sense. Terani was the Messenger for the Twins.

Of course! And you are the beloved of Staul's Messenger.

Terani turned her head, paying attention to something Katerin could not see.

My time speaking is done. I have said all that I am allowed. Remember my journal, my daughter, my Banisher of Shadows. You will know what you seek when you see it.

The figures in front of Katerin vanished.

"What was *that?*" Doryits asked.

"A manifestation of Karnoi, Cirdel, and their Messenger," Katerin said slowly. She urged Rainin forward. "I need to think on what I was told—and then spend some time in the libraries. We are safe now, but just barely. I want out of this forest."

She sensed Doryits's impatience, even as Linyet nodded in understanding. At least Doryits didn't pepper her with further questions as they galloped along the road.

The sight of the Hidden One and Haran leading the rest of their army was a welcome relief.

ADALANE

At least we're halfway through our last day on water!

Rekaré's hand tightened on the railing. Despite the headache remedy that Betsona had given her this morning, she was just waterstruck enough that the right side of her head pounded, a throbbing ache that echoed throughout her body. The bright sunlight on water didn't help the pain. And yet—this didn't quite feel like being waterstruck. It felt more like *benghaalph* wanting to run wild, writhing just beneath her skin. And yet it wasn't entirely *benghaalph,* either.

Rekaré closed her eyes.

No relief. Brightness still radiated through her eyelids.

What is this?

Part of her desperately wanted to curl up on her bed and ride through the ache. Hide from the cacophony that raged around her, both magical and nonmagical.

Gods, there was *so much* here. She wanted to pull her sword and lean her head against it. That had given her peace in Varen. Not so here—and Giolanth would not do something like that.

Just like she couldn't retreat below decks. It wouldn't stop that dull throbbing in her torso and the ache underneath her skin. Giolanth would not do that, and until the time of Challenge, Rekaré was not about to do anything different from Giolanth's typical behavior. Not when they were coming under increased scrutiny as they drew closer to Adalane and the Festival.

This morning had seen yet another paper inspection and vessel search by Chatain's lackeys. Was this the third or fourth time she needed to present papers for her and Sesenth to pass as Giolanth and Estarel since they started up the river? Each time they encountered Chatain's inspections, the shrill din in her ears intensified.

There would be at least one more aboard ship once they arrived at Adalane proper, and then who knew how many more as they went about the city? She wasn't used to this level of scrutiny at all, much less the numbers of people on both land and water.

After Zauril's death, most of Varen had returned to the usual informal way stations at the borders. She was accustomed to either being recognized and waved through border stations, or able to work her way around check sites without being seen. Not this constant check, check, check amongst swarms of people. Daran was definitely more populated than any of the nations of Varen—or at least that appeared to be so on the Islands and now on the river.

That's not what is bothering you and you know it.

Was it *benghaalph* that whispered this in her ear, or was it the alluring song of the *something else* that had been stirring within her ever since she set foot on Lanivar Island? Rekaré shook her head to banish that whisper. But it was growing stronger, the closer they came to Adalane.

At least Betsona's presence seemed to keep the inspectors from looking too closely when searching. Most had been eager to gain her favor, the whole tone of the inspections changing once Betsona hobbled onto deck. However, this last batch of lackeys had been suspicious and threatening, poking in their trunks and papers to a greater extent than before. Betsona hadn't been able to avoid this search like she had the past ones, either.

Sesenth's hand brushed against her arm. "I think I've recovered enough from the morning's inspection to take a stroll around the deck, Giolanth dear."

Rekaré took Sesenth's gloved hand and tucked into the crook of her elbow. "I am sorry that the inspectors were so harsh with you, beloved." She patted Sesenth's hand, the only public affection that Giolanth and Estarel commonly showed for each other. "It makes for a challenging time for your first Progress. I wish it had not been so."

Something else cackled in her thoughts. Was it some artifact of Chatain's presence, now that she was on mainland Daran? Betsona had insisted they stay in character even when by themselves on the ship. Now Rekaré was grateful for the practice. It was harder to present as a Darani lord than she had thought. Most difficult were their overnight stays when custom demanded that she linger in the common room to drink and game with the other lords traveling to Adalane for the Festival, while Betsona and Sesenth retreated upstairs. Betsona's gentle coaching had been a help, that and the general lack of knowledge about the Ourigny Islands on the mainland.

On the other hand, by now she knew to bristle and snap at the inspectors like any other Darani noble when they got too familiar with Sesenth. These last ones had retreated in the face of her annoyance.

They made their passage around the deck. Sesenth's presence fed Rekaré more strength, and the *something else* retreated to a dim mutter at the back of her thoughts. Maintaining the glamor over the daranvelii had been an especial challenge this morning. Normally Basnen's own magic was sufficient, but today's inspection had pushed their limits. She had needed to supplement Basnen's shielding.

Maybe that was why she ached so badly, why her head throbbed. Not a mysterious other presence that wasn't *benghaalph*—though *benghaalph* lurked close beneath the surface.

"Do you think the searches will be as bad when we land in Adalane tonight?" Sesenth maintained the breathless, fretful tone that Estarel had taught her.

"Oh dearest. It may be worse, since we are arriving at the Festival."

She hoped not, but was prepared for anything. At least the number of ships that were also on the river with them meant that the inspections could not take too long without creating a backlog of annoyed Darani nobles. Rekaré paused them in the *Morning Star*'s bow so they could look upriver.

"And perhaps not." She waved at the line of ships ahead of them, a line that had grown longer with each day they had been on the river. "Look at all those ahead of us! And there's as many if not more behind. Who knows how many more impatient ones will pass us before we reach Adalane?"

Tomorrow night was the banquet before the Festival opening. Tomorrow night she would see Chatain in person.

"Do you think the Festival will be as grand as Betsona says?" Sesenth asked as they resumed their stroll.

A ship sidled past them, its occupants also strolling the deck. Several waved at Rekaré and Sesenth. As they waved back, Rekaré recognized them as lords that she had gamed with the last two nights.

Deomar, Kithry, and who else? Those two had stuck in her mind as also being young, impatient, and quietly commenting on Giolanth's good fortune to be traveling with Betsona. Neither appeared to be passionate supporters of Chatain, but were careful speaking openly around the others. Rekaré had earned their confidence—easy enough to do after paying for a few drinks the first night and saying just the right things to lull any suspicions not soothed by her traveling with Betsona.

Both came from lands further north, along the Daraelen River on the other side of the mountains. Deomar's family—the Tiramarn—owned a vineyard, and he muttered about two years of poor production. Apparently they had appealed to Chatain for a blessing, but been dismissed. Kithry's family—the Winast—raised horses, but their bloodlines had been severely depleted due to Chatain's tribute demands for some of their best producing bloodstock.

Rekaré as Giolanth had been able to join in the complaints, thanks to Giolanth talking her through the complexities of the sugar cane and rubber crops his family cultivated.

Young nobles not happy with the current regime.

Was that why Chatain was so persistent about annexing Medvara—and perhaps more of Varen? Was he looking for an escape? Or just a place to send contentious nobles, as Etikar had done with her ancestor Alexran?

They are but part of the story, she reminded herself as her aches throbbed through her again. There were enough nobles—primarily cronies of Chatain who had been raised from the merchant class to nobility—who were equally satisfied with the state of affairs. Kithry and Deomar's caution in speaking their grievances testified to that.

"Kithry and Deomar seem to think so," she said to Sesenth. "They've been to more Festivals than we have. I hope they're right."

"Look! Betsona comes out for the sun," Sesenth said, tugging gently to lead them to where Seijina had settled Betsona on a chair provided by one of the sailors. Hovering over Betsona was behavior that would be expected from Giolanth and Estarel.

Rekaré helped Sesenth sit in another chair near Betsona, glad that she didn't have to cope with the complex garments that Senth did.

"How do you fare today, lady Betsona?" she said in Giolanth's concerned, affected drawl.

Without Sesenth's hand in her arm to lend her strength, she felt the fatigue from the use of magic during the morning's inspection. But Giolanth would not lean against the railing, nor would he sit in the presence of Betsona without being invited. So no matter how tired and achy she was, she still needed to stand.

Betsona smiled as she closed her eyes and turned her face to the sun. "I am grateful to be off of the ocean, and nearly at the end of our travels. The *Morning Star* is a lovely ship, but all the same, it is a ship and we are on water." She traced a cloaking spell. "I have invited your new friends Deomar and Kithry to stay with us," she said after it settled. "They will provide us with good cover before tomorrow night's banquet."

Rekaré frowned. She had hoped for private time so that she could shed Giolanth's façade. Maintaining it took a lot of energy.

"Much as I enjoy their company, I worry that the extra commotion will add to Estarel's distress."

Betsona waved off her complaint. "They will be staying in my house's guest wing, not in ours. Estarel need not see them except at meals." She rubbed her fingers together, and Rekaré felt the cloaking spell weigh heavier. It didn't seem to ease her aches. "Rekaré, they will be useful once we go to the banquet. They are part of my network. I had hoped that you would connect with them on the trip upriver. I was very glad when you found them."

"I see."

"Deomar and Kithry can teach you the men's Festival procedures that I do not know."

"So we will disclose ourselves to them?" Maybe she could drop her façade as Giolanth for a little bit after all.

"They are trustworthy. More than that, you will need their

assistance as seconds before the Challenge. Such would be expected, and they need to know who you really are."

"You couldn't tell me that they were my potential seconds before now?"

"I did not know if you would be able to meet them until tonight," Betsona said. "The timing of river traffic and the limitations of my communication networks…" she shrugged. "And I dared not work this spell to allow us to talk until we were past that last checkpoint."

"So do they know who I am?"

"No. I dared not trust such information to messages. I told them that Giolanth would be my champion, but that we could not discuss it until we were safely in my Adalane house. They volunteered to be your seconds."

That certainly put another aspect on her evenings with those two.

"They're very good at hiding their intent. I'm assuming they meant to connect with me if possible?"

"I directed them to do so, yes."

"They're good at keeping secrets, then," Rekaré conceded. "I had no idea."

"They are some of my best agents." Betsona sighed as another ship passed them. "Enough! We dare not cloak for too long should we attract unwanted attention. Those families—" she jerked her head toward the ship that had just passed them. "—are among Chatain's strongest supporters, and there are magicians amongst them." She snapped her fingers and the cloaking spell faded.

"It should make for an interesting evening," Rekaré said in Giolanth's slow drawl.

"That it should," Betsona said. She raised one hand. "Giolanth, dear. Now that I'm out on the deck I feel a small chill from the wind. Much as I would prefer to remain in the sun, I fear the difference in warmth between Adalane and the Islands could lead to an illness, which we don't want during Festival. Estarel, would you begrudge sharing your beloved's arms?"

"Not at all," Sesenth said, smoothing her skirts.

Rekaré helped Betsona up, then Sesenth. They made their careful way below decks, Betsona to her cabin, Sesenth to the one they shared.

Rekaré sighed once they were alone in their cabin. Her headache was definitely better below decks, away from the sun's glare on water, though the whole body aches persisted.

"I would prefer to stay here, but...." She let her voice trail off.

"You must be seen, Giolanth," Sesenth said. She took Rekaré's head in her hands and kissed her forehead. Just that gentle touch further eased the pounding in her head. "I am grateful that you desire to spend this time with me—but you must be seen."

"Thank you, dear heart." Rekaré straightened up, steeling herself for the return above decks.

Gods, she hoped all was well with both Witmara and Katerin. Her hands tightened into fists as she once again took her position on the rail.

I am coming for you, Chatain. Do you feel me yet? I feel you.

Perhaps her awareness of Chatain was the cause of her aches. She could only hope that she was inflicting the same sort of suffering on him.

"Lady Betsona! We are pleased to see you back!" Tenthras, the majordomo of Betsona's Adalane house, stood by her mechanical wheelchair as she wavered on her canes.

Betsona inhaled deeply before she answered Tenthras, closing her eyes and savoring the crisp sweet scent of the early-blossoming dandybush. Its exquisite tiny yellow-edged pink flowers smelled sweetest right at dusk. Gods, she had missed dandybush. The Islands were too hot and wet for it. Another breath, and more dandybush scent.

Home.

Her real home, unlike the houses in Daraelen and Lanivar.

Home.

She sighed and opened her eyes. There were still things to do before she could indulge herself in memory and the joy of being home.

I never want to leave it again.

"I am glad to be home in Adalane, Tenthras." She eyed the wheelchair, and clucked a command to it. The chair rolled forward, and she sighed with relief as Seijina helped her collapse into its familiar contours, her body fitting into the comfortable and *just right* padding. Her chair on the Islands didn't fit like this. "I bring the guests I had written about."

Tenthras bowed low. "Welcome to you, Giolanth and Estarel."

Rekaré bowed to just the right depth in response—Gods, it had taken too long under decks to pound into that stubborn woman's head that Varen's egalitarian notions did not work for Daran.

"And welcome to you as well."

"Our other guests should be arriving soon." Betsona tapped the starting sequence on the wheelchair's right arm. "They paused to purchase some items for their ladies for Festival."

"The guest wing is prepared for them," Tenthras said.

Betsona steeled herself for more contact as her chair glided toward the row of servants waiting to greet her. Tired and achy as she was after spending several days on water—the Varenese term *waterstruck* was a perfect description of the magician experience on water—she wanted nothing more than to retreat to her own suite and soak in a tub of warm water. But this greeting routine not only endeared her to her people, it allowed her to discern who might be one of Chatain's spies—or another foe seeking power in the Courts.

Just because you own them does not mean you are beloved, she reminded herself, as she always did when she greeted her staff after an absence. More than Daraelen, Adalane would be the likely place for Chatain to insert spies into her household. He knew how much she loved it here. Was probably gambling on her love of the place to be less watchful. This was not a process she could skip.

Most of the faces were familiar. She maintained this house at full staffing, hoping that someday she would be allowed to return. During Festivals, she rented it to Island nobility and close friends from Daraelen who did not have their own places in Adalane. Sometimes that included performers.

Just another way to earn more favor amongst her people, even when she could not be there. But she missed those days when the house was busy with a mix of performers and nobility, pulsing with the energy of actors and musicians and poets. Rehearsals and performances and practices, the occasional scandalized noble reaction at the habits of the creatives, and above all the excitement of the unexpected that could occur at any moment.

Perhaps that can happen again under Witmara.

She'd dared not invite any more visitors than Deomar and Kithry this time, much as she wanted to feel that surge and flow of creative energy through this house. There was too much at stake, and Rekaré's growing tension worried her. Anticipation of facing Chatain? Worry about Witmara? Whatever it was, the woman was getting even more prickly.

Tenthras, followed by his assistant Althen, led her down the line of servants. Betsona took each servant's hands after they bowed to her, sampling their auras and confirming their loyalty as she introduced each one to Rekaré and Sesenth before dismissing them. With limited exceptions, she did not tolerate any whiff of magic amongst her people. Fortunately, most of her staff were old and familiar—but even then, she had been gone for two years. Much could happen to devoted servants in that time. Once they reached the newer servants, Tenthras introduced her to each one and told her their specialties.

Betsona sensed Rekaré's growing impatience as she took the time to speak with each new servant before dismissing them to their duties. Rekaré had wanted to settle her daranval and her riders during the greetings, but Giolanth would not have put his horse first and would have understood why Betsona, as a magician of her stature, needed to check the people she owned to see if they remained true to her. But then, he didn't have the ties to his mounts that Rekaré had with her mare.

As they reached the end of the line, Betsona slowed down even more, appraising these newcomers. Several women, skin almost the same shade of gold as hers, were at the very end. She frowned.

That's new.

Few of the Ternarese women given in tribute to Chatain and his followers ever left Daraelen, and most possessed some magic. She would need to check them carefully. She paused.

"Tenthras," she said quietly. "Why do we have Ternarese on staff? You know how I feel about magicians around me. Especially my mother's people."

"None of these slaves have magic," Tenthras reassured her. "Of that I am certain. They came certified from the auction as non-magical, and all three are excellent staff. They can all serve as bedwarmers as well as chambermaids and washwomen. One is a reasonably skilled healer."

Chambermaids and washwomen—and gods only knew, the Ternarese were held to be the best bedwarmers. And one with healing skills.

Nonetheless, she hadn't allowed her mother's people to serve as slaves in her house before. Magic rested too easily upon them, and it would take a sorcerer of her skill to detect a cloaked Ternarese magician. Even if they were certified by an auction, she still wanted to check.

Better yet, she wanted to send them back. Now.

"Were there no others to be had?" she asked. "You know how I feel about enslaving my mother's people."

Tenthras coughed uneasily. "My lady, there's been a flood of Ternarese women on the market of late. It's difficult to purchase any non-Ternarese who can be discreet, work well, and stay healthy. I've had to sell on too many non-Ternarese this past two years because of health or inefficiency."

Since I was exiled.

"I see." That was a major change in the slave market. She wondered what that meant.

What is Chatain up to?

Perhaps that was one reason he was looking to expand the Empire overseas—a dearth of non-Darani to enslave. From what she could tell, most of the Varenese were dark-skinned and easily identifiable, as opposed to the lower-class Darani. Hadn't the possibility of a potential new slave source been why Etikar had exiled Alexran to Varen and started this whole mess? And Alexran's rebellion had removed Varen as a potential source of slaves?

What is going on?

She'd been too isolated on the Islands to notice these trends. Two years didn't seem like enough time for this kind of change to happen.

And yet it had.

"Lady, you need to finish this," Seijina whispered in her ear, interrupting her brooding. "Let these people go back to work."

"Yes. Just—thinking about these last three. Tenthras, I'm not sure I want to keep them on."

He shrugged. "It is a problem that we will need to learn to deal with, my lady. Markets."

"I—see." Well, after the Challenge she needed to look into this situation further. Hopefully Witmara or Rekaré would dispose of Chatain, and she would be able to stay here and straighten things out afterward.

But for now, her distant kin awaited her approval.

A strange reluctance flooded through Betsona as she approached the three women still standing in line.

"Kinswoman," she greeted the first Ternar woman in Ternarese. Her skin was a lighter gold than Betsona's. "Your name?"

Distress crossed the woman's face. She made a strangled noise.

"We call her Kara," Tenthras said. He hesitated. "Her tongue has been taken. She is a chambermaid and bedwarmer, with nursing experience."

Rekaré and Sesenth tensed as they stood by her. Rekaré frowned, staring at Kara.

"What happened to her tongue?" Rekaré asked.

Tenthras raised his hands. "I do not know. I was not able to trace her provenance completely, as she has gone through several owners. I have been able to determine that the change in ownership is not her fault. I have assigned her to Giolanth and Estarel's quarters."

"We will be just fine," Rekaré said sharply, her accent slipping for just a moment. "We would prefer our own people to serve us." Her lips tightened as she glared at Tenthras.

"What happened with her previous owners?" Betsona asked, before Rekaré could say more. *Something* about Kara clearly bothered Rekaré. The lack of a tongue? Her previous employment—or her role as bedwarmer?

"The two most recent owners were elderly, and used her as bedwarmer and nurse. Lord Nofarth, of the Meneth, and Lord Dunet, of the Wiltenils. Both men were in failing health."

Nofarth and Dunet. Powerful opponents of Chatain, despite their advanced age. Were their deaths accidental?

"Did one of them remove her tongue?"

Tenthras shook his head. "I do not know. I can confirm it was gone when she left Lord Nofarth's service, at his death." He leaned closer. "We got an excellent price on her because of her history, Lady Betsona. And there was simply not much choice in the market when these three became available—I bought them as a package."

So why had her tongue been cut out? To keep her silent about things she had seen—or done—in Nofarth's house? Suspicious that she had served both Nofarth and Dunet before their deaths.

Am I to be her third victim? Or Rekaré?

"What caused Nofarth and Dunet's deaths?" she asked sharply.

Rekaré remained on alert, studying the woman. She bent to whisper to Betsona. "She possesses magic. You should be careful of her."

Betsona nodded to acknowledge Rekaré's comment.

"They both died in their sleep, of natural causes," Tenthras said.

"I see." Betsona reached out to take Kara's hands. Kara backed away, shaking her head. Tenthras growled and reached for her. Kara backed away faster. The other Ternarese women blocked his path.

"I will see you punished!" Tenthras snapped. He shoved aside the other women and grabbed Kara's arms.

One of the women pulled a dagger out of her sleeve and stabbed him in the back. He screamed and clung to Kara as he sank to his knees. Kara tried to pull away but Tenthras held her tight, even as he gasped for breath. The stabber yanked her dagger free and impaled him again. The third woman grabbed

Kara by the shoulders, trying to pull her away from Tenthras's grasp.

Before anyone else could react, Rekaré drew her sword. She beheaded the woman who stabbed Tenthras with a surprising strength, and clubbed the woman trying to free Kara with the sword's hilt, kicking her away from Kara as she collapsed. Sesenth seized Kara in a most un-Estarel-like move, holding Kara's upper arms tight. Rekaré stood there, her sword glowing a faint magenta shade, features oddly different as she glared at Kara.

"Give me one reason why I shouldn't finish all of them," she growled, her voice unfamiliar. *Something different* looked out of her eyes and made Betsona shudder.

Rekaré Kinslayer.

Oh, now she *understood.* Rekaré wrestled with her Kinslayer side as they drew closer to Chatain.

"We need to know why she attacked Tenthras," Sesenth said, tone mild and soothing. "Dearest. You have dealt with the immediate issue. Easy."

Rekaré blew hard, panting slightly. Then tension seemed to evaporate from her, making her seem smaller.

"You are right, dear one," she said, wiping the blood off of her sword and sheathing it.

Detaluna rode up with five of the Mer Galad, jumping off of her daranval.

"Bind them," Rekaré growled, somehow still managing to sound like Giolanth in the midst of the chaos, though what stared out of her eyes was anything but Giolanth. "Estarel, my beloved, thank you. Our private practice sessions have been useful."

Quick thinking and a good explanation for Sesenth's action. Still, not something a Darani noblewoman would do. Even from the Islands. It is a good thing that most of the staff have gone about their work. I'm not sure I want Althen to know about Rekaré just yet.

"I am very glad that you had us practice," Sesenth said as she backed away while the others seized Kara. "I did not believe you when you said it might be necessary in Adalane. I thought this place was more civilized."

Seijina knelt by Tenthras as Kara was dragged away. She ripped part of her underskirt free and used it to staunch the flow of blood as Tenthras moaned.

"What shall we do with the survivors?" Detaluna asked.

"Question this one." Rekaré gestured toward the stabber. "I will take care of this one." She pointed at Kara. "Take her inside to our quarters—Betsona, who can guide them?"

"I will," said Althen. He swallowed hard as he looked down at Tenthras. "Will he survive?"

"I will do my best to save him," Seijina said. "But it's unlikely with a gut injury, even with magic."

Betsona hesitated, torn between staying with Tenthras and following Rekaré inside to see just what she intended to do with the tongueless woman. Seijina looked up, as always seeming to sense her dilemma.

"Go with Giolanth," she said quietly. "His anger is roused, and Estarel may not be able to restrain him. After all, what information can he get from one whose speech is taken away? Your sorcery may be able to help. I will deal with Tenthras and the aftermath." She nodded at the dead woman who had stabbed him.

Their eyes met. *Rekaré Kinslayer* could pull that knowledge as quickly if not faster from Kara than Betsona could. But Giolanth—no. If "Giolanth" went off by himself with a woman who could not speak, that would certainly raise questions as to just how "Giolanth" could manage to question her.

"Giolanth, would you like my assistance? Since Kara is part of my household, I think it would be best if I were present. I apologize for this inconvenience."

"Such problems go along with maintaining several households," Rekaré growled. "I apologize for killing one of your household. As always, I am even more in your debt, dear Betsona." The sharp edge in her voice was almost enough to break the façade of Giolanth. Almost.

"Such a thing should not happen." Betsona cued the wheelchair to follow along with Rekaré and Sesenth. Two of the riders yanked Kara along while Detaluna and the other two bound the other woman. Kara struggled against their restraints until one of the riders slapped her. "I apologize for my breach of hospitality. Should Tenthras survive, he will answer to me for this incident."

She wanted to linger in the Great Hall as they entered, have a moment of welcome back to her favorite home, but it was clearly not meant to be. Instead, they climbed the stairs, her wheelchair spluttering and shooting out fumes as an oil-fired engine took over from the magic that motived it.

Needs maintenance. It's been too long since I was here. What else is not up to my usual standards?

Rekaré raised a brow as the chair chugged up the stairs beside her, but said nothing.

Althen opened the double doors to the family wing.

"I can take over from here," Betsona said, switching off the stinky engine and back to magical power. Even that short climb using the engine had given it time to recharge. "Return to Tenthras and Seijina, Althen."

He bowed and left. Betsona led them down the hallway, past her suite to the library. "This should work for questioning."

Rekaré glanced around the room. "Good." She selected one of the tall-backed, heavy wood chairs by a desk and easily spun it around. "Put her there. Restrain her."

The riders dragged Kara to the chair and tied her to it.

Sesenth said something in Varenese to the riders. Betsona didn't know exactly what she had said, but she had heard the language enough to understand some of the key words. The man argued back, clearly objecting to leaving them alone, until Rekaré cut him off with a sharp retort and order to leave. The Mer Galad riders retreated, leaving Rekaré, Betsona, and Sesenth with Kara.

A cold chill of uneasiness crawled through Betsona's gut as Sesenth stripped off her veils, revealing gray-scaled brown skin. Kara cringed away as Sesenth stalked toward the chair, pulling off her gloves to reveal hands that were all scales, no skin. Sesenth bared sharp teeth at Kara, sharper than Betsona had realized.

"Are we ready, my dear?" she asked Rekaré.

What did they intend to do? The casual way that Rekaré struck down Tenthras's attacker made Betsona nervous. A good feature in her Champion—but gods, she hadn't realized the woman was so ruthless.

That's why she is called Rekaré Kinslayer.

And yet there was something else about her. Something—which God or Goddess did Rekaré serve? It almost felt like she stood next to one of them, but Betsona didn't recognize this as the manifestation of any God she knew.

Rekaré strode across the room and took Kara's chin in her left hand.

"And so, here you are," she said in her normal voice, not Giolanth's slightly deeper tones. "So far, it has been convenient that you cannot speak. I am certain you believe that will keep your secrets safe." She leaned in closer, until she was a hand's width away from Kara's face. *"And you would be wrong,"* she snarled in a tone that made Betsona's gut clench in sympathy as Kara shuddered.

Kara's eyes widened even further. She made grunting and squealing sounds as she tried to push herself further against the chair to escape Rekaré's grip.

"What do you intend to do?" Betsona asked.

Rekaré straightened up. Kara trembled as Rekaré bared her

teeth in a predatory smile colder than anything Betsona had seen on Chatain's face, even during his most intense rages.

Gods, she is *a Miteal.*

"Why, I fully intend to make her speak, in spite of her lack of a tongue."

Kara blanched, whimpering.

"How? I have means to gather that information, but it would be hard on her."

"*Benghaalph* can do it." Rekaré eyed Kara. "It may not leave her with much of a mind, but then again, given the fate of her past two employers, I seriously doubt you have many concerns about that."

"Nofarth and Dunet had a history of opposing Chatain in the Council."

"I thought that might be the case."

"Do you need assistance?"

"Thank you, but all I need is Senth's help. I will summon *benghaalph* to speak for Kara and I require protection from someone who is familiar with how *benghaalph* manifests. That is, if you are able to do it, Senth."

Sesenth snorted from the chair where she was unlacing her boots. She yanked them off. "A moment while I get rid of some of this cursed clothing."

As she pulled off her socks, Betsona saw the cloven feet, unable to stifle a shudder at how alien they seemed.

What is this woman?

Sesenth stripped off her outer clothing as best as she could without help. Then she crossed the room to rest her hands on Rekaré's back. "I am ready."

"Translate for Betsona's sake. I will try not to manifest a simulacrum to speak unless I have to." Rekaré bent back over Kara. Silver and magenta light shimmered over her, Rekaré's body tightening. She spoke harshly to Kara in a language that was *not* Varenese, full of sibilants and growls.

"She asks Kara if she was supposed to kill you like she had Nofarth and Dunet."

Squawking noises in response. Betsona's hands twitched on her wheelchair arms. The woman was clearly resisting, despite the clear note of compulsion in Rekaré's words. *She* didn't know if she could resist if Rekaré spoke to her like this.

Rekaré repeated the question. Kara spat at Rekaré. Rekaré wiped off the spittle, growling something else.

"Enough is enough. She will make Kara cooperate," Sesenth said as Rekaré released Kara's chin and *reached* deep inside of her chest.

The woman screamed. Her eyes widened even further. Then Kara sagged against her restraints while Rekaré pulled a miniature Kara from her abdomen. Rekaré straightened up and held the squirming miniature high, clenched tightly in her left fist.

"You have killed," Rekaré growled. Betsona blinked, surprised, as she suddenly understood what Rekaré said.

"You have no proof!" Miniature Kara shrieked.

Rekaré shook her. To Betsona's shock Kara flailed in the chair, as if it were actually her and not a simulacrum in Rekaré's fist.

"How did you kill Nofarth and Dunet?"

Miniature Kara stuck her tongue out at Rekaré, scars clearly visible on her tongue.

Rekaré placed her right thumb and index finger on the simulacrum's chin and forehead. She spoke a single word, and both Karas convulsed. Rekaré lifted her hand as both Karas gasped for breath.

"Now," her voice low and menacing. *"Who is your real master? How did you kill Nofarth and Dunet? Who is your target in this household?"*

It took several more treatments before the simulacrum began to talk, a gabbling stream of words spewing frantically from her.

"Chatain needed absolute silence. I offered my voice to him. He took it but not my tongue. Nofarth took my tongue when I would not speak under interrogation. He suspected that I was spying on him. Then he caught me in a projection to Chatain. Chatain struck him down for that. When I went up for auction Chatain made sure that I was attractive to Dunet. I poisoned Dunet slowly."

"Who is your target in this household?"

"Betsona's champion Giolanth."

The questioning continued, until the simulacrum faded out of Rekaré's hand. Kara slumped in the chair, eyes wide and staring sightlessly at the ceiling, not breathing. Rekaré collapsed to the floor.

Sesenth looked at Betsona. "That is all we will be able to get out of this one."

Rekaré groaned. "I did not want to do that. Gods. I will be good for nothing but sleep. So much to be done. I—am sorry. I sensed that Tenthras may be compromised, but I could not get the details out of her. I wish I could have—Betsona, I am sorry."

"You could not have pushed further?"

Rekaré buried her head in her arms, unresponsive.

Sesenth gathered Rekaré up from the floor, hugging her hard as Rekaré slumped against her. "Beloved. You did well." She kissed Rekaré's forehead, then glared challengingly at Betsona. "She will need quiet, food, and sleep. Can't you see how much this has taken from her? This is more than being waterstruck. This piece of filth drained Rekaré and drug her along as she died. Rekaré is spellsick. Not even *benghaalph* could protect her."

"I—" Betsona began, but Sesenth waved her off.

"Rekaré's done *enough* for now, especially after being on water for so many days!" She rose to a squat. "Come on, dearest. Let's get you to bed before the spellsickness gets worse." Rekaré groaned. Sesenth gently shook her.

Rekaré mumbled something, but managed to gather her feet under herself, and stagger up with Sesenth's help.

Sesenth fixed Betsona with a steady gaze. "Show us to our rooms," she said, her commanding tone brooking no argument.

Betsona obeyed the firm pitch in Sesenth's voice, suddenly aware that there was more to this woman than just being Rekaré's shadow.

And Tenthras may be compromised.

That information must have been buried deep in Kara's memories.

If Tenthras is compromised, then what about Althen?

Betsona sighed. That would be for her to figure out. Clearly Rekaré would not be in any shape to question him before the Challenge.

I hope this didn't interfere with her ability to handle the Challenge.

Otherwise, she would be dependent on Witmara arriving on time. Ever since Chatain had demanded her return to Adalane, she hadn't received any messages from Petronin. That worried Betsona.

Gods. Gods. I burn.

Rekaré staggered down the hallway, Sesenth's steady support the only thing keeping her from bouncing against the walls. Her head pounded worse than ever and it seemed as if waves of heat and cold crashed over her. A burning, scorching scent filled her nose but her blurred vision didn't show any smoke in the hallway.

This wasn't all *benghaalph*. This was the *something else* that had kept poking at her since they arrived in Lanivar. More worrisome, this wasn't just the Kinslayer, either.

At last they stopped.

"Just a few steps more and we're in our rooms," Senth said, her voice soothing. "Come on."

"I—I don't know if I can make it past the doorway," Rekaré gasped.

Gods. Or was this the result of the magic she'd just performed? Gods. What she had done to that woman? Killer though she was—what Rekaré had seen in her mind should have justified her actions.

And yet. Kara had been enslaved. Willingly, as part of something Rekaré couldn't quite see in her thoughts—a tribute to Chatain. And Kara had gone along with his schemes.

But Kara was still a slave, not her own person. She had ripped Kara's mind apart as if it were nothing. In return, Kara had hooked her hard enough to drag her to death's door. While she might be able to blame what she had done to Kara on that *something* that had flooded through her, pushing her harder and farther than she would have gone on her own—the reality was that she had gone too far in shredding Kara's thoughts, trying to trace down that one little piece about Tenthras being compromised, for Betsona's sake.

Gods.

Rekaré's knees buckled and she collapsed on the carpet, gasping, fighting back sour bile as her stomach tightened. Spellsickness. She'd only encountered this a couple of times before.

This was not the sort of magic I should have performed. I know better. I thought I knew better.

Heat. Cold. Heat. Cold.

Quick steps. Cold cloth on her forehead. Then Sesenth's arms lifting her up, holding a cup to her lips. Sweet over bitter taste as the syrupy liquid poured over her tongue—MagicEase, a potion known to Shadowwalkers for spellsickness. Reluctant swallows.

It burns it burns it burns.

But the MagicEase soothed the burning, snuffing it out slowly, like a heavy snowfall would do to a stubborn forest fire.

It still hurt, aches lashing throughout her body. Oh Gods, this was worse than anything she'd gone through before.

Dovré, Dovré, what have I done?

Rekaré silently implored the Goddess as she leaned against Sesenth and closed her eyes, not expecting much of a response in this land of Daran. Had she finally gone too far?

A different gentle touch on her forehead, something that was not Sesenth. A soothing, healing, warmth that finally eased her pain.

You fell into her trap,

her mother's voice whispered. Rekaré's eyes shot wide open and she stared at the translucent form that stood above her and Sesenth.

M-mother? How can this be?

Alicira ea Miteal smiled gently at Rekaré, her shadowy form that of her younger self and not the pain-wracked shell she had been at her death.

I am Dovré's Speaker,

her mother said.

I do not normally have permission to reach for you—too many threads depend on you being independent of the Goddess. But in this situation, she granted my pleas to comfort you and help ease your pain. So much is at stake and you need to recover more quickly than you would otherwise.

Her hand stroked Rekaré's forehead. Rekaré closed her eyes again, instinctively wanting to reach for her mother. But she knew better—she would not feel anything substantial, and might even compromise this visit.

I wish I knew—something was pushing me. I would have pulled back sooner otherwise. It's not benghaalph. Do you know what's haunting me?

That I cannot tell you, daughter, much as I wish I could. I am forbidden to speak of the whole. But the part I can tell you—Kara baited you to act in this manner. That woman had many compulsions placed on her, and sought death when you defeated her will. She also saw a means to harm the one who would force that information out of her so aggressively. It will take you several days to recover fully, even with my help.

So I have failed in my goal to overthrow Chatain, through my own stupidity.

You will still be able to match Chatain. However, it will be more difficult, and you will pay a price that you might not have needed to pay otherwise. Oh my daughter, can't you ever do anything the easy way?

It appears not.

From somewhere she found the strength to sit up and study Alicira further. Gods, it was good to see her mother at a normal weight, eyes bright and not dull from fighting pain and sickness, movements free and easy.

> I give thanks to the Goddess for allowing me to see you, Mother. Especially like this and not as you were as the end.

Her mother kissed Rekaré's brow.

> I cannot linger. I can only grant you the gift of a good night's sleep without pain to build your reserves. A mother's indulgence that the Goddess was willing to allow. Sleep well, my dear.

> Mother—

Sleep already pulled at her, drowsiness a welcome relief from the agony.

> Will I see you again?

> Not in this life, my dear. Too much is at stake.

Her mother kissed Rekaré's forehead again, then faded away.

"Who was that?" Sesenth asked.

"You saw her too?" A huge yawn cut off anything further Rekaré might say.

"I saw a shadow of a beautiful woman—Aireii, who looked a little like you."

"It was my mother," Rekaré said sleepily. "And she wants me to rest. Sleep."

"That sounds good. Can you get up now?"

Rekaré struggled to her feet. "She's Dovré's Speaker now," she said as Sesenth guided her to the bedroom.

She collapsed on the bed, and fell over sideways when trying to wrench off her boots.

My mother is Dovré's Speaker.

She wanted to think on that but her thoughts were sluggish, sleepy.

A wry smile spread across her lips. She recognized this spell. Her mother had used it during her childhood when Rekaré had overstrained herself during magical training. It was familiar. Reassuring. And, much though a part of her wanted to fight against it, to do what was necessary to help fight this incursion into Betsona's household, she just didn't have the strength to continue resisting.

Sesenth helped her undress and put on a nightgown. Rekaré crawled deep into the covers, pulling them tight around her neck.

"Good night," Sesenth whispered, and gave her a kiss before leaving the room. There was still a sense of another presence in the room—thankfully not that *something else* that had been nagging her. Rekaré half-opened her eyes, and thought she spotted a shadowy presence standing guard over the bed.

But she could not determine if it was her mother or the Goddess who stood watch.

PANCAKES AND PROBLEMS

THE FIRST LIGHT OF DAWN ROUSED WITMARA FROM DREAMS OF Chatain pursuing her, memories colder than the damp fog that surrounded their camp. Her hands clenched tightly as she stared at the pines above the bedroll she shared with Toran. Tonight, they would reach Adalane. The day after tomorrow was the Festival opening and the Challenge to Chatain. Far too tight a schedule for her comfort, but it couldn't be helped.

Once the word had spread about her actions at Marinset, the villages along their route had come out to greet Witmara. Some stared and turned away, but many pushed close, longing for reassuring words and promises of *change* from this exotic potential leader. Others wanted to follow them to Adalane and it had taken fast talk and hard riding to discourage them from joining her entourage. Witmara encouraged them to travel to Adalane on their own, by more direct routes.

The more supporters the better.

At least this part of Daran wanted Chatain to be gone. She'd heard enough tales about the extremes of too much attention from the throne for small infractions to insufficient concern about genuine threats from Ternarese raiders to think this was a minority opinion.

Gods. It was so close now. The day after tomorrow she would either become Empress—or fall. Witmara shivered, wanting to wake Toran just to feel his arms around her.

Now that the actual moment of challenging Chatain was almost here, she had doubts.

Could she rule this nation? Daran had so many more problems than Medvara. It would be a life's work to make things right in Daran again.

Could she do it? Or would she fail?

Daro roused, sending her reassuring thoughts. He would not let her fail. Not when she rode a king amongst daranvelii. She would not falter.

She returned wordless thanks to him, imagining scratching his favorite spot under his forelock.

He gave her a friendly nuzzle in return, followed by a wistful thought about *grain* and *cookies*.

Daro's thoughts of food made her stomach grumble. Light, fluffy pancakes sounded very good, and making them herself was just the thing to settle her nerves. Did they have the makings? They had picked up supplies in Keronin, the village they'd passed through midday yesterday. While Chaye had been stashing food in the panniers, hadn't she seen flour and a small crock of starter amongst the foodstuffs?

It was definitely worth checking, and if not, Witmara still thought she could concoct good pancakes without starter. She slipped into her clothing carefully, not wanting to wake Toran after his early morning watch, and kissed his forehead. He murmured and rolled over as she crawled out of the bedroll, doing her best not to let cold air waft in where she had been.

Witmara sat on the fallen log next to their bedroll and eased on her cold-stiffened boots, intent now on *pancakes*. After slipping off in the woods to relieve herself, then pausing by the creek to wash her hands, she approached the tiny fire. Petronin rose.

"Is something wrong, my lady?"

"I'm hungry, so I'm going to start breakfast."

His brows shot up, startled. "I can wake Chaye to cook."

"I'm fine. Let her sleep."

She didn't need a servant to fix *breakfast*. And this morning, she wanted to be treated as something other than the future Empress. Something to center herself.

Petronin frowned in clear disapproval of a fine lady doing her own work as she dug in the panniers for the big iron frying pan and cooking grease. But he stirred up the fire just enough for cooking, raking the hottest coals into the corners of the fire ring where there were flat rocks that would support her pan.

She paused from her search. "Thank you, Petronin."

He nodded, focusing on the coals.

Once she found the pan and the grease, she set the pan on the rocks to warm, then dropped a dollop of grease to melt in it. While that happened, she returned to the packs. She found the small crock. As she had hoped, the faintly sour scent of starter rose from the bubbling liquid. She poured a small amount into a wooden bowl, added flour and water, and mixed it up. The batter gurgled, just like it would back home in Varen.

How long had it been since she had made pancakes while traveling?

Too long, she decided, her lips tightening. And once she became Empress....

No. Don't think about that now.

She was doing this to distract herself from those worries.

Witmara sprinkled a tiny drop of water in the melted grease. It splattered, telling her it was hot enough to cook the pancakes. She delicately spooned palm-sized batter dollops into the pan.

They bubbled and firmed, her mouth watering as the delicate odor rose. She flipped the pancakes, letting them cook briefly before putting them on the plate and handing it to Petronin, sneaking one for herself before beginning the next batch.

His brows rose as he took a bite. "These are *good*, my lady. Better even than Chaye's."

She smiled at the praise as she gobbled her own pancake. She had not lost her touch.

Chaye started up from her bedroll near the fire. "My lady, you don't need to do that!"

"But I am. Get dressed, and you can cook that ham we got at Keronin."

Chaye dressed in her bedroll, then went off to the woods. On her return, she pulled the ham out of the panniers and another pan, placing it in the other cooking corner. She cut generous slabs of ham into that pan.

They cooked silently together, the other riders rousing at the smell of pancakes and ham, rising and going off to feed the horses and other camp chores. The wisps of Witmara's dream about Chatain slowly faded as she cooked. Her stomach settled and she thought she could face this day.

"There you are." Toran's hands rested gently on her shoulders, and he kissed her forehead. "Smells good."

She grunted at him and he laughed.

The riders gathered round, plates in hand. But they did not serve themselves, not even Toran's men. At last, exasperated, she brushed a strand of hair out of her face and glared at them.

"Serve yourselves before food gets cold!" she snapped. "Haven't you seen a woman cook before?"

"Not—not one of your stature," Tiernin ventured.

She waved the spatula at him. "Eat! All of you!"

Toran chuckled as he returned. "You insult your lady by not eating."

"We just wanted to make sure there would be enough for her," Tiernin said.

"I'll make sure she has food." Toran stooped, and placed pancakes on two plates, along with a generous slab of ham on both. The men crowded in once he sat next to Witmara.

At last she used the last of the batter, scraping the bowl dry as best she could. Chaye took the pans and other utensils.

"I'll wash up."

"Make sure you eat first," Witmara said. "We have a long ride ahead of us today."

She rose and stretched, then took her plate from Toran. They sat on the log by their bed. Toran had already rolled and tied the bedroll, ready to be loaded on one of the pack mules.

He quirked an eyebrow at her. "What brought this on?"

Witmara shrugged. "Nerves. I woke thinking of pancakes, and for once I didn't want to be treated like an Empress."

He reached over and rubbed her shoulders. "I should have gotten up with you."

"Why? You had a late watch."

"I know you had a rough night with bad dreams. You called out several times when I was on watch."

Witmara grimaced as the memory of her dreams came trickling back. "Nervous dreams about Chatain pursuing us. I suppose it is to be expected, given we're riding into Adalane today...but it all seems so very much more than real, suddenly."

He nodded solemnly. "I feel the same way."

"Toran, am I really going to be able to rule this place?" she asked softly, keeping her voice low so that no one else heard her doubts. "There are so many problems. Things here are worse than I thought."

"I have faith in you," he said as he lifted a chunk of ham to his mouth. "And I hope you intend to involve me in your plans."

"Of course! There's just so much to think about." She stared at her remaining pancake and lump of ham. Toran had been more than generous in dishing up. Did she really want to finish it? "So many complications. So much to learn."

"The land is with you. Have you spoken to it about your worries?" He finished his pancakes. "I would think it would be first to let you know if you had overstepped. Then me."

Of course.

How could I be so foolish?

Then again, Daran tended to be silent, not constantly picking at her like Medvara did with her mother. Witmara set her plate aside and bent over to rest her palms on the ground.

Am I really going to be able to rule you?

she asked.

I feel—overwhelmed.

You are my choice,

came back to her, along with reassurance.

You will be the one to listen to my people and right their wrongs.

But—Chatain....

You will not face him alone. You have much support. You will do the right thing.

The land stroked her palms in a caress, then faded.

Witmara sat back up. "The land seems to think I can do it."

"So there you are. You have the land's support." Toran gestured toward her plate with two more pancakes. "Are you finished, or should I toss that out for the birds?"

She looked at the food, and shook her head, no longer

hungry, the pancakes sitting heavy and hard in her stomach. She pushed herself up as Toran took their plates. They had a long ride ahead of them today—and Gods only knew what else awaited them tonight and tomorrow.

Darkness cloaked Witmara and her riders as they entered the Noble's District of Adalane, on a hillside above the Fenras River. The great amphitheater where the Challenge would be held day after tomorrow was directly below the District. Witmara didn't look at the hulking structure glowing white in the moonlight.

Time enough to check it out in daylight.

They took a roundabout way to the District. Petronin brought them into Adalane through a common side gate for merchants, not the one the nobles normally used. Chaye's presence seemed to ease their way through the gate, and past the patrols within the city as she rode in the lead next to Petronin.

Witmara kept the hood of her cloak over her head, letting Toran speak for her as she observed the city around them. Adalane was much, much more busy and crowded at night than Medvare-the-city. The well-lit commercial district they rode through bustled with crowds of foot traffic, carriages, and riders. Some of the carriages moved without being drawn by horses, emitting black clouds of foul smoke as they clattered along the streets, often faster than the horses that startled as the great metal machines clanked by them.

It stinks here. Not good smells, but sour,

Daro complained as one big contraption rattled past them, flicking up his lip to express distaste at the smoke it spewed.

The daranvelii seemed to tolerate the mechanical

contrivances better than the other horses. Perhaps that was due to the faint traces of magic that emanated from the big carriages —obviously whatever created the foul-smelling smoke did not provide sufficient power to run them.

> It is part of what we have to live with if we are to rule here,

she told him.

He blew hard through his nostrils and shook his head to express his disapproval.

Witmara patted Daro on the neck for reassurance. She found the stench and noise bothersome herself. Chatain and his technologists were supposed to be good at magitech. Couldn't they find a better means of powering those carriages without so much noise and smell?

Oh well. Another thing she and Toran would need to figure out.

The smells and noise diminished as they rode up the hillside to the Noble District. The houses kept getting bigger and bigger as they rode uphill, on larger lots. At last they came to the final house on the street, the biggest of all. A long driveway led to the front of the house. Petronin took them around the back, where the stables were.

Tears she didn't expect came to Witmara's eyes as they led their mounts into the stable to find Detaluna and several of the Mer Galad riders cleaning saddles and bridles by the tack room next to the entrance.

Quiet, homely, *familiar.*

"There you are." Detaluna set aside her bridle. "At last something's gone right."

"What's happened?" Witmara's heart sank. Daro nuzzled her reassuringly and Toran rested a hand on her shoulder.

"This has been a difficult day. The river passage was crowded. Rekaré wore a man's glamor all the way here from

Lanivar. And then, when we got here—betrayal. Betsona's household has been infiltrated by Chatain's spies." Detaluna startled as Chaye joined Witmara and Toran. She pointed at Chaye. "She's one of *them*! Bind her!"

"No!" Witmara took a step forward. "She has promised herself to my service. She told us about the Ternarese spy networks."

"One of *them* killed Betsona's majordomo," Detaluna growled. "Rekaré killed the woman who stabbed him. The other two Ternarese women resisted questioning. Rekaré exhausted herself interrogating the one who could not speak. Betsona grilled the other one and then her majordomo's assistant— luckily the corruption did not extend to him. But both Betsona and Rekaré have been drained at the worst possible time before the Challenge."

"You are right. This is not a coincidence," Chaye said. "What was the name of the one who did not speak—Kara?"

"Yes. You know of her?" Detaluna tensed, her nostrils flaring wide.

"Kara was trained to be an assassin," Chaye said. "We were in the same crèche. So she is dead? *Good.* That will make our task of elevating Witmara to be Empress easier." Her lips tightened. "I feared I might have to fight Kara if she survived. She was intended to support Charis and entice Chatain."

"What do you know of these Ternarese networks?" Detaluna relaxed slightly.

"A handful of us within the networks had organized a resistance to our Mothers' goals. Ultimately the intention of our Mothers was to subvert Chatain's reign, turn the tables on our conquerors and rule Daran ourselves." Chaye bared her teeth. "But some of us find the Mothers' methods to be equally as abhorrent as anything that Chatain dreamed of doing."

Detaluna glanced at Witmara. "You trust this one?"

"She has been very helpful ever since we freed her at Marinset," Witmara said. "I would have had many more problems getting into Adalane without her presence."

"All right." Detaluna exhaled. "I'll escort you to the main house. Rooms are ready for all of you."

"I need to report to Betsona," Petronin said. "I'll go up now."

"Good luck with that," Detaluna said. "She has retired for the evening, like Rekaré."

"Is Seijina available?"

Detaluna nodded.

"Then I will speak to her." Petronin handed his horse's reins to one of his riders and left.

"Let me show you the stalls for your mounts," Detaluna said. "There's plenty of room. Tenthras may have been unfaithful to Betsona in the hiring of those three, but he kept things operating properly here." She paused. "There are two other families staying in the house, allies of Betsona who are meant to be Rekaré's seconds. Their names are Deomar and Kithry."

"Do they know about me?"

"I do not know what Betsona has said about you to them. It's been chaotic since we arrived. The infiltrators tried an attack as Betsona was greeting her servants." Detaluna wrinkled her nose. "Not servants, *slaves*. Even Betsona owns people." She spat.

Witmara nodded, too tired to react. She led Daro down the alleyway of the stable, Toran following her and Detaluna. It was a clean, well-kept barn with a faint scent of manure and urine but not stinking, with bars covering the open part of the half-walls facing the alley. She spotted windows on the outside walls. About halfway down the alley, Rekaré's Basnen came to the front of her stall and whickered at Daro, hay sticking out of her mouth. The buzz of daranval communication tingled in Witmara's head as Daro chuckled back at Basnen. Clearly the daranvelii were speaking about their separate travels.

Detaluna stopped two stalls down from Basnen. "Your stalls start here."

Witmara led Daro into the stall and stripped off saddle, saddlebags, bridle, and halter, hanging the halter and lead rope on a peg outside the door and dumping saddle, bags and bridle on the floor outside of the stall. He plunged his nose into the water bucket and drank, then turned to his hay as she brushed him.

At last she was done. Leaving Daro with a pat, she found Detaluna's rider Jesseth, one of the Saubral Shadowwalkers, picking up her saddle and bridle.

"I'll clean these for you," Jesseth said.

"Thank you. I was going to wipe those down myself."

Jesseth shrugged. "I have the time, and they need to be thoroughly cleaned, anyway, after a trip like this. Detaluna wants us here in the stable watching our horses, not in the house. I need to move around after several days on water, and have nothing else to do. You have enough obligations."

"Thank you, again, Jesseth." She was too tired to argue the point. Bath and bed sounded wonderful.

Witmara slung her saddlebags over her shoulder, now noticing that other members of Rekaré's Mer Galad were doing the same for her riders. At least it wasn't just for her.

Toran and Chaye joined her. Chaye took the saddlebags off of Witmara's shoulder.

"I can carry them!" she protested.

"Things have changed," Chaye said. "We're in Adalane. Time for you to start acting like an Empress."

"I suppose," she sighed. They walked to the stable entry.

"Our riders will stay with yours," Toran told Detaluna. "I spoke to them. Petronin's people have a bunkhouse, and our riders want to stay with the Mer Galad."

Detaluna nodded. "So just the three of you in the main house?" She eyed Chaye. "You will not be popular there, especially in the servant quarters."

"I understand," Chaye said. "I can handle that. I am not a

slave but a free woman. Witmara has freed me, and I serve her of my own choice."

"You'll want quarters for her near you, Witmara?" Detaluna asked.

"That would be best," Witmara said.

"All right."

They walked up the main pathway to a big house whose outlines were shadowed in the moonlit night. Many lights shone out of the windows of one wing, fewer out of another. Guards with torches stood at the passageway into the main courtyard.

"Detaluna." One of the guards acknowledged her.

"I bring the Lady Witmara and her people," Detaluna said.

A shawled figure stepped forward. "Petronin told me. I'm here to take you to your rooms."

Witmara recognized Seijina's voice. "Is Rekaré all right?"

"She sleeps," Seijina said. "As does the lady Betsona. Come on."

They left Detaluna to talk to the guards and followed Seijina. "I have a Ternarese freedwoman who needs rooms close to me," Witmara told Seijina.

Seijina halted. "A Ternar freedwoman? How did that happen?"

"We—*liberated* her and others from a smuggler named Klendaus."

"Hmm!" Seijina raised her brows. "You defeated Klendaus? That took some doing. Who is this person that you have liberated?"

"Chaye." Witmara waved Chaye forward. "She has been most helpful in telling me about the Ternar spy networks in Daran."

"Too bad we didn't know about them before today," Seijina said.

"Detaluna told us what happened." They entered the Great Hall. Seijina started to lead them up the stairs but Witmara heard clacking noises and low, masculine voices coming from a side room.

"Who is that?" she asked.

"Deomar and Kithry, who will be Rekaré's seconds in the Challenge day after tomorrow," Seijina said.

Witmara cast an apologetic glance at Toran. "I would like to meet them."

"I'll come with you," Toran said.

"As will I," Chaye added.

"Introduce us, and then you can take us to our rooms," Witmara said.

Seijina sighed, but led them to the side room. Two well-dressed Aireii men held long sticks, the dark haired one standing beside a table with raised sides. Brightly colored ceramic balls sat on a green fabric. The red-headed one squinted down his stick to stare at another ball, before tapping it with the tip of the stick. It knocked another ball into an opening in the center of the table.

"Lords Deomar, Kithry, I present to you the Lady Witmara ea Ralsem," Seijina announced. "And her companions...." Her voice trailed off.

"Witmara ea *Miteal*," Witmara corrected. At least she'd had enough practice in the common Darani by now that she didn't need to resort to the Old High Aireii. "I am the great-grand-daughter of Alexran ea Miteal, and have no blood connections to the Ralsems beyond that."

"Toran int Mershaunten, husband to Witmara and youngest son of the Mershaunten of Larij," Toran said, as fluently as Witmara.

"Larij?" the redhead asked, raising his brows. "Mer—mer-shaw-ten? By Artel's glass eye, whatever are those?"

Toran drew himself to his full height. Witmara stifled a smirk as he glowered at the redhead. "Mer*shaun*ten. That is the title of the ruler of my nation of Larij, in Varen, to the north of Medvara. My father."

The redhead raised his hands, gesturing appeasingly. "I am sorry, Lord Toran. I meant no offense."

"Good," Toran said.

The redhead's companion eyed Chaye. "And who are you? Another Ternarese? Why should we trust you?"

"I can understand your concern," Chaye said smoothly. Witmara admired her composure. Training or was this Chaye's own nature? "I am Chaye ni Saras, of the motherline of Vespla, and freedwoman of Daran." Chaye said.

"Freedwoman?"

"Witmara liberated her from Klendaus," Seijina said.

The redhead snorted as he turned his attention back to Witmara. "You defeated Klendaus?"

"His body hangs from a tree near Marinset," Witmara said evenly.

The redhead nodded approvingly. "And, Bane of Klendaus, you are Witmara ea Miteal? Great-granddaughter of Alexran?"

"Yes, I am."

He exchanged glances with the other man, then both dropped to one knee before Witmara, bowing their heads.

"My lady. I am Deomar en Tiramarn," the redhead continued. "I am delighted to be able to witness the return of the Miteal to Daran. I pledge myself to your service."

"Likewise. I am Kithry en Winast," the dark-haired man said, glancing up quickly at Witmara before looking back down. "I am honored to serve you, Lady Witmara. Betsona has spoken to us about you for several years now. You, your mother Katerin ea Miteal, and the lady Rekaré ea Miteal."

"Who we didn't know was appearing as our newly-met friend Giolanth that Betsona had asked us to befriend on his first Passage," Deomar said. "We did not know that Rekaré wore

Giolanth's visage until Betsona told us tonight. Betsona also said you might arrive in time for the Challenge."

"Nonetheless, Lady Witmara, we are both eager to swear to your service," Kithry said. "We had hoped to talk to Rekaré tonight, but things have gotten into quite a stir."

"Get up," Witmara said, gesturing. "There's no need to kneel to me yet!"

"You will accept our vows?" Was that a begging tone in Deomar's voice?

"As much as I have Chaye's and others on my way here. Please. Rise. It's not yet time to proclaim formal vows and such to me as Empress. There's still a title to be won."

"Nonetheless, I am yours to command, Lady Witmara." Kithry rose.

"As am I," Deomar said.

Seijina cleared her throat. "Excuse me. Lady Witmara, did you wish to go to your rooms now or later?" She gave Witmara a pointed look. "I have had hot water prepared for baths. It will get colder if you talk too long." Her nose wrinkled to emphasize the need for baths.

Bath sounded very good right now. Witmara bowed slightly to the men.

"Deomar. Kithry. I am pleased to make your acquaintance, but we've been riding for many days…."

"Understood," Deomar said. "We will meet in the morning, Lady Witmara?"

"Yes. Hopefully all of us will be able to talk then," Witmara said. "And please. Just call me Witmara."

"Sorry, La—Witmara," Deomar said.

Kithry bowed low. "Rest well, Witmara. I look forward to talking with you tomorrow."

Deomar copied Kithry's bow. "It has been a pleasure, Witmara."

They followed Seijina out of the parlor. She led them up the stairs and down a hallway.

"Rekaré is here." Seijina pointed to one door. "Here are your rooms, Witmara." She nodded at the door next to Rekaré's. "And I apologize, Chaye, but the next suite is not as fine as the others, nor has it been fully prepared for guests. I have not had a fire started in there."

"That is all right," Chaye said. "I can manage." She handed Witmara's saddlebags to Toran.

"I will start your fire and order hot water for you after I have settled Witmara and Toran."

"I thank you," Chaye said, and went on to her rooms.

"Will you need attendants?" Seijina asked as she led them into the main parlor. To Witmara's relief, glow lights glimmered here, still not as bright as the ones they had in Varen—*but that can be fixed. Eventually.* Warmth radiated from a small iron stove and wood was piled in a rack nearby.

Witmara shook her head. "As long as the bath is ready, Toran and I can manage for ourselves."

"You will need to change that behavior as Empress," Seijina muttered. "But yes, the bath has been prepared for you." She led them into the bathing chamber, also illuminated by glow lights, and pointed toward a finely embroidered bell pull. "Should you need assistance, all you need to do is pull that cord. You do know how to shut off the glows?"

Toran went over to one of them and tapped it off, then tapped it back on. "I think we can manage."

"Good," Seijina said, stroking her chin thoughtfully. "I don't think there's much else to show you."

"Thank you." Witmara itched to get Seijina out of there.

She eyed the steaming water in the copper tub. It looked delightful—and was big enough for two people. They could get *clean.* They had *privacy.* Gods, she was still newly wed, and between being abducted and then traveling here, they hadn't had nearly enough private time together.

"All right." Seijina left the bathing chamber and looked around the rooms. "I suppose the rest of this is apparent? Oh." She opened the door to the bedchamber and pointed toward a wardrobe. "You will find clothing in there for both of you. It should fit. Betsona sent sizes ahead so that you can dress appropriately. Let me know in the morning if you need assistance in dressing."

"I will—the bell pull?"

"Yes." Seijina bowed and finally, *finally*, left.

Witmara stood in the center of the main room, heaving a heavy, relieved sigh now that they were alone and she could relax. This main room held overstuffed couches and chairs like those she remembered from the old Leader's House in Medvare-the-city. But unlike the garish décor of the old House, the wallpaper colors in here were muted and soft, a floral print featuring small blue and pink flowers against a tan background. To her relief, it wasn't the same pattern she had noticed in Lanivar. Also capable of monitoring? Probably.

Paintings of actors on an outdoor stage hung on the wall. Were they set in the great amphitheater? Witmara didn't want to take the time to examine them. *Bath* sounded very good right now.

She went into the bath chamber, settling on a bench first to unplait her hair, untangling it with her fingers, then to pull off her boots. They needed to be cleaned—but that could wait until the morning. Then she sat for a moment, hands on her thighs. Gods, she was exhausted.

Toran sat down on the bench next to her. "Do you want help, dearest?"

She leaned against him. "Just a moment to settle my thoughts. To rest. How long has it been since we started traveling?"

"Counting from your abduction or before?" He wrapped his left arm around her and pulled her close.

"Before."

"A month and a half, at least. How do they track days in Daran?"

Witmara snorted and sat back up. "You know, I haven't taken the time to figure that out yet."

Another thing to learn.

With a groan, she pulled off her socks, then stood, unlacing the top of her tunic and pulling it off. She paused to briefly admire Toran's bare chest, then took off her trousers and small-clothes. Going over to the tub, she dangled her fingers in the still-steaming water.

Just right.

A bar of tan-colored soap sat in a wire holder, between two bottles, one blue, one green. She stepped over the side and sniffed the blue bottle, pouring a bare fingertip's worth into her hand. Lavender scented oil. She poured a dollop into the tub and stirred it, smiling as the fragrance rose. The green bottle held a cream. She didn't check it further, but replaced the bottle in its place and eased herself into the water until her head rested on the back of the tub, closing her eyes for just a moment to savor the warmth and the lavender scent.

Her eyes popped open as water sloshed against her chin when Toran stepped into the tub. She pushed herself up so it wouldn't splash on her face. He settled into place, groaning, then twined his legs with hers.

"This feels good," he said. "It's not warm enough to enjoy a steady diet of river baths."

"If I'm tracking time right, the seasons should be similar to Medvara's." The heat felt wonderful, but if she didn't start moving she would fall asleep. She wanted to linger in the tub— but not tonight.

Witmara held her breath and dunked her head under the

water. Then she reached for the soap and lathered her hair, handing it off to Toran before she rinsed. Toran got out of the tub first and held a towel to wrap her before taking care of himself. There were combs and brushes on a counter for both of them, and robes hanging on the wall. She slipped into the robe —more of that silken stuff, finer than anything smugglers had ever brought to Varen—and combed out her hair.

Toran took her in his arms when he had finished with his hair.

"If I wasn't so tired…." he murmured into her neck.

She held him tight. "There will be time."

She hoped.

THE GODDESS TERAT'S FAVOR

Katerin leaned back in her chair, rubbing her eyes, then stretching. Another day spent poring through Terani's references and cross-checking them with the tomes in Kintarit's library—Gods only knew that it had taken long enough to find the right books. At least her table faced a window, looking away from the Gate and over the rooftops of Nere. In the distance she saw farmers plowing for spring planting. Dust motes twisted in the slanted sunlight of late afternoon.

But at least she *thought* that she and Doryits had finally discovered her mother's key. It was so simple once she eventually came across it—she had found a scrap of paper in Terani's handwriting stuck into a spellbook dedicated to Nitel. There had been a matching torn page in the journal. Reading journal notes and the cryptic spell seemed to identify a means for defanging that goddess, more elaborate than the working her mother had performed to banish Nitel.

Now they just had to figure out how to implement it. The spell was complex, and the difference in details between Terani's journal and the records here in Nere were significant enough that Katerin wondered if the discrepancies had been the

300

cause of her mother's ultimate absorption. Terani's notes omitted a section of the spell that was clearly marked as protective in the books.

Was that because she had done it by herself, or because she was so desperate to rid Waykemin of Nitel that she would risk casting it without protection? What had caused her desperation? Waykemin had been aware of the threat the Divine Confederation presented for many years. Was that it? Terani had visited Nere for a time—not something that Katerin remembered happening in her childhood. Had Terani been here before the dalliance with Alame that had led to Katerin's conception?

Katerin rose and went to the window, pressing her hands against the small of her back and continuing to stretch as she thought about this spell. Doryits had gone for Linyet. It would take all three of them to cast this working, if she went by the Nerean books and not Terani's journal.

One mistake Terani made—doing this casting on her own.

Katerin sighed. It was unlikely that she would know her mother's reasoning. She certainly didn't want to petition Karnoi and Cirdel to summon Terani. Time to think about something different—and another worry was swift to replace her concerns about the spell—something she hadn't really had time to consider until now.

I wonder what is happening in Daran? Have Rekaré and Witmara been able to move against Chatain? She hadn't felt any stir in magic to suggest that they had confronted him yet. *Terani did say that we had two days to match their schedule. Gods, I hope she was right.*

The door creaked open behind her and she turned to face Doryits and Linyet.

"You found the key?" Linyet asked.

"Yes," Katerin said. She gathered up the notes that she and Doryits had made, checking each page to make sure it was in order. "Read this. Don't vocalize any of it. That will trigger the spell." She placed the notes on the table in front of an empty chair. "It needs to be read in order."

Linyet nodded. He sat. Katerin eased herself into her chair, leaning on her elbows as she watched Linyet read through the notes. Doryits stood at the end of the table.

At last Linyet finished the final page. He leaned back in his chair, tapping his fingertips on the arms, so much like what Rekaré often did when thinking that it sent a pang through Katerin.

Will Rekaré return to Varen? Will I see Witmara again?

She shoved those worries away. No time for such maudlin thoughts.

"So?" she asked.

Linyet pulled off his headband and fingered the Gift of Terat. "It's a complicated working. I wish that Grandmother—*grandmothers*—both of them—were here." He glanced at Doryits. "You will have to be part of the working, as Sariost's father."

Aha. I had overlooked that piece.

But then again, Linyet had spent the last seven years under Heinmyets and Inharise's tutelage. The sorcery they had worked together differed from what Katerin had learned, and what was common in Medvara.

"I missed that. Thank you."

He flashed a smile so much like that of his father Cenarth that another pang struck Katerin.

Cenarth should not have died in Forsim.

And yet it had been Cenarth's choice to protect her and Rekaré in the battle of Forsim, when they confronted the Witches of Waykemin and destroyed their Council.

"Different eyes," he said. "And Terat spoke to me while I was reading. There are meanings that may be hidden from followers of Artel and Dovré." He rustled through the papers and brought out a page from the middle. He ran his finger along one sentence. "See this?"

Katerin focused on the words. This passage had not made sense to her on first reading.

The Sea-goddess lies dreaming in inland pools, awaiting her awakening. Rise, oh beloved of the seafoam, rise from dirt and dust to your true nature.

"Doryits, are there any bodies of water in that forest?" she asked.

He shook his head. "None close to the wall on either side. We have to bring water supplies to the Gate."

"It's not literal pools," Linyet said. "It refers to hidden teachings of the Goddess. Keep in mind that water arises from the earth in springs and wells. The Goddess is present in those small sources of water that become rivulets, then creeks, then rivers that join the ocean. It makes sense to me—but there are further teachings which I cannot share outside of Clenda."

"All right," Katerin said. "So this means—what?"

Linyet pushed back a stray strand of dark hair that had escaped his braid, and slipped the headband back on so that it kept the strand from falling into his eyes.

"To begin with, I read this as meaning that one dedicated to Terat will need to be present at this working. Me."

"And then?"

"There are bonds that restrict manifestation of the other Gods in the forest, right?"

"Yes," Doryits said.

Linyet smiled grimly. "Because of Terat's nature and presence in the waters under the earth, in the trees and brush, those bonds do not restrict *her*." He paused. "She can manifest herself through me in a manner that Dovré and Artel cannot through you two. So we can call upon her presence in tomorrow's fight. The Outcast God will not expect Terat to appear."

GODS, SHE STILL FELT DRAINED, EVEN THOUGH SHE HAD SLEPT most of the day. Rekaré helped Betsona, then Sesenth into the horseless carriage that had been sent by Chatain, the flickering torches only adding to her fey mood. Basnen's distress at Rekaré leaving without her was strong enough to roil Rekaré's thoughts as she climbed into the carriage, especially since Rekaré was leaving in a conveyance provided by *he who hates us.*

I cannot bring you, beloved,

she mindspoke to the daranval.

You know this to be true.

More fussing came back.

You have Daro nearby. Use his help to monitor me. I will return later tonight.

Basnen continued to worry. Rekaré sat back and blocked the mare's presence in her thoughts. She hated to do it, but she did not need this distraction. Not tonight. And she dared not bring a daranval anywhere near tonight's banquet. No need to tip off Chatain before the morning.

Besides, Basnen and Daro together could break through that block if necessary.

"Are you ready?" Betsona asked as the carriage started. The carriages carrying Deomar, Kithry, and their wives followed theirs.

"As ready as I can be," Rekaré answered. She had spent the part of the day that wasn't sleep either cramming with Deomar and Kithry, or choreographing Witmara's appearance at the Challenge after Rekaré had—hopefully—dispatched Chatain.

Betsona traced a masking spell in the air. "I'm not sure whether these carriages have listening devices in them or not."

"Better to assume they do."

"Agreed." Betsona pressed her lips together tightly. "Your spells are solid?"

"I've gone through every working in detail," Rekaré said, irritated.

Too much time to think and second-guess what we are doing. Gods, I miss having Katerin at my right hand. She knows when to stop thinking and start doing!

She was tired of Betsona's constant fuss over details, over and over and over again until she wanted to scream.

"And if Chatain sees through your disguise?"

Rekaré rested her hand on her sword's hilt. "Then I suppose it will come to battle sooner than we thought."

"We need to avoid that," Betsona said sharply. "Witmara needs to be there, too."

"I know!" Rekaré snapped back. "But if there's some flaws in our spells...." She shook her head. "We don't need to be thinking like this. He will expect us to be nervous, of course. But not like this."

Betsona drew a deep breath. "You are right." She exhaled. "And not having Seijina by my side is fretting me. But that should prepare me for tomorrow. She won't be able to support me at the Challenge."

"Right." Rekaré forced herself to relax next to Sesenth. "The game is in play. We can do nothing but walk through our parts, and deal with the consequences."

Betsona raised her brows at Rekaré. "Have you been reading my play collections? That sounds like something Atalanthe would write."

Rekaré shrugged. "I *have* been reading that book of plays you gave me when we left Lanivar."

"That was a collection of Atalanthe's work."

"Then I like her writing very much."

"His," Betsona corrected.

Rekaré shrugged, feigning a casualness she didn't feel. "I thought you might have given me those for a reason."

"Indeed. Atalanthe is the feted playwright this season." A smile played on Betsona's lips. "Perhaps if we are lucky he will write of our deeds."

"Perhaps." Rekaré looked out the window as they left the Noble District.

Was it her imagination or did she see stealthy sneaking forms glaring at their carriages from the shadowy streets? Rekaré shivered and looked away. Her hand slipped into Sesenth's gloved one. At least her cover story allowed Senth to be with her for support, so she wasn't totally alone. Chatain had forbidden Betsona from bringing Seijina.

And as for those sneaking forms—their carriages wore Chatain's sigil. After having heard Witmara's account about conditions on the border with Ternar, she wasn't imagining those angry stares coming from people on the street. Rekaré tapped her free hand's fingers on the armrest, wishing she were riding Basnen instead of sitting in this strange conveyance that she didn't trust in the least.

I thought things in Medvara were bad before I abdicated. This feels much, much, worse.

But what did she expect in a land that resorted to slavery? Zauril's death curse had haunted every thing she did as Leader in Medvara. Too bad that it was Betsona sitting across from her instead of Katerin. She could trust Katerin without reserve—would know what Katerin intended, could anticipate how Katerin would react. No. That wasn't entirely true.

Chiyan. She hadn't expected Katerin to be ready to burn that village—*and yet, there was an explanation for Chiyan,* she reminded herself. Katerin had still been in shock after the news of Witmara's abduction, and she *had* held back from that initial impulse, had been able to listen to Yitlisk and control her rage, because her goal was to bring down the Witches of Waykemin, not wreak havoc.

She couldn't be certain of that ability to step back and consider consequences with Betsona. Some of Betsona's actions and behaviors suggested that she enjoyed stirring things up for her own entertainment.

Either that or she plays a devious game to seize the Empire for herself.

What *would* happen if Chatain saw through Giolanth's façade? Would Betsona turn on her—or defend her?

Best to be prepared for betrayal.

As if Sesenth was reading her mind, she squeezed Rekaré's hand. Rekaré smiled at Senth and raised her hand, kissing it. Her role as Giolanth allowed her this much intimacy, at least.

"I am here, dearest," Senth whispered in Rekaré's ear.

"Thank you," Rekaré whispered back.

Was she surprised at how that simple affirmation bolstered her spirits? Senth had her back—and even though she was only partway through her Shadowwalker transformation, the love and support of a powerful Shadowwalker was no small thing.

And they were not alone. Witmara waited at Betsona's house, with Toran, Detaluna and the Mer Galad standing watch over her. If Rekaré were to falter or fail tonight—Witmara might be young. But she had the land of Daran behind her, and that strength would serve her well against Chatain.

If it weren't for the vengeance I seek...I would leave this task to her.

That thought took her by surprise, coming out of nowhere. The journey had been harder than she thought. And if it hadn't been for all of those that Chatain had taken from her, she wouldn't be here.

But Rekaré Kinslayer has one final task to perform. And after that —well, she had promised Heinmyets to return to the Two Nations. If she survived. She didn't think she would.

And there was more to this than a simple desire to be the one to confront Chatain, she admitted to herself. Better that Witmara ascend to the throne of Daran with as clean a pair of hands as possible. Better that she not start her rule under the sort of shadows that haunted Rekaré when she became Leader of Medvara. Witmara would be justified in killing Chatain—but better she didn't.

I should have left Zauril's death to others.

Hard to admit it now. She had underestimated the power of the Ralsems, and the strength of their death curses, especially upon one who was part-Ralsem like she was.

She would not, *could* not, let Witmara bear this particular burden. Not if she could help it.

IF IT WASN'T FOR THE UNFAMILIAR SURROUNDINGS, WITMARA could almost imagine herself back at home.

No, not home, no place in Varen can be your home ever again, she corrected herself. *Daran must be your home now.*

She and Toran had retreated to their suite while the others went to the Festival's opening banquet. Detaluna and the Mer Galad patrolled the house to keep them safe. Seijina fussed over small things while Betsona was gone. Toran read a book of plays that Seijina had given him as Witmara studied an obscure magical tome, *A History of Darani Magic and the Empire*. Betsona had brought the book to her that afternoon, commenting that *I just stumbled across this, you may find it useful*. A phrase she had used often when sending books to Witmara.

The book made for fascinating reading and cleared up some questions she had. The Goddess Terat featured in many of the chapters. Witmara had read several accounts of the trials that Sorcerer-Captains went through to prove themselves worthy of a ship—the tone of one story reminded Witmara of a few things that Vered had said about her trial. However none of the Captains were named.

But there was one phrase repeated over and over below the headings of the chapters about Terat that didn't seem to make sense. It had to be important, but what did it mean?

The Sea-goddess lies dreaming in inland pools, awaiting her awakening. Rise, oh beloved of the seafoam, rise from dirt and dust to your true nature.

How did Terat get inland? For that matter, how was it that she was the patron of the nation of Clenda, so far inside the interior of Varen? Granted, the great rivers Chellana and Kitskan formed Clenda's northern and eastern boundaries. And there was the lake at the heart of Clenda, which few non-Clendans had ever seen. She had been born next to that lake. That should be enough water for the Goddess's strength. But rising from dirt and dust to her true nature? Whatever did that mean? Linyet knew the hidden details of Terat's worship—but he was in Varen, not here.

Witmara pushed the spell book aside and got up. The puzzle still hadn't revealed itself, and staring at it wasn't working. Perhaps if she did something else for a while. She collected her staff and a knife, then sat down to work on its head. The knot was beginning to take the form of a long-haired woman with as yet indefinite features.

Chaye had found her a clear oil made from a boiled seed common here in Daran, sweetlace, to polish it. It had mild magical properties. Witmara rubbed the sweetlace oil on the staff after each session. The oil soaked deeper into the wood with each application, darkening and smoothing out the wood.

Witmara followed the grain in the knot, narrowing the shape of the woman's face. Several times she stopped to look at the form emerging from the wood. It was close to being finished, except for the woman's features. A strange reluctance to add those details had slowed Witmara's work, and now she wondered if she should do any more.

> Are you finished?

she thought at the staff.

She had found herself thinking at it more and more, as if it were a living thing still. Magic did pulse through the staff, but so far, it hadn't responded to her thoughts.

The staff warmed in her hand. The woman's face shook itself, as if she were trying to break free from the wood. Witmara carefully set down her knife, waiting for whatever would happen next. Features slowly formed on the face.

> Lady Witmara. I am grateful for your patience and tact.

The voice in her mind was somehow familiar, with the cadences of a Clendan.

> It was the right thing to do,

she answered.

> Why would I rush things of magic? My beloved and I have worked with magitech in our homeland of Varen. I know how to wait for sorcery to reveal itself.

The familiar tones strengthened. Not Inharise, but definitely Clendan in the easy rhythm and grace of her thoughts.

> Not all who work with my blessed items are as respectful.

Witmara bowed her head in respect.

> Goddess Terat, I am blessed with your favor. I thank you for considering to shower your favors on one who is not of your patronage.

She paused, considering her next words before thinking them.

> This is not a form I would have expected to see you wear, Sea-goddess.

The features on the staff became more prominent. Terat laughed.

> Ah, but this wood is from groves by the Sea— not that it would matter. I am Terat of the Waters, and that means all waters, including the sap that once ran through this branch.

> I was not aware of that, Goddess.

She had never heard of this attribute of Terat until now.

> Why has this never been spoken of?

> You are not one of my acolytes from Clenda, and my time had not yet come.

The Goddess's voice grew stronger as the staff's shape began to expand and grew heavier in Witmara's hands.

> You may place this manifestation of myself down—it will be easier for you in the long run.

"Darling?" Toran looked up from his book as Witmara put the staff carefully on the floor. "Oh." His eyes widened as the staff turned upright, growing until Terat stood before them in its place. He bowed low. "Goddess Terat. We are honored by your presence."

"Your time had not yet come?" Witmara asked out loud.
The Goddess nodded.

> My ways are the quiet ones, discreet enough to lull those who expect me to behave as my siblings do, with great, dramatic gestures. I am the one who works behind the scenes—an apt phrase, for being here in Adalane.

Toran laughed, a rueful note in his mirth. "Goddess, I have just been reading of such things in the playwrights of Adalane."

> I have revealed aspects of myself to them. Nonetheless. This staff comes from a tree harvested to make one of My ships. It has been waiting for one such as you to take it up.

"What would you have me do?" Witmara committed herself.

> There is a battle between the Gods.

"I have seen parts of it, Goddess."
Terat nodded.

> You were born as part of this battle. We cast out one of our own years ago, which took much of our strength.

She sighed.

> That was during the time you call the Great Plague, which struck down many not just in Varen and Daran, but in lands throughout the world that you do not know. Our former brother took power in lands to the east of Waykemin.

"I do not know of those lands."

You would not.

Terat sighed again.

It is a long story, and one that need not be told at this moment. We are reaching a key point in our current struggle, both here and in Varen. Your mother and her allies prepare to confront our ancient foe and brother, while you and your cousin ready yourselves to challenge Chatain.

"I—see." Witmara swallowed hard, a lump forming in her throat. She switched to mindspeech as she didn't think she could speak out loud with that lump pulling tighter and tighter.

What does my mother face and when?

Tomorrow, at midafternoon where Katerin is— dawn here—she will face the full aspect of the Outcast God. It will be at about the same time that Rekaré confronts Chatain. My—

her face twisted in an emotion that Witmara couldn't clearly identify—shame? Dread? Sorrow? All three?

—sister Nitel is crucial to the strength of both the Outcast One and Chatain. It is important that her focus be split between them. Otherwise, she will ally with the Outcast.

I see.

She didn't know what else to say. More was at stake here than she had thought.

"That's interesting timing," she said out loud, through the lump.

It has taken some juggling to have everyone in place at the right time,

the Goddess said. She tapped the spell book that Witmara had set aside.

There is a spell in this book that you must read and learn, to be able to use it tomorrow morning. If you do not master it, I cannot answer for the consequences.

"Dire words, my lady Terat."

Making certain that you understand what is at stake.

"I am well aware of that!" Witmara picked up the book. "So which spell?"

Terat touched it. The book opened and pages flipped until they settled. Witmara studied the open page—a spell for concealing an embedded exorcism of Gods within a sling, an arrow, and…a staff. She looked up at the Goddess.

"And this will be my role in the fight against Chatain?" she said, voice rasping as her throat tightened again.

Terat nodded.

Rekaré does not know the degree to which Nitel strengthens Chatain. No opponent can strike Chatain down without banishing Nitel from him first. No human magician possesses the strength to do both. One of you must smite Nitel. The other—Chatain.

"Wouldn't it make more sense for me to meet Chatain in the Challenge, and Rekaré fight Nitel?"

Rekaré bears the curse of the Kinslayer. That weakens her against Nitel. She will be stronger against Chatain—and will keep you from the death curse of the Ralsems. You are the granddaughter of Terani-the-God-Killer and the daughter of the Banisher of Shadows. It is in you to have power against Nitel.

Witmara looked back down at the spell, then up at the Goddess. "And is it you that I am carving into this staff?"

The Goddess laughed.

No. Staul is your patron and ever shall be. She who it commemorates has not yet emerged as her true self. You will see when it is time.

She paused.

My time here is done. Fight well, oh daughter of Katerin and Metkyi. My blessings lie upon you.

The Goddess faded away, and the staff started to fall, once again just a staff. Witmara grabbed it before it reached the floor. She exhaled, and turned to Toran. "You heard her?"

He knelt and kissed her hand. "Every word, my dear one. Every single word."

Witmara turned back to the spell book. "I need you to help me gather what we need to create this spell." She ran her finger down the list of ingredients. "We have glimmer dust. Cirelen powder."

"Should we use Coos berry liqueur instead of starberry?" Toran frowned. "I don't like the idea of using starberry."

"It's from here, so it's probably not from the Divine Confederation...but yes. I like that idea. I feel better using a berry liqueur made from *our* magic, not theirs. And both are distilled from berries, so—like to like."

Toran grabbed a scrap of paper. "Let me make a list of what we don't have or can't substitute because we don't have a match."

Together they pored over the spell book.

❧

"BETSONA MY DEAR! IT'S BEEN *SO LONG*. WE'VE MISSED YOU—HOW dreary are the Islands? Such an exile must be dreadfully boring."

Betsona exchanged cheek kisses with an impresario connected to one of Adalane's smaller theaters. What was his name? He had asked her for money to finance several productions. But the plays he produced focused more on forgettable blood-and-thunder melodramas than what she preferred to support.

Tersontet, she finally remembered, before the lapse became embarrassing. Gods, she had forgotten so much after only two years at Lanivar! How many more memories would she lose if she remained there?

I will not return to Lanivar. I will die instead.

Which might happen.

"I am doing well," she said to Tersontet, forcing a cheerful smile. She waved Rekaré forward. "Tersontet. This is Giolanth en Stanil, from one of the Island families, here on his first passage."

"Ah. Pleased to meet you, Lord Giolanth." Tersontet let go of Betsona's hands and turned to face Rekaré. "Are you interested in drama?" He extended one hand but Rekaré ignored it, clasping her hands behind her back. Tersontet slowly dropped his hand, frowning slightly.

"I am not shaking hands tonight, sorry," Rekaré said, affecting Giolanth's idle drawl. "I'm afraid I'm much more concerned with cane production than dramatic productions, however. And weather."

"Ah, ah, ah. A planter from the Islands." Tersontet smiled appraisingly at Rekaré. "I may have just the play for you to support—the playwright is a young man from your area. Features a heroic sea captain who battles pirates and smugglers, and finds the love of his life as a pirate captive who just happens to be a Ternarese princess."

Betsona stifled a snicker as an expression of shock mixed with appalled fascination crossed Rekaré's face—almost identical, she thought, to what the *real* Giolanth's expression would have been.

"I—I'm not looking to sponsor any productions," Rekaré said. "Estarel and I are investing all of our proceeds into improving our holdings. I'm afraid we're not the kind of investor you're seeking."

An almost letter-perfect version of what Giolanth would say.

"Not even if we add lots of bawdy scenes?"

"*Especially* not bawdy scenes," Rekaré said firmly, exchanging a glance with the heavily veiled Sesenth. "Estarel would not like that and I respect her wishes."

Tersontet shook his head regretfully. "Lady Betsona?"

"Alas, me neither," she said.

Before Tersontet could press his cause further, the call to dinner sounded. Tersontet scurried away to take his place at a lower table. Rekaré guided Betsona's wheelchair as close as she could to their assigned seats at the end of the table. Then she stowed the wheelchair and offered her arm to help Betsona up the steps to their place at the high table—an honor that had not been granted to Betsona since Dunaran's death. But she didn't miss the worried glances from below as she took her seat, flanked by Rekaré on one side, Sesenth on the other. The only relatives Chatain usually placed in that particular seat were those undergoing the Challenge—and to date, none had survived.

Still, the buzz and gossip amongst the tables made Betsona

realize how isolated she had become in Lanivar. Gods, she missed the flirting and the gossiping and the sheer energy that came from the wordplay amongst the playwrights and actors! Betsona closed her eyes for a moment to pretend that this was all normal and back to what it had been when she was younger, that any minute the heralds would announce that her father Dunaran was entering the hall and not Chatain, that the past few years were nothing more than a bad dream....

Trumpet fanfare. Betsona's eyes popped open to see Chatain standing in the doorway.

"All rise for the Emperor Chatain, Conqueror of Ternar and Elbfar, Lord of Daran, Regent of Varen—" Rekaré flinched at that one, quickly concealing her reaction.

Betsona missed the rest as she struggled to rise. Rekaré and Sesenth gently helped her up. She clutched their arms, steeling herself against whatever spectacle her brother had cooked up. At least this time he wasn't using the backs of Ternarese slaves as stairsteps to the high table, like he had in previous years.

"Cha-tain, Cha-tain, Cha-tain," the servants began. At first the lower tables picked up the chant, clapping along with each syllable. Chatain marched forward in pace with the claps and chant as servants unrolled a golden carpet in front of him. The chant processed through the room, and yet—was it fainter than it had been before?

Betsona mimed clapping and mouthed the chant.

Here I am in the place of Sacrifice. So clichéd, straight out of too many historical plays that Tersontet would produce. It would be funny if so much weren't at stake.

From the side glances her friends gave her, it was clear that most of them understood this context. Tersontet stared at her as if he were mesmerized.

Oh Gods, he's going to commission one of his horrible plays about this Challenge if I die!

Reason enough for her to survive.

Chatain reached his seat. He gestured for the chant to continue, his face stormy as the volume dropped rather than rose.

Oh, he's in a foul mood now.

This crowd was the quietest she had heard for one of Chatain's staged entrances, and he knew it. At last he dropped his hands. He gazed around the room.

"So here we are, my people," he said at last. "Tomorrow at dawn we kick off Festival with a Challenge that will be the most worthy of any I have done." He smirked at Betsona. "Many of you are familiar with my lady sister Betsona." He gestured to her. "Tomorrow she—or her champion that I see beside her?—will face me in the Challenge, to open the Festival before the Great Invocation."

There was no mistaking the swiftly indrawn breaths from around the crowd. Or the distressed, worried looks cast in her direction, now direct instead of sideways glances.

"My lady Betsona, would you care to introduce us to your Champion?" Chatain asked, barely concealing the sneer in his voice. "Or are he and his lady wife merely your bedtime companions?" He smirked as shock crossed the faces of about half the attendees.

Betsona's hands tightened into fists.

Damn you, Chatain. I will love seeing your expression when you face the Kinslayer and Witmara tomorrow. Meanwhile...do not react, do not react, do not let him goad you.

Betsona cleared her throat before speaking with the sharpest, most vitriolic tone she dared use without provoking an immediate fight. "My dearest companion Seijina remains at my home, *as you have requested,* dear brother, even though by all rights she should be with me at this banquet."

"Ha!" Chatain snorted.

Before he could say more, Betsona continued, softening her tone. "I introduce to all of you my dear friend Giolanth en Stanil, a simple planter from the Islands with some magic and skill with the blade. Giolanth has agreed to stand Challenge in my stead. And this is his very lovely wife Estarel." She nodded at Rekaré. Sesenth stared down at her plate, and freed one hand from supporting Betsona to pull her veils forward so she could hide her face further.

"I—see." Chatain glowered at Rekaré. She met his gaze steadily, not flinching. "So, Master and Lord Giolanth en Stanil. You think you have the magical and fighting ability to meet me in Challenge?"

"My dear friend Betsona asked it of me," Rekaré said, voice level but sharp. "She was very kind to my dear Estarel when she was ill. How could I turn her down?"

"Even if it means you harm?"

Rekaré raised her chin defiantly. "Especially then, my lord." The sudden sneer in her voice belied the compliant words. "Though I would not be standing here if I thought I was defenseless against you." She patted Betsona's hand. "I have faith in my lady's ability to shield me."

"*Fool.*" Chatain glowered at Rekaré. He gestured with one hand, and Betsona sensed cloaked tendrils of magic radiating from it. Rekaré idly deflected the threads with a light flick of her hand, diffusing them as if they were nothing. Chatain raised his brows in surprise at the ease with which she wielded magic.

She passed the first test.

And the glamor that disguised Rekaré as Giolanth didn't waver. Not surprising given the strength of Rekaré's sorcery, but it was still a relief to see.

"A wise man would have been mindful of his family before accepting such an invitation," Chatain grumbled.

"None have accused me of ever having wisdom, alas," Rekaré

said. She smiled, baring her teeth at Chatain. "And I owe a debt to Betsona. She saved my Estarel's life when she was struck by the plague. How could I turn down her request to be her Champion?"

"Is that what it takes to gain your loyalty? A healing that any competent magician can do?"

"And where were *you* when plague struck the Islands two years ago?" Rekaré snarled back. "As Emperor, shouldn't you have come to the aid of your subjects? The Islands were *short* of competent magicians at that time. Despite her infirmities and her recent move, the Lady Betsona risked her own health to help stop the plague. I—" She choked that back.

Gods, Giolanth told Rekaré about that!

But furious undercurrents roiled through Rekaré, her hands tightening on Betsona's arm as she glowered at Chatain.

"You dare criticize me!"

"I do."

Chatain simmered and power stirred around them. She felt Rekaré's rage rise in response, resisting his sorcery and gathering power of her own to counter Chatain. His brows rose, a brief, puzzled expression flitting across his face before the scowl returned.

"Dearest," Sesenth breathed. "Don't push it. Please. Apologize. Tonight is not the time." She added a phrase that Betsona didn't understand.

Rekaré answered softly in the same guttural language. Then she spoke louder, in immaculate High Aireii instead of Darani. "My dear lady advises me to apologize, so I will. Until tomorrow at dawn, when we meet on the dueling floor. I plead that I spoke unwisely and rashly because I was briefly overtaken by emotion at the thought of losing my lady."

"I *will* utterly defeat you, Giolanth en Stanil. And then destroy your family."

"We shall see. Meanwhile, even the condemned deserve a hearty meal."

Chatain guffawed. "And do you have seconds?"

Rekaré gestured to Deomar and Kithry, seated with their wives at the second table. "Lords Deomar and Kithry have given me that honor."

Chatain focused on them. But when he would have cast more magic in their direction, Rekaré coughed.

"I believe your attention should be on me, not on those who are simply seeking to be of assistance to one not fully aware of the proper protocols," she said.

Chatain snapped his head back toward Rekaré. "Do you accuse me of interfering with your seconds?"

Rekaré raised one brow. Betsona frowned.

Not a gesture that Giolanth would make. Gods, Rekaré, don't falter now!

"I only know that a casting was thrown in my direction, and someone appeared to be giving my seconds a similar treatment." Rekaré seemed to exaggerate Giolanth's drawl. "If not you casting that spell, I would ask that whoever did not treat my seconds like that, as they are not sorcerers."

Chatain bristled. "You insult me."

"Do I? Such was not my intent."

Is she trying to provoke him into fighting right now? Gods, that would be a disaster. I warned her against trying that!

"We can fight now, if you'd rather not wait." Was that uneasiness she heard in Chatain's voice?

"Is that what you *really* want, Lord Chatain?" Rekaré countered. "Is it wise to keep our companions away from their meal? And what about innocent bystanders? I don't know about you, but I would prefer to conduct our Challenge as part of the accepted process, where innocents are not at risk." A faint smile touched her lips. "And that would include neither of us interfering with the other's seconds. Speaking of seconds, who are yours?"

They glared at each other. At last Chatain turned and gestured to the second table. "Lord Egrik, and Lord Senfas."

The two men bowed to Rekaré, then Deomar and Kithry.

Chatain thumped down in his seat, still scowling at Rekaré as the servants began to deliver the first course. He snarled at the unlucky slave who brought him a cup of wine and tossed it down in one gulp, throwing the goblet back at the cringing man with a growl.

"That was a gamble," Betsona whispered to Rekaré when Chatain looked away from them.

"I needed to distract him from probing me too deeply," Rekaré murmured.

"Do you think he suspects anything?"

"No. I think he was more concerned that I was Witmara in disguise. But if I hadn't responded like a bold young lord who's yet to meet his match, he'd have been more suspicious."

Betsona nodded. They watched Chatain drain another cup. "I would be careful about how much I drank."

"I am." Rekaré sipped from her goblet, placing it down carefully. "I'm checking each cup for potions and poisons. I'd suggest you do the same."

She hadn't thought about that. Chatain smirked at them as she cast a small spell to check her drink.

"Did you honestly think I would poison you the night before Challenge, sister?" he called down the table. Those around them stopped talking.

Betsona glared at him. "I would not rule it out."

He scowled. "You think so little of me?"

"I remember what has happened to our kin since you became Emperor," she said. "At the least I prefer to make sure that neither my Champion nor myself will be impaired for tomorrow's Challenge."

Chatain bellowed a laugh in response. "I do not need potions or poison to ensure my victory, sister!" He raised his third—or was it the fourth?—cup high. "A toast, in anticipation of finally being rid of my meddling curse of a sister!"

Uneasy mutters came from the crowd. A few—very few—hands raised their goblets. Rekaré tensed next to Betsona.

"Don't do anything," Betsona breathed.

Rekaré growled and did not relax.

"What?" Chatain roared. "None of you will join me in this toast?" He glared at the reluctant guests. But apart from the very few who had already raised their cups, no one else moved.

Chatain drained the cup and threw it at a servant. "I'm done with all of you! You'll pay, once I'm done with Betsona!" He shoved his chair back and stormed out of the banquet hall, followed by Egrik and Senfas. Stunned silence hung over the room after the doors slammed behind them.

Betsona reached for her goblet with a shaking hand as low murmurs finally rose from the audience. It felt like everyone stared at her. But before she could do anything, Rekaré rose.

"I offer a toast to Betsona ea Ralsem," she said. "And I ask the Lord Artel and Lady Dovré to give us the victory in tomorrow's challenge!"

"Victory to Lady Betsona! Lord Giolanth!" Deomar and Kithry leapt to their feet. Most of the others joined them, chanting "Betsona! Giolanth! Victory!"

Rekaré sipped her cup, bowed to the crowd, then sat. Betsona fumbled for her crutches. Rekaré turned to help her and she waved her away. Slowly, Betsona pushed herself to her feet, steadied herself, then reached for her cup, waiting as the clamor diminished.

At last it stopped.

"My lords and ladies," she said quietly, yet projecting her voice as strong as she could. *There are many assets to befriending actors,* she thought wryly as the crowd hushed. "I thank you very much for your vote of confidence. I thank you for your bold words, Lord Giolanth."

"Betsona! Bet-so-na!" The chant started and she shook her head roughly, mouthing "no."

"Silence!" Rekaré bellowed in the carrying tone of an experienced field commander. "Let the Lady Betsona speak!"

Silence fell.

"Thank you, Lord Giolanth." She inclined her head toward Rekaré. "I appreciate your faith in me. Please, though, remember that even should my brother lose the Challenge tomorrow, he will still remain Emperor. We must be mindful of that reality." *Only if he lives.* She paused to catch her breath. "For tonight, let us enjoy ourselves. Tomorrow the Festival begins. We reaffirm our dedication to our Emperor, as Dovré decreed to the House of Miteal so many years ago."

"The Miteals are gone!" someone yelled from the crowd—that cluster of Chatain loyalists that earlier had raised their cups to her demise.

Betsona raised one brow. "Are they? There are Miteals in Varen."

"And what have they to do with us?" another from that same group bellowed.

Betsona raised her hand to forestall any further comments. "Enough! Let us enjoy this evening. Festival begins tomorrow. Eat well, and I will see you tomorrow."

She let herself down with a thump. The servants sighed with relief, and began serving food again. With Chatain gone, they came to her first, then Rekaré and Sesenth. Betsona fell back into the routines she knew from presiding over the feast in previous years. For a little while she could pretend that nothing had changed, that she was back in the good old days.

Except that Rekaré slumped in the chair next to her, in a most un-Giolanth-like behavior, staring at the doors. She barely ate, frowning. Halfway through the third course, an exquisitely tender filet of venison with savory fried vegetables, Rekaré startled. Then she gestured at Deomar. He came to the table and Rekaré whispered something in his ear. Deomar blanched, then nodded. He rejoined Kithry and spoke to him in a low voice. They gathered up several of their men and left, pausing to talk to several other lords who rose and joined them.

Rekaré leaned over. "I just was warned by Basnen and Daro that something is not right with our transport. Magical interference. Chatain's soldiers are gathering around the building as well. We need to leave quickly. Deomar and Kithry are arranging safe conveyances."

The savory vegetables Betsona had been chewing seemed to turn to ash. She swallowed them and gulped a mouthful of wine.

Another capability of those daranvelii that I did not expect.

"He wouldn't dare," she breathed.

Rekaré coughed a short, sharp laugh. "He is a Ralsem, and without honor," she snarled, menace weighting every word. "Just like my father was." She pushed herself up.

The words struck Betsona harder than she expected. "But—" She found herself breathing hard.

What kind of spell did she just project to affect me so?

Rekaré looked down at her with a distant, appraising expression that Betsona hadn't seen on her before. "Present company excepted, of course. Betsona, Esta. I will be back to escort you to our new carriages. We need to leave. Promptly."

"Be careful, Gio," Sesenth said.

"Always, Esta." Rekaré's expression softened for just a moment. Then she turned and strode for the door, marching down the golden carpet Chatain had used, radiating an aura of power that silenced those she passed in a most un-Giolanth-like manner.

Betsona shuddered and stared after her, uneasy at what she sensed.

Kinslayer.

This was the face of the Kinslayer. It had to be. But there was something further in that presence than just the Kinslayer, something creepy and alien. Then Sesenth leaned over.

"*Benghaalph* rides that person right now," she said. "That is what you sense in her—and may the Lord Staul help us all, should it completely dominate the Kinslayer."

DAWN OF BATTLE

SHE STARTED UP IN HER BED, GLANCING AROUND TO PLACE THE voice that had roused her. But there was no pale telltale shimmer of a sorcerous projection. None of the ponderous weight and warmth that signaled the presence of one of the Gods. Only the distant cry of *"four bells, and all's well,"* from the watchman at the front door of the Leader's House, and the response of *"all's well"* from the street watch.

Katerin grimaced. All was certainly *not* well. Not with what lay ahead of them.

"Goddess?" she asked into the dark.

No response.

"Witmara? Rekaré?"

Still nothing.

Perhaps she had just dreamed the voice. Or—was Doryits crying out in a dream, calling for help because Sariost had reached for him again? Katerin fumbled for a glow on her nightstand, kindling it to its brightest light before she stepped into her slippers and pulled on a robe. She hurried to her sitting room where Doryits slept on the couch.

He snored quietly, no sign of Sariost's presence or any indication that he had been the speaker she heard. Katerin dimmed the glow so that she could study the room for any unusual light that might reveal a projection trying to conceal itself.

Nothing.

It must have been a dream. She sighed and turned back to her room. Too awake now to go back to sleep. Perhaps that was all for the best. She could meditate and prepare herself for today's battle. Her hand was on the doorknob when Doryits's snores stopped.

"Katerin?" Doryits's voice was low and raspy. "What's going on?"

"I thought I heard a voice calling me." She faced him. "But there's nothing I can see. Not in my room, not in here."

"I just heard a voice, too. Yours, calling me. Did you try to wake me?"

She shook her head. "When I saw you were sleeping undisturbed, I decided to go back to my room to contemplate before the morning meetings. I can't sleep."

"May I join you?"

"I don't see why not. I'll dress and be right back." She went back into her bedroom to dress quickly in her fighting leathers.

A quick look in the mirror, a deep breath at the drawn face reflected back with dark circles under her eyes, the long stare in her gaze. She looked like a warrior and not a healer—*you have been a Leader for almost seven years, what would you expect*, she chided herself. Still, sometimes the change struck her harder than other times. She reached for the Spear of War and Unmaking, in its normal spear form, and studied it.

No. More was needed for this contemplation, and she knew what it was. She returned the Spear to its holder and went to her trunk. She hadn't known why *this time* she needed to bring along her ceremonial mask. It hadn't traveled with her for years. Late in the night before they left for Keratil, she had suddenly risen and wrapped the mask in an old cloak of Metkyi's, along with his heartstone. She pulled it out, leaving it and the stone wrapped in Metkyi's cloak for now. Then she picked up the Spear.

Doryits waited silently by the couch, holding his unsheathed sword, ready for pre-battle meditation.

Katerin silently went to the table. She placed the Spear down first, then the wrapped mask. Slowly, carefully, she spread the cloak wide on the table, resettling the Spear on it. Then she picked up the wooden mask, holding it high in two hands. Carving and painting the mask had been a significant element of her first year at the Healing House, as part of her turning thirteen and attaining the first stage of magical majority. The blue-painted mask depicted a sleeping woman with white stars dotting the forehead and cheeks. The paint reflected her ties to the Blue Starry Robe clan that had taken her in when she first came to the Two Nations. At that time she had engraved the sigils of the Healers on its forehead and cheeks, to signify her choice of that vocation.

Since then, she had added the pale blue star outlined in green that was the sigil of the House of Miteal to the forehead, to reflect her new calling as Leader of Medvara. Wavy purple lines on its cheeks spoke to her role as the Banisher of Shadows. But to her surprise, silver and gold now edged the big star on the mask's forehead as well as the purple lines.

What is this?

The mask would change and evolve to reflect her transformations throughout her life—but those gold and silver lines had not been on the mask when she packed it. Katerin drew a deep, shuddering breath that caught in her throat with a gulp. Another change in her fate that had come on without warning.

What would you have me do now, oh Gods?

She lowered her hands and kissed the mask's forehead. It stirred in her hands and grew warm.

Soon, she promised it, laying it gently on the cloak. She placed the Spear below the mask. Metkyi's heartstone went next to the Spear. Her token from Medvara, the many-noduled malachite stone, she placed above it, next to her mask.

"Here." Doryits handed her his unsheathed sword.

She nodded thanks and laid it across the Spear.

Doryits held up a thick white candle from her stores—she had left them on the shelf where he could see them. She nodded again, and he lit it, murmuring a prayer to Artel that she couldn't hear. He handed the candle to her and she placed it above the sword and Spear. He lit three more candles and she set them around their weapons and her tokens. She sprinkled a pinch of her finest glimmer dust over them. Then she picked up her mask and held it to her face.

"Goddess Dovré. I humbly ask your blessing on our weapons. You know what is at stake and what we face. Guide us, lead us, strengthen us."

Fingers gently took the mask from her grasp, placing it over the crossed Spear and sword. The Goddess smiled at Katerin, then bent to kiss her forehead. She faded away slowly as Katerin, then Doryits, knelt before the impromptu shrine.

The mask and weapons began to glow. Katerin kept her eyes fixed on them as calmness descended on her, breath coming easy and steady, the buzz of her thoughts fading until all she was aware of was mask, Spear, and sword.

For better or for worse, the fate she had evaded in many different forms over the past eighteen years would be resolved this coming day. This was what she had been fated to face.

I am the daughter of Terani-the-God-Killer. I am the Banisher of Shadows. I am the Champion of Varen. If I fail, then Varen falls and the Outcast God goes free.

But she did not intend to fail.

ALMOST DONE WITH ALL PRETENSE.

Rekaré moved through her sword practice forms while waiting for the others to join her in the library.

She was Rekaré Kinslayer, and this would be the day that reckoning would be paid. Oh, she would wear Giolanth's glamor into the amphitheater, but more than that aspect of him —no. She was done with all deceptions.

For this I was named Sorrow, and this day I will bring sorrow.

She had been cursed ever since her first kinslaying, justified as it was, and the curse that would undoubtedly fall upon her after she killed Chatain would shorten what life remained to her.

But she could keep that reddest of fates from Witmara. Her cousin could become Empress without that taint on her soul, the same red doom that had condemned Rekaré's leadership of Medvara.

Rekaré paused. She studied her sword, exulting in the power and strength radiating from it. It wasn't named, wasn't the power source that Katerin's Spear of War and Unmaking was.

Nonetheless, it had served her well over the years. She held it high, gazing lovingly at it. Her Heartfather Heinmyets had commissioned it for her when she was small. This sword had taken the life of Gegarth, the Shadowwalker who had killed her great-uncle and mentor Alame, Katerin's father. It had killed her father Zauril. Her cousin Chiral. And now—if everything went as planned, it would kill an Emperor.

Did my family know this was to be my destiny?

She had to wonder. Heinmyets sometimes *saw* things.

Thank you, Heartfather.

It was a royal gift from the man who was more her father than the one who had spawned her. The hilt stirred in her hand

—the first time the sword had done anything more than glow when she wielded it.

Her weapon deserved a name at last.

"I name you Emperor's Bane," she softly whispered. The sword glowed and murmured happily. She kissed it near the hilt, giving part of herself to the blade, as she had been doing gradually ever since *benghaalph* had first come upon her.

No turning back now. I am yours, and you are mine. Today will be the final kinslaying.

Blue-white light flared even brighter, and she felt as one with the Bane, the presence of Dovré filling Rekaré as it never had before.

I am with you today,

the Goddess whispered.

You carry our hope.

I am humbled, Goddess.

Light fingers on her head, *familiar* fingers as she recognized the touch of her mother. Rekaré blinked back tears. She did not turn her head to see if the Goddess was indeed appearing as her mother.

Go forth as our Champion, Lady of Sorrow,

the Goddess whispered. Then the sense of her presence faded.

The library door opened. Rekaré lowered her sword and sheathed it as Witmara entered the room, followed by Sesenth, Deomar, Kithry, Toran, and Betsona.

"Are you ready?" Betsona asked.

"As ready as I'll ever be." And more so than she had expected, as the Bane lent her strength. She hadn't slept well last night, but at this point it simply didn't matter. If she survived this day she would have plenty of time to sleep.

"We need to plan our choreography," Betsona said, fingers picking at the arms of her wheelchair. "How are we getting Witmara on the dueling floor?"

Rekaré inhaled sharply.

No. It's not safe for her. That puts her within range of Chatain's death curse.

"Is it wise for her to be there?"

Surely they were aware of that curse's potential?

"It is if you want the land's assistance," Witmara said. She held the staff that she had acquired since arriving in Daran.

"I don't need the land."

"How do you plan to neutralize Nitel?"

"I've battled Nitel before. I've carried her and I've helped banish her." Rekaré snorted. "I don't need any help to deal with her!"

"This is different," Witmara insisted. "You're facing Nitel as the patron of a ruling Emperor."

"And how is it different from what I faced with my father, who was also a devotee of Nitel?"

"He didn't have Chatain's power."

Rekaré laughed. "Zauril had enough to restrain my mother's magic and murder my great-grandfather!"

"Still not the potency of an Emperor's magic."

Rekaré pointed her finger at Witmara. "And you are barely come into your full strength! What makes you think that you can stand up to Chatain alone, much less Nitel?"

Out of the corner of her right eye she saw Betsona lean forward, lips parting in an anticipatory grin.

"What makes *you* think you can do it alone? You had my parents to support you when you took on Zauril!"

"And look where it brought me and your mother. No. You need to wait until I have either finished him or have fallen!"

"And what would my mother think of me if I held back to sacrifice you?"

"Your mother would not forgive me if I let him kill you or burden you with a death curse!"

"Nor would she forgive me if I let you do this all by yourself." Witmara raised her staff. "Listen. I do not dispute your cause with Chatain. You have lost much, much more to him than I ever had. And his death curse…." Witmara gulped, swallowing hard. "I don't like that you may end up bearing it. Still. You are probably better suited to be Empress than I am—except for the land. But Nitel is *mine* to deal with. I will accept the risk of Chatain's death curse because I believe the land will protect me."

Rekaré's nostrils flared. "It is good that the land accepted you because I will not, cannot, become Empress. Only if something happens to you…." her voice broke. "Gods, Witmara. Do you have the faintest understanding of what you are taking upon yourself by battling Nitel?"

Betsona sat back in her chair, brief disappointment washing over her face.

Witmara nodded. "It will not be easy. But it must be done. You cannot fight Nitel—you have danced too close to her in the past. She must be neutralized here, not just for our battle for the Empire but for my mother's battle against the Outcast God."

"Witmara, I—I can't let you do this. Not put you that close to Chatain."

Her cousin's lips tightened, then moved silently. A faint blue-green light akin to the glow of ocean waves flared from the head of her staff, where Witmara had carved an as-yet faceless woman.

She does not walk alone.

The face took the form of the Goddess Terat.

Rekaré bowed.

I did not expect you to patronize a follower of Staul, Lady Terat.

I owe the Lady Witmara a favor. You dare not be distracted by Nitel. You have been too close to her in the past, and as a daughter of the Ralsem family as well as the Miteal, it is dangerous for you to engage with her at this time. Witmara is the daughter of the Banisher of Shadows. Granddaughter of Terani-the-God-Killer. This is her task, to keep you safe from Nitel, as your task is to keep her safe from Chatain's death curse.

I see.

Good.

The Goddess's aspect faded from Witmara's staff.

"May I make a suggestion?" Sesenth said. "Can Witmara take the aspect of an aide to Deomar or Kithry? That would get her on the dueling floor."

"That would work," Betsona said. She smiled, half smile, half grimace. "It's a classic from the old plays, though."

"I would also like to be on the floor," Toran said. "Perhaps in the same role?"

"I'll take Witmara," Deomar said. "Kithry, Toran can be your assistant."

"So what does that entail?" Witmara asked.

"You will need to hand over weapons to us, both magical and non-magical," said Deomar. He went on to explain, but Rekaré tuned them out. She exhaled slowly.

Sesenth rested a hand on her arm. "Here we are, at last," she said in Saubral.

"Are you certain you want to witness this, dear one?" Rekaré answered in kind.

"I would not miss the fulfillment of *benghaalph* for anything." Sesenth drew herself up. "One of us has to carry back the story to the *quixnafal* of Saubral." Pride and sorrow mixed in her voice.

But sorrow dominated her expression.

THE SUN HOVERED HIGH ABOVE THE ARMY AS KATERIN LED THEM into the forest. Doryits rode at her left hand, Linyet at her right hand, and the Hidden One beside him. Kintarit and Haran followed.

Gods be with us, she thought as the darkness closed around them, the shadows blocking even the light from overhead.

As they halted to light torches, Katerin thought she spotted the shadowy forms of the Hunt, Terani pacing peacefully in the middle of the pack. The Karnoi wolf caught Katerin's eye and bared his teeth, tongue lolling out in an enormous canine grin.

The Six against the Outcast God...and Nitel.

Katerin's hand tightened on her torch as they rode forward.

THE END OF GODDESSES
AND EMPERORS

"Lady Betsona." Kolkex, the impresario of the Great Amphitheater, bowed low before their party at the royal entrance as the pale light of dawn glowed to their east. "Are you and your Champion ready for the Challenge?"

Betsona cleared her throat, fighting back the hoarseness that wanted to choke off her voice. "We are ready, dear Kolkex."

He grimaced. "Your wheelchair is not allowed on the dueling floor."

"I know." The roiling currents of Chatain's magic were such that Betsona didn't want to risk him co-opting the magic driving the chair. "I brought crutches."

She snapped her fingers and Witmara silently brought them, in her guise as Deomar's assistant.

Besides, hobbling into the Amphitheater would only emphasize her frailty and reflect poorly on Chatain. Witmara assisted Betsona to her feet, then faded back to the cart. Her daranval Daro pulled it, also concealed under a glamor. Witmara had insisted that Daro be present.

"Are you ready?" Kolkex asked. "Protocol requires you and your party to enter first."

"I am aware of the protocols," she snapped, harsher than she had intended. "This is not the first Challenge I have seen, Kolkex," she added, more softly. "Just my first time in the ring."

His expression softened. "I wish you and your Champion the best of luck, Lady Betsona."

"I thank you for that, Kolkex."

She appraised her supporters. Rekaré stared ahead. A heavily veiled Sesenth stood next to her—she would join Betsona on the observation platform. The others wore grim expressions, as if they marched to their deaths.

"The Gods walk with us, friends," she said softly. "Let us remember that."

Back at the house she had thought that Witmara would challenge Rekaré. Then the Goddess Terat had appeared, and—no. There was something about these people from Varen. A solidity of purpose she envied.

Either one of them are more worthy to be Empress than I am.

A sobering realization.

Betsona set her chin firmly and hobbled into the dueling ring. Loud cheers erupted from two-thirds of the stands as Betsona shuffled toward the observation stand. As they reached the stand, Rekaré helped first Betsona, then Sesenth onto the platform, then turned to face the other royal entrance, waiting for Chatain's arrival.

Deomar and Kithry stood beside Rekaré. Witmara and Toran moved by the cart Daro had pulled into the ring. It held other weapons, water…and a pallet to carry away the fallen.

Gods, I hope we don't have to use it for Rekaré or Witmara.

BOOM! BOOM!

The drums Chatain used to announce his arrival at a Challenge began to thunder, sending a cold chill as always down Betsona's back. Icy fingers of fear gripped her gut. *She* was the one at stake this time. What would happen if both Rekaré and Witmara failed?

Sesenth patted her hand, seemingly aware of the dread that gripped Betsona. The contact tingled as Sesenth gently extended the pat into a grasp—a gentle chill that was of Staul.

What does it mean that she's a developing Shadowwalker?

Both Rekaré and Sesenth had evaded any explanation of Shadowwalker powers.

The royal entrance doors swung wide. Chatain strode into the ring, flanked by his Seconds and their cart attendants. He wore plain leather armor instead of his usual showy garb, and moved with a quiet competence that Betsona rarely noticed in him.

Then again, considering how many of our siblings he's killed in Challenge....

She had missed the Challenges of the last two years. Perhaps this was how he dressed for one these days.

Chatain marched to the flat circle-shaped stone in the middle of the ring, carved with Ralsem sigils and marred with divots where the Miteal sigils had been gouged out of the rock. His seconds stood beside the stone. Chatain raised his arms and the Ralsem sigils glowed green, edged with magenta.

"I, Chatain en Ralsem, Emperor of Daran, raise my side of the shield, to protect the innocents in this place," he chanted as a shimmering green and magenta light rose behind him. "Are you ready to meet your doom in the name of Betsona ea Ralsem, Giolanth en Stanil?"

Rekaré laughed and stepped forward onto the stone to face Chatain. As she raised her hands the guise of Giolanth dropped from her form. Blue and silver shimmered in the gashes where the Miteal sigils had been, as if they had never been chiseled out. Chatain's eyes widened in recognition and he took a step back as Rekaré bared her teeth at him.

"I, Rekaré Kinslayer, former Leader of Medvara, daughter of both the House of Miteal and the House of Ralsem, *benghaalph* and *quixnahi* of Saubral, raise my side of the shield, to protect the innocents in this place," she chanted. Blue and silver rose behind her and met Chatain's green and magenta. "I bring your doom from Varen in the names of Betsona ea Ralsem, Alicira ea Miteal, Melarae ea Miteal, Inharise of Clenda, Alame en Miteal, and Cenarth of the Two Nations amongst others!" She laughed again and drew her sword. "Meet the Bane of Emperors, *Chatain the foul!*"

Silence fell over the amphitheater.

A fearful expression that Betsona had not seen since their accident crossed Chatain's face as he lifted his sword to meet Rekaré's.

KATERIN'S FACE FELT STIFF AS THEY RODE THROUGH THE FOREST, as if her mask had conformed to its shape.

Sorcery.

The mask was in her rooms back at the Leader's House, still resting on Metkyi's cloak.

If it wasn't for the Light of Clenda shining bright on Linyet's forehead their passage would be much more gloomy. Katerin brought the Eye of Dovré out.

Be a light for us, oh Goddess.

The more light from their magic, the better.

The gold threads in the clear quartz emitted a faint golden glow that radiated ahead of them. Suddenly an opening emerged from the shadows. Rainin snorted, shaking her head and pulling for more rein, eager to leave this dreary forest.

"Are we ready?" she asked the others riding with her.

"As ready as we'll ever be," Linyet answered, eyes unfocused as he fixed on a distant vision, his lips parted. "My mother has stepped up to battle Chatain."

"Then it is time." The Hidden One cackled. "We must support *benghaalph.*"

Katerin glanced at Doryits. He nodded, lips grimly held tight.

"For Varen!" she yelled, and gave Rainin free rein. The bay mare leapt into a gallop, settling into a bold stride as they charged out of the forest to face the rows of skeletal riders facing them.

But Katerin's primary focus was on the woman who led the undead riders. Nitel's green and magenta colors threaded around her, along with the dark red of an alien presence. Rainin charged toward Sariost, ears pinned flat against her head. Katerin drew her sword, and it shifted shape to become the Spear, the spearhead glowing bright blue and silver.

WITMARA'S FINGERS CLENCHED HER STAFF AS CHATAIN AND Rekaré clashed, mixing spells and swords as they battled. Would the exorcism spell actually work? So far, Nitel had not manifested herself as the two battled, alternating between casting spells and using their swords. Rekaré and Chatain broke apart and circled around the central stone. Rekaré hobbled on her bad right leg from a kick to her knee, but Chatain had to keep wiping blood out of his eyes from a forehead cut.

"Is that the best you can do, bastard daughter of the Ralsem?" Chatain sneered. He paused, fingers twisting in a summoning spell.

"You have not even begun to see what I am capable of."

Rekaré snapped her fingers and his spell spluttered out.

She raised an enchantment of her own and flicked it at him. A giant desert scorpion landed on his face. Chatain yelped and batted at it, managing to keep its stinger from striking him. At last he was able to chop it in half with a dagger and pull it from his face. He blasted the writhing scorpion pieces with his magic, crisping them into smoky shells.

At some point he had to summon Nitel's aid. He *had* to do that. But when? Witmara knew Rekaré's fighting style well enough to see that she was holding back, waiting for that moment. But Gods, Rekaré was tiring. Chatain did not appear to be.

Patience,

the Goddess Terat whispered to her.

It is not yet time.

Witmara's fingers tightened even more on the staff.

It still might fall to her to kill Chatain.

The land stirred at that thought, pushing against the restraints Witmara had put on it.

It was ready to be freed from Chatain's grasp.

SKELETAL RIDERS CHARGED BETWEEN KATERIN AND SARIOST while Sariost retreated. Rainin screamed and struck at those in their way while Katerin stabbed at them. It would make more sense for the Spear to reform itself into its sword shape, but it stubbornly refused to do that.

At least Doryits and Linyet fought next to her, the three of them working together. Katerin blocked a blow meant for Linyet as Doryits struck down a fighter who stabbed at Rainin.

Then, by all the Gods, they were *through* the ring of fighters who had gathered around Sariost. She had dismounted and was tracing a summoning spell in the air. Katerin bailed off of Rainin, loosing the ties to her pouch of glimmer dust with her left hand. She seized a pinch of the dust and hurled it at Sariost.

It fell short, cascading to the ground in a bright shimmer as it outlined the form taking shape between them. Green and magenta lights glowed menacingly around the outline.

And then it solidified, Nitel sneering at Katerin.

"I defeated you once and I will again!" Katerin shrieked. A red sword took shape between them. Nitel clasped it.

She kissed the blade, and to Katerin's shock it momentarily took the form of a skeletal man—*no, a God*—dressed in blood red leathers before resuming the appearance of a sword.

Katerin raised the Spear, preparing to strike at the Goddess. *You have done this before,* she told herself. *And then you did not have the Spear.*

But then Metkyi had been by her side, to drag her back from the dreamless sleep. Who would step forward to save her now?

BETSONA'S FINGERS CURLED TIGHT AROUND THE ARMS OF HER chair as Rekaré and Chatain circled, engaged, broke apart, circled, engaged, and broke apart. For once Chatain was up against someone who was his equal in both sorcery and sword work. He had several slashing wounds on his legs and arms, and even though he was using sorcery to staunch the blood flow, he still moved more slowly. Rekaré's wounds were less severe.

Sesenth was murmuring. Was the Shadowwalker casting

spells to support Rekaré? None of the warning wards flared to indicate that was happening.

The crowds around them remained quiet, not even the slightest murmur coming from the stands.

This battle has already gone longer than any other Challenge Chatain has faced.

That spoke to Rekaré's strength not just as a magician but a warrior. Gods, the woman was a fighter.

A groan drew her attention to Witmara. Had that come from her or from her spouse? So far the young woman had maintained her glamor, though she clutched that staff of hers tightly. At the moment she leaned against her daranval—at the moment wearing the guise of a lowly carriage mule—seemingly relaxed. Not so Deomar and Kithry, who leaned forward to watch the battle. Perhaps one of them had made the noise.

Suddenly Witmara straightened up, raising her staff at the same time that power shimmered between Rekaré and Chatain. Magenta and green flared, and then Nitel stood between Rekaré and Chatain.

I did not ask you to summon me now!

Nitel shrieked at Chatain.

You fool! I am needed elsewhere!

"You must end her quickly!" Chatain bellowed back. "Why do you think I summoned you?"

Goddess and Emperor glowered at each other. Rekaré stood at the edge of the great stone, breathing hard, looking exhausted and drained.

Gods, no.

Betsona tried to summon her own magic to aid Rekaré, forgetting the wards.

"Ow!" she gasped as it stung her.

"No interference, sister!" Chatain yelled.

"I would aid my Champion against Nitel!" she screamed back.

"That was before I knew I battled Rekaré Kinslayer and not one of your pets!"

I cannot stay to help you!

Nitel snarled, her form starting to fade.

"NO!" Chatain seized the Goddess.

That evoked shocked gasps from the stands at his presumption. The Goddess tried to twist away as he slapped a wooden bracelet on her wrist, glowing bright red.

Darkwood, Betsona realized as they continued to argue. *I did not know he had become powerful enough to wield darkwood against one of the Gods!*

If he were truly that powerful, then they were lost. Betsona shook her head, despairing. Then her lips tightened. If she had to fight him herself, she would make Chatain pay. She would not die easily.

Sesenth's mumbling grew louder. She raised her hands, power radiating from them. How could she cast spells? Or was Chatain simply not aware of the woman?

Meanwhile, Rekaré stood still, her whole body shaking as she wheezed for breath. But there was something not quite right about her...Betsona squinted hard, then covered her mouth to stifle any sound that would alert Chatain. The exhausted Rekaré was but an illusion.

She could just barely see the outline of a feral-looking version of Rekaré circling behind Chatain, most definitely *not* exhausted.

Sesenth cackled softly next to her and pulled off her gloves to reveal completely gray-scaled hands.

"Hear me lord Staul," she whispered. Her voice made the hairs on the back of Betsona's neck rise at its vehemence. "It is *time* for Chatain to face his fate. *Benghaalph* rises." She pulled off her veils and stood.

Gray scales completely covered her face.

BEFORE KATERIN COULD STRIKE, NITEL'S SHAPE FADED SLIGHTLY, though the sword in her hand still glowed as bright as ever.

> I cannot stay!

the Goddess shrieked.

> Chatain calls me!

The sword transformed again, the God within it glowering.

> Betraying me yet again, sister? I should have known better than to trust you!

He slapped Nitel.
Nitel collapsed to her knees.

> No. Not that. He dares to bind me!

She thrust her hands up for the Outcast God to examine, a bracelet glowing red on her left wrist.

> What? He dares? Then he will be the first to fall once I am freed!

The Outcast God wrestled with the bracelet, trying to pull it off of Nitel.

Now!

Terani's presence suddenly manifested next to Katerin, the Hunt materializing around Katerin, Doryits, and Linyet, the wolves growling and snapping at the skeletal riders who lunged forward.

Now!

The Goddess Terat's visage overlaid Linyet as he struck Nitel with his sword.

The Outcast God whirled to attack Linyet. Doryits stepped between them, driving him back as Nitel writhed on Linyet's sword. Katerin stabbed Sariost with the Spear. She screamed and pushed forward onto the Spear, to tear at Katerin's face with her claw-like fingernails. Terani's hands rested over Katerin's, helping her hold the Spear fast as Sariost shrieked and twisted. Pain writhed through Katerin, power draining from her as she kept Sariost impaled. She gasped for breath, staring straight into the wraith's eyes.

Sariost faded. Bit by bit, her movements slowed. Then her skeletal form transformed to that of a pale-skinned, emaciated young woman. She collapsed, eyes dull and staring straight up. Katerin knelt and checked for a pulse—though did the undead have a pulse?

Behead her. It is the only safe way,

Terani said.

Katerin nodded. She wrenched the Spear free. Sariost jerked, awareness returning to her eyes. The Spear transformed to the Sword and she swung hard, severing the head. Sariost's body crumpled into ash.

The Outcast God disappeared with a shriek, leaving Linyet

and Nitel. Linyet shoved his sword deeper into the Goddess. He bellowed in pain as she writhed and twisted.

Katerin staggered to his side, the Spear back to its usual shape, and plunged it into the Goddess's chest above Linyet's sword.

Gods, it hurt even more than ever. But at least this time it was a shared ache, not like it had when she had banished Nitel from Keldara. Perhaps the two of them could keep each other from being drawn into the dreamless sleep as Nitel faded.

REKARÉ SPRUNG ONTO CHATAIN'S BACK, YANKING HIM AWAY FROM the Goddess.

"Witmara, *now!*" she screamed, letting go of her feigned exhaustion. Fierce joy pounded through her.

No more holding back. It is time.

Chatain shook Rekaré off and whirled to face her, his first stroke going wide. But he still moved quickly enough to block her.

You owe me a death, Chatain.

Rage gave her new strength even as he had clearly tired, looking at least twice his age—how much of his power had he poured into that summoning?

Chatain paused. A smirk tightened his lips as his sword glowed red. Then he was upon her, aiming for her right arm, angling to slash her with the very tip of his blade. Her leathers deflected his blow from her upper arm but that tip found a tiny gap at her elbow. Fleeting strike, barely enough to draw blood—*and it burned.* He danced away, grinning wide as she grabbed at the sharp, biting pain with her other hand, gasping now for real. The bitter, sour scent of Essence of Darsnai rose from her injury.

Poison.

She would die soon. Rekaré blinked hard, drew in a shaking breath as Chatain's sneer grew.

Gods, if ever you chose to smile upon me, now is the time.

And then the flow she had come to recognize as *benghaalph* poured through Rekaré, coupled with the power of a new Shadowwalker.

Senth has fully transformed.

The flow overrode the burning agony raging out from that scratch, temporarily lending her strength. She charged at Chatain and drove him away from where Witmara dueled with Nitel.

There. Goddess guide me!

She swung hard with the last of her strength, beheading Chatain. A surprised expression crossed his face as she struck and she wanted to laugh as his head rolled away, his body collapsing. But she was aflame now, the Essence of Darsnai burning through her veins as *benghaalph* faded, this time for good, leaving only Sesenth's distress.

She allowed herself one final shriek before she collapsed on the stones, muscles tightening hard enough to break bones, a pain greater than she had ever known, burning, burning, burning.

And yet a fierce joy pulsed through the agony. It was done. She had succeeded.

For you, Mother. Cenarth. Melarae. Inharise.

If she strained hard enough, she could almost see them now, Cenarth's hands reaching out for her along with Melarae's as pain crested, eating every bit of her in white-hot flames.

Rekaré gladly reached for them, her only regret that Sesenth remained behind.

And yet—a veil still lay between them, keeping her from her beloved dead. She sobbed into the darkness that fell around her, barely aware that Sesenth held her as awareness faded.

NITEL LAUGHED HYSTERICALLY AS HER ENERGIES SWIRLED AROUND Linyet's sword and the Spear of War and Unmaking. Katerin held the Spear firm. It vibrated with the intensity of the energy it was extracting from the Goddess, but it was taking a long time to drain the Goddess's essence—longer than Katerin had experienced before.

What has Chatain done to her?

Your mother has died, along with Chatain!

Nitel screeched finally.

Which leaves you for my vengeance!

She reached out with bony fingers that elongated, stretching toward Linyet. He held firm, not flinching away.

"I banish you from Varen in the name of the Goddess Terat!" he yelled back at Nitel. Though he had gone gray under brown, testifying to his exhaustion, his grip did not weaken, even as Nitel grabbed the sword with both hands to try to wrench herself closer. Katerin shifted her hold on the Spear, pinning the Goddess so that she could not advance further.

Fur brushing against her arms. The Hunt crowded in around them, Karnoi-wolf biting down on one of Nitel's arms, Cirdel-wolf the other.

You would betray me, my children?

Nitel whimpered.

Doryits bellowed. Katerin looked up in time to see Terani's visage settle upon him as he raised his sword high. He neatly decapitated the Goddess. Karnoi-wolf and Cirdel-wolf dove upon Nitel's head, growling as they chewed and worried it. Makri-wolf was the first of the Hunt to lick at the blood spewing from the severed neck. Katerin pulled the Spear out and stepped back, along with Linyet, as the Hunt dove upon the Goddess's form. Terani's shape separated from Doryits and stood over the Goddess, watching as the Hunt tore at Nitel's corpse.

This, too, was new.

"Are you all right?" she asked Linyet.

Gods, she was tired. Utterly exhausted, like she had been all those years ago after banishing Nitel and the Twins from the Two Nations. But the disassociation that had gone along with banishing Nitel did not drag down her limbs this time, did not cover the world with a fog leaving her separate from those around her.

"Tired," Linyet said. He wiped his forehead with a forearm. "And what was that she said about my mother?"

"That she was dead," Katerin said. She tried to reach out for Rekaré, and felt nothing—just like she had ever since Rekaré had left for Daran.

Linyet gazed into the distance. Doryits staggered into Katerin. She grabbed him and they leaned against each other.

"Sariost?" he gasped.

"I took care of her," Katerin said. "She is no more."

"At the end—was she skeleton or body?"

"Body. Very pale."

Doryits heaved a relieved sigh. "Then they did not totally consume her soul." He rested his head on Katerin's shoulder. "Thank you. She is at peace now. Thank you, Leader Katerin, Defender of Varen, Banisher of Shadows. Thank you for doing what I could not."

"You did what I could not, carrying Terani. Thank you for that."

He nodded and raised his head again. They watched as the Hunt consumed the last pieces of Nitel's body.

Karnoi-wolf and Cirdel-wolf followed Terani to stand before Katerin, Linyet, and Doryits. The wolf forms transformed, until the Twins stood beside Terani in their full divine glory.

Katerin did not kneel or bow to them, though both Linyet and Doryits bowed their heads respectfully. Terani chuckled.

As strong-minded as ever, daughter.

"I can be no other way," Katerin answered. "And the Twins and I have a difficult history."

Very true, Lady Katerin,

Cirdel said.

But, for today, we are allies. And we thank you and your supporters for what you have done.

As Rekaré collapsed and Sesenth ran to her, Nitel pressed close to Witmara, suddenly seeming to grow stronger.

Now I am in one place!

she exulted.

And I can crush you just as my servant has crushed your Champion!

It is time,

Witmara whispered to her staff. "In the name of Staul, I banish and exorcise you not only from Daran but from his world!" She raised the staff high. "In the name of Terat, I call upon Daran to completely renounce your presence!"

You can't do that!

The Goddess's eyes widened as blue and silver glowed from the inlays in the staff, where Witmara had woven the spells into it.

You do not have the authority!

Witmara laughed, unable to control the slight hysteric note creeping into her voice.

"I AM WITMARA EA MITEAL," she screamed. "Daughter of Katerin ea Miteal, who is in turn daughter of Alame en Miteal, son of Alexran! The land of Daran is *mine*, and I claim it in the name of the House of Miteal! Daran, do you tolerate this interference?"

Silence. Then cheers. "Witmara! Witmara ea Miteal! WITMARA!"

Witmara swung the staff hard at Nitel. As the head contacted the Goddess, Nitel shrieked yet again. Bright red light blinded Witmara, but only for a moment.

When she blinked again, the Goddess was gone. Witmara looked around, at Chatain's headless body and Rekaré's still form as Sesenth sobbed over her body. The crowd still cheered her name, but the roars seemed to come from a distance. Then Deomar and Kithry, followed by Chatain's seconds, knelt at her feet. Daro, apparently freed from his harness by someone—probably Toran, trotted over to

Witmara and nudged her. Toran quickly knelt next to Deomar.

The cheers changed. "Betsona! Betsona! BET-SO-NA!"

Was she going to become a betrayer? Witmara did not turn to face Betsona, choosing to focus on the crowds. And Daro did not seem worried so perhaps—

Betsona hobbled past the kneeling men, leaning hard on her crutches. She would have knelt, but her knees wobbled as she started to descend, one crutch falling from her grasp and it threw her off balance.

Witmara dropped her staff and caught Betsona before she landed, trying to pull her back to her feet. Betsona shook her head, sagging in Witmara's arms until she landed on her knees. She took Witmara's hands in hers and kissed them.

The crowd roared even louder.

"WIT-MAR-A! BET-SO-NA! WIT-MAR-A! BET-SO-NA!"

Betsona smiled up at Witmara. "I give thanks for what you and Rekaré have done—my lady Empress. You have freed Daran."

"So what has happened to my cousin? My daughter?" Katerin asked the Twins. "We have all been fighting Nitel's manifestations."

> Our mother is no longer,

Karnoi said.

> Your strike has weakened the Outcast God. Our father will need to find a new patron, and a new host to fulfill his ambitions.

"You mean we've actually killed Nitel?" That didn't seem

right, based on all Katerin knew about the Gods and how they worked. "Does this mean you are now the Six Crowned Gods, not the Seven?"

Nitel's death was not just your work,

Cirdel said.

Chatain's binding spell weakened our mother. And then your cousin's sacrifice, coupled with the strength of your daughter—

She broke off, bowing low, along with Karnoi.

—And we are still Seven.

Overwhelming pressure and heat forced Katerin to her knees as first Artel the Judge, then Dovré and Staul, followed by Terat, joined the Twins.

—On this day we welcome a new Goddess to the Seven,

Artel pronounced.

THE CHEERS OF THE CROWD SUDDENLY CUT OFF AS THE RUMBLING, heavy warmth that announced the manifestation of Gods pressed down upon the amphitheater. Witmara slowly sank to her knees alongside Betsona as first Artel, then the remaining five Gods of the Seven, appeared next to Rekaré's body.

—On this day we welcome a new Goddess to the Seven,

Artel pronounced. He reached down and took Rekaré's limp hand as Staul gently pulled Sesenth away from her.

Rise, Lady of Sorrow, Rekaré who once was Kinslayer.

Witmara gasped as Rekaré's body moved. Transformation rippled over her body, the hurts fading as she slowly rose to her knees, then pushed herself up.

I am not worthy of this honor, Lord Artel,

Rekaré said.

I am no Goddess, even though my father possessed that ambition.

The God laughed.

Lady Rekaré, who would be better to replace Nitel? You are the Lady of Sorrow. You will be a comfort to those who struggle with loss, and the champion of those who are downtrodden. Who better to replace our late foolish sister than you? Prophet of the Saubral. Bearer of Emperor's Bane. Yes. You.

And the fate of those I have loved and want to be with again?

We all need Messengers and Voices,

the God said.

Melarae your daughter will be your Voice. Cenarth your husband will be your Messenger.

He gestured and two forms appeared—Witmara gulped at

the sight of Melarae, *healthy*. Her cousin smiled shyly at Witmara before joining her father beside Rekaré.

> And Sesenth my other love, she who has been devoted to me as wife?

> Her fate is not yet done.

> And my son Linyet?

> Linyet Lightbringer has his own fate that is still unfolding.

Rekaré sighed.

> Then he has survived?

> He and your cousin Katerin were crucial to weakening our late sister so that Witmara could strike the final blow. Linyet Lightbringer along with Katerin Defender of Varen have many things left to do in this life. Now is not their time to sleep.

Rekaré bowed her head to Artel.

> I did not seek divinity, even though my father did as well as—

she gestured at Chatain's still form.

> —my distant cousin.

> Which is why you are the one we have chosen to replace Nitel,

Dovré said.

Goddess, I am honored. And I accept. But oh, Senth—can you forgive me?

Sesenth eased herself free from Staul's grasp. "With my lord Staul's permission—I will gladly serve you as priestess, beloved and Lady."

I release you from your oaths, Sesenth,

Staul said.

My new sister will have need of you.

The new Goddess and Sesenth stared at each other. Then Rekaré strode over to Sesenth. She placed both hands on Sesenth's face, kissing first her forehead, then the tears rolling down her cheeks, before kissing her hard on the lips. Then she stepped back. Cenarth's form came forward to kiss Sesenth as well. Then Sesenth rose.

"I will speak of your fate to my Shadowwalker kin," she said.

I thank you, beloved.

Rekaré turned to face the crowds.

Carry these tidings far and wide, and be warned. The Lady of Sorrow will not tolerate ill treatment of the downtrodden, including the oppressed and enslaved. This is a new era, and a new world.

Then she turned to Witmara.

Lady Witmara, Empress of Daran. Go forward and do what is right. But do not forget your earliest lessons.

"I will not forget," Witmara promised. And she meant every word.

Her eyes widened as she looked at her staff. Rekaré's face stared out from the uncarved portion of the knot.

WHAT COMES AFTER BATTLE

It was done. So why didn't she feel better?

Katerin heaved a heavy sigh as she gazed around the battle-field, still trying to take it in. Not the events of the battle—that was tangible and real, as the cries of the wounded and the stench from the fallen skeletal warriors testified.

Soon enough she needed to join Linyet and Doryits in triaging the fallen. Even though the Outcast God was gone for now, those who had been maimed by his followers were still at risk of possession.

But she had a moment to consider what she had seen in that vision from the Gods.

Chatain fallen, and Witmara as Empress—those were tangi-ble, although a small part of her sorrowed that she would most likely never see her daughter again. She doubted Witmara could leave Daran now, just as Katerin could not leave Varen, even if she wanted to cross the ocean.

Harder to accept was the ascension of Rekaré to Goddesshood.

Memories spilled through Katerin's thoughts as she twined her fingers in Rainin's mane and buried her face in the mare's neck, fighting back sobs. Small Rekaré, the wild young horse-woman that Katerin had seen once in her early days as a circuit Healer in Keldara. Adult Rekaré, who had ridden with Cenarth to save Katerin and Metkyi from an attack by the Hunt. Rekaré her cousin, the Leader of Medvara. Rekaré, the anguished mother of a daughter killed by sorcery. Rekaré Kinslayer, the leader of the Mer Galad, dedicated to creating unity amongst the people of Varen, starting with defanging the Saubral threat. Rekaré, mourning Cenarth's death. The grim, fell expression she wore after he died in Waykemin.

Rekaré become Goddess? Hard to believe. And yet, there it was.

Familiar, spectral hands stroked her neck. Rainin nickered a welcome.

I told you our daughter was Witmara of the Promise,

her late beloved Metkyi whispered. Katerin startled and turned away from Rainin. Metkyi smiled at her, solid like he hadn't been for ages.

"Beloved," she choked, wiping away the tears that blurred her vision with her least blood-and-ichor-splattered wrist. "I thought you could not appear to me again."

His hand cupped her cheek, feeling solid, warm, *alive.* But she knew better.

This is the last time we can speak, until you join me,

he said.

She dared to reach up and rest her hand over his. It did not fade away, even as more tears made it hard for her to see him.

"Now what?" she asked. This was the final goodbye she had been dreading over the past few years. She swallowed hard. Gods, even after eighteen years—it was only now that she realized the degree to which she had clung to the visitations with Metkyi at Staul's shrines that had been allowed them after his death.

He leaned forward and kissed her.

> Remember that I love you beyond the grave. This parting is only temporary.

Katerin sniffled. She reached to wipe her eyes again so that she could see him more clearly, but he gently did it for her.

> You still have things to do. You are the Defender of Varen. Mother of an Empress.

"No you. No Witmara," she whispered. "Not even Rekaré. Am I to always be alone except for my daranval?" *You're whining,* she scolded herself. Wasting precious time with Metkyi. After all, she had been alone except for her daranval before, while riding her healing circuits. She gulped. "Forgive me."

> For good reason, dearest. I do not want you to feel like you have to be alone. That has never been my wish.

She gulped. "There's been no one to capture my heart but you, Metkyi. Not even Senai." And Senai had never appeared to Katerin after her death.

> I know. But you don't deserve to be alone.

"I have Medvara. And Rainin."

> Will the land comfort you? A daranval bond is good, but is it enough? Open your eyes and your heart, Katerin. Do not deny yourself should someone come along.

His hand stroked her forehead.

Promise me this. You have lost much—and with both Rekaré and Witmara gone to you—I would not have you be alone, beloved.

Anguish twisted his expression.

"If the right person comes along," she finally whispered.

He pulled her into his arms without saying anything more. She held him tight while he kissed her forehead, her cheeks, and then her lips.

Farewell for now, beloved,

he said, gently separating from her.

She blinked back more tears as he faded slowly away. Then she took a deep breath and straightened up. She had duties.

"Katerin." Doryits's voice startled her, from the other side of Rainin.

"I'm coming."

He came around Rainin's head, pausing to rub her forehead. "Are you all right? I saw—was that Witmara's father?"

She nodded, choking back another sob. "Yes. He is the Messenger of Staul now." She swallowed hard and coughed. "A moment, and I'll be ready to help with triage."

He shook his head. "The Hidden One and her people have taken on that task. You, Linyet, and I are to take the survivors back to Nere."

"We shouldn't."

"She insists, as we bore the brunt of the attack. The Saubral Healers are doing a good job. I've checked." He paused. "They have not been visited by ghosts like you and I have."

"Your wife?"

He nodded. "And our son, and—Sariost."

"I need to speak to the Hidden One. And check on the wounded."

"You need to care for yourself, too, Defender of Varen," he said. "Katerin, you cannot do it all. We leave things in good hands."

She drew a deep breath. "I want to check for myself."

"Gods, you're stubborn." But a soft smile touched his lips. "Come on, then. Let us check, and then take our people to a well-deserved rest."

Tired,

Rainin added, turning her head from Doryits's scratching to shove her nose hard against Katerin.

All is well.

Further thoughts of a stall heavily bedded with straw where a tired daranval could lie down, with as much hay as she could nibble on, came to Katerin.

"I can't fight both of you!" Katerin sighed. "All right."

"Both—oh." He smiled at Rainin and rubbed her forehead again. "Come on. We'll go to the Hidden One together. Linyet is gathering all who can still ride."

They walked together toward a tent that had been erected in the middle of the battlefield. Katerin glanced around. Shadowwalkers worked alongside the other peoples of Varen, some bringing wounded toward the tent while others burned the dead.

Seven years ago this would have been an unlikely sight. Now the Shadowwalkers are our allies.

But this unity had been Rekaré's doing—and, she finally admitted, her own.

"I don't know what to do now," Witmara said softly to Betsona as she helped Betsona regain her feet. Chatain's seconds loaded his head and body onto the waiting pallet and silently carried it away, while Rekaré's body had disappeared. "I understand one of us needs to perform the renewal rites. But what do I *do*?"

Temptation pulled briefly at Betsona. Here was her chance at power. She could take over the responsibility of invoking Dovré at the Festival, could still leave herself open as a conduit from the Goddess to the land. After all, why would one dedicated to Staul know the rites? This was one ruling task she could take from Witmara, one thing to be postponed until the next year.

And yet, as she considered it more, the less she wanted to step into Witmara's place. Gods, she was already exhausted. The land throbbed eagerly under their feet, and she could see its power pulsing not just through Witmara but through the wooden staff she carried.

More than that, the anger and passion that had fueled so much of her life was ebbing. It felt good to realize that she didn't have to defend herself against Chatain. Ever since Witmara had stuck down Nitel, the constant low-level sensation of *threat* had faded, and along with it any desire Betsona felt for assuming the title of Empress.

How much of my feelings were shaped by Nitel's presence?

Seijina would be happy if they returned to their quiet lives in Adalane and Daraelen.

She cleared her throat. "Kolkex has a ritual book. I will have him bring it to you." Betsona gestured to the impresario hovering at the edge of the ring, noticing that he already had garbed himself in the ceremonial robes and carried the book.

I trained him well.

A mild satisfaction at that thought. She still had work to do, and Witmara would need her guidance.

Kolkex bustled over to them. Betsona stepped back as he bowed to Witmara.

"Lady Witmara."

"The lady Betsona says that you have the book for the consecration ritual?"

He nodded eagerly. "You will need to stand here, my lady." He gestured to the central stone. Witmara's nostrils flared as she gazed at the stone. Then she sighed, and stepped forward.

"Show me the way, Kolkex," she said. Toran followed her.

Betsona turned to hobble back to the platform. To her surprise, Sesenth gently took one elbow and helped her back to their seats.

Witmara raised her hands high and began the chant.

Betsona had never seen the sigils in the stone glow so brightly—Ralsem and Miteal alike.

"WIT-MAR-A! WIT-MAR-A!" THE CROWD ROARED AT THE END of the consecration ceremony. Kolkex smiled at Witmara, clearly happy to see that he hadn't needed to prompt her too many times. The ceremony *was* somewhat familiar, after all. She had originally read it in the library at Medvara, amongst the few records recovered from Alexran's reign. Not even Zauril had dared to burn that book. There were minor differences in words and pronunciation of the old High Aireii.

Power throbbed through her as she studied the people—*her* people now. Witmara drew a deep breath. Now would come the hard work. But she had Toran at her side, and Daro—and Betsona.

Betsona. Until she had children, Betsona would be her heir. She should be standing on her other side.

"Kolkex," she said quietly. "The lady Betsona needs to stand with me. She is my heir, after all."

The quick smile he gave her before scurrying off to help Betsona to her side was reward enough.

And the louder cheers as Betsona slowly made her way to Witmara told her she had made the correct move.

"Are you certain you want me here right now?" Betsona asked. "It is your victory, after all."

"I couldn't have done it without your help—and until Toran and I have children, you are my heir."

"Are you certain?" Betsona repeated. "Wouldn't you want a fresh slate, with no ties to Chatain or the Ralsems?"

"I am very certain," Witmara said firmly.

So this is what it is like to be a Goddess.

Rekaré's vision was divided between Witmara performing ceremony, Katerin riding slowly back to Nere, Basnen's sudden collapse back at her stall, and the new presence of her divine now-siblings as they hovered above the land. The vast views of Daran, the ocean, and Varen were almost enough to invoke vertigo—*if Gods could develop vertigo, that is,* she thought wryly.

"Come," Staul said. "We have a ceremony of our own, sister. For now, we can let them be. They have their own paths to forge."

She let herself be drawn away. A loud, familiar nicker made her turn back. Basnen galloped toward Rekaré, her coat a bright, burnished glowing gold, starlight reflecting off of her silver mane.

Rekaré laughed and ran toward her daranval, wrapping her arms around Basnen's neck even as Basnen curled her head around to wrap Rekaré against her shoulder. They stood there for a moment, then Rekaré swung up on Basnen.

"Now I am ready, Lord Staul!"

He shook his head, a slight smile twitching his lips as Dovré joined him, that Goddess's smile as big and as bright as Basnen's coat.

"Sister, I suppose we have to allow this," he said to Dovré.

Dovré raised her brows. "My gift to our new sister."

Staul snorted. Basnen echoed his snort, shaking her head. Rekaré urged her on. With Staul at one side, and Dovré on her other, she rode ahead, into a shimmering rainbow veil of light.

THE END

NEWSLETTER

Like this story and want to know what's coming out next, or what deals Joyce is offering on her book?

Check out Joyce's monthly newsletter at

https://joycespublishingnewsfromwideopenspaces.kit.com/a65eaa89cd

And get a free download snippet from the Martiniere Multiverse!

ABOUT THE AUTHOR

The work of Joyce Reynolds-Ward includes themes of high-stakes family and political conflict, digital sentience, personal agency and control, realistic strong women, and (whenever possible) horses. She is the author of *The Netwalk Sequence* series, the *Goddess's Honor* series, *The Martiniere Legacy* series, *The People of the Martiniere Legacy* series, and the recently published *The Cost of Power* trilogy as well as standalones *Klone's Stronghold, Alien Savvy, Beating the Apocalypse*, and *Federation Cowboy*. Joyce is a Self-Published Fantasy BlogOff Semifinalist, a Writers of the Future SemiFinalist, and an Anthology Builder Finalist. She is a member of the Science Fiction and Fantasy Writers Association and a member of Soroptimists International.

BOOKS AND PUBLICATIONS

Goddess's Honor

Beyond Honor and Other Stories: Goddess's Honor Book One
Pledges of Honor: Goddess's Honor Book Two
Challenges of Honor: Goddess's Honor Book Three
Choices of Honor: Goddess's Honor Book Four
Judgment of Honor: Goddess's Honor Book Five

The Cost of Power

Return
Snippet: Outtakes from Philip Martiniere
Crucible
Snippet: The Criminal Injustice Interview
Snippet: Sibling Warfare
Redemption
Omnibus Ebook Edition

The Martiniere Legacy

First Meetings: A Martiniere Legacy Short Story
Inheritance: The Martiniere Legacy Book One
Ascendant: The Martiniere Legacy Book Two

Realization: The Martiniere Legacy Book Three

A Belated Christmas Honeymoon: A Martiniere Legacy Short Story

The Enduring Legacy: The Martiniere Legacy Book Four

People of the Martiniere Legacy

The Heritage of Michael Martiniere: A Martiniere Legacy Novel

Broken Angel: The Lost Years of Gabriel Martiniere: A Martiniere Legacy Novel

Justine Fixes Everything: Reflections on Mortality

The Martiniere Multiverse

A Different Life: What If?

A Different Life: Now. Always. Forever.

A Very Multiversal Christmas Miracle

Netwalk Sequence Author Preferred 2022 Editions

Life in the Shadows: Book One

Netwalk: Book Two

Netwalker Uprising: Book Three

Netwalk's Children: Book Four

Learning in Space: Book Five

Netwalking Space: Book Six

Bright Star Fair Witches

Becoming Solo: A Bright Star Fair Witches Novella

Non-Series Titles currently available:

Alien Savvy: A Western SF Novella

Klone's Stronghold: Reeni

Beating the Apocalypse

Bearing Witness

Fabulist and Fantastical Worlds: A Short Story Collection

Federation Cowboy

Vision of Alliance

Vella Titles:

Falcon of the Martinieres (part of *Justine Fixes Everything*)
Bearing Witness
Beating the Apocalypse
A Different Life—What If? An Alternative Martiniere Legacy Novel
Becoming Solo
A Different Life—Linda's Story: An Alternative Martiniere Legacy Novel
Federation Cowboy

Audiobooks Available:

Alien Savvy: A Western SF Novella

Released from other publishers:

"Queen of the Snows," in *Once Upon A Winter: A Folk and Fairy Tale Anthology*, edited by H. L. Macfarlane

"My Man Left Me, My Dog Hates Me, and There Goes My Truck," in *Black-Eyed Peas on New Year's Day: An Anthology of Hope*, edited by Shannon Page

"Lost Loves," in *All Worlds Wayfarer*

"The Wisdom of Robins," in *Whimsical Beasts: A Campcon Anthology*, edited by Joyce Reynolds-Ward

"The Cow at the End of the World," in *Well...It's Your Cow*, edited by Frog Jones

"To Plant or Pull Up Stakes," in *Pulling Up Stakes: A Campcon Anthology*, edited by Joyce Reynolds-Ward

"The Notice," in *Children of a Different Sky*, edited by Alma Alexander

9 780989 847346